Temptation overwhelmed him . . .

"Damn you, Cassandra. Stop this. *Now.*" His voice was as unsteady as his fingers. He took her by the shoulders and gave her a hard shake. "You will regret this come morning."

"I might," Cassandra conceded. "But it's not morning yet, and there cannot be many more nights here on this cay. I fear leaving here, Rafe, and wondering for the rest of my life why you never kissed me when I knew you wanted to. I dread living the rest of my life wondering what it might have been to be touched by you, held by you."

"Cassandra." He closed his eyes. "I can't . . . just kiss you."

She recognized desire rising within her. It had stirred between them that first night in the school garden, had simmered hotter on board the ship. She was awed, excited, shaking. Trusting.

"I'm not afraid, Rafe," she whispered.

He was thinking less and less clearly. She was so beautiful . . .

MOONTIDE

DIANNA DEVLIN

DIAMOND BOOKS, NEW YORK

This book is a Diamond original edition, and has never
been previously published.

MOONTIDE

A Diamond Book / published by arrangement with
the author

PRINTING HISTORY
Diamond edition / September 1992

ISBN: 1-55773-769-X

Diamond Books are published by The Berkley Publishing Group,
200 Madison Avenue, New York, New York 10016.
The name "DIAMOND" and its logo are trademarks
belonging to Charter Communications, Inc.

PRINTED IN THE UNITED STATES OF AMERICA

10 9 8 7 6 5 4 3 2 1

To Katie Leahy and Linda Miller who said
You can do it,

To Kim Bush, Susan Coppula, and Linda Wallerich who said
You can do it better,

And to Sue Clark and Peggy West who said
Just do it,

Thank you.

MOONTIDE

Chapter One

France, 1863

SOMNOLENT. SERENE. MID-MORNING. July.

Heat rose in shimmering waves off the thatched and red-tiled roofs of the village Denoir, the day's hot breath rustling the wilted vines along walls and winding fences, the sun's unblinking gaze pressing, permeating. In sun-splashed doorways, young mothers smiled and hummed softly to dark-eyed babies. Barefoot youngsters sprawled under apple-laden trees, scraped elbows shielding or cradling sleepy heads.

Against the high walls separating Denoir from the good sisters' convent and school, Josephus and Pierre sat as usual. Their gnarled hands hung limp between arthritic knees, Pierre's pipe lifeless between his remaining teeth. Beyond the convent wall, the drone of insects rose from well-tended gardens. The scrubbed cobblestone courtyard baked in the sun. A loud bang destroyed the reigning quiet.

"Finished." Cassandra Mortier, her student pinafore soiled, dark mahogany curls clinging in damp curlicues to her flushed cheeks, spun clear of her trunk.

"The remainder of my worldly effects," she intoned, sweeping her arm dramatically toward the fair-haired girl sitting on the bed, "I hereby bequeath to Miss Lucinda

Hammond, my ever-stalwart defender and comrade in exile."

Undaunted by her friend's unchanged expression, Cassandra hugged herself and twirled like a toy top released from its string. It made her dizzy. She staggered to a wobbly halt and collapsed, loudly, onto the room's straight-backed chair, the third such chair since Cassandra's rambunctious habitation.

"I've been waiting, *praying,* for this day. *Forever,*" she sighed when the whitewashed walls stopped turning. "It's a miracle!" She learned forward. "Do you believe in miracles?" Her laugh, as spontaneous as its mistress, floated up and danced in the air with the dust motes her spinning had ruffled moments before. "Of course you do. Why else would you persist in trying to reform me?" She was rewarded by Lucy's indignant sniff.

"Since April is forever? You're exaggerating again."

"See?" Cassandra leaned forward wagging a slender finger. "You're reforming again." With characteristic abruptness, she changed both position and mood, jerked her stocking feet into the chair's seat and plopped her chin on her knee. "I almost ignored Sister's summons this morning, thought Old Mat—Sister Mathilde," she amended at Lucy's look, "was only wanting to start in again about yesterday." She pinched her lips and looked down her nose primly. "Even I have limits."

Lucy shook her head. "I believe Sister *is* still furious. Rightfully so! Climbing the steeple tower? With your skirts hitched up to your waist, no less? What did you expect?"

"To see into the village and not to be seen?" Cassandra offered innocently.

Lucy's eyes filled, ready tears dissolving her tight control. "What I can't believe is that you might truly be leaving, Cass." Hope glimmered through her despair. "Sister didn't say your grandfather was coming for you, only that he's coming out. For a visit."

"Right," Cassandra acknowledged, standing. "But"—her apron sailed into a corner—"*this* time I'm leaving with him when he goes." Her dress and petticoat followed the apron.

"Cass, be reasonable. You can't just—" Lucy bit off her words. Reason never got very far with Cassandra, and using the word *can't* was always disastrous. Lucy sighed, watched her friend plucking out the pins holding up her thick hair. Yesterday's escapade was typical, even tame fare for predictably unpredictable Cassandra Mortier. Few of the nuns and none of the other students save herself saw past "Cassandra the Alabama Hellion." Cassandra guarded herself well, too well. Only Lucy was privy to Cassandra's strange dreams, knew the depth of Cassandra's aching homesickness, or understood how fierce was Cassandra's devotion to her grandfather.

"He wouldn't take you with him in April," Lucy said quietly.

Cassandra glanced up but kept her second stocking on course down a shapely, suspiciously sun-pinkened calf. "This time will be different. I've got it all planned." At Lucy's groan, Cassandra gave her stocking a toss, skirted the tub taking up the center of the room, and bounded onto the bed. "No more tears," she ordered, hugging Lucy. The rope-strung mattress creaked, its straw stuffing crackling as Cassandra shifted to sit cross-legged. She grabbed Lucy's hands and squeezed them tight. "Lecture me if you must, but please, please, please don't look so sad."

Cassandra frowned, suddenly serious. "It's important I be with my grandfather. You saw him last time, Lucy.

Something's wrong. He's not . . . himself. But"—she shook her head once, jouncing the dark mane of hair tumbling down her back—"*he* still sees *me* as a child chasing cats on roofs giving poor Lalie fits, I think. I'm seventeen!"

Lucy's cheek dimpled. "True. A woman grown who now only climbs steeples and gives nuns fits."

Cassandra laughed and flopped back on her pillow, letting her legs dangle from beneath her chemise over the side of the bed. "Well, I am grown now, whether this infernal War Between the States is over or not and whether Grandpapa realizes it or not." She lifted her head and looked down her nose at her high, rounded breasts pulling her chemise uncomfortably tight. Her nose wrinkled. "I get any more grown and it'll be embarrassing." Lucy giggled, and Cassandra rose up on her elbows. "I mean it. Being female gets worse all the time. My balance is off. That's why I slipped, you know. And I'd have been fine even then, but for that devil-take-it chunk of rotten stucco."

"Which landed on Sister Mathilde's head," Lucy added.

Cassandra grimaced. "She was supposed to be in the sewing room."

Lucy's brow arched. "So were you."

"No." Cassandra fell back onto the pillow, the change in her mood jarring. "Not one day longer, Lucy." Her grey eyes narrowed, became fierce, not forlorn. "I've been stuffed away in this suffocating school sewing up smocks for orphans and street urchins five horrid years so Grandpapa could ruin his health worrying about Alabama, not me." She stopped, hating the tremor she heard in her words. Lucy stared down at her hands, the silence heavy and strained between them. "He needs me,

Lucy." Cassandra sat up, curling her legs beneath her. "And we both need to go home, to Leeland, where we belong."

"But the war," Lucy protested. She was almost knocked off the bed by Cassandra's bear hug.

"Stop fretting," Cassandra whispered, squeezing Lucy hard and sitting back. "Be reasonable," she mimicked her friend. "If I can handle Sister Mathilde and Grandpapa can handle me, don't you think between us we can handle a few irritating Yankees?"

Lucy closed her eyes. Cassandra frowned, studying her protective, protesting friend. They couldn't be more opposite, couldn't be more close. Lucy opened her eyes, met Cassandra's look, and smiled at last, a crooked, sad smile that tugged at Cassandra's heart.

"Your bath water's getting cold, Cassandra Anna Maria Mortier."

Cassandra grinned, leaned forward, and kissed Lucy's pug nose as she bounced off the bed. "And I miss you already, Lucinda Catherine Hammond." Yanking her chemise over her head, Cassandra eased into the tub and scooted down, careful to keep her hair from getting wet. "Sweet Mary," she sighed. "When I get home, I'm going to soak in a tub every single day—ten times a day if I feel like it." She raised her head and eyed the crumpled apron Lucy was picking up off the floor. "Leave it. Or keep it, burn it, throw it away. I never want to see it again."

"It's a perfectly good pinafore," Lucy said. "You're going to lounge in tubs all day? Never do another bit of dusting or gardening or—"

Cassandra sat up, sloshing water onto the floor. "If you must be doing something, there's a gown rolled up in a sheet under my bed." She pointed impatiently when

Lucy simply stared at her. "It's a respectable traveling gown I've been working on just for Grandpapa." Her eyes twinkled. "Part of the plan."

"What's it doing under the bed?" Lucy asked.

"Waiting for someone to shake it out?" Cassandra laughed. "Spread it on the bed." She lathered her arms and neck absently and watched Lucy tug out the sheet containing the gown Cassandra had finished, providentially, only two nights before. Rich, grey taffeta spilled out of the bed linen's folds as Lucy stood up. The girl gasped, struggling to gather the slick material into her short arms without crushing it or letting it brush the floor.

"Wherever did you—" Lucy started, then stopped. "This is the material your grandfather had sent to you when—" Her head snapped up, her expression stricken.

"When my father was killed at the First Manassas." Cassandra nodded calmly. She stood up, wrapped a length of toweling snugly about her, and stepped gracefully out of the water. "I used it after all. Do you think Sister Mathilde will be pleased?"

Color was returning by degrees to Lucy's chalky face. She opened her mouth and closed it without speaking, turning instead to the bed. "I've never seen you working on this," she said, smoothing the gown's skirt.

"I could hardly see *myself* working on it." Cassandra's voice came muffled from the clean chemise she was wiggling over her head. "Votive candles may be fine for sick rooms and praying; they're nigh useless for sewing light." Her head poked through. "Well?" she asked. "Do you think it needs pressing?"

"Pressing!" Lucy squeaked. Cassandra's gaze jerked from the bed to her friend's again white face. "What *were* you thinking of when you cut this out? It's . . .

it's . . ." She waved plump hands in distress.

Cassandra grinned. "Not exactly schoolgirl attire?"

"Not exactly respectable!"

"Good." Cassandra's smile widened. "I want Grandpapa to see me as a grown woman, not the twelve-year-old hooligan he shipped off to France grown taller, don't you see? It's time he realized I don't belong in a convent school any longer."

"Cass," Lucy wailed. "He'll take one look at you in . . . in this and think you belong in a *cloister*." The lesson bell rang. Hurried footsteps sounded along the tiled dormitory hallway, and Lucy moved reluctantly toward the door. "My lace bertha!" She turned, her eyes hopeful. "It'd be perfect and—"

"Your first gift from your first beau?" Cassandra cut her off, horrified.

Lucy colored to the roots of her pale hair. "Raymond is a friend—my brother's friend. They spent all of one afternoon here, and you did all the talking."

Cassandra laughed. "Whatever were Clayton and I to do? Sit there and watch you two blush at each other, sweet as it was? And then come Christmas, you got a gift from Raymond and I got a postscript from Clay." Cassandra posed. " 'Regards to Christina.' " A fresh surge of blood brightened the other girl's cheeks, and Cassandra relented. "Go on or you'll be tardy. I'll try this on in the daylight, and if it is too revealing, I'll fix it. All right?"

"Promise?" Lucy pleaded.

"Go." Cassandra pushed her friend into the hall and watched until Lucy disappeared down the stairs. Turning, she stepped back inside her room, shut the door, and stretched with most unladylike abandonment in the rare peace of having the entire floor to herself and being released from lessons she forever fluctuated between knowing backward and forward or knowing not at all. Leaning against the door, she studied the gown she'd fashioned with such careful stitches and determined resolve, its billowing skirt spilling over the rumpled cot.

Cocking her head, Cassandra traced its lines and grinned. She knew exactly how it fit. How well the puffed-sleeved, full-skirted creation with its tight bodice and plunging neckline had come together still amazed her. No mourning rag this. Her grin hardened at its edges. Hadn't she mourned her father an entire childhood? She'd grieved his loss from the day he'd left Mobile when she was but five to the morning she'd arrived in Le Havre where he managed the family's French holdings a long seven years later, to be exact. Leland Mortier had sent a rented carriage to take her on to Denoir, had declined her tentative invitations to visit her via his business secretary, and had neither come nor sent for her once in the three years they'd been but a morning's carriage ride apart before he returned home to die a *hero*'s death. Cassandra swallowed, the grey material blurring. "But Grandpapa is coming." Her grin returned. "Today."

Cassandra jerked away from the door. Scattered garments and damp toweling whizzed through the air, landing in piles to stay, piles to go, piles to . . . pile. Stopping for breath, she snatched up her feather-filled pillow from home, buried her face in its soft thickness, and recalled, unbidden, her first major battle with Old Mat. The infamous Goose Feather Fracas her grandfather dubbed it now with that so familiar, so endearing shake of the white, white hair he boasted was his crowning achievement for raising a child alone in his old age. Cassandra frowned.

She'd not raised a fracas when this pillow had disappeared for the lumpy convent's version; she'd waged all out war. An ocean away, Randall Mortier had received a nonstop torrent of letters accusing him of desertion, callousness—cutting, terrible things. Cassandra closed her eyes, seeing the entire incident with painful hindsight and feeling an aching remorse that would have warmed Sister Mathilde's heart.

Sister Mathilde. Cassandra grimaced and crushed the pillow tightly against her chest. Home. The word bubbled up, sang in her blood. Home. Home. Home. Grabbing the pillow's sides, she held it at arms' length and twirled around the room. "We're going home. We're going home."

Captain Rafael Dominic Buchanan stared out the open window of the tumbledown waterfront tavern, his dark eyes scanning the jumbled, gently bobbing masts of vessels, great and small, crowding the Le Havre harbor. Late afternoon sun silhouetted his straight Gallic nose and uncompromising jawline. The play of light and shadow repeated a pattern preordained from conception in the man's tawny hair, sun-bleached and wind-combed, coupled unexpectedly with eyes the shifting shades of midnight. His seaman's face twisted into a scowl.

Black this day with their blacker thoughts, his eyes narrowed on the taller masts of the American-owned but French-registered clipper ship *Good Fortune*. Distance-shrunken Frenchmen and familiar crew moved back and forth, up and down her gangplank, oblivious to his seething scrutiny. A tall, lone figure standing on deck turned, stared dockside a moment, then turned again. A muscle jerked along Rafe Buchanan's locked jaw. He hefted his tankard, found it empty, and slammed it down on the table.

"Does this hellhole serve ale with its flies?" he roared. The middle-aged serving maid wiping gouged tables and straightening uneven-legged benches in the afternoon lull shot the only occupied table a sour look. Her face smoothing instantly, she hurried with another tankard.

"You've had enough, Rafe. Let's get out of here. Go for a walk, *aihn?*"

Rafe looked at the scrawny older man who sat across from him shuffling and reshuffling a frayed-edged deck of playing cards. Dominic Veasey's ebony eyes stayed with his cards, his expression blank, the set of his bony shoulders relaxed. The irony of his uncle, first mate, and friend being so serene and himself in a state of seething anger felt strange enough to check the rage churning in Rafe's gut. Frowning, Rafe stared down at his drink, his fingers squeezing the soft pewter mug.

"Since when do we need a supercargo aboard, Dom?" Rafe said, his deep baritone even, dangerously so. "That's not how Bernard planned it, I don't like it, and I don't have to go along with it." He shoved his tankard aside. Dom's quick hand snatched the mug when it would have toppled. "I'm going down there."

"Sit still," Dom growled.

Rafe's black eyes bored into those of his uncle, so like his own. "It's my ship."

Dom grunted and went back to his cards. The deck fanned like a peacock displaying for a mate. They flashed again, then disappeared beneath his veined hands. "It is his uncle's ship, yes?"

"Entrusted to me! Those supplies they're loading right now." Rafe's callused index finger pointed toward the wharfs. "Lawrence Hadley was to have them collected and ready to board—*that's all.* Bernard holds us responsible for getting them safely to Nassau, nobody else." At Dom's raised eyebrow, Rafe hunched forward and lowered his voice but not the tide of anger surging through it.

"I don't need some pompous jackass telling me *he'll* see that *his* cargo is properly stowed away." Rafe's ruddy face darkened. "And I sure as hell *won't* be told who is and who isn't shipping on as crew!" He retrieved his ale and drank deeply.

"Po yi," the crusty Acadian sighed, watching him. He winced when Rafe's tankard thudded back onto the table. "So Bernard's fancy-pants nephew mebbe wants a piece of the pie. So who does not, *aihn*? So he wants to play supercargo." Dom turned his leathery palms up and shrugged. "So let him."

"Let him!" Rafe exploded. The serving woman scurried behind the bar at the opposite end of the room. "A supercargo hires the vessel and can hire and fire the captain, dammit, but the captain hires the crew. Did you see what slunk on with him? By the Virgin, Dom, if I needed riffraff and rummies, I wouldn't have sailed out of Nassau shorthanded to begin with."

Dominic Veasey's uncharacteristic calm gave way. The veins running down his neck stood out. His Adam's apple bobbed once, twice. "You were happy enough, you, when Bernard offered you the *Fortune* and a chance t' sail t' Havre!" He cursed, stuffed his cards into the inside pocket of his tattered jacket, and cursed again. "The sea in yer blood drowns the brains in yer head. Would you listen t' Dom then? *Non.* The gulf it is not the open sea, you rant. The centerboard, her, she is not a clipper true. Bah! So now you have yer fine ship an' yer high seas—an' a supercargo along with 'em!" The old man's spine stiffened. He planted his palms on his thighs and became the fire-breathing first mate that he was whenever a sailor dared become careless, cocky, or—the saints protect him—too slow.

"Listen t'you!" Dom spat. "You are no saint, *non,* but pride has never been one of yer sins. You shame yer maman."

Temper flashed in Rafe's eyes. His jaw set as Dom leaned toward him across the table, the Acadian's misshapen, thrice-broken nose a vivid red.

"We sail for Bernard Cramer an' he is a good man, yes. We run the blockade, an' we are makin' good money, yes. But the man an' his money, they are not why we are here." Dom's hand slapped the table. "That medicine they are boardin'. It is for boys—friends, them, yers an' mine!—dyin' this very day for the lack of them. Who cares who stows it so long as we get it to them, *aihn*? You are so proud all of a sudden that who you sail under and who you sail with is more important than why we sail at all? Bah!"

Rafe wanted nothing so much as to leap up and throw the table the length of the tavern. Instead he watched the square, brown thumb of his left hand trace and retrace the grey rings upon rings staining the tabletop, the grueling discipline bred into him in his ascent from cabin boy to captain buying his mind the time it needed to sort through his chaotic emotions.

Dom's dressing-down hurt, Rafe realized. His hot-tempered uncle raged as easily and about as often as he dealt cards. When it came to Rafe, Dom's short fuse had ever tended to ignite sooner and blaze hotter, but his rantings had long ago lost their sting. Rafe frowned. Dom's words hurt because they were true. *Damn.* Rafe's finger stilled and curled with his hand into a hard fist. Lawrence Hadley's arrogant face came to mind. Merely recalling that man's haughty, self-inflated manner tightened Rafe's gut. With an effort, Rafe forced his hand open and pressed it flat on the table. Other memories stirred, other faces. Intended and unintended humiliations. The silent screams of powerlessness. Hate. Rafe held his breath, willed his mind blank. He breathed out slowly. The veins on top of his large hand smoothed.

"It's not sailing under a supercargo I mind, Dom," he said at last, his deep voice steady, tired. "It's being around the likes of Lawrence Hadley."

"Ah." Dom sat back on his bench slowly. Sunlight flashed golden in the younger man's hair, and something akin to pain crossed the old man's grizzled face. "Coton," Dom began. Rafe glanced up at the use of his childhood *ti* name. "They are everywhere, them."

Rafe held up his hand. "Don't. I know." His hand fell to the tabletop, and Rafe smiled, his smile haunted at its edges. The two men held each other's gaze for a long moment, the bond stretching between them stronger than words. Rafe's smile reached his eyes. "To the *Fortune,*" he said, taking up his tankard, "and to Bernard's money waiting in Nassau when we get her there." His mouth quirked. "I've a feeling we're going to earn every—"

"Maman!"

The tavern's door slammed against the wall as a wild-eyed youngster, all arms and legs and flying hair, slid into the room, crashed over a bench, and sprawled on the littered stone floor.

"Dieu me garde," the woman screamed. Her tray of mugs clattered onto the bar. Hiking her skirts, she scrambled around the bar's end. Another winded participant filled the doorway and joined her race, each of them

reaching the sobbing boy at the same time.

"Maman!"

The thrashing child's howls shrilled higher as his head was clasped between frantic maternal hands and his arms pinned by strong masculine ones. The man won out, his eyes blazing, teeth flashing white in his sweat-shiny black face. Shoving aside the screeching woman, the heavyset Negro yanked the boy to his feet, then off them, shaking the waif violently in midair.

"Maman!"

The child's ragged sobs set off a storm inside Rafe as sudden and as violent as any norther off the gulf coast. He reached the man and child in two long strides, one arm circling the ragamuffin's waist, his other arm's huge fist burying itself in the stranger's ample midsection. The Negro doubled over, staggered backward. Freed, the lad twisted from Rafe's hold and leaped toward his mother. Rafe lunged for the black man's shoulder, wrenched the man around, and in a blind rage delivered three punches before his victim could draw a single breath.

"Rafe!" Dom's sharp voice cut the air.

With agility that belied the iron-grey curls hugging his head, the Negro recovered, bellowed, and broke Rafe's hold. A table split and crashed beneath the two men's wrestling weight. The serving woman screamed and yanked herself and her son behind the bar where the lad, wide-eyed, gaped over its edge. The stranger fought hard, his meaty fist splitting Rafe's lip, finding Rafe's rib cage with accuracy, but his brute strength was no match for the younger man's sailor reflexes and longer reach. Rafe straddled him, pinning him to the floor with his weight astride the black man's heaving chest.

"Enough!" Dom's gnarled fingers clamped around Rafe's wrists as Rafe's fingers circled the Negro's neck. "*Enough,*" the Acadian shouted.

Rafe looked up, his hair and the perspiration running into his eyes hiding Dom's face inches from his own.

"I . . . can't . . . breathe. . . ."

Rafe released his grasp. The room and the man beneath him swam into focus. Rafe pushed his hand through his hair, willed his breathing to slow. "Who are you?" he asked in French.

The Negro's eyes snapped open, his breathing labored, loud. "I'm Jim," he panted. Rafe blinked, the black man's English registering for the first time.

"American?" the younger man rasped. Dom swore beside them.

Jim nodded his head in a jerky motion. "A freeman. American."

Still coiled and wary, Rafe shifted off the man's chest to the side opposite Dom, who knelt eyeing Rafe with equal intensity. Ignoring them both, the black man sat up and twisted to stab an accusing finger toward the two staring from behind the bar. "You!" he croaked. The boy jumped. His mother's arm clenched about his thin shoulders. "You're a half-pint French thief!"

"*Merde,*" Dom groaned and sat back on his heels.

Rafe's brow drew together. He glanced to the boy, then to Jim, then leveled his gaze back on the youngster. "Did you steal from this man?" he asked in clipped French. The boy's eyes bulged. His greasy curls danced wildly in mute denial, and he glanced nervously over his shoulder toward a door opening in the wall behind the bar.

"Hold," Rafe ordered. Wincing, he got slowly to his feet. "You will stand and answer, mister." The boy made a choking sound, whirled, and fled.

"Hey!" Dom bounded to his feet, evaded the screeching French woman's clawing fingers, and sprinted through the back doorway after her son.

A lioness protecting her cub, the mother spun around and slung her ale-soaked slop rag when Rafe moved to follow Dom. With stinking, stinging accuracy it hit Rafe full in the face. He yanked it off in time to bat away a spinning tankard. Behind him Jim yelped as the remaining pewter ware from the spilled tray took to the air. Sidestepping maternal expectations was second nature. Rafe ducked. Maternal wrath was a new experience, he reflected, not without humor, and ducked again. A tankard bounced off his forehead. Rafe swore, leaped the bar, and captured the woman's flailing arms.

"Madame," he said, hard-pressed to hold her without hurting her and not get his eyes clawed out for his trouble. "Madame," he repeated above her screaming epithets. "We mean your boy no harm. *Ouch,* dammit!"

Dom reappeared, out of breath, his knit cap askew. He raised an arm and waved a flat leather pouch. Rafe released his captive and a great breath of relief simultaneously. The woman lurched backward, regained her balance, and tumbled Dom hard against the door frame in her haste to run after her sticky-fingered offspring.

"Dominic!" Rafe roared. Groaning, he tore after his livid uncle, cutting short the irate man's second chase in as many minutes. Incensed at the interference, Dom swung. Rafe grinned, stooped, and hefted the bellowing first mate over a broad shoulder. Retracing their route, he deposited his thrashing load onto the bar's top.

"Stow it, Veasey," Rafe laughed, yanking Dom's cap down past the man's scarlet nose. "You've enough vices without taking up chasing skirts in a foreign port."

Dom stiffened. "Chasin' skirts!" A string of Acadian profanity fogged the air as he jerked his cap off his head. "You should know, you, yes? You cocky half-breed—" His eyes fixed beyond Rafe's shoulder. Cursing, he shoved the younger man aside and jumped down from the bar. Rafe looked, then hurried to kneel with Dom beside the sprawled black man's still form.

Dom's fingers probed gingerly for the wound responsible for a pool of blood spreading beneath the unconscious man's head. The stranger moaned, and the older man grunted as an ugly cut, its crescent shape matching the sweat rings on the tables, showed itself above and behind a split and swollen ear.

Rafe grimaced. "She got him good, looks like. How bad is it?"

"You got him not so bad, you, more than once afore her."

Rafe's mouth tightened into a straight line. He held the man's head steady as Dom pressed a leathery palm against the cut to slow the bleeding.

"How bad?" Rafe repeated when Dom remained silent.

Dom shrugged. "I'm not Doc, me, but I think it is not so bad as—ah." The man between them moaned, then tried to roll onto his side. "Easy, mate," Dom cajoled, holding him still.

"Jim?" Rafe pressed hard against the man's chest to restrain his groggy movements. "Jim." He leaned closer to the Negro's face. "Can you hear me?"

The man stopped struggling and opened his eyes—or eye. His left one had swollen shut. "I'm Jim," he said thickly. "I'm a—" His lid fluttered closed.

"A freeman," Rafe prodded. "An American." When Jim failed to respond, Rafe sat back on his heels. His gaze traveled the black man's torn and bloodied checked shirt and came to rest at the puffy flesh encasing Jim's eye. "One bashed-up American," Rafe muttered. His left hand fisted and pounded his thigh.

The corner of Jim's bruised lip quirked. "An' you're the French-talkin' American what bashed me up."

Dom hooted. The Negro's eye opened and fixed on Rafe.

Rafe shook his head. "I'm sorry," he said, the inadequacy of his words smiting his ears.

Jim smiled outright. "No. You got the right instinct. You just picked the wrong—" He started. "My letter! Got t' get back—"

"We got it." Dom scrambled to his feet and retrieved the leather packet from the bar. Jim grabbed it, relieved but no less agitated.

"Lost an hour easy," he mumbled, pulling himself up. He clutched his side and fell back, gasping. "Meetin' . . . meetin' with that snake t'night. Got t' be . . . be back." He heaved forward and swayed to his feet, sweat mixing with the fresh surge of blood from his cut and staining his collarless shirt. His knees buckled. Rafe leaped to steady him.

"Here." Rafe hooked a bench with his booted foot and lowered Jim onto it. "Let Dom wrap your head before you bleed to death." The Negro struggled to rise. Rafe pushed him back down and held him there. "Sit still. I'm the basher, remember?"

Dom straightened from behind the bar and crossed the room ripping a dingy but clean wipe rag into strips. When Jim nodded his reluctant cooperation, Rafe stepped back and leaned against the edge of an overturned table. He folded his arms over his chest and studied the American freeman Jim.

The stranger's muscular shoulders drooped. His good eye closed, and his facial features sagged. The corded muscles across Rafe's back tightened. *Mon dieu.* Jim was a powerful, strong-armed, stubborn . . . old man. Rafe looked away.

"Mister Ran, he'll go alone if I don't be back." He clutched his leather-cased papers. "That's good enough."

"Quit squirmin', you," Dom growled. He glanced to the younger man and measured the set line of Rafe's jaw. "You ain't goin' t' miss yer meetin'."

"No." Jim started to shake his head but stopped, wincing. "I got t' deliver this here letter first." He stood, and Rafe reached to help him. When Jim stiffened, Rafe stepped back and let him stand on his own. The three got as far as the front door before Jim fell heavily to his knees. He let Rafe and Dom help him up and didn't protest when they positioned themselves on either side, balancing him between them.

The trio maneuvered outside, the afternoon sun bright after the tavern's cool dimness. Rafe felt the large man shudder and was glad for Dom's scrawny strength holding up Jim's other shoulder. Tossing his hair out of his eyes, Rafe looked toward the wharves and loading docks. "So where do we take this letter?" he asked, praying it was someplace along the waterfront and Jim didn't pass out before they got both message and messenger delivered safely.

"Denoir. A village. Fifteen miles outside o' town."

"Fifteen miles!" Dom squawked. Rafe shot him a look. Dom glared but clamped his mouth shut.

"Denoir?" Rafe repeated. "Dom and I were just heading out that way." Dom's mouth dropped open. Rafe ignored his uncle and grinned down at Jim, who was squinting up at him.

"You know it? An' the nuns' school there?"

"Know it?" Rafe shook his head, the sunlight catching in his hair, warmth flashing in his dark eyes. "It's my mother's home village, Jim. Can you believe this? Why, my aunt's a nun at the school."

Dom spit into the powdered dust at the road's edge, and the black man's look narrowed. Rafe read Jim's expression and became serious.

"Think, Jim. It makes no sense for you to make this trek and risk missing whatever it is you're worried about missing when we're going there anyway." His voice softened. "I owe you, Jim. Let me do this."

The older man, silent in indecision and growing weakness, leaned more heavily against Rafe's side. He weighed much heavier on Rafe's conscience. Respecting the Negro's inner struggle with a fierce pride, Rafe looked away. He measured the lengthening shadows, judged the light left in the day, and waited, cursing himself more roundly than even Dom would have dared for his heavy-handed misjudgment and Jim's undeserved misery.

An unplanned thirty-mile excursion inland bothered him not at all. In truth, Rafe welcomed the diversion. He needed it. Lawrence Hadley's overbearing presence on board the *Fortune* coupled with the French youngster's hysterical cries had ripped, unbidden, the scabs off wounds long buried and best forgotten. When they set sail from Le Havre at dawn, for the sake of their precious cargo so desperately needed back home, Rafe would need his wits very much about him, his iron will again in force. He sighed. Once under sail things would be right again.

Tilting his head, he drank in the sea-salted air, filtering out the stink of decaying fish and human slops that permeated crowded port cities everywhere, ignoring for a moment his own perspiration at war with the cloying scent of ale from the rag missile. The sea. It filled him: his nose, his pores, his soul. Rafe closed his eyes. Long before he'd ever laid eyes on his father, before he'd escaped from the plantation, before he'd rejoined Dom, before the mad dash to California had changed the course of lives, his and Dom's among them—always Rafe had dreamed of, longed for, belonged to the sea.

"You are a Southern boy."

Rafe turned his head. Jim, his broad face beginning to puff and purple with the last hour's abuse, was studying him. Rafe met his scrutiny safe in the knowledge that his own face mirrored nothing but a patient, passive waiting. "Aye," Rafe answered, though he'd not lived in the South nor on any solid land anywhere since he'd shipped out of New Orleans a ten-year-old runaway.

Jim frowned. "You give me your word you'll deliver this here letter? To the school?"

"You have my word," Rafe said.

"Today. Got t' be today."

"I'll have it in Denoir before sunset."

Jim nodded. His eye closed. His head dipped to his wide chest. "Get me t' the warehouse, then. I'll just wait there, ahead o' them. Rest." Rafe bent closer and caught the old man's slurred directions before Jim weaved and crumpled into unconsciousness. Rafe swung around to catch the black man's full weight, not without difficulty.

"Lend a hand, dammit," he grunted.

"So? Do you swear at yer *'tante* the nun' or only at yer poor Nonc Dominic?" Dom bristled but moved quickly to help. "First you are crazy mad. Then you are crazy stupid," the Acadian muttered as they laid Jim gently on the ground. "Your maman, her. *She* should have been a nun!"

Rafe grinned and stood up, dismissing the still fuming first mate to scan the road. An ox-drawn, wooden-wheeled farm cart led by a sleepy-eyed peasant was lumbering toward them. Rafe raised his hand, a command, not a query. The farmer blinked, checked, and nudged his plodding charge in Rafe's direction.

"So?" Dom pushed to his feet and slapped at the chalky dust clinging to his wide-legged trousers with his cap. "Now what, Monsieur Do-Good?"

Rafe shrugged. "We get this man to deliver Jim, and we deliver the letter."

The tiny veins along Dom's nose enlarged and throbbed. "Why can't we deliver the mate an' find someone else . . ." His voice faded at Rafe's look. "But"—Dom's eyes blazed—"but that is thirty miles!"

Rafe grinned. "So he said."

"You are crazy!"

"So you said." Rafe's grin widened into a smile that guaranteed palpitations in the skirted half of the population and always sent Dom into spasms of quite another nature. "You were the one who wanted to go for a walk. Remember?"

Chapter Two

CASSANDRA, HER STUDENT pinafore twisted in the folds of her dowdiest day gown, lay on her stomach, her face buried in her pillow. The sun was setting, the day ending, and Randall Mortier had not arrived. Her throat ached with swallowed tears; her head throbbed.

"Something came up. He'll be here tomorrow. I know it." Lucy's voice sounded far away though she sat beside Cassandra on the narrow cot.

Cassandra nodded into her pillow and wished Lucy would leave. What had happened? Her grandfather was innately considerate, intractably conscientious, and cautious to a fault. If there'd been the slightest doubt of his coming, he would have never sent word ahead. And if something unforeseen had occurred, he would have . . . Cassandra raised her head. Morbid pictures flashed in her mind's eye: a coach accident, highwaymen—

"The bell!" Lucy was yanking at Cassandra's arm. "Someone's here!"

The distant gong of the bell above the garden gate at the convent's school-side entrance reached Cassandra's ears. *He'd come.* Cassandra leaped up and ran for the hall, letting loose a jubilant, blood-curdling rebel yell.

Sister Mathilde, dozing over a book in her room, jerked awake. Startled heads poked from behind doors, and Mother Superior, pensive the entire evening, broke into a beaming grin that threatened to pop the spectacles off her short nose.

"What the—" Rafe extended a long arm and stilled the bell's clapper overhead. "Did you hear that?"

Before Dom could disentangle himself from the vines winding the garden wall where he'd slumped in exhaustion, muffled, running footsteps sounded beyond it. The heavy gate swung back, Rafe took a deep breath—and lost it as Cassandra cannoned into him, threw her arms round his neck, and burst into tears.

"What happened?" she choked. She squeezed tighter, struggling to speak coherently. "What took you so—" She froze, thick hair, taut muscles, her feet not touching ground registering. "Long?" she finished into a wide, hard chest. Her head fell back.

The man, his face bronzed by twilight's last, red-orange glow, stared down at her as stunned, as still, as she. Cassandra unlocked her hands from behind his head and felt herself sliding down, guided by strong hands circling her waist. Her stocking feet stood again on the path, the stranger's hands stayed in place, and Cassandra, senses spinning, remained suspended. There was no garden behind her, no village beyond melting into night shadows. She saw only his face—and the blackest, most beautiful eyes she'd ever seen. His hands moved, and Cassandra trembled as wide, gentle palms slid up her arms, traveled across her shoulders, teased her neck, and came to rest on each side of her face.

"Next time," he said, his thumb skimming, feather-soft, over her wet cheek, "I'll walk faster."

He spoke English, Cassandra's mind registered. American. Her heart lurched in her chest. He was a Southerner! Her fingers tensed where they spread against the stranger's shirt. "You know my—"

"Yer *tante* is coming," a voice grunted from the vines beside them, and Cassandra started.

The dark-eyed man looked up, a shorter figure separated from the garden wall, and Sister Mathilde's wide bulk filled the gate's opening. "Cassandra!"

The stranger's eyes darted back to Cassandra, became onyx gems in the light of the nun's lantern as Sister Mathilde's fingers bit into Cassandra's sleeve, pinching to the bone. He glanced down. Cassandra looked and saw that her hand still rested on his chest. The good sister yanked at her other arm, and the stranger stepped back at the same moment. Cassandra's hand hovered in midair, her fingertips throbbing. Abruptly, she pulled her hand behind her back, her face heating for no reason she could identify.

Beside her Sister Mathilde raised the lantern higher. "Who are you? What business brings you to this place at this hour?"

The stranger met her demand with unruffled, blatantly challenging silence. Cassandra held her breath, felt Sister Mathilde stiffening, and steeled herself against the wrath about to be heaped on this man's light-haired but unfortunately witless head. His eyes narrowed and he suddenly looked dangerous, not witless.

"You're hurting her," he said quietly, nodding to Sister Mathilde's hand clenched about Cassandra's slender forearm. The nun gasped, Cassandra stared, and the grip about Cassandra's arm eased.

"I'm Captain Rafael Buchanan of the *Good Fortune* in Le Havre, Sister," the man continued in French as if nothing untoward had happened. Cassandra swallowed, her jumbled thoughts tumbling. Tall before, in the lantern's harsh light the sea captain looked a giant towering over them with wild hair glinting gold, a recent cut above his eye, a bruise marking the hard line of his jaw.

"I have a letter." He paused and looked back to Cassandra. She felt her eyes widening. "For you," he said, reverting to English, his words and his look for her alone. His gaze traced her burning cheeks, lingered on her softly parted lips, and recaptured her eyes. Cassandra watched his brow lift and was mesmerized by the masculine shape of it. "By way of"—he paused—"Jim?"

"Jim!" Cassandra darted from the nun's clasp and pounced on the packet that he'd pulled from his wide belt. She clutched the letter to her chest and looked up. "Thank . . . you." She stood so close that the seaman's size and her senses undid her no less than before, but Sister Mathilde's fingers folded over Cassandra's shoulder and broke the spell.

"*Merci,* Captain Buchanan. Give our regards to Monsieur Mortier." The nun was speaking in dismissal, her grip turning Cassandra forcibly. Cassandra twisted, her feet stumbling in one direction as she looked back the other way.

"Wait," she called out, searching the stranger's face too quickly receding into shadow. "I'm coming with you. Everything's packed, ready. *Please.*"

"Stop this." Sister Mathilde's arm closed around Cassandra's shoulders. "You have your letter," she chided, not unkindly. "Come inside."

Cassandra planted her feet. "No!" Instantly she was jerked tightly against the nun's thick side and half carried through the gate opening. Cassandra struggled, strained to look over the determined nun's shoulder. "Wait!" she called back.

The tall captain frowned, stepped forward. Her heart soared, but the shorter man yanked his friend's sleeve and stopped his advance.

"Please," Cassandra pleaded. "It's all right, Captain Buchanan. It's all been arranged, I promise you, and as soon as—"

"Silence!" Sister Mathilde gasped. Cassandra bit her tongue at the nun's hard shake. The shorter man was gesturing wildly, as upset as Sister Mathilde scolding furiously in Cassandra's ear. Cassandra ignored them. The captain was turning, going back to his ship, Le Havre, her grandfather.

"Wait!"

The gate swung closed.

"Falsehoods and fabrications!" the nun panted, dragging Cassandra through the garden. "They fall from your lips like rain from heaven." Cassandra tripped. Sister Mathilde slowed, the anger in her voice giving way to dismay. "Will it never end! Can you never learn?"

"Grandpapa would have agreed," Cassandra argued, too numb, too empty of a sudden to care if she raised more wrath. "Once I explained, once he knew how badly I want to be with him, then—"

"Cassandra." Sister Mathilde stopped, took a deep breath before speaking. "Even if I believed that, even if your *grandpère* had told me himself to send you to him, do you think I'd have let you go with that"—she shuddered—"that sailor? The man reeked of ale—can you not smell it still? And he looked every bit as rough as he smelled."

Cassandra lowered her eyes, thankful the shuttered lantern's light faced ahead of them. She didn't need Sister Mathilde to tell her how Captain Rafael Buchanan looked. She felt again his eyes on her lips, his thumb brushing her cheek.

"See now?" Sister Mathilde's arm tightened protectively. "You've gone and taken a chill."

Hustling them through the side door still ajar from Cassandra's flight and the nun's lumbering pursuit, Sister Mathilde set down the lantern but took the stairs with her charge firmly in tow. She dismissed a round-eyed Lucy from Cassandra's room with a look and didn't let go of Cassandra until she'd sat her down on the cot.

"I'll brew a cup of hot . . ." The woman's voice trailed off as she straightened, looking about the room. "What is this?"

Cassandra tensed as the nun took in the empty clothes pegs on the walls, the trunk, the lumpy carpetbag. Though the light from the hall sconces failed to reach as far as the discarded gown draped over the chair in the corner, Cassandra stood up before Sister Mathilde looked in that direction. "I'm very tired, Sister," she said. Cassandra willed the gathering questions in the nun's eyes to remain unspoken. "I don't need anything. Truly. I only want to go to bed." She swallowed. "If I may."

Sister Mathilde sighed and laid a heavy hand on Cassandra's shoulder. "Tomorrow, my child. You will feel better tomorrow. We will talk." She waited, but Cassandra stood statue still, her stony gaze fixed on the floor. Sighing again, Sister Mathilde turned, the rattle of the rosary beads clipped to her belt loud in the silence as she moved across the room. They quieted when she paused in the doorway, waiting, but Cassandra would not look up. "Remember your prayers." The door closed.

Cassandra sank down on the edge of her cot and stared at the long, grey square at her feet where the rising moon peeked over the forested hills into her room. Prayers, she scoffed. What good were prayers? Disappointment and anger warred in her head. If only her grandfather had come as he'd planned, promised. She turned the leather sheath over in her lap, examined the frayed ribbon tying it closed, and tossed it onto the bed beside her. If only Jim had delivered the letter. Her childhood protector-champion and her grandfather's servant-companion would do anything Cassandra asked of him, and Old Mat could not have objected overmuch. Her pulse quickened. If only Captain Buchanan had come alone, without his grunting, grumpy shadow—her mouth twisted wryly—and come not stinking of ale. . . . Her eyes narrowed. Could she have persuaded the lion-maned, gentle-eyed captain to take her back with him?

Cassandra eased back onto her pillow, heat spreading through her, settling in her stomach, not unlike the time she'd sipped liberally from the forbidden decanters in her grandfather's study as a child. Captain Rafael Buchanan. She closed her eyes and felt his hard frame pressed against her as she'd clung to his neck, saw again his black eyes catching fire in the lantern's light. The heroines in the furtively passed-about novels Monique Desmond secreted back to school from her Parisian home had almost magical powers over men. Cassandra wrinkled her nose and dismissed the thought. Her childhood dream's faceless phantom was more real to her than those silly heroines and even more silly heroes. She stared up at the ceiling. Any firsthand knowledge of the real-world give-and-take possible between adult men and women was equally lacking, since she had grown up in the company of her grandfather, his elderly, mostly men friends, and a houseful of doting servants. And nuns and schoolgirls.

Scowling, Cassandra flipped onto her stomach and closed her eyes. Unbidden, Annalee Maria Mortier's stunning portrait hanging in the library back home came to mind and with it the stories begged from Lalie over and over about the mother Cassandra had missed as much before the beautiful woman died as afterward. Too late Cassandra opened her eyes, hating her memories of the dashing, adoring Leland Mortier and his worshiped Annalee. Cassandra's bottom lip trembled. Whatever her mother's great attraction, it'd been a quality she'd obviously failed to pass on to her daughter. But for Lalie and Jim, Cassandra might as well have been an orphan in her own home. She smiled suddenly. Not so in New Orleans, though, not when she was with—

"Sweet Mary mother of God!" Cassandra scrambled to her knees and snatched up the leather packet, ripping the ties free. Her fingers slowed to remove the folded, wax-sealed sheets of stationery tucked inside. In the shadows enveloping her cot, she read a scrawled "Cassandra" instead of her grandfather's familiar, elegant hand. Cassandra stood and hurried to the window. She frowned. In the moonlight her name on the outer sheet remained a hasty, almost illegible scribble.

Breaking the seal, Cassandra scanned the first page, stopped, and began again more slowly. The knot of fear that had loosened in Captain Buchanan's presence returned and wrenched Cassandra's stomach.

If the words were hard to decipher, the urgency with which they'd been penned was not. Since her grandfather had arrived in France over a year ago Cassandra had seethed inwardly and argued openly that he see her as a woman grown. To no avail. Now, in short, direct sentences, he wrote as an adult to an adult—and Cassandra closed her eyes. "My God," she breathed. Swallowing, she forced herself to keep reading. It was much harder to force herself to believe what she was reading.

Her grandfather sought her forgiveness for telling her

in a letter and not in person his true reasons for sending her away and for coming to France himself, and Cassandra forgave him. But when he begged her understanding of why he'd chosen to stand against the Confederacy, chosen to risk arrest and imprisonment using what influence he had to block a Southern alliance with France, Cassandra slumped to her knees, her legs no longer capable of holding her weight.

She stared at the floor, thoughts spinning, heart pounding. He could be arrested? *Imprisoned?* Her clenched hands threatened to rip the letter they held.

"I *love you,* Randall Mortier," she seethed. "The devil take the Confederacy, the Union, *and* France! I don't believe this!" Pushing to her feet, Cassandra circled her tiny room three times before she was calm enough to stand still again at the window.

"With news of the fall of Vicksburg," her grandfather's letter continued, "I feel the Confederacy's hopes for aid from France have been dashed and my service here is no longer necessary." Cassandra's breathing slowed, and she vowed to make sure he quit for good and forever his, she swore, service.

"Ironically, since arriving here it has been my business affairs, not my clandestine politics, that have nigh broken my health," she read on and recalled easily his tired eyes, his uncharacteristic preoccupation with his thoughts, and—she winced—her pique with him concerning both. "As Jim and I were preparing to set out for Denoir, evidence presented itself that unravels a snarl that has grown only more tenacious the harder I've worked to right it. I can tell you now, with greatest shame, that I've harbored a deepening dread this last, torturous year that your father, my own son, left this life an embezzler. A thief. I can tell you this because"—

Cassandra squinted to make out the words written in renewed haste, or with great emotion—"because he was not. He was not."

"He was not a lot of things," Cassandra muttered. Leland Mortier. Dead and buried, he was still breaking the hearts of those who still loved him. Damn him. Taking a deep breath, she forced herself to go on to the last page.

"Listen well, my dearest. I must move on this matter immediately. I would see the true master larcener, this destroyer of decent men, prosecuted and brought to justice. To that end I am closing the Le Havre offices as of today." Cassandra gasped. "I will see this man arrested this night but I will not subject you to the scandal that must ensue. This I cannot bear. I shall come for you within a fortnight, and we shall quit France and make a beginning somewhere else together. Be patient. Be ready. Your ever-devoted grandfather, Randall Mortier."

The expensive stationery slipped from her fingers. Clamping her hands over her mouth, Cassandra twirled about the room, stubbed her toe on the trunk, and, holding her foot, half hopped, half danced to her cot.

"Ready?" she giggled. "Be ready?" She jumped up. I'm ready, she wanted to shout. She stopped before the window, her heart slowing, eyes scanning the moon-washed garden to where the high wall cast its edges in shadow. Night-dark eyes pierced her thoughts. She shivered. "Two weeks might as well be two years," she moaned.

Be patient, her grandfather's words chided.

"No." Cassandra's eyes narrowed against disjointed thoughts that pulled first one way and then another in league with her conflicting emotions. Slowly, her mind stilled. A smile tugged at her full lips as a single idea took shape and began growing, becoming clear, possible. "Of course!" she laughed.

Spinning from the window, Cassandra hauled the carpetbag over to the bed, turned it upside down, and shook furiously. Petticoats and pantaloons, her pearl-backed brush set, chemises, nightgowns, hairpins, a sewing kit, and assorted wadded-up ribbons thumped and bounced onto the coverlet. Lighting her forbidden candle and working with hasty, haphazard disregard, she repacked only what she deemed necessary on a daily basis. Working more carefully, Cassandra folded the grey satin gown and began easing it into the near-empty bag.

"Devil take it!"

Cassandra stepped back and eyed the billowing taffeta spurting out of the valise like Vesuvius over Pompeii. She dared not leave the dress behind; Lucy would "forget" to send it with the rest of her things.

"Well," she sighed. "When all else fails." She stepped forward and began pounding the skirt into the carpetbag, feeling like a cook gone berserk punching down a triple batch of bread dough. It worked.

Out of breath but smiling, Cassandra scribbled a quick message to Lucy, yanked off her apron, and draped her cloak over her shoulders. Without a backward glance, she picked up the valise and slipped into the hall. She stooped at Lucy's door and slid her note beneath it, tiptoed past Sister Mathilde's room, and crept, step by step, down the stairs. Once outside her heart left her throat, and her feet took flight. Giving no mind to the slippery, dew-dampened turf and sharp pebbles that pierced her thin-soled shoes, Cassandra didn't stop running until Denoir was lost behind the road's first bend.

Cassandra stopped to catch her breath, exhilarated. The

night's quiet sang in her ears: crickets droning, a summer breeze sighing in the orchards, her uneven breathing. She leaned her head back and filled her lungs with air. It was sweet with the taste of adventure, sharp with the new tang of escape. Laughing out loud, she twirled. Her carpetbag pulled her off balance. Staggering, she giggled and regained her footing. *You forever speak without thinking. Act without thinking. . . .* Cassandra grimaced and banished Sister Mathilde from her thoughts. Her grandfather would understand her need to be with him. Cassandra frowned. Captain Rafael Buchanan might not be so understanding. He could decide just as easily to escort her back to Denoir as to allow her to return to Le Havre with him. Cassandra shook her head. He would help her. She was sure of it.

An owl called. The road beckoned, a full moon a beacon lighting the way. Smiling, Cassandra brushed her hair from her eyes, shifted her valise to her other hand, and followed the moon, her light steps padding in beat with her heart.

Jim groaned. His face felt twice its normal size; the roaring between his ears was hurricane loud. Peering through the slits left for his eyes, Jim frowned. The warehouse was pitch-black. He'd not meant to sleep so hard, so long. Struggling to sit up, he cursed, gasped, and fell back onto the sawdust-coated floor. If he outlived this afternoon's madness, he meant not to tangle with any more young bucks again either.

"*You* would lecture *me* of justice?"

Jim came instantly awake, his head twisting toward the voice and the high, cruel laugh that came with the words. His eyes fixed on the door at the far end of the room, the closed panel but a yellow outline cast by the lamp-lit room on its other side. He tensed, his every sense alert, his injuries forgotten. He knew the voice, knew the snake that owned it. And if *he* was here, Mister Ran was with him.

"I would do more than lecture you, you Satan seed, you worst kind of avarice-riddled, mud-crawling coward."

Jim stumbled to his feet. His friend, weighted too long by guilt, rocked too often with grief, now pushed too hard alone. The authorities. Where were they? Why hadn't Mister Ran waited for them, waited for *him*? Jim's knees buckled, and he grabbed at a crate to save himself from falling, his noise drowned by the loud voices beyond.

"Fool! You think I didn't know why you called me here, didn't know—to the column sum, to practically the exact hour—when you would find me out? I've been ahead of you, old man, have led your chase and am captor, not captive, at its end. It is *justice* that it be so. Leland Mortier paid but his just penance for his crimes."

"Crime? Blackmail is the crime! But it is his murder that I hold you—"

"*His* murder!"

"It was his life you stole more than his money, damn you to hell. He fled France to die, not to fight. These ledgers will see his death avenged. I will see you—"

A pistol shot exploded.

Jim cried out. The door crashed open. A tall form, his black cloak billowing behind him like the wings of death, darted from the room. Jim lunged.

They rolled on the floor, the man's muscled, hard length yanking free. Jim grabbed, his meaty hand locking about the other man's tailored trousers, the expensive material ripping. Strong hands fisted in the Negro's torn shirt, shoved. Jim flew backward. Crates crashed, splintered. He straightened, whirled, only to double over and sink to his knees. With a bellow he pulled the knife free where it had buried in his wide girth. Choking, dragging in air, Jim lifted his head—and saw the flames. They were engulfing the room beyond the door. Roaring. Leaping.

"Mister Ran. *Mister Ran!*"

Chapter Three

"FIRE! FIRE!"

The alarm echoed along the wharfs in a half-dozen languages. Running feet pounded behind Cassandra. Cursing, she squeezed into the hidden space between a cart and a waiting stack of iron-bound kegs and sank to her knees. The men tore past her. Cassandra groaned and slumped against the crates lining her back. What else could possibly go wrong?

She'd been so sure she would catch up with Captain Buchanan before ever reaching Le Havre, had pushed herself beyond endurance to that end. But she'd not overtaken him, had only just found the cursed *Good Fortune* after heart-pounding, nerve-stretching scurrying from shadow to shadow. And now all hell had broken loose and running men were spilling out of beds, bunks, and bars, making for the blaze flickering in the distance.

"Now what?" she breathed, forcing her voice to sound calm though her confidence was waning with the moon, her mood destroyed hours ago.

Shifting tortured muscles, she eyed the swaying outline of the *Good Fortune* ahead of her. Gilded silver in the fading moonlight, it seemed to stare back at her, aloof and self-assured, aware of its beauty compared to the squat-bodied vessels on either side. Cassandra shuddered, pulled her cloak tighter against the damp, fish-rank air, and cursed her throbbing legs and Rafael Buchanan's long ones for all her trouble.

If it were the Mortier-owned *Annalee* that rocked in front of her, Cassandra could simply board, find an unoccupied cabin, and sleep until daybreak. She'd played above and below its decks often enough as a child. Cassandra scowled at the *Good Fortune*. The *Annalee* would not stare down its nose at her, making her feel unknown, unsure.

That her grandfather was planning to sail on Captain Buchanan's ship did not surprise her. An established, wealthy merchant, he'd combined business with pleasure and made several crossings between Le Havre and New Orleans in the years before he'd joined Cassandra in Mobile. Ever the shrewd entrepreneur, he'd preferred crossing on vessels sailing for other merchants and had gained more than one good captain for the Mortier trade doing so.

"Damn." Cassandra winced, a painful cramp scattering her rambling thoughts. She stood up and leaned forward, massaging the knotting muscles in her calf with icy fingers. Fear, not cold, made her shiver. She was not so dull-witted as to be unaware of how fortunate she'd been to get this far without mishap. Or worse. She glanced at the orange glow lighting the night sky. To tarry longer on the wharf was tempting fate. Turning, Cassandra swallowed and measured the distance between herself and the clipper ship's gangplank.

For the thousandth time she wished she could go directly to her grandfather's boarding house, then shook her head. She knew his address; she didn't know Le Havre. Cassandra's hood fell back, and she ran her hand tiredly through her hair. "Think," she groaned.

She couldn't think, not clearly. No one aboard the *Good Fortune* was expecting her, obviously. But for the tall captain and his companion, no one would know who she was, let alone think she had a right to be boarding, unescorted, like some thief in the night. Sighing, she leaned back against the cart. Explaining her presence to Captain Buchanan was going to be awkward. The thought of having to go through it all first with a groggy-eyed, completely strange sailor made her head ache along with everything else.

No. Cassandra straightened in decision. She could face neither captain nor crewman right now. Her body was too tired, her wits used up. Tonight she would simply steal on board, hide in the hold . . . and sleep.

Rafe scanned the bank of low clouds gathering overhead as the *Good Fortune* made the open sea and left the channel and shores of France behind. He was thinking of the girl again, had not stopped thinking of her, his mind haunted by those stormy grey, grey eyes, by the girl looking out of them. Child, he corrected himself and decided he'd been at sea too long—or not long enough. Frowning, he tuned his senses to the *Fortune,* to the creak of cloud-scraping canvas, the whine of wind-whipped rigging. His blood quickened, mind calmed. Storms meant wind; wind meant speed.

Every muscle in Rafe's lean frame came alert, made visibly so by the stiff head wind molding his full-sleeved shirt and trousers to his skin. His feet apart, his hands riding his hips, Rafe became one with the infinite sea and ship beneath him, with the towering masts and endless sky above him, all needing nothing but the wild, tearing, life-giving wind. He glanced to Dom beside him on the poop deck.

"Looks like we're going to find out how many true sailors we shipped out with right away." He had to shout to be heard. Dom scowled, and Rafe grinned. "Hold your cards, Veasey. This blow will deal us the upper hand." He broke off to shout an order. The seaman fumbled to obey. Dom cursed and bellowed the directive more bluntly. One of their original centerboard crew dropped from the rigging and shoved the first sailor aside.

Dom's expression matched the darkening sky. "I've been watchin', me," he shouted. The deck tilted, and three men toppled, rolling the width of the main deck below where Dom and Rafe stood. *"Po yi."*

"Aye," Rafe agreed. Recalling the argument with Lawrence Hadley that had resulted in Rafe's being sent ashore until he was needed to set the ship to sea this morning soured Rafe's mood. The permanent crease between his eyebrows deepened. "They're a sorry lot, Dom," he said more to himself than to the first mate. "But they'll be a sorry lot of sailors before we reach Nassau." He bent closer to Dom's ear. "The storm. Pray it's a good one." His uncle shot him a look. "What these men wouldn't do to make a living they'll be only too happy to master to stay alive." Dom shrugged, his eyes scanning his crew. With a curse, he clattered nimbly down the steps, sidestepping the elderly man maneuvering toward the same. Rafe frowned and followed Lauchlan Collier's stumbling advance.

"Rafe," the old man wheezed, making the poop deck at last. Rafe's hand shot out, saving the surgeon from spilling down the steps he'd just cleared.

"It's too rough, Doc, and getting rougher. Go below."

Doc, his wiry white hair standing on end, pinched his spectacles down tighter upon his nose in a nervous gesture. "Lad," he shouted into the wind. Rafe bent closer to hear. "The crates? In me cabin?"

Rafe straightened abruptly and looked away. Was it blasphemous to pray the coming storm would not only help whip his crew into shape but wash a certain Lawrence Hadley overboard?

"Our illustrious supercargo overloaded the entire ship, Doc. Take a look." Rafe swung his arm in a semicircle. "He's taken over every space not allocated for cargo, not only your cabin. It's out of my hands, and I'm keeping clear of it." Rafe looked up and bellowed to a sailor ninety feet over their heads. When he turned back to Doc, the elderly man looked more agitated than he'd looked before Rafe had spoken. Doc opened his mouth, and Rafe cut him off.

"We got more than we came for." He wasn't above being grateful that Dom was no longer standing beside him, but neither was he ashamed to repeat his uncle's sound advice. "Let's accept the added medicines, ignore our added super, and be done with it."

Doc closed his eyes and took a deep breath. "I pray ye're right, lad, but"—his next words came in a rush—"I've a bad feelin' we didna take on . . . medicines."

"What?" Rafe's head snapped around to the surgeon. He glared, giving the man his full attention. "What did you say?"

"The dockhand Hadley's man nigh mauled to death while ye were ashore?" Doc, his eyes owlish behind his spectacles, hurried on at Rafe's impatient nod. "Cuffey jus' told me why that Navarre pirate jumped him."

"He was helping himself to cargo was how I heard it."

"Ye hear what he was helpin' himself to? Wine, Rafe. Expensive French wine."

"What?" Rafe was already moving, giving the deck over to Dom and heading for the companionway.

Doc struggled to keep his footing and keep up with Rafe's much steadier, longer strides. "I patched him up, had Cuffey take him ashore," he panted. Rafe checked long enough to grab up an iron crowbar. "But"—Doc stopped to follow Rafe's hasty descent down the four steps of the companionway—"Providence forgive me, lad, I didna ask questions at the time."

Rafe halted at Doc's cabin and wrenched the door open. He paused, letting his eyes adjust to the weak daylight from the single porthole, forcing his voice to remain even. "It's not your job to ask questions, Doc." It was the captain's job, his job. And he'd better get the right answers or he'd have Hadley's head on a platter if it meant dancing with that cur's hulking henchman Navarre first to get it.

Rafe knelt down and jammed the crowbar into the nearest crate's nailed-down lid. His knuckles whitened around the cold metal. Wood splintered as the top yanked free. Brown paper shredded apart. Rafe swore. He shoved the box aside and opened a second one, a third, a fourth. He stood up, his long length threatening the cabin's ceiling. A scattered chaos of fine linens and luxurious silks, gold-threaded brocades and reams of lace, circled his feet, taunting him with their presence. Rafe whirled to Doc, who stood rigid and mute in the doorway.

"Did these come on separate from the rest?" Rafe asked, but knew the answer before Doc shook his white head. The older man stepped inside the cabin and sank down on the edge of a crate.

"D'ye think . . . Ye don't think . . ." Doc looked up to no one.

"You! Sailor!" Rafe bounded up the companionway steps, grabbed a startled crewman, and hauled him toward the first mound of lashed-down tarp securing the deck cargo. "I want these crates opened." He shoved the crowbar into the mate's tar-stained hands. "Now!" Rafe turned, shouting, and two more sailors leaped to help. Swiping the hair from his eyes, he glanced up at the purpling, roiling clouds. The tarp snapped free, whipping in the rising wind. Rafe looked, saw the top crate tilting. It toppled, crashed to the deck, splitting, spilling its contents. *"Mon dieu,"* he breathed.

For a moment the air was thick with the cloying aroma of Normandy's prized apple brandy. Then the wind swallowed it, and the deck ran with it. Rafe swooped down and picked up one of the few unbroken bottles rolling drunkenly toward him and lobbed it overboard with harpoon force.

"What's happened?" a voice shouted.

Rafe whirled. Lawrence Hadley stood in the companionway opening, his eyes blazing. The sailors slowed at their task, their eyes flitting uncertainly from captain to supercargo.

"I said, open them," Rafe barked. "All of them."

"Stand to!" Hadley leaped on deck, his fluid balance and nautical command at odds with his jeweled stickpin and manicured nails. "What's the meaning of this?"

Rafe swore and kicked aside a loosened lid. "This?" he shouted, digging in with his hand and jerking out a filmy swath of sheer material. The savage wind yanked it from his grasp. Hadley cursed as it sailed overboard. Rafe lunged for another crate. "And this?" Ladies' chemises, satin ribbons and all, billowed and flapped as Rafe continued emptying the crate with rising disgust and raging fury. "And this? *And this?*"

Hadley shot forward and stayed Rafe's arm. The crewmen rounding the half-dozen opened crates scattered.

"Are you mad? This wanton destruction of valuable cargo—"

"This is the 'valuable cargo' you were charged to purchase?" Rafe shook a fistful of frothy satin beneath Hadley's aristocratic nose.

Hadley, his shorter-cropped hair as dark as Rafe's was light, stepped back, straightened to his full height, and met Rafe's fury eye to eye.

"Rafe!" Dom called out.

Rafe scooped up the crowbar at his feet and turned in a single motion. The Frenchman Navarre was emerging from the companionway. He moved with ominous grace for his size, unaffected by the rolling sea, the molded muscles across his massive, naked chest contracting as cold salt spray beaded on his skin. He stopped, his expression unreadable, his threat unmistakable.

The hairs at the nape of Rafe's neck rose. Tattoos covered the other man's trunk-thick arms. Grotesque mermaids with obscene proportions sported with the reptilian creatures of someone's demented, mayhap demonic, imaginings. Their sport was obvious, their effect lurid, ludicrous to even Rafe's jaded eyes long accustomed to the art form. Rafe's look narrowed, his hand testing the bar's iron weight. *Pirate* was too tame a word for Navarre, but he doubted even Dom knew a name low enough for the thieving peacock the man served. Alert and wary, Rafe looked to Lawrence Hadley.

"Answer me true, Mister Supercargo. Is this all we're carrying?"

Hadley stiffened, his blue eyes like ice. "You've no right to question my—"

"I'm questioning it!" Rafe exploded. "You arrogant, usurping—"

"Rafe!" a sailor yelled from the rigging.

Rafe spun but not in time to block Navarre's lunging attack. The two crashed to the deck, taking Dom and Hadley with them. The supercargo rolled clear and sprang to his feet shouting. Sailors surged forward. Rebel yells pierced the air.

Below them in the ship's murky hold Cassandra jerked into a tight ball. In sleep, her hands fisted against her ears. "Go away," she moaned. But it was back, and she couldn't stop it, and she knew she wouldn't wake up, not in time. It was the dream.

The vision, benevolent, bewildering, came sometimes on horseback, on a steed powerful and pounding that thundered from the mists of sleep into her mind. He came sometimes on the mists themselves, silently, secretly. This time, for the first time, he came in the guise of the moon. Always he came searching for her. *Why?* she'd pleaded asleep and pondered awake as a child. Why could he never see her and never be seen? She reached out a slim hand in her sleep, drawn to him, pulled by him, the tide to his moon, but his features remained hidden. He drew back, fading. Cassandra tensed. Shouting, wordless voices raised in anger assaulted her from within. She gasped in fear, in confusion. And then in panic. The other face. Oh God. That hideous mouth, grinning, taunting, shrieking—

Cassandra sat straight up, her scream swallowed by the noise and wailing wind overhead, her senses disoriented by the unfamiliar shadows. The hard surface beneath her tilted. Her eyes widened as her whereabouts crashed back into consciousness. "Sweet Mary," she gasped. "We're at sea."

An exploding fall on deck rent the air. Cassandra shrieked, twisted onto her hands and knees. "I'm awake," she chanted, her words drowned out by the chaos overhead. Scuffling, cursing, another plank-splintering impact. Cassandra scurried backward until the crates lining the ship's bulwark blocked her retreat. The pitch-blackness there only magnified the fiendish noise she'd sought to escape. Shouts. Thundering, running feet.

The screeching above became one with the pounding splitting her skull. Why weren't they anchored in Le Havre? What had happened? *What was happening?* French oaths in an unfamiliar dialect rose above the mayhem and set off more scuffling, renewed cursing. The strange words silenced, as though snuffed out like a candle. Cassandra lurched forward. Judging by the savage violence on deck, her angel-eyed Captain Buchanan might have been no more than a mixture of moonlight and overwrought imagination, but she had to confront the man, immediately. Why had they left Le Havre? Where was her grandfather? The jammed-together boxes, her long skirts, and her heavy cloak hampered her progress but not her rising panic.

The floor beneath her seemed suddenly to stand on end. Cassandra screamed, careened wildly, and was toppled against the stairs leading to the open booby hatch when the ship dipped again with a violence that matched Cassandra's churning insides. She jerked blindly at her tangled cloak and groped up the steep ladderlike steps, her alarm growing apace with the wind that screamed in her ears as she fell through the hatch onto the slick deck.

Salt spray stung her cheeks, burned in her eyes. The wind tore at her hair, billowed her cloak with yanking force. Oblivious to the heaving elements, Cassandra struggled to regain her footing. Sea foam swirled about her hands and knees, soaking her as it washed over the deck. Gasping, she stood up, clutched the hatch for balance, and turned around.

"Dear God."

Sailors, some stumbling, some running, weaved amid floating, splintered wood; loose, tumbling crates; rolling kegs. Cassandra stood unnoticed in the frenzied confusion, deep-pitched shouts and the wind's roar loud in her ears. The scene, bucking up and down with the roughening sea, looked as if it were the aftermath of a sea battle. It was, she realized, her breath catching at the sight of a rumpled form facedown in the swirling foam, a knife in his back.

Arms lunged around Cassandra's waist, snatching her off her feet. Cassandra screamed, kicked, twisted with the strength born of terror.

"Release her! *Navarre!*"

Her feet tangled in her cloak. The arms pinning her let go, and Cassandra landed full force on her hands and knees. Sharp pain shot up her arm from her hand. Crying out, she pulled her hand free from the swirling water. She was cut, bleeding. Feet sloshed into her vision, a pair of long, lean, muscular legs. Cassandra jerked her head back—and stared up into eyes blue, not black, to a stranger bending over her, pulling her to her feet, swearing quietly but quite fluently in blistering French.

"Who are you? Who brought you on board? Who is responsible for you? *Who?*"

Her blood still roiling with the fear let loose moments before, it was another moment before Cassandra realized she was expected to answer. The ice in the man's look as he took a breath to speak again released her tongue.

"No one," she said quickly in French. "I came on alone. Last night." Her true situation and very great need washed back with chilling force. "You must help me! There's been some terrible error and—"

"Quiet," the tall man snapped. He closed his eyes, his look, insanely, reminding Cassandra of Sister Mathilde. "Come with me." He began hauling her, more in haste than in anger, toward the companionway.

"Wait! You must listen to me."

He ignored her, barking orders instead, first in French, then in English. Crewmen jumped to his bidding, retrieving cargo, scaling ropes. He wrenched open the paneled doors of the companionway and called into the dim passage.

"Collier! Doctor Collier!"

"Please." Cassandra pulled on his strong arm with all her strength. "We can't be that far. There's been a mistake," she shouted above the wind.

"Aye." He finally looked at her. "This entire morning's been a comedy of errors. I've lost a small fortune in destroyed or damaged cargo; we've two crewmen killed, the rest bloodied; we are without a captain and first mate, and have a storm breaking over the bow threatening to blow us to Hades. But"—he whirled from Cassandra to a white-haired man Cassandra discovered staring up at them from the bottom of the companionway steps—"in all of this, my Bible-spouting Scotsman, your all-seeing God has seen fit to gift *you* with a nurse!"

"What?" Cassandra and the old man spoke in unison.

"We've a stowaway," the man at Cassandra's side bellowed. "Here!" Strong hands shoved Cassandra into the passage, ignoring her resistance.

"Wait!"

"Get her below, Collier, and keep her out of sight. *I mean it.*" The doors slammed shut.

Cassandra twisted on the top step, her palms striking the wood, sobs gathering in her throat. She didn't care that the stranger behind her might see her cry, that the tall stranger on deck might toss her overboard. Her pride was gone, and Sweet Mary mother of God, this nightmare vessel *had* to turn around.

"No, lass!" The man pulled her back when she reached to open the door. The ship tilted. Cassandra stumbled down the step between them, her momentum taking them both down the last two steps where she regained her footing and reached without thinking to help the old man recover his. Her eyes adjusted to the dimly lit corridor, took in the closed cabin doors lining it, the brighter, skylighted saloon showing at the passageway's far end. She raised her hand, pushing her matted, sea-soaked hair out of her face, pressing her hand to her forehead against the throbbing behind her eyes.

"I'm not a stowaway—or didn't mean to be."

"Ye didna mean t' board this ship?" The man's shaggy brows pulled together above his eyeglasses.

"No. . . . Yes!"

"Ye're bleedin', lass." Firm hands captured Cassandra's wrist, turned her hand palm up. "Ye've been cut." Cassandra tried to tug free, but the man, his grasp stubborn, eyes serious, shook his white head. "Ye can talk in me cabin where I can see t' yer hand." Given no choice, she followed him to one of the doors closest to the saloon entrance. Opening the panel, he stepped back and let her enter ahead of him.

"My God." Her first shock when she'd turned from the hatch topside returned full force. Cassandra swallowed. A man sprawled on the floor atop a rumpled length of gold-threaded scarlet brocade, the material's rich hue no brighter than the angry, egg-sized welt on the sailor's forehead. But it was the other still form, his length too long for the cabin's bunk, that caught—and kept—Cassandra's stricken gaze. Captain Rafael Buchanan.

"Sit on that crate, lass. I canna offer ye better." The old man shut the door and picked his way through the debris to the bunk and the washbasin next to the captain's head. "Here. Clean that cut." He tossed her a cloth and turned back to the man on the bed. Pulling down the blanket, his hands began working gently, quickly. "Let me finish here. Then I'll see to ye proper."

Cassandra's stomach lurched. The wet cloth slipped unnoticed to the rocking floor. She recalled the tall stranger's words concerning the ship's captain, remembered his shouted summons into the companionway. She began trembling violently, saw why this ship was without its leader and this man in need of a nurse. Doctor Collier was sewing Captain Rafael Buchanan's shoulder shut. Cassandra squeezed her eyes closed.

"What's yer name?"

Cassandra hugged herself against the chill seeping through her from the inside out. "Cassandra." She kept her eyes closed. "Cassandra Mortier from Mobile, Alabama, sir, attending school outside Havre." Rafael Buchanan's strong arms holding her weight in the garden came to mind, and she shook the memory away. It was her predicament that needed her concentration. She shuddered, cleared her mind. Captain Buchanan had delivered the letter. Her grandfather'd said they'd be leaving France. But in a fortnight. Not now. Her thoughts blurred, scattered. She wet her lips. "Doctor Collier? Are . . . are there any passengers on board besides . . . me?"

The surgeon grunted from across the room. "Only ye, Mister Hadley who brought ye t' me, an' a pack o' French reivers passin' themselves off as crew. Look at me, lass." Cassandra opened her eyes, careful to look only at the old man, not at his patient on the bunk. "However it happened an' for whatever reasons good or ill, ye've boarded a misnamed vessel, lass, an' there'll be no turnin' back if that be what ye're thinkin'."

Cassandra took a slow breath. No passengers. No turning back. Randall Mortier was in Le Havre, clearing his wretched son's name, closing his business, and believing his granddaughter safe in Denoir packing her trunks. Her hands fisted in her lap.

"If it's a comfort, we be a Confederate ship Nassau-bound. The captain"—the doctor's voice tightened—"he's one o' the best. He'll get ye through the blockade home to Mobile, lass. I promise ye."

Cassandra stared at him, his words rocking her no less than the sea tossing the ship. "Sweet Mary," she groaned under her breath. She'd followed the wrong man, boarded the wrong ship, was headed the wrong direction. . . . She shook her head. "The *Good Fortune* is a . . . Confederate ship?"

Cassandra's laugh startled them both. She felt herself sliding from the crate's top, its slatted side pressing through her cloak bunching up behind her, tissue paper crackling as she landed amidst it on the bucking cabin floor. Covering her face, Cassandra leaned her head back against the crate and laughed harder, higher.

"Lass! Miss Mortier!" Hands closed over her shoulders and shook her. They moved to capture her wrists. The man's grasp penetrated Cassandra's senses. "Look at me."

Cassandra blinked, hiccuped.

"D'ye ken that a man's life be in the hands o' Providence an' no one elses?" he charged, squeezing her wrists tighter. Cassandra's eyes widened. With his wiry white hair sticking out in every direction, his bushy brows furrowed together, and his ferocious, magnified eyes, the man kneeling beside her looked like Moses come down from the mountain. "D'ye?"

Cassandra nodded.

"Then ye must ken from the outset that this man's life or death be God Almighty's work, not yers, even though ye be the one carin' fer him."

"Me?" Cassandra sat upright, nearly knocking the elderly man over.

"No! I don't know—"

"Listen t' me. Ye just may be heaven sent into hell, lass, if ye'll only keep yer wits about ye. These next hours be vital." The intensity burning in his owlish eyes behind his thick spectacles was frightening. "The lad needs care, from whatever quarter he can get it. Ye can help, Miss Mortier. He's a stour man, a good man."

The good man was Captain Rafael Buchanan. Cassandra saw him in Denoir, tall, strong, his hair gilded in lamplight; she saw him on the bunk beyond them, his shoulder bloodied, body limp. "No." She shook her head, closed her eyes. "You're the surgeon. I don't know—"

"Ye can help me; *ye must*. Rafe deserves a fighting chance."

Rafe. The name made him a man, not a mysterious, moon-washed captain, made his hurts real. Her desire to help warred with her fear, her revulsion.

"I'll try, Doctor, but . . ." Her words trailed off.

The surgeon nodded. "That's all any o' us be asked t' do." His eyes gentled. "An' I be Doc, lass, nothin' more an', God willin', nothin' less." He released Cassandra's hands, his manner turning brisk. "Let me dress yer cut, an' then I'll show ye what needs t' be done."

Chapter Four

TWO DAYS LATER Rafe remained sprawled on the bunk in Doc's cabin, but it was Cassandra, curled tightly into a ball on her side, who lay on the floor. The first mate, furious and foul-mouthed, had returned to his duties. The scattered cargo had been repacked into the crates cramping the cabin's space, and the wind still howled outside.

"Fils d' putain!"

Cassandra tensed, the captain's garbled curse dragging her out of the blessed respite of sleep. "No," she groaned, dreading the battle ahead. No more. Her every muscle and nerve ending pleaded for mercy. Cassandra raised her arm and let it fall back down across her eyes. Two silent tears rolled into her hair.

"I'm not a nurse," she choked through clenched teeth. Devil take it, the man outweighed her by over one hundred pounds. If there was a way to get Rafael Buchanan to swallow the laudanum Doc insisted was vital save by jamming the spoon halfway down the twisting captain's throat, Cassandra hadn't discovered it. It's only the fever, Doc had assured her during his one fleeting appearance since a sailor had been blown from the rigging and the surgeon had been forced to amputate the crewman's leg. Cassandra shuddered. Still, fever or no fever, it was Captain Buchanan's hands that fought her, Captain Buchanan's eyes that burned her with their glazed hate, Captain Buchanan's savage oaths that drowned out Cassandra's pleas. Her apologies.

There was the muffled bang of a door and hurried footsteps came down the companionway steps. Cassandra sat up, shoving her hair away from her face and swiping at her cheeks with the backs of her hands as the cabin door opened.

"Doc?"

It wasn't the surgeon. In the cabin's darkness, Cassandra tensed. The light from the hall silhouetted a form she didn't recognize. As surefooted as a cat, the man crossed to the lamp and the room blazed with light. Cassandra blinked, frowned. It was the first mate. He shrugged out of his slicker, stepped over Cassandra's legs without a glance, and bent over Rafe.

"It is Dom, me. I come as soon as—Coton. Oh, Coton."

A ragged half-sob, half-oath shook the man's thin frame. Cassandra shifted uneasily. This Dom was the other man from the garden in Denoir. She knew it without knowing how she knew, just as she felt the man's physical anguish for his friend. Coton? She let go a tiny prayer, her spirits lifting with it.

"He's . . . he's been delirious," she said. Dom ignored her, his attention now on Rafe's shoulder. He tightened the bandaging here, loosened it there. Cassandra felt herself flushing, as if her efforts were being examined and found wanting. She pushed the feeling aside. "He needs more laudanum."

"Non!" Dom exploded. Cassandra shrieked as he whirled and came toward her, his ranting louder, faster, his index finger jabbing closer and closer to Cassandra's

nose. She recognized the strange French she'd heard while still in the hold, recognized it further as the French patois of the Acadians she'd overheard when visiting in New Orleans as a child.

A persecuted people, she recalled her grandfather telling her. A proud people. Dom paused, out of breath. Cassandra slapped his finger away from her face. Proudly and proficiently profane, she seethed. "Hold your filthy tongue. Your friend—"

"No laudanum. *Non!*" Dom hissed. He stepped forward, and Cassandra shoved him out of her way as she scrambled to her feet.

"He needs his strength to fight the fever, not pain." Her voice rose with her temper. "Doc said—"

"You will listen to Dom, not Doc!"

"*You* listen!" They were nose to nose. "It's time to give him his medicine. You're here. And damn your surly"—Cassandra flung out her arm, words failing her in her fury—"ignorance! You're going to help me give him—" She screamed and grabbed for the bunk's edge as the floor tilted. Dom stumbled forward. They cracked heads. The Acadian swore and jerked back. Cassandra clung to the bunk, the cabin spinning.

"Dammit, who's at the helm?"

They both whirled to Rafe, who was straining to sit up in the bunk. He collapsed, sweat pouring down his face, glistening across his shoulders in the flickering lantern light. Cassandra forgot the first mate, forgot her anger in her fear.

"Lie still! You must—" She stopped, stunned by the humor dancing in Captain Buchanan's black, fever-bright eyes. It vanished when he looked from her to the hovering first mate.

"Get topside. That's an order."

"I am where I belong, me. And I swear before your maman I will kill him for—"

"She's listing. I can feel it!"

The Acadian's thick moustache quivered beneath his veined nose. "I go," he grunted. Turning, he made a great, and to Cassandra's mind unnecessary, ramming and rattling about gathering up his raingear. His hand on the cabin door's latch, he glared over his shoulder at Cassandra. "No more, that." Cassandra, rubbing the tender lump forming on her forehead, glared right back at him. "I will be back."

"Not if—" The door banged shut on her words. *"Oh."* If she'd had something in her hands, she'd have thrown it. "What a blasphemous . . . belligerent . . . *awful* man!"

"Hardheaded, too."

Cassandra looked down. She stood beside the bunk, one hand still clutching its ledge against the storm's battering assault. Captain Buchanan lay watching her, but even cast in the shade of Cassandra's shadow she could make out the darker twin pools of his eyes and the white of his teeth—grinning.

Cassandra stared. He was awake. He wasn't fighting, rolling, screaming obscenities. He was talking, talking sense. Grinning? The fear that had wound tighter and tighter in her chest since Doc had been called away eased. Her eyes filled, for no reason she could name. Relief. Release. It didn't matter.

"Don't. Don't . . . cry." Rafe's voice was low, hoarse. His hand groped for her arm. "Come here." Cassandra stepped back, shaking her head. If his voice was weak, his grip was not. "Come here."

"No." He was guiding her down, tugging her gently onto the bunk beside him. Cassandra's heart thudded, but her arms and legs seemed of a sudden leaden, the bunk's cramped width a haven drawing her against her will. "No," she said more forcefully. "I should rewrap your—"

"If it needed doing, Dom would have done it." His good arm came around her waist and, shifting, cursing under his breath, he settled her awkwardly against his uninjured shoulder with her head tucked under his chin. "There," he grunted. "Go . . . to sleep." Cassandra swallowed, closed her eyes, and struggled to breathe evenly. The heat radiating from Rafe's long bulk pressed to hers registered, obliterating every other distress.

"You're still burning up!" She raised her head, straining against his arm circling her back. "Let me go." She jerked her head back. Rafe swore in pain. Cassandra froze. They both lay silent, still, their breathing loud in Cassandra's ears, rasping breaths dragging in and out in tandem with the whine and roar of the storm above them. She offered no resistance when the captain moved, slowly, and resettled her against him, her head again firmly beneath his chin.

"Merde," he sighed into her hair. "I'd . . . lay odds . . . Dom's head hurts worse . . . than yours does."

His breathing slowed but it was shallow, labored. She'd hurt him. Again. "I'm sorry," she choked.

"About Dom's head?"

His gentle humor cut deep, much deeper than any accusation could have done. Cassandra trembled. Rafe's hold tightened.

"Don't," he ordered. No, soothed. Cassandra closed her eyes. Sweet Mary, what a mockery: her charge in charge, him comforting her. This shouldn't be happening. But . . . "That's right, little one. It's all right." His voice rumbled in his chest against Cassandra's ear. She opened her eyes but didn't protest when his hand covered hers. Her muscles relaxed in her arms, down her legs. She felt . . . safe. Which was strange, even silly. She let the thought drift away. He was so warm. She was so cold, so tired. Her eyelids drooped shut. What a nurse, her brain roused itself to taunt. Cassandra jerked her eyes open.

"It's time for more—"

"Non." The man beside her shuddered. "All I need . . . is sleep. And you . . . as much . . . as me."

"The medicine is important, Captain Buchanan. You've not gotten down nearly what Doc instructed I—" Cassandra stopped. He was slipping into unconsciousness. She sensed it, irrationally, instinctively. His arm pinning her to his side pressed heavier, trapping her. "Captain?" Concern stabbed through her, shooting out tendrils of fear. "Rafe?" She raised her head.

"Thought . . . thought . . . I . . . was dreaming." His words were slurred. Cassandra strained to hear him. "If . . . if I wasn't dreaming . . . you've been . . . living a nightmare." His callused thumb brushed the top of Cassandra's hand beneath his, a feeble movement that set off an aching in Cassandra's heart. "I'll make it . . . right." Cassandra wanted to tell him to stop, tell him he bore no responsibility for her foolishness or for his delirium. But no words could push past the lump in her throat. She lay mute and miserable, lulled by the steady beat of his heartbeat and hers, rocked by the storm, feeling trapped, feeling helpless—yet safe. Warm.

They slept.

The dream.

Cassandra moaned in her sleep. Her specter floated above her, hidden in shadow but for his eyes. She wasn't afraid, not of him. She'd never been afraid of him. It was the other face, the other—Cassandra stiffened. She had to wake up. Now. Before *he* came. She was so hot. Burning hot. Suffocating. Her eyes opened to the rocking blackness of the cabin, and it was a full minute before her heart slowed, before she recalled the dream and how the fear of the nightmare and the sweltering heat had dragged her from sleep. Captain Buchanan shuddered, and Cassandra remembered where she was. Twisting, resting her weight on her shoulder below his, she tried to make out his face. One look, even in the cabin's gloom, and Cassandra was scrambling out of the bunk. The burning heat had not been a dream.

The captain was drenched with perspiration, as was the front of her gown and the coarse bed linens. "God. Oh, God," she panted, prayed. He tossed, began trembling violently. Beating down her panic, Cassandra relit the lamp and tried to think. Nothing Doc had explained had foretold Rafe's newest agony. His teeth began chattering. Biting back a sob, Cassandra grabbed up the two moth-eaten blankets someone had brought for her use and added them to the captain's covering. She bathed his face, his neck. The water in the tin basin turned as hot as his skin. Still he shivered uncontrollably, giant wrenching shudders that surely robbed him of what strength he had and shredded what hope she'd felt when he'd broken free of the delirium. Slapping the rag back into the basin, Cassandra pushed her hair away from her face, pressed her fingers to her throbbing temples. What else did she know to—"The laudanum! I didn't give him the laudanum!"

"It's here. I know it's here." Cassandra flung aside the dented spoon and pillaged the box containing Doc's supplies a third time. But the vial of laudanum was gone. She circled their cramped space on her hands and knees, groping with shaking fingers into the cracks between the cargo crates, the indentations gouged in the planked floor. Her throat was dry, her pulse racing. Her forehead banged into a crate in her haste. Dom.

"He *took* it." Damning Rafe Buchanan's "friend" for a thief and a murderer, Cassandra pushed up from the floor and stumbled drunkenly to the door. Rafe tossed behind her, his groans swallowed by the door's crash against the wall as Cassandra flung herself into the narrow passageway. "Doc!" She turned one way, then back the other. "Doc!"

A youngster, his *café au lait* skin soft in the lamplight, hurried toward her from the saloon. Eyes wide and black with alarm searched her face.

"Missy? Is it . . . is it . . . ?"

"Get Doc! Quickly!"

Nodding, almost knocking Cassandra into the wall, the boy lunged past her and disappeared up the companionway steps at the far end of the passage. She heard the wind, the doors bang open and closed, and sank to the floor. Rafe called out from the cabin, garbled prayers—or blasphemies. "Hurry. Hurry," Cassandra breathed, her words lost in the folds of her skirts as she sat with her forehead resting on her knees. What if it was too late? She began shaking, suddenly certain the captain was dying, dying a terrible death.

"Miss Mortier? Lass!"

Chaos rained down on her as first Doc, then Dom, another sailor, and the young mulatto tumbled into the passageway. Someone moved her bodily else she be trampled. Huddled in the hall outside the open door, she didn't try to follow them into the cabin. She couldn't, couldn't move, couldn't help. She couldn't watch him die. She covered her ears. Did all sailors always talk all at once—at the top of their lungs?

"Miss . . . Mortier? Is that your name?" Large hands closed over Cassandra's shoulders and squeezed gently, insistently. "Can you stand? Let me help you."

Cassandra raised her head from her knees and let the tall man bending over her help her to her feet. Her knees buckled, and he caught her weight easily, his raingear rattling loudly in Cassandra's ears.

"Come with me." Without waiting for her reply, the stranger guided Cassandra toward the saloon, his arm firmly about her waist.

"The captain," she said weakly. "I . . . I think he's . . . he's . . ."

"Don't. Don't upset yourself further." The man's manner was resolute, his words soothing. "You've been through enough, Miss Mortier. I am partially to blame, and I trust you will allow me to make some effort at amends for this"—he paused—"mistake." His words surprised Cassandra from her fogged thoughts. They were standing in the doorway of the larger room at the end of the hall. She looked up and realized she was staring at the man who'd so curtly handed her over to Doc. Some scrap of spirit returned with the recollection.

"*I* called it a mistake, sir. You called it a comedy."

The tall sailor's dark, wildly curling hair glistened in the lamplight, but it was his eyes that Cassandra watched. She'd seen them icy. Now they were clear, piercing. Her remark hadn't angered him, she decided, but his look still chilled. As if he'd read her thoughts, the man looked away and motioned her ahead of him into the room.

"Sit down, Miss Mortier." He led her to one of the heavy chairs pushed under the long table taking up the saloon's center. Seating her, he moved to her side and leaned against the table's ledge, his arms crossed over his chest, his gaze once more studying Cassandra until she looked up and studied the skylight above them to keep from squirming in her chair. The skylight added no light to the room but much noise as the rain clattered and drummed against it. Cassandra was grateful for the racket in the stretching silence. The tall man cleared his throat. Holding her breath, Cassandra looked at him.

A dark, finely shaped brow cocked above arresting blue eyes. "This storm"—he glanced up—"whether it sounds like it or not, is blowing itself out." He smiled. Cassandra straightened in her chair, unsettled by how it softened his chiseled features. "We seem to have gotten blown off course at the outset along with the ship. May we begin again?"

Cassandra looked away, stared sadly at a lamp secured to the wall. What she wouldn't give to begin again—and do differently. She sighed and faced the sailor as well as reality. "I am Cassandra Anna Maria Mortier, sir. Captain Buchanan delivered a letter to my school. From my grandfather. I"—she paused, hearing her own foolishness and hating it—"I ran away from school and boarded this ship thinking my grandfather was taking it out of Le Havre." She stared at her hands clutched tightly together in her lap. "Obviously, I was . . ."

"Mistaken." Cassandra nodded, felt the man's gaze on the top of her bent head. "Did Buchanan know this?" She shook her head. "Does anyone know?" Cassandra started to shake her head again and stopped.

"I left a note. At school. Lucy will know I followed Captain Buchanan, and Sister Mathilde might remember the name of his ship." That by now her grandfather had certainly been notified and was in a state of pure panic over her disappearance rolled over Cassandra like a wave. Her eyes filled. "He's . . . frantic by now." She watched her hands squeeze tighter in her lap but didn't feel anything but remorse. Choking, churning remorse.

"Would your grandfather happen to be Mister Randall Mortier?"

"You know him? You know my grandfather?" Cassandra toppled the chair jumping up from it. The man beside her stood up with her, frowning. He shook his head, held up his hand to stop her advance and spurt of questions.

"I know of him, Miss Mortier." He turned abruptly and crossed to a cabinet. Cassandra followed him, watched him pour amber liquid into a glass. "Mortier is a name well established among Le Havre merchants," he said, turning to face her, "and I am a buyer for my uncle who is an established merchant in San Francisco." He met Cassandra's look and smiled. "Unfortunately, I've never had the pleasure of meeting one so esteemed as Randall Mortier in the short time I've been in Havre." Cassandra frowned. He looked much more sailor than businessman in his dripping oilcloth and sodden clothes. Her look must have said as much because the man glanced down his front before he turned away stiffly and downed his brandy in one swallow.

"My name is Lawrence Hadley. The *Fortune* sails for my uncle Bernard, and I boarded as supercargo, not seaman."

"I . . . I see," Cassandra said. Struggling to assimilate this new information, she crossed back to the table and stooped to right the overturned chair. Lawrence Hadley moved quickly and picked it up himself, then stood at attention behind it, waiting for her to sit down. Cassandra shot him a look. He certainly hadn't the manners of a common sailor. "Shall I ring for the butler, Mister Hadley?"

"Cuffey is the ship's boy, Miss Mortier. He's hardly a butler, but he does what he's told well enough."

No sense of humor either. Sighing, Cassandra sat down.

"Can I get you anything? Have you eaten?" The tall supercargo moved to his place beside her, leaning his weight against its edge. Cassandra met his gaze and thought no more of joking.

"Can you get me back to my grandfather inside of a fortnight?"

"No." His answer was immediate, final. Cassandra looked down at her lap. "Miss Mortier. Now that I am aware of who you are and your true situation, I will do everything within my power to make this up to you, and I vow—"

"Turning back is not within your power, Mister Hadley?"

Hadley pushed away from the table and crossed the room where he removed his slicker and hung it on a hook. Cassandra followed his deliberate movements. Lawrence Hadley was a young man with powerful shoulders and natural grace. His black hair curled over the collar of his expensive linen shirt. Without his outer wear, he looked the gentleman he was, although there was a restlessness about him that seemed at odds with his refined manners. And, her chin raised, merchant's granddaughter that she was, she knew damn well that as supercargo Lawrence Hadley had the authority to change their course.

"You are a daughter of the South." It was a statement, not a question. Cassandra nodded though she loathed his choice of words. The rhetoric of "The Cause" that had banished her from her home, glorified her father as a martyred hero, and stolen her place in her grandfather's life disgusted her. "My uncle is"—the tall man paused and studied Cassandra a long moment—"a philanthropist, I suppose. He feels a great responsibility to right the wrongs of mortal humanity whenever and wherever and however an opportunity presents itself."

Cassandra stopped listening. Lawrence Hadley's uncle was no concern of hers; her concerns were of as little interest to Lawrence Hadley. She leaned wearily against the oak chair's back. Her head was throbbing, stomach unsettled. She shivered—and, rubbing her arms for warmth, remembered Captain Buchanan. An aching sadness pressed down on her, adding its weight to her misery. The raised voices from Doc's cabin next door had ceased. Did that mean—she shook her head, a surge of nausea forcing her to swallow. She glanced up, not wanting to listen, think, know. Lawrence Hadley was still speaking. She'd not heard a word.

"So he resolved to come to the aid of the wounded in the South and redeem his long-lost sister's son in one fell swoop as it were." Hadley lifted a long, strong index finger. "Not that I didn't appreciate the opportunity to better my circumstances or disagree with sending aid through the blockade." His eyes turned a deeper blue in the light of the lamps. "I only tell you all this, Miss Mortier, because I fear Captain Buchanan might have led you to believe I was"—he frowned—"less than exemplary in my duties regarding my uncle's charge. Whatever the captain's opinion of me or my opinion of my uncle, I *have* boarded the medicine requested, and I *am* committed to delivering it to Nassau ahead of my own personal investments also boarded."

This entire speech made little sense to Cassandra. The fact remained that they were going to Nassau, not Le Havre. She was too tired to argue her case further. In truth, she was feeling much worse than tired, and the longer she sat the worse she felt. Lawrence Hadley began talking again. His voice sounded muffled, far away.

"You have my solemn word that I will see you safely returned to your family as soon as—Miss Mortier? Miss Mortier!" The supercargo leaped forward and caught Cassandra as she slid from the chair. Swearing, he hefted her into his arms and strode to a door off the saloon, his bellowed "Cuffey!" ringing then fading in Cassandra's ears.

Chapter Five

CASSANDRA OPENED HER eyes and blinked at the brightness flooding the cabin. She let her lids flutter closed. The light was soothing, warm, like—her eyes snapped open—like sunshine. Her other senses came awake with a jolt. The skylight was propped ajar overhead, and fresh, sea-salted air teased her nose. The *Good Fortune* rocked gently to the creak and snap of rope and canvas, the storm's absence deafening. Blessing the mattress beneath her no thicker than the one she'd cursed nightly at school, Cassandra let her eyes roam the unfamiliar room.

It was bigger than Doc's cabin and not cluttered with cargo. The white walls soaked up the sunlight and radiated a heat of their own. From the built-in bunk, she gazed over at the cabin's longer wall. A railed bookshelf boasted a half-dozen dog-eared volumes with cracked spines. A sea chest, as well-used as the books, sat beside a desk that captured her attention. Ornately carved, a study in scrollwork and inlaid ivory with polished brass and porcelain pulls, the desk was worthy of a place in her grandfather's study back home at Leeland. Cassandra frowned. Was this the ship captain's cabin?

She closed her eyes. This ship no longer had a captain. The bunk was suddenly hard, the sun's welcoming warmth gone.

"Miz Mortier?"

Cassandra jumped, turned her head. The youngster who had run for Doc sat cross-legged on the floor opposite the desk, his thin shoulders against the closed cabin door. He smiled, shyly, his cheeks dimpling in his round face.

"Doc said I was t' stay till you woke up. I'm Cuffey." His chest puffed out under his yellowed cotton shirt. "Ship's boy."

Cassandra took a deep breath. "Cuffey," she repeated, stalling, not wanting to ask but needing to know. "Captain Buchanan. Tell me. What . . . when. . . ." She stopped.

Cuffey beamed. "Woke up long enough t' drink some broth an' was hisself enough t' call it bilge slop just 'fore daylight."

"What?" Cassandra struggled up on her elbows and stared across the room. "You mean he's not—" She stopped, the boy's words taking hold. "He's all right?"

"Oh, no, Miz Mortier." Concern hushed the boy's voice. "Doc, he say he's still plenty bad off an' weak as Samson after Delilah." His teeth flashed white against his soft brown skin. "That's Doc's way o' talkin'—an' good thing, too."

Cassandra sat all the way up in the bunk, tugging the top blanket with her. She could feel her heart racing beneath her hands.

"But for Doc I mighta had t' stow away, just like you." Cassandra was only half listening. She wished the cabin boy gone. She had to go check on the captain. "But Mama learnt he was a preacher man's son an' all. Yessir." Cuffey's melodramatic sigh snagged Cassandra's attention. "Doc's way o' puttin' things saved me a thrashin' I was sure enough not lookin' forward to." His black eyes were so round Cassandra grinned and forgot her impatience. "I'm beholden to Doc, Miz Mortier. Sure as sure."

"I see." And she did. Hadn't Jim done the same for her regularly? Not that Lalie hadn't won her share of confrontations. Cassandra's smile faded. Only Lalie had stood steadfast in the face of her small charge's very large capacity for willfulness. Not for the first time, Cassandra wondered if that stern black woman still kept an ever vigilant eye from her well-earned reward in heaven. Sometimes the thought comforted. Cassandra grimaced. Today was definitely not one of those times.

"I'da had it comin'," Cuffey said. "Captain Rafe, he don't say what he don't mean. No sir."

"*He* promised to beat you?" Cassandra stared at the cabin boy. Mothers and mammies were one thing, but grown men, gentlemen and gentle men like her grandfather and Jim, would never threaten violence to children.

"Aye." Cuffey shrugged, nonplussed, and stood up. "He knowed I was set on sailin' with him." Shooting her another grin, he turned and opened the door. "I best tell Doc you're all right." Before Cassandra could say more, he'd disappeared. Before she could toss the covers aside, Doc appeared: brisk, brusque, and blunt.

"Are you telling me I'm confined to this cabin?"

"Ye're t' be commended for all yer help, lass, but we didna know ye were gentle born—"

"Gentle born! Since when? Says who?"

"Mister Hadley seems t' think ye're in need o' coddlin' an' . . . protection from the common elements, t' use his words."

"Is that what *you* think? Do I look in need of"—she almost choked—"coddling?"

"I be too common meself t' appreciate our Mister Hadley, true enough, but"—Doc's bushy brows drew together ominously over his spectacles—"*I* think ye look a sorry sight o' skin an' bones in need o' rest, food, an' quiet, an' *I am* confinin' ye t' that bunk till I see high color in those cheeks not put there by a temper more fittin' a first mate than any gentleman merchant's granddaughter."

It was like arguing with Old Mat. Cassandra flopped back on her pillow, tight-lipped and, she was sure, flushed to her hairline. The surgeon changed the dressing on her hand in like silence, slammed his supplies back into his box, and left.

Seething, Cassandra stared at the ceiling, at the closed door. She got up and paced, climbed back into the bunk and tried to go back to sleep. Giving up, she stared again at the ceiling, tired but no closer to accepting this unexpected turn of events. She sighed. Not that any events since she'd opened her grandfather's letter had turned exactly to her liking. Cuffey arrived with dried apples and beans, her carpetbag, his welcome smile, and more welcome information. Captain Buchanan was still sleeping; Doc had taken his own advice and was snoring loud enough to wake the dead in the crew's quarters near his other patients; Lawrence Hadley was overseeing the salvaging and securing of what was left of the deck cargo. It took several loud yawns, but Cuffey finally judged Cassandra was more in need of sleep than food. He left, promising not to let anyone bother her the rest of the day. She was digging through her bag before the barefoot cabin boy's light tread faded down the passageway.

"Close your eyes, Lalie," she mumbled, yanking into a clean change of clothes. Tossing her brush onto the bed, Cassandra shrugged her heavy, single braid out of the way and grinned as she peeked out the door and up and down the corridor. Lalie would not have approved.

•

Doc's cabin had no skylight, but sunshine poured through its open porthole. Cassandra leaned lightly against the closed door, content to measure the captain's steady breathing with her ears, trace the sunlight tangling in his hair with her eyes. She'd never seen him in this much daylight. Cassandra swallowed. It'd be a sight she'd not soon forget.

The blanket had slipped to his waist, leaving his wide, sun-bronzed chest bare but for the bandaging. The hair matting his chest was as she remembered it, a cinnamon-brown glinting copper. How well she knew the width of him, the hard strength of the muscles down his arms, across his shoulders. Stop it, she lectured herself. She'd only come to see for herself that he was all right. Gentle born was a bit thick, but surely she was above . . . ogling.

Maybe not.

She couldn't keep from studying his face, was unable to resist marveling at this man's ability to appear so strong, his strength a tangible presence even in sleep and physical weakness. Why Captain Rafael Buchanan affected her the way he did was a mystery to Cassandra. She only knew that he did, that he had from the moment in the garden when she'd stood looking up at him, his hands circling her waist. She cocked her head, her thick braid heavy against her back. Maybe that was . . . whatever this was. The mystery of it. Her need to know had gotten her into as many scrapes as her stubbornness had won for her spankings.

On tiptoe she crossed to rearrange his blanket. Her hands moved awkwardly; heat crept up her neck when her fingers brushed the hair on his chest. Sweet Mary. Up close merely watching him breathe made her own breath catch in her throat. The door behind her creaked.

Cassandra whirled, her gasp ending in a groan. It was Dom. "He's asleep." She stopped, steadying her voice under the first mate's black glare. "He needs quiet."

Dom grunted and shut the door. "He needs his ears boxed, him." Cassandra's eyes narrowed, and Dom scowled at her look. "I been seeing after his needs since he was in wet clothes, *aihn*? Stand to."

"Stand to?" Cassandra bristled. "What does that mean? Ignore your threats? Your thieving interference?"

The two took each other's measure a full minute, the captain's breathing the only sound in the cabin, the *Fortune*'s gentle swaying the only movement. Squaring his shoulders, the Acadian moved to the bunk beside Cassandra.

"I do not come to rearrange his ears," he grumbled. He stared down at the sleeping man. His voice softened. "It is a waste of time."

Cassandra stepped back—and told herself she was being considerate, not cowardly. She willed herself to relax, but this man put her teeth on edge. No matter his obvious concern for his friend, the first mate's ignorance was . . . dangerous. Her anger resurfaced. "Doc will replace the laudanum, you know. Taking it again will be a further waste of your time."

"Po yi." Dom turned, his movements tired, old. Cassandra bit her lip and fought to hold on to her anger in the face of the weariness etched into every crevice crisscrossing the man's walnut-dark features. He leaned back against a crate and looked at her.

"Doc . . . he's a surgeon. He knows . . ." His look stole her words, his black gaze never wavering. The silence dragged out between them.

"He almost died, him."

Cassandra jumped at Dom's low, strangled words. His eyes moved to the sleeping captain's face, but Cassandra sensed his thoughts looked elsewhere.

"They flushed out the poison, yes. But not the pain. *Non*. The taste of it, it bleeds in his soul." Dom's voice dropped to a hoarse whisper. "Forgive me, Coton."

Cassandra frowned, glanced from the older man to Rafe. Coton. Of course. As light as the grown captain's hair was now, it had surely been cotton-white as a child. Rafe was Coton. Was Dom Rafe's father? Cassandra's look swung back to the wizened, ill-humored Acadian with his ugly nose. Before she could decide how to ask, decide if she even wanted to know, Dom spoke.

"The laudanum. It is . . . poison."

"Poison." Cassandra stared. "Dom," she began.

"I come back, me," Dom went on as if Cassandra hadn't spoken. "Always I go to Fronie and Coton right away. That Anton. Bah! He is a good trapper, him, but good for nothing else. I know they will not starve, but that is all. Always I try to make her see, make her come back, her. Anton, he is nothing to her, to even himself, yes? And what he has he owes to Fronie's hands more than his own. But *non*. She will not listen. *Ah, la quinche*. She will not hear, her. Buchanan. It is him. She is afraid." Dom shivered, his chill in some way passing to Cassandra, sending a shudder down her spine though she stood in the porthole's sunshine. "You were right, my littlest sister," Dom said, his voice hushed. "You were right to be afraid."

"You are his . . . uncle," Cassandra breathed, struggling to follow Dom's jumbled story. He looked back at her for the first time, his eyes black with pain.

"Aye. It was with me the planter Buchanan first saw Fronie. Bah!" He stared down at his gnarled hands. They fisted against his thighs. "I did not know, me. *Non.* I go to sea. I come back. Little Fronie, she is—" He stopped, his face twisting. "The *Américain,* I want to kill him. I would have"—one fist pounded his leg—*"should have."*

Dom leaned his head back and closed his eyes. Cassandra held her breath, waiting. "For Fronie, I do not. She loves him, she tells me, weeping in my arms like the child she was but for his seed in her belly. Him! Him who is already taking his *Américain* bride to his papa's plantation, his promises to our Fronie as recalled as last summer's rain." Dom spat into the corner and fell silent. It was Cassandra's turn to study her hands clasped tightly in front of her. Her fingers were trembling.

"I took Fronie with me, to New Orleans. Away from our family's disgrace, and with her babe, the light, it come back into her eyes. Little, little at first, but her Coton, he is her light, yes? And then"—Dom swore—"the *Américain,* him, he want that too."

Cassandra gasped. "He took her child away from her?"

"The holy saints, them, they led him to me, not her. His wife, he tell me, it has been three years. She is barren. A just thing, I think, but I am silent, me. I take his money, let him think I will sell my own Coton, that Fronie, her, she does not matter to me because she does not matter for him. And we run, go deep, deep into the bay marshes." Cassandra swallowed and sank onto her knees, not trusting her legs to hold her weight. Barataria Bay. It called up pictures at once: murky waters, pirates, creatures never seen in daylight, a childhood of Jim's begged-for, best-loved stories.

Dom leaned forward from his waist, the plea in his tortured words cutting through Cassandra's memories. "Fronie, she will not come back, her. I cannot stay. So. I let them go with Anton. I will go to sea. I will come back. Fronie, she will be ready then, *aihn*?" He straightened back against the crate and sighed wearily. "This I tell myself the first time, the second time, always. Anton, I do not like him, *non*. But Fronie, she feels safe, her. And Coton"—Dom's face softened—"the marsh, it is a part of him like the sea in his blood. So." Dom shrugged.

"At sea I make a vow that Fronie, she will do as I say, put away her woman's fears. But always I come back and they are safe, happy. I leave them again with Anton. *May he burn in hell with the Caller's fire on his head.*" Cassandra froze, not wanting to hear more yet straining forward to catch the Acadian's raspy words.

"I come back. They are gone. I am a crazy man, me. I track Anton, but his black waters are for him, against me. I learn Fronie, she is dead. A fever. A sickness. I learn"—Dom's voice strangled—"Anton, he has sold the boy to the *Américain*."

"Sweet Mother of God." Cassandra couldn't look longer at the old man's memory-ravaged face. She focused on the man asleep beyond them, her eyes burning. How terrifying it must have been—how wrong!—for a child to lose his mother and be so suddenly yanked into an alien world all at once.

"How . . . how old was he?" Cassandra's mother had died when she was three; her father had left her when she was five. Though she'd deny it to her last breath, too well she remembered the loss.

"Six years." Dom sighed. "Seven, maybe. Too young to go to sea else, I swear by Fronie and the Virgin,

I would have gone for him." He groaned. "I was a fool."

The catch in Dom's voice brought Cassandra's gaze back to him. He had covered his face with his hands. His words, when they came at last, came muffled. "Buchanan, he was the boy's father, yes? Rich, him. With a new wife, a new, young wife. A maman for Coton, yes? So. I went back to New Orleans, me. To sea." He raised his head from his hands, perhaps unaware but unashamed of the tears that tracked his lined cheeks. His black, black eyes bore into hers. Cassandra trembled. Rafe's eyes. "To this day, him, he tell me nothing about his father's house. Only that he ran away. A cabin boy at ten, a seaman grown when next I see him. But Cuffey's maman, her, she was with him there. She tells me what I know." Dom took a deep breath and stared out the porthole. Cassandra waited.

"The *Américain*'s new wife, she is not barren, her. The babes, they come. All girls. In her witch's mind, she blames her husband's bastard seed in her house, vows to purge her husband's sin by . . . by poisoning Fronie's Coton."

"No." Cassandra felt her mouth going dry. Dom met her stricken look with eyes again hard, fierce.

"With laudanum." Cassandra closed her eyes. Stop, her mind screamed. She didn't want to hear any more, couldn't face what she—"Look at me," Dom ordered. She raised her head. "You will listen to Dom, not Doc. No laudanum. *Non*." He pushed away from the crate, yanked open the door, and was gone.

Cassandra bent forward from her waist clutching her stomach. She saw again the naked hatred in the captain's pain-glazed eyes, understood at last the savage desperation fueling his war with her spoon. Captain

Rafael Buchanan. Rafe. Captain Rafe. Coton. Like flotsam caught in an eddy his names swirled in her mind. "I didn't know," she whispered over and over. "I didn't know." Wave after wave of emotion rocked her, leaving her shaken and spent. And numb. She straightened. Slowly the room and its crates and hard floor tilting rhythmically with the sea returned. Cassandra shuddered. She should go back to her cabin. She didn't belong here, no longer wanted to be here. She didn't move. She sat, the sea rocking her gently, and stared down at her lap at nothing.

Rafe woke slowly and knew without opening his eyes that the worst was over. Like a ship riding out a storm, the sea was still heavy, the sky leaden, but it was over. With his eyes closed, he let his thoughts drift, unconsciously taking inventory, consciously flexing his hands, limbs, assessing the dull ache behind his eyes, the stabbing pains at his shoulder. His ears caught the whisper of a sigh, and he stilled, came fully awake. Cassandra. Rafe turned his head.

She sat a few feet away framed in the splash of sunlight spilling into the cabin unaware of the picture she made. The pain inside Rafe's head eased. He held himself perfectly still, wanted time to look and assess. And admire. She'd braided her hair but not tamed the dark curls escaping at her nape and temples. Rafe's fingers itched to redo the braid, the heavy rope swinging against her slim back a haphazard effort to his sailor's eyes. Her loose hair's glorious thickness brushing against his hands as he'd disentangled himself in Denoir came to him. He shook the memory away but couldn't ignore the reality of her presence. She was beautiful.

She was a child. A schoolgirl. A convent schoolgirl. His headache returned. What was she doing on board the *Fortune*? Rafe closed his eyes and forced his brain to function. The name Mortier came. That harbormaster in a habit had bid him give regards to a Monsieur Mortier. And the girl. The way she'd looked up at him, the way it had felt circling her small waist with his hands. Rafe wondered if he'd remember that for the rest of his life—and why. He frowned, irritated, and steered his thoughts back to the problem at hand. She'd begged him to take her back with him. Rafe opened his eyes and studied Cassandra again.

She was still beautiful, but now he saw that she also looked drained, pale. Her simple day gown was a common caramel color unworthy of her much darker hair and striking features, but it was quality cloth and clean—and hopelessly wrinkled. His eyes narrowed. As if it had traveled stuffed, not packed carefully away. The ache in his head made him clench his teeth. *Non,* he fought the obvious conclusion forming in his mind, but his thoughts broke loose, luffing like untended sails flapping in high wind. A stowaway. He cursed silently. First Hadley, then the fiasco at the tavern, then the cargo, then his shoulder, and now . . . By everything that was holy, was there any other way this voyage could become any more of a goddamn disaster?

"Merde."

Cassandra's head snapped up. Her stomach lurched. If her moonlit, gentle giant had pulled free of delirium to offer comfort before, Cuffey's forbidding Captain Rafe was glaring at her now. Angry black eyes squashed any doubts Cassandra harbored about the man's capability for child beating. She scrambled to her feet, moving as quickly from remorse to self-defense.

"Captain." She squared her shoulders. "I was only trying to . . . to help you."

"Help me!" Cassandra jumped. "To what? An early grave? *How in the hell* was your—"

"Don't yell at me!" Cassandra screamed. She stormed toward the bunk, her rage fueled by guilt as much as temper. "Yes! *Help you.* How was I to know any differently? Nobody listens on board this damnable ship! Nobody *explains* anything. They just bark orders and"—she flung out her arms—"and disappear!" Rafe reached for her hand. Cassandra snatched it free. He cursed. "And swear!" she railed, regaining momentum.

"Cassandra."

"You think I chose this? Any of it? To be nurse? To be Nassau-bound? To be—"

"Hold, dammit." He captured her hand. She yanked, yanked harder. He laughed, his amusement at her powerlessness the final indignity.

Cassandra let loose a string of curses the likes of which she'd not used—nor heard, for that matter—since she'd used them in front of Lalie and romps up and down the Mobile docks with Jim had ceased to brighten trips to town. Captain Buchanan sat straight up, grabbed her with both hands above her elbows, and cut her off with a well-aimed, hard-planted kiss.

Cassandra's entire body went rigid. Her shriek reduced to a sputtering, feline hiss, she was propelled forward as Rafe flopped back onto the bunk. He released her mouth with a loud *smack*, and Cassandra jerked her head back. The room was reeling, her heart crashing in her chest—as was his beneath her, she realized. The blood roared in her ears. There was no cabin. No walls, no streaming sunshine or muted shouts above. There was only the captain, staring up at her as she stared down at him. A tremor rippled through him. Or was it through her? Cassandra tried to shake her head, shake free. She shivered, opened her mouth—to speak? To breathe? To be kissed again.

She pulled back instinctively, then melted against him as naturally under his gentle onslaught. Groaning, she closed her eyes and her fingers curled about a muscled shoulder, her hand going still when she came to the bandaging there. He shook his head as his lips continued to trail soft kisses over her cheeks. *"Non,"* he mumbled. "It's . . . all right." He found her lips, and Cassandra gasped when his tongue nudged inside. She was floating—and then swirling. How . . . strange, some part of her mind still pondered. His long fingers cradled her head. Hard palms pressed at each side of her neck, and Cassandra leaned more fully against him, no longer thinking. Her senses drank in the softness of his furred chest pressed against the thin cotton of her summer gown, the taste of him, the texture of his lips. Unshaven these last, torturous days, his beard stubble scraped her face, and she cried out and lifted her head. The captain jerked back at the same time, but it was his look, not his sudden stillness, that brought the cabin crashing back about them.

The change in the tension between them was too abrupt. Confused, Cassandra looked down and felt heat rushing up into her face. The captain's hands dropped suddenly back to her arms. Was he reddening? Cassandra sat up, tried to stand.

"Wait." His good arm stayed her.

Her confusion was running quickly to embarrassment. She couldn't meet his eyes, couldn't fathom how, in the space of a heartbeat, she could careen from feeling somehow cherished to feeling downright churlish. Her chin squared. No. It was much worse; she felt as she had the time she'd belched during evening vespers: mortified and, she cringed mentally, childish.

"I . . . apologize." He lifted his hand from her arm, put it back. His sigh was deep, and not a little irritated. She stole a look. His brow furrowed, at odds with his shrug. "It was either kiss you or spank you to get you to—Cassandra!"

Rafe watched her fly from the cabin and winced as the door banged shut. He cursed. He cursed some more. His shoulder was on fire, his head throbbing. It was the truth: he'd kissed her without thinking, wanting only to shut her up.

The first time.

Shame assailed him. *Mon Dieu,* he could feel his face heating, which shamed him more. His fist pounded the bunk's mattress and pain shot up his arm. He welcomed it. He should be flogged for what he'd just allowed to happen. That what had happened had actually happened seared through him, with no redeeming justifications and double the guilt. Dockside whores had never enticed him, but neither had virgin innocents. Rafe groaned, clenching his teeth against the pain splitting his skull. He couldn't think, couldn't take in a breath without feeling his body scream in protest from his head down.

The cabin swirled about him. He shut his eyes. He hurt. Everywhere. He'd hurt that girl. That knowledge pained him. That he'd wanted her, wanted her like he'd no business wanting her, and for precious, delirious moments acted on that desire . . . unnerved him.

"Damn," he groaned, giving in to the rushing tide of exhaustion tugging him under. "Damn, damn . . . damn."

The voyage had just become more of a disaster.

Chapter Six

CASSANDRA EYED HER reflection in the glass of the closed porthole. The glass was too small to show much more than the shoulder-baring décolletage of the exquisite evening gown draping her slender frame. If material was missing above the waist, the yards and yards of shimmering ice-blue satin and deep lace flounces that made up the billowing skirt well compensated for the oversight.

"Devil take it." She turned abruptly from the porthole. This gown made her grey frock still stuffed in her carpetbag look a nun's habit. "One more thing not of my choosing," she grumbled to no one.

Lawrence Hadley had insisted she accept this dress and three others as tokens of his esteem and desire to redeem himself. They had arrived—along with all the accessories from ribbons and hair pins to color-matched, soft kid slippers—draped over Cuffey's skinny arms. Cassandra had sent Cuffey back to the supercargo with the entire lot. But Lawrence Hadley was not a man to be so easily dissuaded. When he returned his gifts a fourth time, Cassandra had accepted them only to save Cuffey from dropsy and herself from the boy's pitiful, pleading eyes.

With a weary groan, Cassandra began winding her

thick, uncooperative hair into an amateurish but passable chignon. She'd accepted his damned dresses. She'd endured his company and insipid conversation for two long afternoons while waiting for Doc to release her from her sickbed. The surgeon had finally pronounced her fit this morning. "Released but not reprieved," she grumbled. Now Lawrence Hadley expected her to begin joining him for the evening meal in the saloon.

"But of course, Mister Hadley," she sighed, her drawl dripping acidic honey. "Dressing formally in a room the size of a closet, with only two hands, no mirror, and absolutely no desire to play primping belle to your prince gallant is what every lady needs to restore her spirits." Cassandra swore. Jabbing her hair back into place, she turned from the porthole and plopped down on the bunk. "You're acting an absolute shrew, Cassandra Anna Maria Mortier, and well you know it."

She didn't need Lucy to point out that Lawrence Hadley was only treating her as a gentleman was expected to treat any gentlewoman. Still, Cassandra wished Lucy there to hear her anyway—so Cassandra could know the pleasure of sticking her tongue out at someone who'd appreciate her present temper and not halo her with tender sensibilities she didn't appreciate and didn't pretend to claim. She gazed morosely down her front. Holy Mary mother of God. Her breasts were barely covered.

Heedless of the fragile satin, she closed her eyes and flopped back on the bunk. She didn't feel like a lady; she felt like screaming, breaking something. And she'd felt so ever since she'd bolted from Captain Rafe Buchanan's presence.

"Damn him."

She knew from Doc that the captain was regaining his strength, his robust health and strong constitution accelerating his recovery. She knew from Cuffey that he was in the devil's own temper, something the cabin boy took in stride and seemed to count a healthy sign. Maybe it was. She opened her eyes and stared at the books lining the wall above the desk. She'd feel a sight better herself if she could rant a while instead of practically chewing her tongue in half to keep from telling Lawrence Hadley to shut up, to go away. She might sleep better as well.

Cassandra's brow knitted. With her childhood dream's return, she'd not slept deeply or well since she'd boarded this cursed ship. Her frown deepened. Once. She'd slept free of her demons once, the night Rafe Buchanan had pulled free of the delirium and drawn her into his bunk, his voice comforting, rumbling in his chest against her ear, his solid bulk pressed to her softer one.

Heat flushed Cassandra's face, and her heart, encased in pinching whalebone and impossible laces, thudded painfully. The gentleness of the captain's comforting paled against the memory of his kisses the second time he'd yanked, not guided, her against his hard chest. For two torturous nights she'd lain in her bunk fearing the nightmare and remembering against her will his lips moving over her face, his tongue invading her mouth setting her senses to riot.

Cassandra stood, swatting at her tangled skirts. Her vision blurred, and she blinked furiously. She was swaddled in this . . . this contraption called a gown and being slowly strangled by her blasted thoughts as well. She straightened her shoulders, took a deep, shaky breath. She was going to explode or asphyxiate.

Stalking to the porthole, she opened it with trembling fingers. Sea-salted night air fanned her hot cheeks. She breathed deep, deeper. Captain Buchanan's parting words smarted as much as his remembered kisses confused. He thought her a child, had only grabbed her in order to still her . . . her what? Tantrum? Her chin jutted up. The mighty captain would yet rue the day he'd mistaken her for some malleable innocent who could be struck dumb with a kiss. "Either spank me or kiss me, my eye," she seethed. "Arrogant . . . sailor." She pronounced his trade like a curse.

How she wished he'd chosen to spank her instead. Or tried. She would have known better how to react to that, would have let him know in short order his mistake, and he would be the one still smarting now, not her. But he'd kissed her. Cassandra's hands squeezed the bottom rim of the porthole opening. And instead of clobbering him, she'd melted in his arms. "Like a swooning, penny-novel nincompoop."

Next time would be different, she vowed. Her stormy grey eyes narrowed. And there would be a next time. Her sensibilities weren't tender, but the Creole blood in her veins demanded satisfaction.

Cassandra took a deep breath, her senses straining for the smells of the open sea, the rush of the waves sluicing against the sleek ship's sides, the song sounds of sails and rigging. Her pulse slowed, mind cleared. She turned from the porthole, and the weight of her skirts set in motion made her glance down. She watched the rich satin shimmer and swirl as it settled. Its blue was the shade of the supercargo's eyes. Cassandra started to grimace, stopped. A wicked mischief sparked. She could almost hear Lucy's groan.

Lawrence Hadley seemed bound and determined to cast himself as gentleman champion and protector. Rather than chafe at his efforts, Cassandra now realized this was a situation that could be turned to her advantage—with far-reaching consequences for one contemptible, condescending Captain Rafael Buchanan. Cassandra straightened her shoulders. Donning a smile that hurt her cheeks and feeling like an actress sans grease paint and memorized lines, she crossed the cabin, opened the door, and stepped over its threshold into the brightly lit saloon. Mister Hadley might have provided the costuming, but she was going to have a say in the script.

"Will the captain be joining us this evening, Mister Hadley?"

"The captain?" Lawrence Hadley looked up from where he stood beside the table. The wine in the crystal goblet he held sloshed. "Dear God," he breathed.

Cassandra watched the man's look disintegrate into disbelief, and her confidence wavered. She had no experience with gowns such as this one and had had one monstrous time fastening herself into it. Was something on backward? Cuffey glanced over his shoulder from where he stood on tiptoe lighting a lamp fixed to the wall above a silver-laden sideboard. The lampshade tumbled from his grasp. Glass shattered. Hadley swung around, spilling his wine.

The supercargo swore and yanked out his handkerchief, dabbing at the red stain seeping into the white linen of his sleeve. Cassandra darted toward Cuffey—and collided with Doc barreling from the passageway into the saloon. He grabbed Cassandra's arm to steady her, then let her go as quickly.

"Good God a'mighty!" he exploded. Doc's flushed face, furrowing brow, and the blatant censure in his scowl as he looked Cassandra up and down calmed Cassandra's nerves. She feared ridicule, not reprimands.

"Dear Doctor Collier." She extended her hand, again enjoying her part in the play. "How nice that you will be joining us."

"Joinin' ye," Doc sputtered, his eyes bulging behind their lenses. He waved a white hand. "What can ye be thinkin', lass, trussed up in that . . . that . . ."

Goaded by who knew what devils in her blood, Cassandra tilted her head coyly and dropped into a regal curtsy. "It is lovely, don't you think?"

"Cassandra!" The old man's fingers shook about her own. "Stand up 'fore ye fall down—or out!"

Lawrence Hadley's strong hand closed about her other elbow. Cassandra straightened. "Neither Captain Buchanan nor Doctor Collier will be joining us this evening, Miss Mortier." Cassandra frowned.

"This wee bairn isn't stayin' either!"

Without thinking, Cassandra whirled. "I am not a—"

"Aye, ye're not a lot o' things by the grace o' God an' Cook's penchant fer bendin' the ear o' anyone passin' his galley. God a'mighty! I go fer tea an' find out *ye're* bein' served up fer—"

"Collier!" Cassandra jumped at the supercargo's voice, her temper doused by the ice in Lawrence Hadley's tone. "You will not cast aspersions on Miss Mortier's reputation." His grip tightened about Cassandra's elbow. "Nor upon mine. Leave us."

"Gladly," Doc shot back. "As soon as I escort the lass here back ter her cabin where she belongs."

Cassandra glanced from the surgeon to the supercargo. The anger erupting between the two men was frightening. She felt responsible—yet at a loss to account for the hatred she sensed fueling it. The muscles tensed in Lawrence Hadley's hand. He stepped toward Doc.

"Wait!" She clutched his sleeve and held him back, her words coming without her forethought or knowledge. "Perhaps Doc is speaking in your interests as much as mine, Mister Hadley. My grandfather is a powerful man, as you must know. I . . . I fear his wrath when next I see him but only now realize how he might hold you responsible for my remaining onboard the *Good Fortune*."

"I had nothing to do with your boarding." The supercargo brushed aside her words.

"Even so," Cassandra hurried on, "it might be better if I remained in my cabin. The less I'm seen the less likely my presence will be remarked upon after we reach a port, and then the . . . the easier it will be for me to—"

"I've told you I hold returning you safely as my personal responsibility." The tall man's gaze was steady. Blue. Chilling. Cassandra's heart thudded. This Lawrence Hadley was no gentleman dandy but the towering, formidable male presence who had first grabbed her from the sea-washed deck. His voice deepened, became sensuous cajolery, and Cassandra stared up at him. "You are a beautiful woman and my honored guest." How easily he became a capable, commanding sailor even without benefit of oilskins and storm-raked hair. "I will see you freed of this present coil with your reputation unblemished. I give you my word of honor."

"Honor?" Doc choked. The supercargo's face darkened, and Cassandra caught her breath. "Herod knew more the meaning o' the word, ye thievin', thrice-cursed—"

"Doc!" Cassandra stepped in front of Hadley to face the surgeon. "I'll go back to my cabin. There's no need for this. None of it."

"An' ye've no need fer this serpent's posturin' poppycock an' empty pleasures!"

Cassandra jumped at Hadley's curse. She was close to choking Doc herself. The man was either oblivious to the supercargo's threat or determined to meet his precious Maker violently.

"Cuffey," Hadley ordered behind her. "Set another place at the table." Cassandra turned. He met her look, but there was more tension than warmth in his smile. "I trust the good surgeon's presence in addition to my pledge as a gentleman will put you both at ease, Miss Mortier?" A muscle jumped at his jaw. "And your grandfather as well, if need be."

Cassandra was surprised by his offer, impressed by the iron self-control it took to make it. She relaxed, her previous foreboding and more previous irritation with the man shifting to a grudging respect. And relief.

"There," she sighed, looking to Doc, pleading with her eyes that he see reason too. "That wasn't so terribly difficult after—"

"I forbid it!" Doc exploded. His refusal to let this horrid evening play out to its miserable end without bloodletting—and the entire farce in *her* honor—snapped Cassandra's nerves a final, fatal time.

"You forbid what?" she charged. Blast Lawrence Hadley's strained temper and Cuffey's wide-eyed stare. She would have an end to it. "You would forbid me my first proper meal, Doc? One served on china at a table and not out of a dented trencher in my lap? Forbid me satin against skin rubbed raw from sleeping in my traveling clothes on the bucking floor? Forbid me the company of this ship's ranking authority and the protection he avails me after what I've suffered enduring delirious captains, detestable Acadians, and surgeons who disappear for days on end?" She stopped, out of breath, out of fire. Doc stared past her at nothing, his rounded shoulders rigid. Beyond them, Cuffey set a goblet on the table, his eyes hooded, mouth grim. She wanted to shake both of them.

"I will stay," Doc said. His gaze raked the supercargo's wary, waiting features. "I'll stay an' hold ye ter yer pledge, Mister Hadley." He looked at last at Cassandra. Her stomach knotted at his stilted words. "I'll not disappear again, Miss Mortier, while ye be in need o' my . . . services."

A week later Cassandra paced back and forth the length of her cabin feeling more like a leper than a lady. Doc had kept his promise. He arrived promptly for meals, ate little, said less, and drank much. Cuffey's disapproval was worse, if that was possible, his downcast looks and loud silence a constant reminder of her new status on board the *Good Fortune*.

Cassandra winced, her bare feet slowing. As if every sailor she passed while parading the decks in all her finery upon Hadley's arm was not reminder enough. How quickly she'd come to know which men had sailed into Le Havre from those who had just sailed out of it. Like Dom, Captain Buchanan's original crewmen turned stiff backs to her. Lawrence Hadley's men stared, grinning and elbowing each other if Hadley was near, ogling her outright if he wasn't. Still, she thought, as she resumed her pacing, at least she was able to be out of her cabin now. And no one was expecting her to do anything save look pretty. And they were back on course and making good time and . . . And she hated it: hated playing the smitten female to Lawrence Hadley the gentleman suitor; hated sighing when he boasted, sympathizing when he bemoaned his heavy lot. There was no point in it. She swallowed. And too much pain.

Captain Buchanan remained sequestered away in Doc's cabin. She'd heard his deep, raised voice on occasion, glimpsed sailors slipping into his room in twos and threes like subjects seeking audience with their exiled king. She'd broached the subject of Captain Rafael Buchanan with the supercargo once—a mistake she'd not repeated. Sighing, Cassandra curled her legs beneath her Indian fashion and wondered what tales were being laid at the captain's feet concerning her and Lawrence Hadley. She made a face. She could care less.

Her eyes made their familiar round about the cabin. With a mumbled curse she hopped off the bunk, crossed the room, and slammed down the lid of the sea chest Cuffey was forever forgetting to close when he'd been in it fetching for his . . . His Worship in her absence. Her aching weariness gone, she resumed her pacing, resenting Captain Buchanan's intrusion into her thoughts. Sweet Mary, she felt surrounded by the man: by his books, his papers on the desk scrawled in a surprisingly schooled hand. She jerked to a halt and glared down at the neatly stacked parchments and charts beneath the room's single candle on the desk's polished top. Bending, she blew out the flame with enough wind to darken Easter Vigil services.

"I've problems enough of my own," she grumbled. She'd not escaped Lawrence Hadley's presence for the day only to plague herself with thoughts of another equally odious man. Lifting her braid away from her neck, she let her head fall back. God, she was tired. She glanced at the bunk. The cooling night air drew her to the open porthole instead.

Folding her hands over the opening's bottom edge, she rested her chin on her fingers and let the gentle swaying of the *Fortune* and the musty night smells and muffled sounds on deck wash over her. They were entering fairer climes, the days blustery and fair, the sun scorching by midday. Hadley's gifts of gowns and trinkets continued to arrive over Cuffey's stiff arms, each ensemble elegant, most of them a nuisance for walking about a ship's cluttered deck, all of them torturously constricting. Cassandra breathed in the pungent air and blessed her loose night shift. She longed to sneak topside, to stand in the wind, feel it clean and sea-misted, tugging in her hair. "And be called Mister Hadley's lady?" she sighed into the night. Or worse. Cassandra squeezed her eyes shut. Her chin trembled.

"Oh, Grandpapa. I've made such a mess of things."

Homesickness, sharp-edged and unrelenting, knifed through her. *Remember your prayers.* Sister Mathilde's last words to her. Cassandra blinked hard and stared out at the star-heavy sky and endless, undulating sea. Was there a patron saint of unintentional stowaways? Her mouth quirked. Jonah, perhaps. Her smile soured. *You're like Jonah reborn, child, running forever counter any will save your own.* Old Mat again. Cassandra rolled her eyes. "God wills us swallow our pride lest it swallow us," she parroted.

"So He does," a deep voice answered.

Cassandra whirled but was snared by long arms that pinned her against a man's chest, her scream blocked by a callused palm. "Hold, Cassandra." She struggled all the harder, fighting her terror with fury. "I didn't mean to frighten you." Cassandra stiffened. Captain Buchanan.

His hand left her mouth, and he turned her to face him so quickly she felt like a toy top released from its string. He caught her up short with two large hands atop her shoulders. Panting, Cassandra stared up into familiar black eyes that defied the room's shadows. That he appeared as shaken as she jarred her no less than her hasty turnabout, but the look vanished from his eyes so suddenly she might have imagined it.

His brow knitted. "Forgive me, but I didn't want you to scream—or bite my hand off."

"Bite you! I should—" His hand clamped over her mouth.

"Quiet," he hissed, glancing to the porthole. Cassandra bared her teeth beneath his hand, and he jerked his attention back to her. His eyes darkened. "Say what you will"—he drew his hand back an inch—"but keep your voice down."

Their gazes locked, midnight and moonlight.

In the space of seconds Cassandra had leaped from panic to outrage. Staring up at the man towering above her now, defiance rushing in her blood, both states gave way to the strange but too familiar tension that seemed to charge the air whenever she was near Captain Rafael Buchanan.

"Let me go," she said, her words strangled. Rafe frowned, both his hands again squeezing her shoulders, holding her against her will. Cassandra trembled.

"You've just cause to be angry, Cassandra. And afraid." Her chin jerked up. "Easy, dammit." His gentle shake was more plea than reprimand. "Hear me out. I was wrong to startle you, and I apologize for being here at all."

Cassandra saw his bandaging where it showed beneath his open collar, and Lawrence Hadley's face came abruptly to mind. From Cuffey she'd learned why the brutal Navarre's knife had laid open the captain's shoulder. From Lawrence Hadley she'd learned that, as far as he was concerned, the knife should have entered five inches lower.

"Please." Cassandra's fingers clutched Rafe's shirtfront. She hated the chaos this man had made of her world, spent a good deal of her waking hours hating him. And enjoying it! Reckless, self-righteous ship captains were possibly predestined to die young—but damned if she was going to be one more *cause célèbre* for this particular captain on his pompous march to vainglorious martyrdom.

"Get out of here. Now!"

"Keep your voice—"

"Sweet Mary!" When Rafe's hand lifted from her shoulder, Cassandra hushed her words but couldn't quell the rising fear prompting them. "Have you forgotten how rabidly your supercargo hates you?" Rafe's disgust showed plain enough, but Cassandra refused to be dismissed. "I'm not one of your fawning crewmen, Captain Buchanan, but—"

"Fawning!"

"Listen to me," she ordered. Arrogant, ignorant man. Rafe laughed outright. "Stop it!" Her hands fisted in his shirt, and Rafe stilled. Concern shaded his eyes, deepened the line between his brows. Shying from his look, Cassandra noticed her hands and, her face heating, let go of his shirt. Hands again at her sides, she took a breath and started over. "All I did was suggest you join us at meals." The urgency reentered her words. "He despises you. You can feel it, it runs so deep, so . . ." She shivered. "So black."

Rafe's serious eyes studied her face a long moment. "Let it be, Cassandra," he said quietly. He shrugged. "The bad blood between Hadley and me is between us"—his finger moved to smooth back a curl that clung to Cassandra's temple—"not you." She jerked back from his touch, and he let her go free.

"You think I don't know what I'm speaking about? Blast you! I wish I *could* forget it!" His grin in the shadows incensed her. "You won't find any humor in anything in a good long while if he finds you here, you cocky—" She stopped, her eyes widening as enraged fire lit Rafe's eyes. He seemed to grow in size before her, his voice, when it came, a low but rumbling thunder.

"Is he in the habit of coming to your quarters at this hour?"

"What?" Cassandra gasped. White rage nigh blinded her. "Is that what they crawl to you to report, your gossiping legions of leering . . . lying—" Rafe stepped toward her, and Cassandra swung. Her fist smashed solidly into his face, with enough force to have broken her hand and his nose but for his much greater height and her wild aim. As it was, he stumbled back, swearing. Cassandra skittered in the opposite direction. "I suppose you blame me for the laudanum too? Damn you! How was I to know about—"

The back of her legs crashed into the bunk, and she toppled backward onto the mattress. Scrambling wildly, she twisted to her knees and faced the room, her heart slamming against her ribs. Only then did she register Rafe's hoarse cursing as he shot out from the shadows and across the cabin. Cassandra froze. She'd pushed too far, said too much. Rafe's cursing stopped. Prayers. She closed her eyes, her hands fisting in the rumpled covers. Remember your prayers. Remember your prayers. Her mind was blank. A hysterical giggle threatened. Old Mat was right again: she was without a prayer. The porthole's latch snapped shut.

Cassandra jumped, opened her eyes. She went rigid, steeling herself as he stepped toward the bunk. He stopped. Moonlight gilded his powerful shoulders as they rose and fell, the rasp of ragged breathing, his and hers, sawing at her nerves. His shoulders squared, stilled. Cassandra held her breath. "I had to see you. Talk to you."

She stared, surprised. He spoke quietly, even gently. Blast you, she wanted to rail at him. Once more he was throwing her into confusion, his unexpected tone even now setting her adrift from her expectations and breaking down her defenses.

"And what in the hell does laudanum have to do with—*merde*." He turned on his heel and swore as savagely as when he'd fought her in his delirium, blaspheming Dom's woman's tongue, Doc's sanctimonious blindness, and an entire litany of saints before coming up short in the darker shadows beside the desk.

"That was it, wasn't it?" he charged, stalking back to where he'd started. "Why you flew out of the hold like the Caller was on your heels and think now you must trust yourself to that—"

"Quiet!" It was Cassandra's turn to worry about the captain's much deeper, angry tones.

"I hold you accountable, Cassandra Mortier"—his lowered voice was velvet iron—"*for saving my life*. It's myself I hold in contempt." He jerked his head up, his entire body going still, listening.

Cassandra's heart lurched. Head-on his face had been hidden by the darkness between them. Now he presented her a perfect profile as stunning as an artist-cut silhouette, a master artisan's chiseled cameo: thick, tousled hair falling over a high brow, sharply defined cheekbones, his straight nose and square jaw, the total image set off against the moon's light and captured inside a porthole frame. He turned back. She blinked. The vision was gone.

"Listen to me." Rafe sighed, cradling his injured arm with his good one. "Most of what I remember I wish *I* could forget. I was out of my head, and you took the brunt of it. Do you understand?" Cassandra nodded, still struggling to recover from the dousing her senses had taken. He sighed, again. His uncertainty undermined Cassandra's wariness further, and she didn't want that. She didn't want him here, didn't know how to make him leave, didn't want to know what might happen if he was discovered in her cabin. She looked down at her lap. She didn't want to see how good he looked standing there either. Well. Strong. Like he'd appeared in the garden. She groaned silently. Idiot, she seethed, shaking herself. He had no business here, and she had less business letting herself think about anything but how best to get him gone.

"How you came to be here," Rafe went on, "and all that's happened since doesn't much matter at this point." Cassandra looked up. It mattered. To her. To her grandfather going out of his mind with worry in Le Havre.

"Turn this ship around." She leaned forward, hating the tremor in her voice but helpless to still it. "That's all I want, need."

Rafe shook his head. "I'll worry about all that, and I'll get you back." His voice heated. "In the meantime, you stay clear of Lawrence Hadley." Cassandra's chin went up.

"I'm fully grown and can take care of myself, thank you."

Rafe threw up his hands, swore. "What you are is *too* fully grown and freshly sprung from a convent, dammit." He stalked toward the bunk, eyes snapping. "You think you're feeding him a line, Cassandra, but I tell you the hook is in your mouth, not his!" He stopped in front of her. She glared up at him, defiant and unafraid. Like a kitten, Rafe thought, a tiny, fragile ball of fluff and ferocity, cornered but not cowered. Foolish. Fearless. He knew a crazy desire to reach out and touch the wild, escaped curls from her braid that haloed her face. To tame them. *Non,* to tangle his fingers in them, to trace her straight nose and stubborn chin, to be the one to watch those grey, grey eyes widen, darken, close.

"Get out!"

The vehemence charging her whispered words was like a seawater dunking after hours aloft under the equatorial sun. It was this girl's reckless fearlessness that captivated him, he reasoned. Such a lack of fear was often foolish, he knew, but more fool the man who allowed this hot-tempered, wild-haired hellion to get under his skin. The mistakes he'd already made this voyage must be undone or endured. He had his hands full as it was, and, he sighed, he was no fool.

"I'm going," he said. "But you must promise me you—"

"I must nothing!" Cassandra lunged forward on her hands, her arms stiff, eyes blazing. "And I promise you only that if you dare enter my quarters again I'll come after you with more than my temper in hand and—" Rafe's grin flashed, shocking her speechless.

"I doubt if you've ever had your temper in hand, Miss Mortier."

"Out!" Cassandra shouted. She scrambled up on her knees. "Now!"

"Quiet."

"Miss Mortier? Miss Mortier!" Lawrence Hadley's voice rose above his pounding on her door. Cassandra lurched to her feet on the bunk as Rafe leaped for the door and flattened himself against the wall beside it. Cassandra took a quick breath and called out.

"It's all right, Mister Hadley. Go . . . go back to sleep." The supercargo stopped banging. She motioned frantically for Rafe to move away from the door. He shot her a look that cut the cabin's shadows cleanly. He didn't budge.

"Let me in, Miss Mortier."

That moved him, closer to the door.

"Would you let me handle this?" she whispered, furious. "I'm all right, Mister Hadley. Truly."

"You screamed."

Cassandra glared at Rafe. "I was having a nightmare." The captain's scowl sweetened her voice. "Forgive me for disturbing you." Her eyes narrowed. "I assure you this will never, ever happen again."

"Open your door, Miss Mortier. I would see for myself that you are well."

Rafe's eyes were murderous. No, he mouthed. Cassandra stiffened. She tossed her braid over her shoulder, glanced from the glowering captain to the door and then back to Rafe. He held her gaze. Slowly, as if he read her mind, he shook his head.

"Miss Mortier?" the supercargo called.

Without dropping her gaze from Rafe, Cassandra pushed off from the bulkhead and began crossing the bunk. "If you insist, Mister Hadley." Her bare feet thudded gracefully onto the floor. She paused. In front of the door a scant six feet away Rafe went rigid. Cassandra smiled and stepped toward him.

"Fire! Fire on deck!"

Shouts took up beyond the porthole, up and down the corridor off the saloon. Doors slammed. Feet pounded. Cassandra heard Cuffey's terrified shouting for Mister Hadley reach the saloon before renewed pounding on her door drowned the boy's voice.

"Open the door," the supercargo shouted. Cassandra lunged forward and crashed into Rafe's chest. He held her fast, shoving her against his good side and locking his uninjured arm around her.

"Stay put," he grunted.

Cassandra screamed. She kicked at his legs, twisted in his hold. She felt his bandaging beneath his shirt, heard him gasp, curse. She didn't care. Lawrence Hadley's command that she go with Cuffey topside filtered through her panic. That the supercargo was leaving her and Rafe's arms were chaining her fanned her fear to hysteria.

"Let me go!" she shrieked. "Mister Hadley! Cuffey!"

Rafe shook her, hard. Cassandra's head fell back.

"It's a ploy, dammit. Look at me." He gave her another shake. "A diversion. For me."

She went still. Rafe's words registered, his words and his wrath. Cassandra stared up at him, her pulse still thrumming, and felt the blood drain from her face. The entire deck ablaze could be no hotter than Rafe Buchanan's black eyes. She stepped back, then gasped as she was swooped off her feet, the dim cabin and those blazing eyes spinning in her vision.

"You may very well die a violent death," he ground out, "but you've nothing to fear from—ouch!" He jerked. "From any fire"—he hopped, cursed—"topside." They careened off balance and crashed with a resounding *whump* onto the bunk, a giant tangle of legs and arms. Pinned by her shock as much as by his weight pressing down on her, Cassandra lay still. Rafe's hot breath was at her ear, their hearts thrashing in tandem. He jerked his head up.

Cassandra closed her eyes. He smelled of lye soap and sweat, of ointment and . . . tobacco? Her hands came up between them, to push him away. His shirt had pulled from his waistband, its loosened folds stretched sideways in their fall so that her fingers brushed the soft hair matting his chest. She heard him catch his breath and opened her eyes.

He was no longer angry. She stared at him, at his face inches from hers. Her thin night shift was little barrier between them. She knew he must feel her as she could him: the hard muscles cording his thighs, the physical length of him, the way he was resting his weight on his good side. She met his gaze and knew he wanted to kiss her. She trembled. She wanted to kiss him.

Rafe jerked roughly to his feet. Without looking at her and with a sailor's efficient dispatch, he bent over her, tugged the covers from beneath her, and stuffed her between them. He straightened beside the bunk. She watched him, cloaked in the night shadows, as he looked down at her. He didn't touch her, didn't need to. She could feel his presence where he stood as strongly as she'd felt his weight moments before. As could he. She knew it.

He didn't like it. She knew that too.

He was fighting it.

As was she.

"If Hadley comes back"—Rafe's voice was husky, forced—"for God's sake, don't let him in." He left the cabin swiftly, as soundlessly as he'd entered it.

Cassandra turned her head to the wall. She hardly blinked when the supercargo knocked at her door later, when her silence sent him away. The night deepened. The moonlight waned. When her eyes closed at last, it was not to sleep. It was to dream.

Chapter Seven

THIS TIME THE dream was different. Worse. The shouting voices and terrifying face came first, not her phantom; the voices seemed closer, the face clearer. Only when she was certain she would not escape, that she would strangle in her terror, did the mist-shrouded presence come searching for her, and she chased him into exhausted, dreamless sleep. When Cassandra next opened her eyes, her breakfast tray was on the desk, and Doc was planted in the chair beside it.

"Ye don't look well, Miss Mortier." The surgeon's hair was more on end than usual, his tone gruff. Cassandra closed her eyes and struggled to break free from the druglike remains of her hellish night. Her head throbbed. And her hand. Sweet Mary, her aching hand.

"I'm fine," she lied.

Doc snorted. "A fine fright, t' look at ye."

"Please, Doc."

" 'Doc,' is it?" he interrupted, pushing up from the chair. "Not 'Dear Doctor Collier, how ever d'ye eat so little an' stay so spry?' " Cassandra winced at her Alabama accents flung back at her with a Scottish burr, a biting one. The old man stepped to her side and pressed his palm to her forehead. "If I could be done with the entire lot o' ye, I'd be a happy man," he grumbled.

Cassandra turned her head beneath his hand.

"I told you—"

"Aye, an' I'm doin' the tellin' from here on out." Doc snatched his hand from her head. Cassandra blinked up at him, fully awake. "I've spent most o' the night half into the morn bein' chewed up one side an' down the other. I wash me hands o' it! I'm not no wet nurse an' no primpin' princess's personal maid neither." His ruddy complexion darkened. "I be a surgeon an' a Godfearin' mortal man, is all. An' an old one at that!" His finger wagged. "Too old fer the likes o' yer shenanigans an' lack o' sense, lassie, an' fer Rafe Buchanan's temper fits as well!" He stomped to the door and turned. "Eat yer breakfast. I'll be back t' see ye did. An' ye're hereby confined t' yer quarters, Miss Mortier. D'ye ken?"

Cassandra sat up. "Mister Hadley will—"

"Hadley be damned," Doc snapped. "I'll tell him ye're at death's door if I have to"—his round eyes bulged behind his spectacles—"an' by God ye will be if ye so much as put one toe beyond this cabin 'twixt here an' Nassau." He jerked the door open, shot her a last blistering look, and slammed the panel shut behind him so hard a thick volume toppled from its shelf onto the floor.

Cassandra jumped and looked over at the book splayed facedown by the desk. *"The Physical Geography of the Sea."* She read its title, then flopped back on her pillow. "That's easy," she mumbled. "Rocky." Wincing, she pulled her hand from beneath the covers. Her fingers were swollen, her knuckles purpling. Holding her breath, she moved each finger. They still worked. Sighing, she rested her hand gingerly on her stomach and closed her eyes. Nassau. Sleep beckoned, and she didn't fight it. If she dreamed, she dreamed, but for some reason she didn't think she would this morning. Rolling onto her side, she blocked out the sunlight by burrowing deeper into the pillow. Her hand throbbed. She fell asleep thinking about Captain Buchanan's face—and hoping it hurt like hell.

Rafe pressed the towel Cuffey held out to him against his jaw and winced. The entire left side of his head felt like an overripe watermelon, and promised to look about as tempting as rotting bananas before the day was out. He glanced at the cabin boy, who stood quietly next to Rafe's bunk holding a dented basin.

"You didn't get into the drinking water for this."

Cuffey's eyes rounded. "No sir. Got it from Cook."

"Wonderful." Rafe grunted. "My face will probably putrefy by sundown." Cuffey grinned. They both turned as the door opened, and Dom entered the cramped cabin. Rafe sat up, tossing the towel into the basin.

"Well?" he prodded when the first mate had settled himself, cross-legged, atop a crate.

Dom grunted, and, glancing at Cuffey, reached for the deck of cards in his jacket. "The captain, him"—he addressed the cabin boy but kept his eyes on the cards fanning liquidly in his hands—"he has the way with women, *aihn*?" Rafe scowled but kept silent. Cuffey did not choose to share his captain's reticence.

"Aye, Mister Dom. They sure do fly right at him, don't they?"

Dom snorted his approval, and Rafe laughed though it cost him sorely. Being more careful to keep his head still, he eyed Cuffey with his fiercest shipmaster's mien.

"I promised your mama I'd look after you like I was your daddy, teach you what you need to know to get by in the world. Listen up, then, sailor." Cuffey snapped to attention, and Rafe couldn't keep back his grin. He leaned forward in the bunk, his hands covering his knees. "Avoid mothers with ugly daughters, barmaids with thieving sons, and all women with mean right hooks."

"Yessir," Cuffey barked, flashing a smart salute.

"Go on, now." Rafe reached out and knuckled the boy's tight curls so roughly water sloshed out of his basin onto the floor. "Get back to your duties before I keelhaul you." Grinning from ear to ear, Cuffey scurried out of the cabin.

Rafe turned to Dom, the change in his manner as swift as it was complete. "He's gone. What happened with Hadley?"

The Acadian's wrinkled visage soured. He stuffed the cards back into his pocket, rested his elbows on his knees, and scrubbed his face vigorously with his hands before meeting Rafe's look. "Bah," was all he said. Rafe arched his brow, waiting. It was a test of wills they'd played a lifetime, one they each played well and both enjoyed more often than not. This morning the silence hanging between them was heavy, both men's humor grim. Dom's eyes narrowed on the younger man, studying Rafe's face the way he scanned the horizon for sails.

"Hadley, he is not happy, him. But"—Dom shrugged—"he is not so stupid that he does not know when to hold, when to fold."

"Good." Rafe grimaced and shifted in the bunk, letting the bulkhead at his back take his weight. It was that or lie down. Damn, he hurt. Dom was watching him, probably getting ready to lecture him. Rafe didn't wait to find out. "So he agreed, then."

Dom snorted. "*Non.* He is holding, not folding. He needs no one, he thinks, him, but he needs to reach port, he knows. For that he needs a crew with its mind on work, not mayhem, and its eyes on ropes, not on rigged-out mamoiselles. So." He unfolded his wiry legs and let them dangle over the side of the crate as he leaned back on his hands. "For today he will leave the girl alone, yes. For today he says he will not seek her out the remainder of the voyage if you do not stir up your men against him or interfere with his plans to return her to her *grandpère*. Bah!" He skewered Rafe with his eyes. "I read him, yes? And I know you."

Rafe ignored his uncle's thrust. He was surprised. He'd been more than half certain Lawrence Hadley would throw Dom out on his ear and not even listen to Rafe's demands. He was relieved. The supercargo's agreement, sincere or otherwise, saved Rafe from confronting the bastard personally. Not that Rafe wouldn't relish the opportunity. His left hand fisted—and pain ripped through his shoulder so intensely perspiration beaded his brow. He released his fist, sucked in a slow, steadying breath. *Merde*. Cuffey could probably best Rafe right now in a test of strength. Rafe swore out loud. He was on board his own ship inside his own body, the master of neither. He hated it, his helplessness roiling, building, eating him up inside.

"We are a long way from Nassau, yes?" Dom's voice broke into Rafe's thoughts. "It suits him to say what he says, him. But"—Dom frowned at Rafe—"words. They are easy to say when it suits us, yes? And this Hadley, if what suits him changes, then . . ." He sat forward, his hands cupping his knees. "His words? They will change." Dom's voice lowered. "Let him be, Rafe." His look burned into Rafe's skin, made Rafe's hair bristle above his collar at the back of his neck. "Fold."

Rafe took a deep breath. Everything in him, his common sense, his experience, his gut instinct, told him Dom was right. Trying to keep Cassandra away from Lawrence Hadley was . . . madness. She wasn't his responsibility. She didn't want his help. And though Doc had given her no choice in the matter this morning, if she chose not to cooperate, she simply wouldn't, and there'd be precious little Doc, himself, or anyone else could do about it short of tying her into her bunk. Rafe closed his eyes, blanking out Dom's uncompromising glare. Cassandra Mortier and Lawrence Hadley deserved each other, he reasoned. He was answerable to Bernard Cramer in San Francisco, no one else. His responsibilities involved getting the *Fortune,* its crew, and its cargo safely to Nassau, nothing more. His stomach knotted. From the moment Lawrence Hadley had boarded in Le Havre, Rafe had let other things take precedence over his job. He sighed, opened his eyes. Other things best left buried in the past. And things like supercargos and stowaways best left alone in the present.

He looked up at Dom. "I need to go on deck, get back to work."

Dom's brow raised. "I go on deck, me. Your work, it is where you are, yes?"

Rafe could argue Dom's point, override the older man's position. He wanted to. He didn't. He didn't because he and Dom both knew that Rafe had spent what strength he'd gained going to Cassandra's cabin last night. His stomach twisted tighter. Dom was doing his best topside, and no one knew better than Rafe that first mate Dominic Veasey's best was as good as it came. But he needed Rafe. They all did. And where was their captain? Rafe swore under his breath and stared blackly at Dom's battered, square-toed shoes knocking softly in time to the sea against the crate Dom perched upon.

"Chasing skirts," he ground out. Along with demons from his past and madness between his ears. That's where their captain was.

"Rafe?"

He looked up, the concern in Dom's face plain, painful. "I'm all right," Rafe said. He shrugged. "Or I will be. Now." Looking away, Rafe thought one last time of Cassandra Mortier, pictured easily how her grey eyes mirrored emotions he didn't want to see, didn't want to know. He frowned. He only saw them because he knew them. Shaking his head, he pushed her away and met Dom's gaze. "I fold."

"Miss?"

Cassandra turned her head at the knock on her door. "Come in, Cuffey." She looked back out the porthole at the leaden sky, yesterday's and today's change in the weather a fitting foil to her bleak thoughts and unraveling nerves. She heard the cabin boy cross to the desk, knew without turning that he was eyeing her supper tray.

The boy's attitude had softened toward her in the days since she'd ceased keeping company with the supercargo, since she'd not been allowed beyond her door, since she'd stopped caring about anything save reaching Nassau and leaving this ship forever. But he still kept his distance. It no longer mattered. Still, Cassandra found it easier to keep her back to him when he came on his errands. She missed his smile.

A heaviness settled in her chest like the pall of thickening clouds spreading in the sky. She missed Lucy's smile even more, and her grandfather's deep, age-cracked laugh. Rafe Buchanan's flashing grin came to mind. She stiffened. "Take the tray, Cuffey. I'm done."

"You're not eatin', Miz Mortier."

"I ate all I wanted." Cassandra made a face at the churning clouds mirroring her stomach's protesting of the hard biscuit soaked in greasy broth that she'd forced down. She armed herself against the concern that had slipped into Cuffey's voice, against his will Cassandra was certain. She was relieved when she heard him pick up the tray.

"Miz Mortier?"

Cassandra closed her eyes. Go away, she wanted to scream. Please go away.

"Mister Hadley say we're in for a blow. A good one. I'm t' tell you not t' be"—he paused—"scared is what he meant. I think. He talks funny, don't he?"

"Funny?" Cassandra turned around. Cuffey stood at the door with her tray, his eyes puzzled, his chocolate brow puckered. He looked at her straight on, his thoughts tumbling into words, his words coming naturally, as they had not come since Cassandra's defection that first night in the saloon. It made her throat ache.

"All them big words when he's all fancied up? Doc say he's a . . . a reiver no matter what he's dressed like, but at least when he's helpin' topside you can understan' his talkin'." He stiffened suddenly and dropped his gaze to his bare feet. Cassandra winced as if she'd been slapped. "Meanin' no disrespect, Miz Mortier," he mumbled. He turned and fumbled with the door's latch.

"Cuffey?" Cassandra's hand shot out. The door banged open, and the boy hurried away without looking back. Her hand fell limply to her side. Turning, she moved numbly back to the porthole.

Air that had clung hot and heavy all day now blew cold, the gusts buffeting her cheeks, raising gooseflesh on her arms. Cassandra shivered, too weary to move away from the porthole, to even shut the glass. She laid her cheek on her hands and closed her eyes. A storm. Good. Maybe they would be forced into a port before Nassau. She smiled. "Any port in a"—she lifted her head, listening—"storm."

The constant thud of landing feet, the pounding of running feet, wind-tossed shouts, Acadian curses, creaking ropes and snapping canvas had long ago become as unconsciously present as the air she breathed, as noticed as the act of breathing. She listened harder, tensed. Captain Buchanan was on deck.

She stepped back from the porthole, the captain's distant, low-timbred shouts seeming to follow her into the cabin. She slammed the portal shut. Turning, she began pacing, her ever-present lethargy these last endless days forgotten. The cabin darkened, the day's twilight leaving with an eerie swiftness, as if some giant, unseen hand had reached out and covered the *Good Fortune,* blotting out the sun. Without warning, the cabin's floor pitched and hurled Cassandra across the room. She grabbed onto the desk's ledge and regained her footing. The supercargo's prediction was proving true.

"Good!" Cassandra said, hanging on to the desk, wincing at the pain that shot from her still sore fingers up her arm. Her vehemence surprised her. It was good. She welcomed a storm, a great, loud, thrashing one. Releasing the desk, she groped for the bunk, crying out when the next wave tossed her the last two feet. Toppling onto the bunk, she righted herself and scrambled under the covers, yanking them over her head. She wasn't frightened, she was ready to burst in the face of her world turned inside out and grabbed out of her control. Let it come, she wanted to shout. Let the elements rant and rage with her, for her, anything if they only blanked out her futile thoughts, her warring emotions, her dream . . . and Captain Rafael Buchanan's voice.

Hours later Cassandra stared into the rocking blackness and admitted she was afraid. The wind had become a continuous, keening howl. She shut her eyes, told herself this ship had proved herself seaworthy before; she would do so again. The desk chair clattered onto its side. It banged from desk to door, back and forth. What sailors' noise still filtered through the storm's mayhem sounded desperate, the shrieks of men at war, not at work.

"We'll ride it out. We'll ride it out," she panted, bracing herself against the bunk's sides to keep from being bucked out of it. "Please, God. Let us ride it—"

An explosion of splintering wood ripped the air.

Cassandra screamed and flung her arms over her head, sure that a mast was crashing in on top of her cabin. But wood masts didn't shriek obscenities at their fate, didn't have shrill laughs that raised gooseflesh along Cassandra's arms. She whirled in her tossing bunk.

A mammoth figure stood bracketed in the unsteady light cast by an oil lamp from the saloon, what was left of her door scattered at his feet. Cassandra recoiled instinctively and slammed against the bulkhead walling the bunk's far side.

"You have been hiding, *coquine,* but Navarre, he does not forget." The man's French was guttural, slurred. "And you? Do you remember me?"

Navarre. Cassandra's mouth went dry. The hulking giant's hot gaze had unnerved her, and Lawrence Hadley had banished the sailor to the fo'c'sle thereafter whenever Cassandra had been about. She'd not seen or thought of him again, but he was not a man easy to forget. Cassandra wasn't sure he was even a man.

"Get out," she choked.

His laugh came again, as demented as the squealing wind. "Out?" he roared. "Where to go? Can't you hear, *coquine*?" His warped humor was replaced with a viciousness that leaped at Cassandra with his words. "The masts are torn away. We are going down!"

"No." She spoke for herself, not him. Sound ships survived hurricane gales. She knew that, clung to that knowledge though her heart hammered harder in her chest. It was only Navarre's fear talking. Cassandra's eyes narrowed as he lifted a long-necked bottle to his lips and drank deep. His fear and his wine. Belching, he raised his thick arm in a toast.

"To Hadley's heiress, eh?"

Cassandra pressed against the lurching bulkhead and watched him down half the bottle's contents. Her stomach cramped. The man was drunk. She had to get him out of here, get help. No one topside would hear her above the storm. Surely if Doc or Cuffey, if anyone save Navarre, was close by, they would have heard the door break and come. She closed her eyes. She would have to protect herself. Somehow. How?

The floor pitched. Glass shattered. Her scream filled her ears as she was tossed forward onto her hands. A vision of the ship rolling end over end came. Pain seared up her arm. The Frenchman's bellowing curses penetrated her panic. He was reeling forward, his feet tangled in the overturned chair. Losing his balance, he careened toward her as he fell. Meaty fingers reached out for her. She shrieked and skittered away. He crashed amidst the floor's clattering debris a foot short of the bunk, but snagged hold of the top cover on his way down.

Sobbing and kicking, Cassandra fought to free herself as Navarre yanked at the bed linens, pulling her toward him. She was trapped. His hand closed around her ankle.

"No!" she sobbed. "No!"

With a heaving grunt Navarre yanked, and Cassandra fell on top of him, hopelessly knotted in the bunk's covers. Broken wood gouged into her shoulder, but it was the sailor's grasping hands that hurt her and renewed her frenzied twisting to break loose of her blanket shroud, fight off his assault. They rolled with the pitching floor, and the Frenchman pinned her beneath him.

"Him," Navarre panted, his stinking breath hot against Cassandra's face. "Always my work, his way. My risk, his gain." Cassandra turned her face away, her struggling crushed by the wall of flesh grinding her into the splintered wreckage beneath them. He tore at the bunched bed covers. "I go to burn in hell, yes. But I will go riding *his* heiress."

He rose up to gain a better purchase just as the ship tilted. Cassandra shoved, he toppled sideways, and they tumbled the length of the cabin. The covers caught on a split fragment of wood and tore free from Cassandra's legs. She rolled on. Her flailing arms smacked against the desk's ornate leg. She grabbed hold. Navarre cursed, dug his fingers into her thigh but couldn't break his own momentum in time. Her dress pulled taut, choking her, the material straining, then tearing in an explosion of cotton threading and seams as Navarre's bulk crashed and skid away from her.

Gasping, Cassandra lunged blindly to her feet. The floor bucked. She wheeled, fell, and stood again. Navarre roared. She sprang away from him, slamming into the wall. The saloon. She had to get past him to the saloon and its corridor. Where was the door? She turned, searching, the room spinning around her. She couldn't find the door.

A hand closed roughly around her arm, yanking her backward. She screamed and kicked free. Bolting blindly away from her attacker, she tripped, fell forward. Light. The saloon. Sobbing her relief, she negotiated the threshold and flung herself through the doorway.

Instinct guided her to the passageway, instinct and the animal bellows of Navarre behind her. She flew down the hall's shuddering, pitch-black length, pushing off the walls when she was thrown against them, oblivious to pain, to everything save escape.

A grinding shudder shook the *Fortune,* threw Cassandra to her knees. She pushed up, ran faster, and collided into the steps at the corridor's end. Tripping, crawling, Navarre's curses propelled her up the companionway. He was so close. Too close. She couldn't get her breath. Her hands fumbled wildly, searching for the doors' latch. The ship tilted, and Navarre's massive weight plowed into her from behind. The doors flew open.

Navarre held her arm in a death grip as they rolled, the waves pouring over the ship's sides tumbling them in their crushing assault. Cassandra couldn't breathe, think. She went limp. This was it, she thought, strangely calm. Water stung her eyes, filled her mouth. From a great distance, as if she were floating above the tumult of wind and waves and screeching chaos and no longer a part of it, she heard a deep shout. Her name. She turned her head, struggled to see, hear. Someone was calling for her. She floated higher, farther away. The voice faded, then the storm. It was sad to leave, she thought, so sad. Still, she smiled. After all these years, her phantom knew her name.

Chapter Eight

WAKE UP. WAKE up. Cassandra whimpered, thrashed, but she couldn't wake up. There was a great roaring in her head. It hurt. And the voices. Screaming. They were getting closer, coming for her through the roaring noise. *Wake up*. The nightmare face. It would come with the voices and—

"Easy, *minette*. Easy." This voice was different from the others. It was low, calm. Cassandra frowned, listening, but when she felt hands pushing down on her shoulders her fear returned. She tried to yank away. It hurt. "Dammit, let her be." Now this voice was angry too. She cried out, afraid. "You're scaring her, Doc. Let her wake up on her own."

"An' if she don't? I told ye, an' I'm goin' ter keep tellin' ye—"

"She's going to be all right."

"An' ye? Not sleepin' yerself won't make her wake up any sooner, Rafe. Ye look worse than the lass."

These new voices faded in and out, chased the nightmare screams away. Cassandra stopped listening. She could sleep now. She wanted to sleep. It didn't hurt when she sank into the midnight oblivion of sleep.

"Lass? Can ye see? How many fingers? Count fer me."

"One, two, buckle my shoe."

"Miss Mortier!" Doc sat back wearily on his knees and sighed. He'd come at a run at Rafe's shout. True enough, the lass's eyes were open. But she wasn't awake. He glanced over at the younger man. Rafe held Cassandra cradled in his lap, his black eyes searching the girl's face. Doc shook his head.

Cassandra giggled. "Don't worry so, Lucy. I know my lessons."

"She's out o' her head, lad. Delirious."

"But her eyes are open," Rafe argued, "and she can hear us. She answered you, didn't she?"

Doc scowled. "She may be hearin' our words, but she's talkin' ter"—he waved his hand impatiently—"Lucy."

"Are the village children asking for me?" At her question, both men looked at Cassandra. Rafe shifted so she looked straight into his face.

"Cassandra," Rafe said. "Can you see me? Hear me? Who is Lucy?"

"I . . . I miss them. So . . . much. I won't teach them any more card games. I promise!" A deep laugh rumbled against her ear, and Cassandra struggled to see who was laughing at her. It wasn't funny. She was good with the children. Even Sister Mathilde had said so. It wasn't right that for one innocent misjudgment they were taking away the single thing Cassandra had found that she enjoyed. "It's how Jim taught me my numbers and sums, is all. Why won't anyone believe me, give me one more chance?"

"We believe ye, lass. Rest now."

They didn't believe her. Cassandra couldn't see her accusers, but she knew them for what they were, knew what they thought, what they all thought. Curse them! "I'm rested unto death! I can't run. I can't ride. I can't even walk slow enough to please anyone. And if Old Mat sends me upstairs to rebraid my horrid hair one more time, I'll—I'll cut it off again. I swear it! And then . . . then—" She stopped, her words escaping her. Tired. She fought the waves of exhaustion dragging her down. What she was saying was important. But she couldn't remember . . . what she was saying. Only that it was . . . important.

"Sleep. That's a good lass."

"No," she mumbled. Lucy was . . . good. Cassandra was . . . was . . .

Rafe laid her gently down on the pallet of survival grass and stroked the side of her face, pushing her matted salt-coarse curls back from her forehead, behind her ears. Cassandra's breathing deepened, but she was tense, her muscles twitching even as she slept. Rafe sat back, his gaze remaining on her pale, pinched face. "She's a fighter, this one. She'll come around. You'll see."

"God willin'," Doc said. He frowned and looked from Cassandra over at Rafe. "Ye don't think she really cut her hair off, d'ye?"

Rafe's grin flashed white in the dimness of the shelter. "To within an inch of her head."

She was warm, enveloped in a gentle, soothing cocoon. She turned her head, snuggled. Stilled. Her benevolent phantom was near. This time it was different. She couldn't see him, but she sensed he wasn't searching for her like always before; he was looking at her. How strange that he could finally see her, but she still couldn't see him.

"Cassandra?"

He'd come. He had found her. He knew her name.

"Listen to me, *minette*. You are all right. You are safe. You don't have to run or hide or stay away. You don't have to be afraid. You are all right."

Cassandra let the deep voice wash over her. "Don't . . . don't go away," she whispered. "The voices. They will come if—"

"I'm right here. Look at me, Cassandra. Can't you see me? *Look at me*."

"Papa doesn't like to look at me. Lalie . . . Lalie says it hurts him to look at me."

"Then your papa is a blind man. You are beautiful, *minette*."

"No." A deep sadness welled up, gathered in Cassandra's chest. Her throat ached. "No." She strained to see as well as hear this gentle, guarding presence with his low voice and soothing words. If she could see him, maybe she could make him understand. "I'm not pretty. Not like . . . like Mama." It hurt to talk, but suddenly she had to explain, make the gentle voice hear her and understand.

"Papa had a visitor, and he brought his son with him. I was supposed to be nice to him. Lalie said he was my guest just like his papa was Papa's guest. But he was . . . a horrid boy. Mean. He hurt Lucifer. I tried to stop him, but he was too big. He almost broke Lucifer's tail!" Her voice dropped to a choked whisper. "I wanted to hurt him back." Cassandra stopped. She sensed her phantom waiting, watching her, and forced herself to tell him the rest. "I did. I . . . I got him back. Good."

"I am sure you did." She could hear his smile though his face remained hidden. He didn't understand.

"No." She shook her head. "I did a terrible thing." Misery stabbed through her, and shame, two more emotions tangling up with the knot of fear and anger and confusion that was flooding back from that other time so long ago. She took a deep breath. "I locked him in the root cellar and . . . and told Papa I saw him going off toward the swamp." Her words came fast, tumbling over each other.

"I didn't say a word. Even when they called everybody out and stayed up all night searching the swamp. And when Jim found him in the cellar the next morning, I . . . I wouldn't say I was sorry. I . . . I didn't mean for him to be so scared, but even if I'd known how he was almost sick from being locked up all night, I still wouldn't have told. And I wasn't sorry. I wasn't! Until . . ." She stopped. "Until . . ." She couldn't go on.

"Until what? Say it, Cassandra. It's all right." The voice wasn't smiling anymore.

Cassandra shivered and sensed as much as felt her phantom gathering her closer. "Until Papa went away," she blurted out and clamped her mouth shut. The sadness pressing down on her became simply weight. Heavy. Leaden. Crushing. Her next words were hollow, lifeless. "I was hateful. Willful. He never wanted to see me again. He never did. Never asked about me in his letters to Grandpapa, never answered my letters, never came out from Le Havre to Denoir. Never once. Never." Her words faded away.

"How old were you, Cassandra, when that boy hurt your Lucifer?"

Cassandra sighed. What did it matter? She didn't want to talk anymore. She wanted to sleep. "I was five. That's why I had Lucifer. He was just a kitten, and Jim gave him to me on my birthday."

"Your father hasn't seen you since you were five years old? By choice?"

He was angry. The numbness pinning her under its weight lifted. He wouldn't like her anymore, come find her, talk to her.

"Please." She reached out, felt her hand clasped in a hard, warm palm. "Don't go away. Don't be angry with me."

"With you, *minette*? *Non.*" His hand slid over hers and stroked her arm gently, up, then down, back and forth. So light. Like a soft summer wind that teased and caressed. And warmed. Straining to see him only made Cassandra dizzy, made her head pound. She stopped struggling to see and welcomed the warmth, relaxed under his touch. His hand stilled and squeezed her arm. "Your father. He's a blind fool, do you hear me?" He paused. "Maybe someday he will know it. I hope so." His hand took up along her arm once more, his voice deepening. "I hope so for you, not him."

"No." Cassandra shook her head. "He's dead." She ignored his low curse, the way his hand jarred still, knew only that the warmth was receding and pain rushing up in its place. She fought to hold back her words but they came of their own volition. "I . . . I refused to mourn him. I was glad—glad!—when Grandpapa wrote that he was d-d-dead."

"He hurt you. You wanted to hurt him back, maybe. It doesn't mean you—"

"You don't understand! I did terrible things, said hateful things."

"Aye, because he hurt you. We all hate being hurt, Cassandra. We fight back. There's no sin in that."

Cassandra shook her head, the darkness imprisoning her began swirling about her. "No. It's wrong to hate." She was angry, afraid. "It's wrong. And I do hate him. I . . . I do." His arms tightened about her and she burrowed deep against him, hating her father, hating herself. Hating. Hurting. Sweet Mary, she hurt so bad.

"He's dead. He can't hurt you anymore, *minette*."

She shuddered and wished it was so. The voice was fading, and she strained to hear it.

"Maybe you only hate him because"—he paused—"because you loved him and needed him to love you back."

"No!"

He was rocking her, his voice low. The urgency in his words seeped through her pain but couldn't stop it.

"Don't be so brave, little one. You will break. It hurts to love someone who cannot love back. It's too . . . hard. Not mean or bad. Just hard. Too hard."

"I . . . hate him." The words became a chant in her mind. *I hate him. I hate him.* Her father's averted looks. His impatient replies. His curt dismissals. They all came back, faster and faster, gushing up like bile. The ignored birthdays. The rented carriage when she arrived in Le Havre. The declined invitations. She curled tighter and tighter against the guarding presence. The letter from her grandfather bordered in black. The mourning-gown material. Knowing, considerate Randall Mortier had sent grey taffeta, not black crepe. She'd flung it across her room and refused to mourn Leland Mortier even out of respect for her grandfather. *I hate him. I hate him.* Dead. Gone. Missing. Forever. It came, then, wrenching, tearing. Oh, God. It hurt. "He . . . didn't . . . love . . . m-m-me."

"I know. I know, *minette*. I'm sorry."

An hour later Rafe ducked clear of the lean-to shelter into the Caribbean night. For the first time Cassandra slept deeply, at peace. No dreams. No delirious jabbering. Her closed eyelids were still, her muscles relaxed. Squeezing the back of his neck with his good hand, Rafe let his head fall back. The inky sky's great dome of stars spread as far as he could see, the sight as familiar to Rafe as the lines etched in Dom's weathered face.

Tonight neither the sky's familiarity nor its fantastic beauty soothed. He glanced toward Doc and Cuffey, darker shadows huddled in sleep beside the embers of their supper fire. Abruptly, Rafe turned and took the down-sloping, serpentine path away from the camp.

A foolish thing, he knew, to traipse unfamiliar, vegetation-choked island wilds by night. He didn't slow. Had the path not been cleared at all and the distance to the beach been long, not short, Rafe still would have gone. He couldn't breathe.

Tear-washed grey eyes haunted him. Oblivious to the drooping coconut palms that slapped and stung his face, he cursed the undergrowth tangling in his bare feet and damned Cassandra's father, wished him still alive so he might send the bastard to hell personally. He quickened his pace.

It was not the girl's pain nor her father's sins that chased him.

The path leveled, widened. Rafe cradled his injured left arm and lengthened his stride, his feet taking up the light, padding cadence of his boyhood. The packed earth loosened, gave way to sand. The cay's beach spread before him, a grey expanse defined by the thick blackness of jungle forest and sea and sky. Rafe broke into a run.

Sweat and sea spray matted his hair, burned his eyes. He ran until the restlessness surging through him changed, became release. He ran on, ran out of beach only to veer, not check, crashing into the surf and clambering over a fringing reef in order to gain more sand. His arm throbbed, lungs burned, and still he ran on and on. Faster. Harder. His stride broke, feet faltered. He staggered onward another sixty yards, then fell forward onto his knees in the wet, welcoming sand. Head down, he leaned his weight on his good arm and gulped down air. His labored breathing screamed in his ears, but it was the waves breaking over the reefs he heard; it was the sea and the sand and the black night sky that he needed more than air in his lungs.

With a low groan Rafe doubled over and retched, spewed bile and vomit like he had not since he'd lain in the mire of a Louisiana rice paddy, and Cuffey's mother had poured bitter gourd cup after cup of gagging muck down his throat. Afterward, he staggered into the surf and dropped to his knees. He dunked his head, raked his fingers through his hair. Sitting back on his heels, submerged to his waist, Rafe cradled his arm, let his head fall back. The waves rocked him. His gaze quartered the sky, his map, his soul mate. His breathing slowed.

Now. Now he too could sleep.

Cassandra opened her eyes. The throbbing in her head receded as her eyes adjusted to the grey dimness blanketing the shelter. Turning her head, she frowned at a canvas-made wall. Weak light outlined the canvas sheet's edges, filtered through its many rips and holes. She closed her eyes. Wherever she was, it wasn't heaven, but it wasn't hell. She swallowed. Or so she hoped. The storm and Navarre's attack came back to her. She shuddered. Her eyes snapped open, her gaze darting about the small enclosure. She was on a lumpy pallet, on the ground. Alone.

Wincing, she rose up on her elbows to better see her surroundings. She was inside a lean-to of sorts, with three bamboo sides and a palm-leaf roof. Cassandra frowned. She'd not gotten here alone. Had the *Fortune* broken up and gone down like . . . She left the thought unfinished, as if even recalling Navarre's ravings might make the Frenchman reappear. She shuddered, thought instead of Doc and Cuffey and Captain Buchanan and Lawrence Hadley, even the foul-mouthed first mate, Dom. Were any of them here with her? Where were they? Where was she? What had happened? Her head throbbed. Holding her breath to keep from crying out, she lay back down and let her eyelids droop closed. That helped. She remembered falling through the companionway, remembered the water, the screeching wind. Trying to recall anything after that made her head hurt worse. She gave up and fell back to sleep thanking all the saints, her guardian angel, and whoever else for seeing to her safety—and praying she'd be glad they had when she woke up.

"Cuf-feey!"

Cursing under his breath, Rafe tossed his hair out of his eyes and glared at the spot where the dense foliage swallowed the path to the beach. His missing ship's boy failed to materialize. "By the Virgin, I gave him credit for more sense," he growled.

"He's hungry," Doc sighed from his perch on a nearby rock. He raised his hand to shield his eyes and followed the younger man's gaze, but looked back down at his lap almost immediately. "A lad's stomach will overrule his head every time."

"I told him he'd have a feast here—of breadfruit and bananas, if nothing else."

"That ye did." Doc pushed off from the rock and landed with a pained *oomph*. "Two days ago? Right after Dom an' Jansen shoved off, it was, if ye'll recall."

Rafe shot the surgeon a black look. Without his spectacles, Doc couldn't appreciate it, but Rafe didn't care. He'd reinjured his shoulder, was bruised everywhere he wasn't rope-burned or battered, and now Cuffey'd gone and disappeared. He shouted Cuffey's name again, this time louder, his curse behind it hotter. He scowled.

Ignoring physical discomfort came with his trade as did the stamina and strength to keep moving on nothing but willpower when necessary. But as horrendous as these last days had been—from the moment he'd stepped on deck to the moment he'd fallen out of the lifeboat into the surf and made the cay's beach with Cassandra slung over his good shoulder—it was not his abused body that was testing him beyond endurance. It was his panic when he'd seen Cassandra tangled in that French monster's arms, his helplessness when he'd watched the rigging crashing on top of them, his fears that she'd slip away in her delirium, his relief when she'd cried herself to sleep in his arms. And now this?

"I'm going to—"

"Find him, Captain?"

Cassandra stood wobbily in the lean-to's opening. Hanging on to the canvas to keep upright, she watched both men whirl to face her. If the sun's white glare wasn't making her nauseous, she might have laughed. Doc, never a fashion plate, looked something washed up with the tide, his hair sticking out from under a home-made hat, his glasses gone. Rafe looked as bad as she felt, she decided. His shirt was in tatters, feet bare, face bruised, arm in a sling. But it was the heat snapping in his black eyes that captured her attention. She was glad she hadn't laughed. Rafael Buchanan looked more dangerous than storm-damaged. She raised her chin.

"Lass!" Doc hurried toward her. He took her arm and turned her back the way she'd come. "Ye shouldn't be up like this. Lie back down, an' I'll bring ye a cool drink."

Cassandra didn't argue. Rafe pushed aside the canvas and entered the shelter with them, his size shrinking the space alarmingly. He helped her down and, squatting beside her pallet, didn't leave when Doc hustled out. Cassandra felt her face reddening under his scrutiny.

"You look"—he paused—"better."

Cassandra closed her eyes, swallowed. The pain in her head was nothing compared to this unexpected, humiliating need to burst into tears. She fought it, hated it. "Don't you think you should go find Cuffey, Captain Buchanan?" she managed.

"He's back," Doc said, rattling the canvas as he returned. He held up a fist full of bananas no bigger around than his thumbs. "D'ye ever try these, lass?"

Cassandra smiled, her unexplained self-consciousness easing in Doc's presence. "Yes. But not since leaving Leeland."

"Miz Mortier!" Cuffey's wide grin popped around the surgeon's shoulder. "You awake? You all right?"

She laughed. "You've been to market, I see."

"Against orders."

At the captain's gruff reprimand, Cuffey's eyes lost their glow instantly. Cassandra's temper sparked.

"He's back, isn't he? And with breakfast, something no one else has thought to provide, it seems." Ignoring Rafe's raised brow, she grinned at Doc and Cuffey. "I'm starving. How long have we been here? And where are we?"

Doc shook his head but couldn't hide his smile. Cuffey beamed, and Rafe, giving all three of them a long-suffering glare, excused himself—to make a breakfast worthy of a native chieftain from the tropical fruits Cuffey had collected.

The morning set a pattern of sorts.

As Cassandra's head bothered her less and less, she ventured from the pallet to the cooking fire, from their campsite to the beach, from the beach to the entire islet, Cuffey her constant companion. Doc watched and warned and shook his head, smiling. Rafe glowered and kept busy and silent for the most part. She stopped worrying about the time. She knew where she was: heaven.

The cay was tiny, uncharted, untouched by habitation. A gift, she sighed, stretching out on the white sand and letting the sun soak into her bones. Cuffey yelled from the surf, and she raised her head, laughed at his antics in the water, and resettled her woven palm-leaf sun hat over her face. Lying so, it was as if Denoir and Le Havre and the *Good Fortune* never existed, as if she'd just been born, and been born to traipse jungle-thick paths and chase metallic-winged butterflies and run barefoot along the white-hot beach. Bird songs called her from sleep into days lush with beauty, filled with new larks and hidden spots yet to be explored. Tree frogs sang her to sleep. Paradise.

"You're going to be as brown as Cuffey if you don't keep out of this sun."

Cassandra lifted her hat and stared up at Rafe. His arm was no longer in a sling. His golden hair was blowing in the ever present breeze, his face hidden behind a beard, an addition she didn't particularly like. It suited him, though, she decided. This solemn, long-faced Captain Buchanan never grinned. She'd wondered about him, missed his laugh, but she'd followed Cuffey's and Doc's lead and stayed out of his way.

"I like the sun," she said finally and covered her face.

Instead of going on to the cliff where he watched hours upon hours for sails or for Dom's return, or ordering Cuffey out of the surf to help fish up their supper, or returning to finish whatever it was he was forever repairing, fashioning, or fussing with, he sat down beside Cassandra on the beach. She raised her hat three inches and studied him, waiting.

"It likes you," he said. At her look he explained. "The sun. It's kissed your nose with freckles, and it dances in your eyes." He met her look. "Your wary, impudent, temper-testing eyes."

Heat stroke. Doc was forever warning her about it. Rafe must be having one. She frowned. "I've no desire to test anyone's temper, especially yours, Captain Buchanan, and"—her nose wrinkled in disgust—"I refuse to have freckles."

Rafe threw his head back and laughed. Its booming timbre vibrated in the air, reverberated in Cassandra's chest. His beautiful, soul-deep laugh. She let her hat flop back over her face, to think. Or hide.

"You like the sun but not the water?" he asked.

"I love the water." Her words came muffled.

"I never see you in it past your knees."

Had he been spying on her? She grimaced under her hat. Asking stupid questions was contagious, apparently. Of course he'd been keeping his nosy, captain's lookout. It was the way he was made. "Make sure Cuffey and Cassandra behave" was probably on his mental list of things to do each day.

"That's because I don't go in past my knees, if it's any of your concern, Captain."

"You don't swim."

He said it as statement, not question. Since it was true and Cassandra didn't care to chitchat, she ignored him. It proved a futile notion.

"Come on."

"What?"

Ignoring her protest, Rafe grabbed her hands and tugged her to her feet. Her hat squashed down on top of her head with one hand, her other hand clasped in Rafe's callused grip, Cassandra was given no choice but to stumble over the sand toward the water's edge. Balking only threatened to pop her arm from her shoulder socket. She lengthened her stride. Cursing would probably only make him laugh, or stop for a lecture. Cassandra grinned. She didn't want him to stop any more than she wanted a lecture. Heat stroke was catching. Laughing, she veered around him and crashed into the water in front of him. Rafe halted her when the water reached her waist.

"Miz Cassie!" Cuffey, his dark curls glistening, his eyelashes water-spiked, bobbed up beside her. "Look at this."

A wave washed against them. Rafe reached forward and steadied her. She regained her footing on the sandy bottom. Rafe's hand remained at her waist, riding her hip. Trapped between the tall captain and excited cabin boy, Cassandra concentrated on the shell Cuffey was holding under her nose. Rafe's long fingers tightened with the next wave. Cassandra frowned down at the shell. His touch was upsetting her more than the sea.

"How beautiful," she said, taking the small conch shell from Cuffey. Its ruffled edge glistened in the sun. "We've not got one like this, have we?"

"Nope." Cuffey shook his head, spraying them all with water. "Must have 'bout ever' kind by now." With a grin and a graceful arch he dove backward and slipped out of sight.

Rafe's long, brown finger skimmed the shell, his hand against hers making Cassandra's head light. "A rooster, they call it." He withdrew his hand. "To get every kind would take longer than any of us care to spend here, believe me," he sighed.

Cassandra looked up. He was eyeing the shell, his expression closed. The laughing Rafe Buchanan who'd dragged her into the sea had disappeared. Cassandra closed her fingers over the shell, almost protectively, stepped clear of his hand, and watched Cuffey pulling a chunk of driftwood up onto the beach as she beat back her disappointment.

"You hate being here, don't you?" she said.

When Rafe didn't answer, she looked around. He was staring out to sea. Something in the set of his shoulders made her pause and look at him more closely.

His unshaven state hid the fine bones of his jaw and chin and coarsened his appearance, but his eyes were the same eyes that had stared down at her in the school garden. Black. Intelligent. She frowned. Weary.

"I hate losing the *Fortune,*" he said, without looking her way. "I hate not knowing what became of my crew save us." He paused, looked down his arm, and shook his head. He faced her at last, his eyes black, more bleak than weary. "One crewless, almost crippled, shipwrecked captain at your service, Miss Mortier." He gave her a mocking, watery bow.

Cassandra wrinkled her nose. "You sound like Mister Hadley."

"And I definitely hate being likened to that bastard."

She met his angry glare head-on. "To Mister Hadley," she corrected him. She raised her chin. "Who was forever playacting the gentleman and bemoaning his assorted and heavy lot in life?" With a frigid smile and stiff nod, she turned toward the beach. Rafe's hand closed about her arm and whirled her about-face.

"I'm not . . . bemoaning."

Cassandra smiled up at him. "Yes you are."

She watched his eyes darken, jaw tense. He looked more ready to dunk her than to teach her to swim, and Cassandra gloried in it. This was the Rafe she'd decided she must have imagined, the captain who could grin and—her smile widened—glower. The time on the cay had evidently healed more than Cassandra's head. It had restored her resolute, rambunctious spirit, a spirit woefully reckless at the most inopportune times. Cassandra shrugged. So be it.

"I've had enough of male sighing and inflated self-importance on board the *Good Fortune,* thank you." She watched Rafe's eyes narrow, noticed for the first time the tiny lines fanning out at their corners, the permanent crease between his brow, the marks of every man who lived his life at sea. But, gazing up at him, she sensed how strain had aged his young man's face as well.

Unbidden, she saw her grandfather's lined brow, recalled his anguish over his son so evident in his letter. Her heart ached. She'd noticed the former and dismissed the latter only as they had affected her desire to leave Denoir. Selfish and spoiled. Old Mat was right again. Cassandra focused on Rafe. But no longer so blind?

Captain Rafe Buchanan was like her grandfather, not like Lawrence Hadley. This tall man with tired eyes felt the weight of his responsibilities not because that made him feel important but because meeting one's responsibilities was important. Cassandra bit her lip, her thoughts overriding her senses when Rafe's hand tightened about her arm. His spirit had been as battered as hers, she was certain, by all that had transpired since Le Havre. She hurt for him but knew instinctively that that wasn't what he needed, from himself or from her.

"Fretting doesn't help, you know," she said.

"Fretting! Now I'm fretting?" Rafe stepped back so quickly Cassandra struggled to keep her balance amidst the wake he stirred about them. "I also champion thieves and assault old men if you're compiling a list!"

Cassandra laughed. "A collection of your shortcomings. It would be every bit as colorful as Cuffey's shells, I've no doubt, and"—she cocked her head—"much the bigger collection."

Rafe opened his mouth, snapped it shut, his jaw visibly clenching. Cassandra watched, happiness and orneriness dancing in her blood. Sweet Mary, he was wonderful to look at with the sun caught in his hair, the sea glistening on his bronzed, furred chest beneath what was left of his shirt. He was more wonderful to irritate. It was so . . . easy. He needed stirring up a bit, and her talents had ever leaned disastrously in that very direction. For once she might be able to put them to a good use and positive end: healing. Healing for him and for her.

"Oh!" she cried out as the breeze caught under her hat. She lunged, floundering. Rafe reached up effortlessly, snaring the palm-leaf concoction and saving Cassandra a dunking one-handed and at one and the same time, a feat Cassandra found irritating. Eyeing her, he clamped both hat and hand on top her head, then tilted her head back so their eyes met, held. Cassandra swallowed. He was easy to aggravate, but he was also . . . big. The sea slid and sloshed between them. Rafe no longer glared. Cassandra no longer grinned.

"You are testing my temper, Cassandra," Rafe said, his voice deep, gruff. His temper, hell. The little sea sprite was driving him this side of insane, running barefooted hither and yon from dawn to dusk, her shredded skirt showing more petticoat than a dance-hall doxy, showing legs long and slender and— He swore under his breath. Fire sparked in Cassandra's eyes, those laughing grey eyes that ignored him or, worse, watched him until he thought he was going to explode with the wanting of her building beyond reason within him.

"And you are testing my credulity, Captain."

"Your what?"

"Is this your idea of a swimming lesson?"

Mon Dieu, she was beautiful. Dressed in Hadley's damnable satin gowns she'd looked a schoolgirl let loose in her mother's wardrobe—if her mother was a wily widow with matchmaking in mind. He'd wanted to throttle Cassandra and murder Hadley, he knew that much. That night in her cabin with her braid mussed, her prim night shift covering her from chin to toes, she'd glowed in the moon's light and looked . . . an angel. Untouched, untarnished, and painfully, powerfully unaware. A fallen angel, he corrected himself, fighting the spell the sight of her had cast, and which threatened still. A fallen angel spitting fire and brimstone and packing a wild right hook.

"Well?" she prodded.

"Fine," he said, glad to be freed from his thoughts. He glanced down and swore. "You can't swim."

Cassandra's eyes rolled skyward. "If I could swim, why would I be needing lessons, pray tell?"

Rafe closed his eyes. "You can't swim in skirts," he said through gritted teeth. He looked down at her, waving his hand. "You might as well be toting an anchor they're so—hey!" He jerked back, too stunned to even swear as Cassandra shimmied nimbly out of her skirt. Catching the sodden mess she tossed his way, he found his voice—and volume—when she began yanking at the petticoat ribbons tied at her waist. "What do you think you're doing?" She didn't spare him a glance. "Cassandra!"

"There." She stooped, stepped, not without difficulty this time, free of the soaking cotton underskirt and stood grinning up at him in her chemise, shirt, and drawers. He blinked. Since when did stern nuns in respectable convent schools allow their demure charges drawers trimmed in wide, wanton scarlet ribbon? Cassandra followed his look and glanced back up at him with a shrug. "It was a dare." She smiled. "I won."

Rafe's look ricocheted, snagged on her hat bobbing atop the waves toward the beach. He stared after it, envied it. Cassandra might as well be standing before him newborn naked the way the wet muslin left on her clung to her skin.

"Get dressed," he choked.

"But you said—"

"I know what I said. Now I'm saying *get dressed.*"

"Captain Buchanan," Cassandra reasoned. "I'm as dressed as you and Cuffey, am I not? More dressed! No one's here to see me anyway, and I really would love to know how to swim." Her small hand closed over his arm. He held himself rigid. "Please?"

Rafe groaned. God knew he was no saint. Cassandra Mortier was no angel, either, fallen or otherwise. She was Satan's daughter incarnate, and he was in soul-deep trouble. The hat sank from sight, not reaching the beach. Rafe took a deep breath and looked at Cassandra who, *damn,* didn't look at all like himself or Cuffey.

"Can you float?" he asked.

"I don't know. How do I do it?"

He stared down into her grey eyes, read her stubbornness, her willingness, and her out-and-out challenge. He gave up. He was going to teach her to swim—and pray he didn't drown in the process.

Chapter Nine

CASSANDRA'S PEALS OF laughter floated to Rafe above the pounding surf where he sprawled half-asleep on the beach. He opened his eyes, rose up on his elbows. Pain shot through his shoulder and down his arm. With a grimace and grunting curse he sat the rest of the way up—and forgot his arm.

Cassandra, the sun flashing like molten copper in her streaming, dark hair, dipped and darted in the waves, eluding Cuffey's chase. Rafe shook his head. She was part fish, a damselfish. No. He grinned wryly. She was tiny and aggressive and fearless, but she was about as harmless as the shipwrecking mermaids of ancient myth, her laugh her siren song.

Rafe flopped back down on the sun-heated, powdery sand. She was swimming, and he was drowning and no longer denying it. To himself, at least. Doc had begun scowling at him like a preacher in purgatory but was saying nothing save what he mumbled under his breath. So far. What could he say? Rafe argued in his own defense.

Rafe had done nothing save spend every free moment with Cassandra. He'd taken her to the caves overlooking the beach, taken her with him when he scavenged the islet for breadfruit and the beaches for driftwood, taken her along wherever he was going to help with whatever he was doing. But he'd not taken her. Not like he wanted to. So far.

Frowning, he stared up at the cloudless dome of sky so bright and beautiful it hurt to look at it. Like Cassandra. He closed his eyes, helpless against the myriad images of Cassandra planted in his mind, imprinted on his senses.

The way her hand fit into his, and how strong it was yet how gentle her touch when she examined the trembling petals of a fallen orchid bloom or cleaned a coral cut from Cuffey's pink-bottomed foot. The way her stride matched his, long, purposeful, graceful, her calves muscled, her ankles slender, her toes tiny and tanned and . . . ticklish? He longed to tickle them. With his tongue. Like he longed—no, ached—to take her high, firm breasts naked in his hands, tease her nipples berry-hard, and suckle, pull harder and harder and wetter and wetter until she ached and arched. Ready for him. Reaching for him. Wanting him. Like he wanted her.

"Fils d' putain." He twisted onto his stomach, his groin tightening, displaying his need. His lust, his conscience smote him. For shame, Doc's frown scolded. Kiss me, Cassandra's grey eyes called to him. He wasn't imagining the permission in her look. She wasn't unaffected, unaware. She was curious, reckless, naïve. She was willing. But she could not be ready for where one kiss would lead. If he touched her like she wanted to be touched, kissed her like he wanted to kiss her . . .

Rafe shuddered in the midday heat. He breathed deep, slowly, and willed himself master over his body and mind. Cuffey's shouts mixed with Cassandra's laughter. The sea's pulsing waves hissed and sprayed. Hidden parakeets scolded and blackbirds cawed in the tangle of green that spread behind them. Surely Dom and Jansen had made Nassau. They should be returning for them by now, before now. His muscles eased. The sun's heat soothed, massaging his shoulder. Surely Dom would arrive from Nassau soon. Today or the next day, it didn't matter. As long as it was soon.

"Good Gawd a'mighty," Cuffey sighed, leaned back against the trunk of a giant palm tree that spread and roofed their campsite, and closed his eyes. "I'm pure stuffed."

"An event to be duly noted in heaven and in the log," Rafe joked.

Doc turned to glare at them. "I'll not be mocked nor listen t' ye make light o' sacred subjects. D'ye ken?"

"Aye, Doc," Rafe sighed and leaned back beside his cabin boy, mirroring the boy's blissful after-supper repose.

"Sorry, Doc." Cuffey mimicked his captain's unconcern.

The surgeon's shoulders stiffened where he squatted by the fire. He raised his hand, let it drop limply. "A matched pair o' good-fer-nothin' heathens, ye be," he mumbled. "Sailors! A full stomach an' a fair wind be all ye know t' care aboot." His brogue thickened, his grumbling continuing under his breath. Across the fire from him Cassandra set aside the remains of her grouper-and-chub fish feast and studied the two heathens.

One light, one dark, one tall, one small, one captain and one ship's boy. Doc was right; they were born sailors. Stomachs full, work done, they'd soon both be snoring and would rival the tree frogs until dawn, she knew too well. She smiled wistfully. They had become her best friends.

A feeling akin to the homesickness that had pressed always against her heart at school came. She would miss them, miss these halcyon days, miss the haze of the surf breaking over the reef beyond the beach and lagoon, miss running wild and unencumbered by clothes, by concerns, by conventions. She would miss it all once Dom returned for them and never likely know such times again. Or these people either. Rafe and Cuffey would go back to sea. Doc would return to New Orleans. It was her turn to sigh.

Doc's squinting gaze searched her face in the dying fire's glow. "Go t' bed, lass. I'll see t' this meself tonight."

Cassandra shook her head and stood up, brushing her skirt. "No. Rafe and Cuffey caught it. You cooked it, and I ate it. I can help clean up at least." Doc protested but not overmuch.

The old hypocrite, Cassandra thought, smiling as she stacked their meager sand-scrubbed utensils in a tarp and folded it closed about them. It was a useless precaution. By breakfast an assortment of insects and one or more hermit crabs would be sleeping in the coconut-carved mugs and shell dishes, all doomed to energetic eviction by a most efficient Cuffey.

"Ye feelin' well, lass?"

Cassandra looked around, surprised. "I'm fine. Why?"

"Ye seem . . . pensive o' late. Somethin's weighin' on yer mind." The surgeon's brow knitted, and he glanced away looking undeniably and very uncharacteristically at a loss for words. Cassandra pushed up from her knees, glad that the sun had set and, away from the fire, her face wasn't readable. Doe struggled mightily without his spectacles, but his instincts were as sharp as ever.

"I'm tired," she lied. "Our signal fire puts Cuffey's appetite to shame. We hauled driftwood up there most of the afternoon."

"Mebbe," Doc grunted. "Ye've no business doin' that sort o' work. Rafe an' the lad—"

"I know. But I enjoy it." Another lie. She enjoyed being with Rafe, enjoyed watching him, watching the sweat darken his hair, drip off the end of his nose, paint his bared chest and sinewy arms with a golden, glistening sheen. Her pulse quickened, but not her conscience.

"Lass." Doc straightened. He was gathering wind, a bad sign. "Ye know I be a common sort not given t' fancy ways nor words either. But"—he frowned down at his feet—"I feel a keen responsibility regardin' yer . . ." He paused. "Yer well-bein'." Cassandra cringed inwardly but met the old man's gaze when he looked up. "I don't need specs t' see there's a heaviness settlin' on those young shoulders. I've kept me thoughts t' meself, but—"

"Doc." Rafe's deep voice from the shadows beyond the fire made both Cassandra and the surgeon start. Cuffey moaned in his sleep and turned onto his side, a soft, curled-up mound beside Rafe's long length in the flickering fire's light. "It's late, and the sun rises early. Cassandra needs her sleep. We all do."

"What the lass needs is—"

"We didn't mean to wake you," Cassandra cut in. "Doc." She turned, taking full advantage of Rafe's interruption. "Could we talk tomorrow?"

Doc looked from her to Rafe and back to her, then shrugged, his irritation loud in the stretching silence. "Good night, then," he said.

"Good night," Cassandra called over her shoulder, making a hasty retreat.

"But no more haulin' firewood, d'ye ken?"

The old man's order followed her inside the lean-to. She dismissed it but couldn't shake her melancholy. It seemed to deepen with the evening shadows. Sighing, she thought to take Rafe's advice instead and busied herself readying her pallet of sweet-smelling survival grass, discarding her clothes down to her chemise. Her petticoat did double duty as her blanket at night. She wasn't wearing her drawers. They were hanging up on a vine clothesline strung near the beach along with Doc's suit vest. She shook her head. Poor Doc would have apoplexy if he suspected she was swimming, let alone in such ragtag swimming attire, so she changed into them at the lagoon, out of them before they returned to camp. She hoped he'd not miss his vest too soon, but until he said something, she'd decided to keep quiet.

"I'm not hurting it," she said to no one. Swimming with Cuffey and Rafe wasn't hurting anyone either. Cassandra lay down and stared out the opening left by the tied-back canvas. Cuffey was oblivious to how she dressed. And Rafe . . . Frowning, she studied the Big Dipper dominating the northern sky, traced its lip to the North Star as Rafe had taught her. Rafe Buchanan was the problem, not swimming or borrowed vests or Dom's return. Doc was a grumpy, grumbling mother hen regarding her, ever worrying and warning. Cuffey was her champion and ready cohort. But Rafe? How did he feel, truly, about her?

Cassandra wrinkled her nose and shifted onto her stomach, resting her chin on her folded hands. How did she feel about him? That might be the better question to lose sleep over. And she was losing sleep over it.

"Blast," she groaned. Her entire life up to Captain Rafael Buchanan she'd gone after whatever had taken her fancy, set off her temper, or piqued her curiosity. Warnings? They went unheeded if heard at all. Difficulties? They merely challenged. Consequences? They were seldom considered and always survivable if they came. But she was not acting herself regarding her feelings for this tall, dark-eyed blockade runner.

He'd certainly taken her fancy. When she wasn't with him, she was thinking about him. If she wasn't with him or thinking about him, she was asleep—dreaming about him. It was irritating to a degree. That she couldn't seem to stop herself she found even more irritating to a much greater degree. Sweet Mary, he was only a man, she lectured herself, rolling onto her back. A man easy to look upon, to be sure. A man easier to be with. So what? her mind raged. So what? So what? So what? She grinned wryly. He set off her temper easy enough too.

Which left curiosity. Her grin disappeared. Rafe Buchanan stirred emotions in Cassandra that were exciting, intriguing. She frowned. Frightening? Fear was foreign to her nature, or so she'd always believed, behaved. Up to now. She was not afraid of Rafe. She knew that. The more she was with him, the more at ease she became. She wasn't afraid for him any longer either. His arm was mending, his strength returning. More important, the long-faced captain was no longer in evidence. Cassandra took no small pleasure in feeling that that was at least partly her doing, so adept she was at raising the man's laugh—or wrath.

She arched her neck and stared up and out at the sky. The stars were brighter, the drone of insects and frog chorus steady, soothing. The breeze that blew playful and pleasant all day turned surprisingly cool at night. Cassandra shivered and reached for her petticoat. She should close the flap before the chill crept into the lean-to and settled in her bones. She should get some sleep; the sun did rise early. She closed her eyes. A dying ember popped and hissed outside. Some night hunter winged over the lean-to, leaving a deeper silence in its wake. Cassandra swore, tossed off the petticoat, and sat up. Bats and bugs and familiar haunts cloaked in darkness had never much frightened her either. She was cold. She wasn't sleepy. She was going for a walk.

Wearing her petticoat about her shoulders like a shawl, Cassandra saw the fine white sand of the beach ahead, aglow in the silver moonlight, and slowed her pace. Shoeless, she had to pick her way carefully along the pitted limestone terrace that ran below the cliff standing guard over the lagoon's beach. Prickly cacti grew in the cracks and potholes here, as well as sisal and leathery-edged shrubs. She reached the tumble of giant, razor-sharp slabs of ancient coral shed from the cliff's face and stopped, the white sand spreading in front of her.

The lagoon looked different by night. The reef beyond seemed closer, the surf louder, the beach lonelier, a protected, isolated pocket of paradise under a star-dizzying cap of blue-black velvet sky. Cassandra closed her eyes, breathed deep—and whirled at a step and the crunch of rock behind her.

"You shouldn't take off alone, especially at night."

"Holy Mary Mother of God." Cassandra expelled a shaky breath. Her heart left her throat. Sinking down on a block of coral, she shook her head and eyed Rafe where he stood in the cliff's shadow at the path's opening onto the beach. "Being alone"—her fright sharpened her words—"isn't what nigh robbed me of life in this world, Captain."

She heard his sigh, watched his tall shadow take form as he strode toward her. She scooted over, and he sat down beside her.

"Couldn't sleep?" he asked, staring out at the water.

"No." She pulled the petticoat tighter about her shoulders.

"Cold?"

"A little."

"Stand up." Rafe stood and took her elbow as she hopped down. "Get out of the wind. Here." He sat down on the sand, the rock at his back, and pulled Cassandra down with him, situating her snugly in the space between his knees. His arms joined her petticoat about her shoulders, his hands clasped loosely in front of her as they faced the sea. "Is this better?"

Cassandra nodded and burrowed closer, letting go a soft, contented sigh. She leaned quietly against him. His measured breathing rhythmic, soothing, as they stared out over the beach toward the reef and night swallowed sea beyond.

"You couldn't sleep either?" Cassandra broke the comfortable silence. "Or did I wake you?"

"I wasn't asleep."

"Are you worried about your uncle and Mister Jansen? It's been so . . . long."

Rafe didn't answer right away. Cassandra waited, could almost feel him gathering his thoughts. She liked the way he took his time when they talked. If her observations made him laugh and her obstinance made him swear, her endless questions never made him lose patience. He explained things simply, expressed his opinions thoughtfully. He took her seriously in a way no one save Randall Mortier had ever done.

"We may be farther out than we calculated," he said. "They might have run into more weather or a half-dozen other things you can't plan on." Rafe sighed, his breath warm, soft, against her hair. "But they made it okay. I feel like I'd know it if they hadn't. Feel it."

"I wish I felt that way about my grandfather, could feel, somehow, that he was all right and knew I was all right."

Rafe's hands moved up to rest on her shoulders. His thumbs traced small circles where they met at the base of her neck. "You told your friend what you were doing—or what you thought you were doing." Cassandra smiled at the residue of exasperation in his comment. Rafe believed there were only two kinds of disasters: those that were unavoidable and those that weren't. He'd made it clear that her boarding the *Fortune* was a disaster of the first water on her part, of the latter variety. "Your grandfather's a merchant with connections and contacts," he went on. "He probably knew before you did where you were and where you were bound. He might be in Nassau right now, looking for you." His thumbs slowed, pressed more gently. "I would be, if you were my granddaughter."

Cassandra giggled. "As much as you remind me of Grandpapa at times, I can't imagine you a *grandpère*."

Rafe's thumbs stilled. "You can't begin to imagine what I can imagine when it comes to you."

Cassandra's heart stilled with Rafe's hands at the deeper note in his voice. The very air seemed to shift, warm about them, caressing her skin and coaxing her senses awake to a new night, a different place than they'd sat in only moments before. She was aware of Rafe's bare chest at her back, of its breadth, its fine coating of hair. She was aware of the thinness of her chemise and her nakedness beneath it, her petticoat her sole article of clothing not transparent from wear and washings in the spring beside the camp.

As was Rafe. She sensed him scrambling for distance mentally, felt his muscles tensing down his entire length wrapped about her. He put his hands on his knees.

"Tell me," she said.

"No." He swore. His hands fisted.

Cassandra reached up and pulled his arms back round her, her fingers curling softly around his thick wrists in front of her. "Please?" she whispered.

"It's late." Rafe bent forward to rise, and Cassandra clasped onto his forearms, staying him. "It's time to go back."

"No."

"Cassandra." Her name was plea, reprimand. Warning. She refused to heed it. "This is"—he paused—"dangerous." He was making it difficult. She rose to the challenge.

"You know why I couldn't sleep, Rafe? Why I got up, came here?"

He refused to answer. He was fighting her, fighting himself.

"Because I was afraid but couldn't fathom what there was to be frightened about. I'm not . . . not usually a fearful person."

"You are a fearless idiot. Come on. Let's go back."

Rafe stood up, hauling Cassandra up with him. The petticoat slipped from her shoulders and landed at their feet. Rafe swore, stooped to snatch it up. The scar where

Navarre's blade had torn into his shoulder showed white and new in the moonlight as he straightened before her, a ragged line that disappeared in the hair on his chest. Cassandra reached up, her hand spreading wide, covering that other man's ugliness so at odds with this man's beauty. She felt his heart, racing. His hands shook as they fumbled to drape the petticoat back over her shoulders. She brought her other hand up to his chest and willed him to meet her gaze.

"Rafe," she said. "I may be an idiot, but I know what I fear, fear with a dread I'd not thought possible."

"Damn you, Cassandra. Stop this. *Now.*" His voice was as unsteady as his fingers. He took her by the shoulders and gave her a hard shake. "You will regret this come morning."

"I might," Cassandra conceded. "But it's not morning yet, and there cannot be many more nights here on this cay. I fear leaving here, Rafe, and wondering for the rest of my life why you never kissed me when I knew you wanted to. I dread living the rest of my life wondering what it might have been to be touched by you, held by you."

Her bald words heated her face and tested her courage, but she did not look away. Rafe's tortured eyes bore into hers, and though his face remained a mask, his stance rigid, Cassandra knew—*knew*—that she was right. He did want her.

"Cassandra." He closed his eyes. "I can't . . . just kiss you."

Her heart raced no less than his. She recognized the desire a woman knows for a man rising within her. It had stirred between them that first night in the school garden, had simmered hotter on board the ship. Here on this isle it had come to this: this night, this time. She was awed, excited, shaking. Trusting. She trusted this man who was Rafe, was choosing to trust the budding woman who was unfolding inside her.

"I'm not afraid. Rafe," she whispered. "It's right. Why else would I feel so for you and you for me?"

Rafe could think of a score of reasons, except that he was thinking less and less clearly. She was so beautiful. The dark circles of her nipples showing through her chemise made him dizzy. The dark desire in her eyes made him ache. He reached out, stroked her cheek, tucked her wild curls behind her ear.

"You should be afraid, Cassandra," he said. Her skin was like silk against his fingers. "I don't wish to be the one to teach you to be afraid."

"Never." Cassandra's arms slipped around his back. She lifted up on her toes and kissed his shoulder, tracing the scar down, down, until she buried her face in his chest, her hug tightening about him. "Not with you, Rafe. I'm never afraid with you."

He was lost, drowning. His arms wrapped about her, his hands sliding, searching, until they cupped her buttocks, and he discovered what a part of him had known from the first time his hands had circled her in Denoir. She was soft and round and made for his hands, formed to fit against him. She was his. If only for this night, this time, Cassandra was his.

His mouth covered hers, and Cassandra welcomed him, grew light-headed with the taste of him and the swelling tide of hot desire his kiss let loose inside her. Her arms circled his neck. Their kiss deepened, and she clung to him. Her hands fisted in his thick hair, hair that had grown with his beard and altered his appearance from shipmaster to coarse sailor to shaggy, untamed pirate. Rafe's lips tore from hers. Her head fell back.

She let her weight rest in his hands that cupped her hard against him, squeezing her yielding flesh, molding her to him. She ached for him, cried out when his head dipped, and he took her nipple into his mouth. Rafe pulled and tugged through her chemise, one breast, then the other, until the pleasure shooting deep into her center became a melting torture that made her throb and shake. She arched, freeing her breasts more fully to his marauding caresses. A wave of desire crested, crashed over her. They became a part of the moonswept night, the pulsing jungle, the pounding surf, the dizzying sky.

"Rafe. Oh, God."

With a last, hungry pull, he drew back. They leaned against each other, holding each other up, their breathing ragged, pulses racing.

"*Jesu,* Cassandra," Rafe panted.

She rested her forehead against his chest, weak, trembling. "I know . . . I know."

He shuddered, and it passed from him to her.

"We should go back."

Cassandra swallowed, nodded. Rafe's hands slid up her back, and she burrowed into his arms, her cheek pressed against his heart. His chin at rest atop her head, they stood thus in the night's embrace, calming, their emotions gentling, spirits touching. They stood finally silent, connected, content.

Rafe swore.

Cassandra smiled without lifting her head from his hard-planed, hair-soft chest. "I know."

He stepped back. Cupping her face with his callused hands, Rafe searched her face. "Do you?" His eyes were black, the fires within them banked but still well able to heat her senses as she held his steady gaze. "*Can* you know?" he asked, his words deep, gruff.

She stood, her hands circling his wrists at each side of her face, and said nothing. Their eyes, their hands, the space they stood in said all there was to say. Rafe took a deep breath, let it go.

"We will regret this, Cassandra."

"Maybe," she said quietly.

"I want you. I won't deny it." The line between his brows deepened. "But I can't offer you anything more."

"I'm not asking for anything more." She smiled. "I want you." She spoke simply. She spoke the truth. "I want this night."

He looked at her a long moment, then pulled her into his arms. Cassandra closed her eyes and drifted, awash in the wonder of this man, this night. The heat thrumming in her blood warmed and was a tended fire, not a rampaging one. Rafe stepped back, his gaze mirroring her wonder, his kiss gifting her with magic, with amazement that a taking so slow, so infinitely gentle could be so thorough, and more thoroughly limb-weakening than his hunger-hot ravishing had been before. He lifted his head, grinned when she wobbled and clutched his arms to keep her balance.

"Do you know how wonderful you are?" he asked. His eyes skimmed her face, her breasts, her length to her toes. Starting over once more, his hands joined the journey. "Your face glows, Cassandra, and feels like finest satin." His fingers moved to the frayed ribbon at her chemise's neckline. He tugged, and the gauze-thin linen loosened and slipped to her waist. "*Mon Dieu,* your breasts. Look, Cassandra. See how beautifully you are made." She looked down, the sight of his hands holding her making her catch her breath, catch it further as his thumbs brushed over her nipples again, and again, and again. Her short nails dug into his arms.

"And such a tiny waist." His hands circled her, riding her hips. "So small. So soft." Her fingers slid up his arms and tangled in the hair on his chest, her chemise floating to her feet unnoticed.

"And here." Cassandra jumped as Rafe's hand cupped the moist mound between her legs. He stroked her, slowly, knowingly, holding her gaze all the while, then dipping his head to take her mouth as his fingers entered her. Cassandra whimpered, rubbed against him in untutored desire. "You are so good," he whispered against her lips. He kissed her deeper. "So good."

He stepped back and doffed his trousers. Cassandra watched as he spread them with her petticoat on the sand. She let her gaze drink in how the moon gilded his wide shoulders, his hard stomach and thick-muscled thighs, felt her eyes widen at his naked maleness. He was beautiful. He stood and his need, so evident and erect, was beautiful.

"Cassandra."

She jerked her gaze up to his.

"I want you."

She closed her eyes, searched her mind for doubt, for fear. She met his look, held out her hand, and followed him down onto the sand, unafraid. This was a gift. This was magic. It was right.

"Sails, ho! Sails, ho!"

Rafe opened his eyes, wincing at the rising sun's rays slanting off the white sand. "What the . . . ?" He sat up, disoriented, frowning down at his nakedness, cursing the stiffness in his shoulder.

"Sails, ho!" The distant shout carried to them.

"*Merde.*" He leaped to his feet and began scrambling into his trousers. "Cassandra! Wake up! Cuffey's sighted sails."

Cassandra curled tighter into a ball, her tousled hair spilling over shoulders kissed the color of honey by her days under the sun. Rafe closed his eyes. Shoulders sweeter to the taste, to the touch than— He swore, opened his eyes. The petticoat lifted in the breeze, showing a round hip, pink derriere. Rafe dropped to his knees and shook her. She rolled onto her back, the petticoat rolling underneath her. Rafe's mouth went dry at the sight she made, naked and nubile, her silken skin shaded by the pink and lavender hues of daybreak. She opened her eyes, smiled.

"Good morning."

"Aye, it's morning, and there's going to be all hell to pay if—"

"Rafe? Rafe!"

At Doc's shout, Rafe shot to his feet, and Cassandra bolted upright, fully awake. "What's he coming here for?" she gasped, yanking her chemise over her head, missing an armhole in her agitation. "He's never come down here." Rafe straightened her twisted chemise, and she jammed her arm through the proper opening. "Sweet Mary, what are we—"

"God a'mighty."

Rafe and Cassandra whirled. Framed by palm leaves and tangled vines and panting from his trek, Doc stood staring at them, frozen in shocked comprehension. His face stained purple, drained white.

"God damn ye for a fool an' a fornicator!" he bellowed. Cassandra stumbled to her feet. Rafe stiffened, his hands fisting as if to ward off a physical assault. "I took ye for a man higher than his rutting animal urges.

An' look at ye!" He turned his wrath on Cassandra, his voice hoarsening. "An' ye, lass?" She skittered behind Rafe, yanking the petticoat tight about her shoulders. "Ye think t' hide? Cover too late what ye've flaunted an' lost forever before man an' Maker?"

"No," she said, but only Rafe heard her. "It's not . . . it wasn't . . . isn't—"

Rafe spun to face her, feeling more helpless than he'd felt when he'd watched the rigging crashing down on top of her head. "Cassandra," he said, squeezing her arms, hating the chill radiating from her skin, the chaos in her grey eyes that had looked up at him seconds before brimming with morning, with warmth and the glow of their loving. "Forgive me," was all he could say. Rage rocked him. Forgive him? What had he done? And at what cost? *"Dammit."*

Doc sank down onto a slab of jutting coral. "Go back t' camp, Cassandra." His words were stiff, old. "Go on," he said louder when she didn't move. "D'ye wish Cuffey t' see an' "—he paused—"an' lose his childhood along with yers? The lad's all upset 'cause ye didna wake him for yer mornin' "—his voice curdled—"swim." Rafe watched pain rush up, brim in Cassandra's eyes.

"Don't," he said, shaking her, forcing her to look away from Doc and back to him. "Don't take on what isn't yours. This is mine to carry, all of it. Do you understand?"

"An' yer seed? If ye've got the lass with child, whose will that be t' carry, Rafe Buchanan?"

"Enough!" Rafe whirled, spraying sand. His shout cut through Cassandra's confusion, his anger and guilt increasing it a hundredfold. She bolted. "Cassandra!"

Evading Rafe's hands, veering wide around Doc in her path, Cassandra gained the trail for camp running blindly, wildly. Rafe's yell followed her, but she didn't check, and it was Doc's words that chased her until she collapsed, stumbling, sobbing, onto the ground inside the lean-to.

For Cuffey she dressed, and calmed, and washed her tears away. For Cuffey she smiled when the camp filled with strangers jumping to Dominic Veasey's familiar oath-blighted orders. With Cuffey dancing at her side, she walked lightly to take her place next to him as they shoved off from the cay. But though she stood beside him, only Cuffey watched the island sink into the horizon as the schooner's sails filled with wind, and they headed, once more, toward Nassau.

Chapter Ten

"THERE." CUFFEY TUGGED Cassandra's elbow and pointed toward the horizon and a dimly discernible blue mist. "See it, Cass?"

"Miss Mortier, lad," Doc grumbled beside them. "We be back t' civilization an' civil ways." He sighed. "Providence preserve us."

Cassandra glanced sideways at the surgeon. He faced the railing with her and Cuffey but with his eyes tightly closed, his shaggy hair and frayed necktie whipping about his whisker-stubbled face, his expression worse than grim: pained. He and Rafe made a matched pair, she decided, Doc slump-shouldered and sigh-heavy, Rafe wire-strung and silent. And absent. She wasn't sure if Rafe was avoiding her or avoiding Doc, who'd hovered sighing and seething at Cassandra's side since they'd boarded. Blast them both. She'd not asked either Lauchlan Collier or Rafe Buchanan to feel responsible for—she wrinkled her nose—her well-being.

She stared back toward New Providence island, watched the tall coconut trees feathering it take form above the haze. She wished she could blink the island away, blot out this entire time since the scene on the beach. She felt cheated in some way she couldn't explain, robbed. Her fingers curled tighter about the wet railing.

Bleak emotion and bald reason warred in her heart and head, but in all of it she felt not one drop of guilt, not one twinge of remorse.

The island blurred. She was glad she'd followed Rafe to Le Havre, she wanted to shout out loud, glad the *Fortune* had not made Nassau, and glad she'd stayed with Rafe at the lagoon. Glad! Willful, selfish sinner! her conscience shouted instead. Fine, she argued back, tossing her hair out of her eyes. She stood guilty as charged. She turned her head and gazed up at the poop deck where Rafe stood, shoulders rigid, legs braced. What she couldn't stand was Rafe Buchanan's solitary sulking, whatever the cause.

As if he read her thoughts, Rafe turned. Their gazes locked down the length of the cluttered deck. Cassandra's heart thudded painfully. He'd shaved, donned the sailor's familiar striped shirt and baggy, calf-length trousers. The pirate was gone, but, sailor togs or no, he looked every inch the master, not the mate. Rafe shouted something to Dom and the captain, then swung down the steps onto the main deck.

Cassandra drew back from the railing and finger-combed her hair. She should have braided it tighter. He was coming toward them, sidestepping cables, scanning the rigging. Cassandra forgot about her hair. Strength and boldness rippled in his balanced, loose stride. Sunlight flashed golden in his wind-tossed hair. Behind her, Cuffey shouted a hello. Rafe ignored it. Doc muttered under his breath. Cassandra ignored him. Rafe stopped, and Cassandra saw only Captain Rafe Buchanan before her, the crease between his brows, his straight nose, high cheekbones, lighter-toned chin, and those dark, guarded eyes looking down at her. She pressed her hands together. She wanted to reach up and touch him, wanted him to touch her. Rafe frowned and looked over her head out to sea. He cleared his throat but said nothing. He cleared his throat again.

Cassandra struggled not to smile. She'd seen Rafe delirious. She'd seen him distracted, deliberate, angry, aloof, but she'd never seen, never even imagined him nervous. Her eyes narrowed. If he was about to apologize, again, for taking what she'd freely given, she'd strangle him then and there and add murder to her list of sins. Her pulse quickened. Maybe he was done apologizing. Maybe he'd come to his senses at last and was about to—

"Dom just told me there was someone at the Royal asking about the *Fortune,* making inquiries about"—he looked at her—"a passenger."

Cassandra stared up at him, his words too much of a surprise to register sense immediately.

Rafe's frown deepened with his voice. "He didn't learn of it in time to check it out, but"—he glanced down Cassandra's front—"*merde.*" That registered clear enough. Cassandra's face heated. She raised her chin. "If it's your grandfather, or even someone sent by your grandfather, we can't have him seeing you like—"

"Grandpapa!" Cassandra jumped forward and grabbed Rafe's arms. "He's in Nassau? Now?" She whooped and spun, tugging Rafe in a complete circle, oblivious to the sailors' hoots and open mouths, to Cuffey's cheer, to Doc's myopic eyes rolling heavenward.

Rafe caught her before she tumbled them both into the rail. "Hold, Cassandra." But he couldn't hold back his grin. Her laugh made him light-headed; the joy and relief and love shining up at him in her eyes made him ache. *Mon Dieu,* she'd bewitched him, he thought. He felt much as he had felt when she'd crashed into his arms, into his life in Denoir. The present crashed back, and he jerked away from her touch, from her spell.

The man and the girl from the garden were no more. He didn't want to hold her now; he wanted to shake her. She could no longer afford to be so unconcerned, unaware. Reckless, untested, Cassandra, he feared, was enamored with wind and speed and heading into a hurricane with every sail unfurled. She hugged him, stepped back, hugged herself. Rafe dragged his eyes from her and glared at three mates who scrambled back to their duties. Cassandra whirled and leaned on the railing. Shielding her eyes, she stood on tiptoe and scanned the horizon, blissfully, completely . . . happy.

Rafe sighed and watched the wind buffet her, billow her sun-bleached rag skirt above her arched feet, tug her curls escaped from the braid down her back into a wild halo about her head, a dark halo streaked with copper by the sun.

"I've a friend in Nassau," he said.

Cassandra smiled into the wind. Of course Rafe would have friends there. He'd have friends wherever he went. Her grandfather would be upset with her, would not approve of what she'd done, none of it. But he'd like Rafe Buchanan. And Rafe would like him. She turned.

"Grandpapa always needs good captains. Maybe you could sail for him?"

"Aye, Cassandra." Rafe closed his eyes. "All the way to Hades once he learns—"

"Learns what?" she challenged. "That you vowed to see me safely returned to him from the very start? That you got me safely off the *Fortune* and to the cay where you—"

"Where I what?" Rafe's eyes burned her to silence. He glanced behind her. "Cuffey. Find Mister Jansen and tell him he's to see you get into some clean clothes—a decent shirt at least. And scrub down. We'll dock looking like sailors, not sea urchins."

"Aye, Captain." Cuffey snapped to attention, grinned, and darted off. Doc bristled.

"Ye'll not be sending me off so easy, so don't—"

"Stop it." Cassandra glared first at Doc, then at Rafe. "Neither of you is responsible for me. I am."

"I agree, Cassandra." Doc's eyes bugged under his bushy brows. "An' ye've been bloody irresponsible, an' well ye know it. As have we all!"

Cassandra tossed them both a mutinous look and turned to watch New Providence's approach. She didn't want to argue, had no patience for doom and gloom. She was too happy. Randall Mortier was in Nassau; he'd send no one else. He was looking for her, distraught, despairing if he'd learned that the *Good Fortune* had gone down in the storm. Her spirits dipped. Rafe and Doc joined her at the railing. The three leaned on their hands or their elbows or their forearms and watched the sea carry them closer to their destination, each silent with their thoughts.

"What's done is done." Rafe was the first to speak. "We need to be dealing with where the winds are blowing us now."

"They can't blow us into port soon enough," Cassandra said.

"An' then, lass?" Doc said. She looked at the older man, but Rafe spoke first.

"Then I find Lenora who will get Cassandra into some clothes befitting someone resembling her grandfather's granddaughter. Then I book passage for you to see Cuffey safely back to New Orleans. Then I find whoever is looking for Cassandra and see she gets safely back to her grandfather."

"What about you?" Cassandra asked. "Where will you go from here?"

"San Francisco." He exhaled. "I've a lost ship, undelivered cargo, and a missing nephew to report to Bernard Cramer."

"An' what o' the lass, Rafe, if she finds out later she's carryin' yer bairn?"

The three stood silently not meeting each other's eyes. Cassandra's face burned. Her fingers clenched the railing. Anything, she prayed, pleaded. Break my legs. Blind me. Give me a blemish—a horrid mole the size of a walnut right on my nose for the rest of my life. But don't let me be with child. Please.

It was a condition she'd never once considered. It was the one consequence she was not sure she could survive: the breaking of her protective, honorable, devoted grandfather's heart. She had been willfully, selfishly, sinfully irresponsible, and well she knew it. Now. She shuddered, felt Rafe shift beside her.

"Dom can report to Bernard," he said. "I'll stay until we know. If I've fathered a child, its mother will have me as well." He paused. "I've damned my father my entire life, Doc, for not doing as much and for doing much worse. But his blood in me has shown true." He swore.

Cassandra winced at the self-loathing in his voice, ached at the past's ghosts and pain she saw resurrected in Rafe's haunted eyes. She was responsible for that too. Sweet Mary.

"There be ways," Doc began, "proven means an' measures not based on superstitions an' ignorance whereby a lass—"

"No." Cassandra and Rafe spoke as one.

Doc eyed them both, then looked out to sea. "I've a need for a stiff drink an' some peace t' sip it in. I'll be below." He turned from the railing, stopped, turned again. "Our best be ever all that's asked. Be it too late or not enough or not done well is ever better than no attempt at all. Ye remember that. Both o' ye."

Cassandra remained at the railing. Rafe, to her surprise, remained beside her. Flying fish leaped and gleamed, the first to greet their return. Then came butterflies darting in the sun, fluttering to rest atop the gear stowed on deck or upon the lines, the railing, on Cassandra's hand. She smiled, glanced up at Rafe, then looked away, the moment and its beauty shaded, her smile unshared. The ship cut in from the sea, passed a white inelegant fort off the port bow from whence a native pilot boarded. He guided them past Potter's Cay, beyond Hog and Athol Islands to the port and anchorage at a wharf below Bay Street where ships were made fast three abreast.

"Sweet Mary," Cassandra breathed, taken aback by the rush of throbbing, thriving commerce that enveloped them. She'd begged always and gone often with her grandfather and Jim to Mobile's waterfront; she'd visited, less often, the wharves of New Orleans. But time had softened the stored sights and sounds of her childhood, and she was too soon away from the untouched cay's serenity and gentle solitude. Rafe took her elbow. She jumped.

"The gangplank's secure. Let's go."

Without waiting for her response, Rafe led her off the ship, stopping only to give curt instructions to Dom. They dodged drays and darted around Negro roustabouts loading and discharging ships. Cassandra clung to Rafe's arm and wondered that they were not run down or assaulted, the pace he set was so fast, his course so oblivious to life and limb. She choked on the pulverized limestone clouding the air, cringed at the shrill screech of the steam donkey engines being used to help empty or load the yawning holds of uncountable ships.

"Rafe," she panted. "Slow down."

"We're almost there."

He didn't slow, but it was relief enough when they turned off Bay Street and she could drag air, not dust, into her abused lungs. Cassandra scanned packed-together shopfronts and taverns. The din of banging drays and bawling drivers at work gave way to raucous laughter and bawdy songs of seamen and dockhands at play.

"Buchanan? Hey!" A sailor stepped out from a doorway into the street behind them. "Rafe! They said you was lost, man."

"Later," Rafe called without looking back or breaking stride. If it was possible, he walked faster.

Cassandra stumbled, cried out as her foot turned beneath her. Rafe scooped her up in his arms and jogged on. He turned up one street, down another. The shop he finally entered smelled of stale rum and coconuts. Cassandra squinted into its cluttered dimness and squirmed to be set down. Rafe shook his head, swung behind a sagging counter. They passed a glass display case boasting delicate shell necklaces and trinket boxes, gaudily-worked headdresses, a shell-framed mirror. Coral chess pieces?

"I can walk. Where are we? Where is everyone? Put me down."

Rafe ignored her, ducked through a low door, and started up a narrow flight of creaking stairs. Shifting her weight, he knocked familiarly on a scarred door at the stairs' top. Cassandra reached up, took the man's stubborn, sweat-dampened face in her hands, and glared at him, nose to nose.

"Put me down," she said, enunciating as if he were deaf. Or dense. Being held like a truculent toddler felt foolish. Being ignored was heating her temper, dangerously. Their eyes met, held. A remembered fire sparked and a different heat seared through her, through them both. The door swung open. They both jumped.

"No one is allowed . . ." The woman's voice faded as her shaded eyes rounded. "My God. Rafe? Rafe!" Cassandra watched the color drain from the woman's face, leaving her rouged cheeks in painted relief. She felt her own blush creeping up her neck when the lady stepped back and stared first at Rafe, then at her. "My God."

The woman's eyes crinkled. "What's this?" She waved a white hand. Her smile came, sultry and knowing, and Cassandra's eyes narrowed, wariness rising in her no less real than her embarrassed flush. "Did you spit in death's eye, Captain, and retain your life but gain a sea urchin for your trouble?"

Rafe set Cassandra down, so quickly Cassandra swallowed her protest.

"In a manner of speaking," he said. Cassandra swung around on the top step where she'd been deposited, but he shot her a quelling look and smiled over her head at the woman framed in the doorway. "Lenora. This is Cassandra Mortier from Mobile. She's been in France, attending school, and"—he smiled, a slow smile that Cassandra had not seen and disliked on sight—"I need your help."

"Of course." Lenora smiled. Cassandra frowned. "Have I ever failed you, Rafael Dominic Buchanan?" Cassandra blinked. This woman with her cat-shaped eyes actually purred. It set Cassandra's teeth on edge.

"Never." Rafe smiled.

Cassandra glared at him. She had claws of her own, but she wasn't sure whom she would most enjoy shredding, Rafe or—her nose wrinkled—Rafe's *friend*

Lenora. They both seemed to have forgotten Cassandra's existence.

"Actually, I'm here to ask a rather large favor, Lenora," Rafe said.

"I'm here to help." The woman matched his smile. Cassandra had seen enough.

"Well, I'm here to find my grandfather. He's not here." Cassandra tried to push past Rafe on the step below her.

"Easy, dammit." Rafe took hold of her shoulders. Cassandra stiffened and went still, stared straight ahead at Rafe's throat. She doubted Rafe talked to Lenora like this, or dragged her the length of Bay Street as though he were a runaway being chased by hounds, or that he'd ever slung her into his arms like his blasted sea chest and—

"You're here because you look the nightmare you've lived since last your grandfather laid eyes on you. You're here"—it was his turn to bite out his words—"because you can get cleaned up here and Lenora can get you into some fitting clothes so that when I come back for you here you can meet your grandfather looking yourself, not sea urchin twice boiled and thrown back with the tide. Do—you—hear?"

Cassandra stared straight ahead, mutinous, silent.

"Answer me."

Rage and humiliation clogged her throat, stung her eyes. "Aye, aye, Captain."

"Can you manage that?" He was speaking over her head again, calm and all charming again.

She ignored them, blanked out their voices, the way Lenora's elegant hand lingered on Rafe's arm, how Rafe smiled for Lenora but frowned at her at his parting. Feeling foolish and forlorn, belittled and betrayed, she turned and followed Lenora's swishing watered-silk bustle into the tiny apartment.

A native servant girl, dark-skinned and silent, appeared and was given charge of Cassandra's toilet, and the tightness in Cassandra's chest eased with Lenora's departure. The tub that was readied for her was a woman's dream: deep, enameled, porcelain-smooth. The water was hot, scented with coconut oil. Cassandra missed the lagoon. She donned underclothes of the softest cotton, hand-stitched with myriad tucks and lace edging. Cassandra tried not to think about who had worn them last, wondered, painfully, if Rafe's strong fingers had undone the ribbon lacings she was knotting so badly that the servant girl waved Cassandra's shaking fingers aside and finished them for her. No corset was supplied. Cassandra was glad—until Lenora reappeared with the gown.

It was a simple dress of light pink muslin sprigged with embroidered flowers the same color. Eyelet lace circled the high neckline, edged the sleeve's cuffs. It was a lovely dress, a party dress. For a child. The surprise that registered in Lenora's eyes when she viewed Cassandra's high breasts and feminine curves was some satisfaction, enough to keep Cassandra silently smug as the woman and girl helped Cassandra into the gown, enough to make Cassandra's refusal firm regarding the wide satin ribbon brought with the dress for her hair. She argued that her hair be pulled up and curled, like Lenora's. They compromised by gathering her hair into a net held in place with a shell-made barrette and curling the hair framing her face into long sausage curls at each ear.

At length Cassandra stood, ready, in the center of Lenora's bedroom. The other woman's appraisal was studied and acute. She straightened an inch of lace here, smoothed a fold there. She'd not spoken to Cassandra directly once since she'd opened her door. She didn't speak now but turned Cassandra this way and that by hand. Sighing, she stepped back at last and smiled, satisfied.

Cassandra felt like a life-sized fashion doll. Lenora was not unkind. She was going to considerable lengths and doing so with a generosity and willingness that Cassandra knew she'd never match were their roles reversed. Lenora was Rafe's friend, a close friend for him to arrive unannounced with such an unusual request and receive such a gracious, unhesitating response. Cassandra swallowed.

Rafe was doing this for her. Was she so . . . lacking in gratitude? Her grandfather would be appalled. Lenora was doing this for Rafe. Cassandra's resentment of this woman was making her feel all of five again, miserable and miserly because Jim was letting their horrid house guest ride Cassandra's pony as long as he liked when it was her pony, her turn.

Grandpapa and Jim. A glimmer of light cut through the gloom enveloping her. She would be with them both again, soon. Rafe might be with them this very moment, leading them to her or coming to take her to them. Cassandra smiled, her first true smile since they'd disembarked at Nassau.

Her smile softened. She no longer looked the nightmare she'd lived, as Rafe had put it. That she looked a first-year student arriving at school all pink and polished and proper didn't change the fact that she wasn't the same schoolgirl who had followed the misidentified, gentle-eyed Captain Buchanan onto the *Good Fortune*.

Doc was right: it was time to rejoin civilization and take up its ways.

Rafe had told her true: after a night's loving such as she'd desired, regrets dawned, unforeseen, and remorse built like storm clouds banking higher and higher along the sea horizon.

But she had been right too, right to follow the moon outside the garden wall, right to follow her heart and remain in Rafe's arms on the moon-washed beach. She'd been right because now when she chafed at constrictions put in her path she would know that contriving to live with them was a wiser choice than conniving a way out of them. She'd been right because, though she knew regret and remorse, she'd tasted loving and being loved. And she was still glad.

She looked over at Lenora where the woman sat at her dressing table overseeing her girl's rearranging of her hair.

"Thank you," Cassandra said. The serving girl's hand paused with the brush in mid-stroke. The two at the table met Cassandra's gaze from the mirror. "I appreciate all your trouble on my account."

And she did.

"No!" Cassandra screamed, her pitch rising to a keening wail as she ran at Clayton Hammond, slammed into him, and beat on his chest in time with her words, with her soul-renting despair. "No! No! No!"

"I'm sorry. Oh, God, I'm sorry." Eyes as blue, as brimming with concern as Lucy's, blurred in front of her. Other hands were pulling her back, turning her. She fought them, swinging and swearing. Screaming. Other faces spun about her. Doc. Cuffey. Dom. Lawrence Hadley. But Randall Mortier wasn't there. Jim wasn't there. They would never be there, never.

Her scream took on a life of its own that kept growing and growing and growing. Her head was forcibly buried in a wide shoulder and pressed, hard, against it. Robbed of of oxygen, her scream snuffed out. Her arms were pinned, her body trapped. Her hysteria quieted to a wracking wheezing, giant shudders convulsing her shoulders.

"We didn't know, Cassandra." Rafe's deep, emotion-thick voice came at her ear. "By the Virgin and all that's holy. We didn't know."

"You bastard! How could you not have known? Spared her this . . . this," the other voice sputtered, swore. She felt Rafe's muscles jerk, tense up.

"Ye've been here a week, Mister Hadley? Did *ye* know? God a'mighty. Ye barged in 'ere uninvited. The least ye can do is talk sense, damn ye, or I'll put ye out on yer ear m'self!"

"It took longer than Rafe wanted to trace Hammond here, him. When we learned he had word of the girl's *grandpère,* we"—Dom's sigh was heavy—"simply left him word when we'd come back with the girl an' where. *Po yi.*"

Cassandra was suddenly limp, a cold numbness robbing her legs of strength, her hands of feeling. But not her heart, not her soul.

"Cassandra?" Rafe bent and gathered her into his arms. "Look at me. Cassandra."

"They burned? Oh, God, Rafe. They . . . burned?" Rafe's face swam in front of her mirroring her pain, her deathly pallor. The room jarred as he sat down, cradling her in his lap.

"I don't think they suffered, Cassandra. Believe that." Lucy's brother knelt down beside her, reached awkwardly to take her hand. "The authorities think the warehouse was set on fire"—he frowned—"afterwards. To . . . to hide . . ."

"Their murders," she finished for him. She shuddered, closed her eyes.

"Murder!"

"Merde."

"Providence preserve us."

The voices came on top of each other, a rumbling murmur of disbelief, dismay. Rafe's silence was Cassandra's armor. She huddled inside his tight embrace keeping the hotel room and the others in it away. Lawrence Hadley's voice came muffled though he stood close by.

"To hide what, Hammond? Do they know?"

"No, or they knew nothing when I left Havre for here." She heard Clayton rising, chairs scraping as the three men and Cuffey gathered about Rafe and Cassandra on the settee. "They don't know what happened, or why," he went on. "But it was evident they'd both been assaulted, seriously wounded." He sighed. "They might have stumbled onto a robbery attempt at the warehouse and not had a chance to get away or—"

"No." Cassandra opened her eyes, focused on the squat, camellialike flower painted on the lamp's globe shade beside them. She forced herself to think, to remember. "My father was being blackmailed, apparently, and Grandpapa finally had"—she frowned in concentration—"had the proof, I suppose. He had what he needed." She looked up at Rafe, into eyes black and steady. Safe. "That's what he wrote me in the letter, why he couldn't come as he'd . . . planned. He was going to take care of everything, first, and then—" She stopped, unable to put into words what could never be, what should have been.

"The mate, him. He was crazy crazy about missing a meeting. Remember, Rafe?" Dom said.

"Aye." Rafe didn't look away from Cassandra. "He said his Mister Ran was meeting some snake that night and he had to be there." The line between his brows deepened; his voice softened. "He was a rare man, your Jim, to feel as he felt, and your *grandpère* must have been a good man to have earned that."

Cassandra stared up at him. His mussed, too-long hair glowed soft yellow in the lamplight. His eyes reflected his compassion, his caring. "Aye," she echoed him. "He was good. They both were." His face blurred, and he pulled her against him. She buried her face in his neck and clung to him.

"Did he say who the man was, Miss Mortier?" Lawrence asked.

Cassandra shook her head.

"He knew but he didn't tell you?" the supercargo prodded.

"Leave her alone!" Cuffey's shout was shrill.

"He didn't tell me." Cassandra spoke into Rafe's collar.

"She doesn't know his name," Rafe said. His chest expanded against her, relaxed. "Whatever evidence there was to be had probably was taken or destroyed in the fire."

Dom swore. "Aye, an' the name of the bastard, him, it died with the mate an' his master."

"Surely the authorities can find something," Lawrence protested. "The man should be tracked down. Hung!"

"I'll tell them what there is to tell," Clayton said. "As soon as I return Cassandra to the sisters in Denoir."

The room fell silent and still.

Cassandra's fingers fisted in Rafe's hair. "I want to go home. To Leeland."

"In Mobile?" Rafe asked.

"How can you, Cassandra?" Clayton said. "The house is closed, the servants gone. Raymond? Your gardener? Didn't he pass on this winter?" He stopped as Cassandra turned and looked at him over her shoulder. He looked sheepish. "My sister is only reserved in person, I'm afraid, not in her letters." A ghost of a grin lit his handsome features. "Trust me. Since she arrived at school she's never had little to write about and most of it concerning her poor, dear, scandalous Cassandra Mortier."

Cuffey giggled. Cassandra sniffed. Shifting on Rafe's lap, she let her head fall back against his shoulder and looked at Clayton.

"How is Lucy?" she asked, her voice tiny, tired.

Clayton's eyes grew serious, his face solemn. "Frantic. And waiting for you."

Cassandra closed her eyes. "I miss her, so much, but . . ." She bit her lip, tensing as tears gathered behind her eyelids, ached in her throat. Rafe's hold tightened. She swallowed. "I don't belong . . . there. I want to go home."

"The war, lass. Have ye forgotten?" Doc said. "Ye can't be in Mobile now. The home ye're needin' "—he paused—"it's only possible to go there in yer heart, Cassandra. For the present time, at least."

Clayton leaned forward. "Your grandfather was a wealthy man, Miss Mortier. I spoke at length with one of his associates before I sailed. Given the war at home and this"—he frowned—"this tragedy in Havre, it may take time to put your grandfather's business concerns in order, but things will come to rights. The man was your grandfather's friend, Cassandra—one of many. You will not be left without means."

Cassandra heard them, understood what Doc was trying to say, knew Clayton spoke the truth. It didn't help. It didn't matter. It changed nothing. "I don't belong anywhere." Rafe shifted. The coldness was returning. She shivered, welcomed it. "I was . . . wrong," she said, her voice lifeless to her ears. "So . . . wrong." Rafe turned her in his lap. She didn't help him, didn't protest. She was a rag doll. Limp. Numb. He cupped her chin with his hand, and she looked up at him. He was frowning.

"I had everything good," she said. "I was bad."

"Cassandra." Rafe's frown deepened.

"I never obeyed. Never listened. Never . . . knew." Her voice began fading. Her eyelids fluttered closed. "I ran away and lost it all. Grandpapa. Jim. Leeland."

"They still would have died, Cassandra, whether you were in your bunk where you belonged or stowed in the *Fortune*'s hold. It would have happened, just the way it happened, however it happened. Look at me, dammit."

"Easy, lad," Doc muttered.

Cassandra opened her eyes. Rafe's eyes were black, angry. Doc hovered over them, new spectacles glinting in the lamplight. Cuffey was at the surgeon's elbow looking small and frightened. They were good, each of them. She was going to lose them too. Maybe Rafe was right. It didn't matter if one was good or bad. It didn't matter. Holy Mary Mother of God, her lips mouthed the prayer. Help me. Help me. Nothing mattered anymore. The faces spun out of focus. The lamp's glow shrank, dimmed.

To nothing.

Chapter Eleven

BAY STREET WAS as crushed as before, the dust as thick, the noise as shrill. Cassandra walked between Lawrence Hadley and Clayton Hammond and didn't look, didn't listen. Cuffey and Doc had sailed for New Orleans three days before. They'd said their farewells to Cassandra at the Royal Victoria Hotel, Doc blowing his nose, bidding her trust in Providence; Cuffey saying nothing, his tight, hard hug saying it all. She'd watched them walk down the steps to where Rafe stood waiting with the surgeon's and boy's meager supplies and donated clothes stuffed into one dilapidated carpetbag under his arm. She'd watched them until they disappeared down Parliament Street, the tall man, old man, and boy—and felt nothing save an ever-deepening emptiness yawning inside her.

"Are you all right, Cassandra?" Clayton bent his head closer so she would catch his words amidst the clattering chaos rumbling about them. "Are you sure this is what you want? It's not too late to change your mind."

Cassandra glanced up at him through the black netting, of the mourning veil draping her bonnet. "I'll be fine," she said. "Tell Lucy I'll write. I promise."

"You'll like San Francisco," Lawrence said. "It's a city all its own, not antiquated and tired like Havre. And you'll like my uncle. He's a good man."

His uncle the philanthropist, Cassandra thought, recalling Lawrence's less than complimentary description of Bernard Cramer on board the *Fortune*. A man who couldn't resist works of charity. She sighed. She had no idea how long it might take for her grandfather's friends to sort out his affairs, no idea what her lot might be once they did. It didn't matter. Just as, if she didn't want to return to school and couldn't return to Leeland, it didn't matter where she went in the meantime.

The jostling on all sides lessened as they neared the gangplank jutting from the ship's bulwark. Lawrence had made all the arrangements. He'd discussed them with her at length over the last week. Cassandra couldn't even recall the ship's name, knew only that it was bound for San Francisco, that she and Lawrence were among its passengers, that Rafe and Dom were among its crew.

They made the main deck, and Lawrence excused himself and pushed on ahead to locate their staterooms. Rafe had come by for her trunk earlier. The trunk, the clothes in it as well as her ticket, had been provided by Clayton. She stood quietly next to him now, weighted by his generosity and wishing she could offer him more in return than her gratitude.

He was scanning the milling fifty or so passengers gathering with them, those along the railing waving hats and handkerchiefs, others clinging, to companions and dabbing teary eyes. He looked young to her, older than she, certainly, but so much younger than Rafe. He was a young man of means exploring the adult world, waiting to be tested, and, if Lucy knew him as Cassandra thought her intuitive friend probably did, impatient for the war to end so his family could return home and his life begin. At the moment, though, he mostly looked worried.

Cassandra reached out and placed her black-gloved hand on his sleeve. "It will be all right, Clayton," she reassured him, if not herself. She could give him that, at least.

He frowned. "But what will you do in San Francisco?"

"What would I do back in France? I can't stay in school forever. I've been in the oldest set for two years already, and"—the tiniest of smiles teased her mouth—"I don't think I'm called to be a nun."

Clayton grinned. The bell announcing all but passengers go ashore took up. The crowd shifted; tears flowed more freely; hankies waved more frantically. Clayton scanned the deck once more and stood his ground as hatboxes and elbows brushed against them.

"Where's Mister Hadley, I wonder?" he said.

"He'll be back. Go on. I'm fine."

With a last concerned look and a spontaneous hug, Clayton turned and was enveloped in the crush of people clogging the way to the gangplank. Cassandra stepped back next to the deckhouse and closed her eyes.

Maybe the numbness was wearing off. She was tired, suddenly, so tired. She'd gone with Lenora and been fitted for her mourning gown and picked out and bought all the required accessories in a record two hours, but only Lenora had collapsed back at the hotel and called for lemonade—iced, for her parched throat, and water—hot, for her abused feet. Cassandra had felt . . . nothing. Just as Cassandra had dutifully tested each item's worth as they had purchased it, from black bonnet, veil, and gloves to black stockings and shoes, fingering the texture, tugging the seams—and felt nothing. Lenora had made every decision. Not so now.

Now Cassandra felt the weight of the veil, the prick of every pin holding her hair, the pinch of her corset, the heat of the deck through the soles of her shoes. But she felt her exhaustion more. Her head ached, shoulders drooped. Her legs were unsteady. Worst of all, tears were gathering behind her eyelids as they had not since she'd huddled in Rafe's lap a week ago. The price of feeling was tears. Cassandra swallowed, straightened her shoulders. The emptiness seeped back. She wanted it back.

"Isn't this exciting, my dear?"

Cassandra's eyes snapped open to a perky face agrin from beneath an oversized, outlandishly extravagant hat. The grin widened, showing tiny, childlike teeth, except that they belonged to a decidedly elderly woman whose ribbon-rampant bonnet barely reached Cassandra's shoulder. The lady's dainty double chins jiggled. "Don't you adore setting sail?"

The dog in the woman's arms barked, and Cassandra jumped, the animal unnoticed at first, its bark high-pitched and insistent. "Sigmund. Hush," the woman scolded, rocking the dog like her baby. It wasn't working. The dog continued to yap, began squirming. "I know. I know," the lady soothed. Cassandra stared. It was as if the two were conversing with each other. "Oh, all right," the woman sighed. She set the dog down on its short legs in front of Cassandra and straightened, clutching a length of satin ribbon the same shade of purple as the bows, the purple ones, aflutter on her hat. The ribbon leash was attached to the giant looped bow tied between the dog's head and wide shoulders, where a neck was expected but failed to be evident.

"Sigmund's a wonderful sailor." The lady transferred her cheery smile from Cassandra onto her pet. "But he can get a little—oh!" The ribbon jerked from the woman's hand, almost pulling her off her feet. "Siggy!"

Cassandra gasped. The dog was running pell-mell down the deck, his short legs pumping, his ribbon streaming behind him. A stevedore, balancing three bandboxes on top the trunk in his arms, was the first victim. The man sprawled, the trunk crashing, boxes tumbling, rolling. Women screamed. A sailor took off in pursuit. Sigmund veered around a coiled mound of rope, shot between the legs of a portly passenger who, in the act of leaping aside, collided with the sailor. The dog hairpinned around the corner. There followed a crash, an explosion of Acadian blasphemy. Cassandra winced.

The inhaled breaths of everyone on deck could have filled the ship's sails. A silence fell so deep it muffled the cacophony of Bay Street beyond and below the railing. All eyes locked on the corner of the deckhouse.

Like an actor appearing on cue, Sigmund strutted into view, paused, lifted his squashed-in mug, and walked with military dignity back the length he'd run. Every head followed him, some shaking, some scowling, most simply staring. Spying his master, the dog broke into a canine grin, shot forward, and landed snugly in the elderly woman's arms.

"Siggy!" the lady breathed, her voice shaking. Taking a deep breath, she smiled up at Cassandra as spontaneously dignified as her dog. "So nice to meet you, dear." She turned, smiling and nodding her head to the other passengers as she walked by them. Cassandra shook her head.

"Do you know that woman?" Lawrence asked, coming up beside her.

"No," she said, "but the entire ship knows Sigmund. The dog," she added at Lawrence's frown.

He sighed, his frown remaining in place. "Undisciplined animals are a nuisance anywhere and should be barred from ships." He nodded toward the stevedore, looking frazzled and frustrated as a woman examined a fashionable poke hat retrieved from its dented box opened on the deck between them. "It's a bad omen."

"That sounds like superstitious sailor talk, Mister Hadley."

He looked at her, strangely, and she recalled too late that Lawrence Hadley was of a serious bent, a man innately critical but sensitive to criticism. "How true, Miss Mortier." It was Cassandra's turn to look surprised. He bowed, still as correct as she remembered him, and offered her his arm. "Let me show you to your stateroom. Everything is in order."

They left the main deck and followed a couple and their two young sons past several doors until Lawrence stopped and indicated Cassandra's room on their right.

"May I come for you later, escort you to the evening meal?" he asked.

Cassandra shook her head, her veil swaying gently. "I'd prefer to take my meals in my room if that's possible."

"Of course it's possible. I'll arrange it for you."

"Thank you, Mister Hadley."

She didn't know why she was surprised again, but she was. Given her veil and the corridor's gloom after the bright sunshine on deck, she couldn't read Lawrence's expression. If she could see him clearly, he would look the same man he'd looked as the *Fortune*'s supercargo, his dark hair as meticulously trimmed, his eyes as pale a blue. There was still an aloofness about his manner; the air still crackled with tension between him and Rafe. And yet, he seemed different. Was it her, or was it him?

"I will see you tomorrow, then." He broke into her thoughts, scattering them. "Sleep well, Miss Mortier."

Cassandra stepped into the stateroom, closed the door, and turned to lean against it. She shivered. Sleep well. She'd barely slept at all since they'd arrived in Nassau. But she'd not dreamed either. She frowned and realized that she'd not had the nightmare since she'd been on board the *Fortune*. This other ship's bunk drew her gaze. Folding her veil carefully back over her bonnet, she undid the bow beneath her chin, and set aside her musings along with her hat. Even the nightmare had ceased to matter.

Her eyes circled the room, its polished wood, burnished brass, a plush carpet. A basket of . . . fruits? Roses? Cassandra crossed to the low table, her steps slow, pulse skittering, and stared at the vellum card tucked under the vase's base. Biting her lip, she picked it up, turned it over.

"Bon voyage," she read, her eyes skipping to the scrawled initials below the words. "L.H."

Her eyes stung, chin raised. She wasn't surprised. It was a thoughtful gesture, the appropriate expression of Lawrence Hadley's ever-solicitous concern. So like him, after all. Her lips trembled.

Rafe Buchanan had made passionate, wondrous love to her on the island, had held her, ached with her, in her pain at the hotel, would marry her if she carried his child. He wouldn't send flowers.

It mattered.

It shouldn't. She knew he cared for her, was worried about her, had ignored Lawrence Hadley's wishes and

Dom's arguments in order that he and Dom ship out on the same vessel with them. She swallowed, raised her chin. She knew where he had stayed in Nassau, and with whom.

In a burst of energy, Cassandra stalked over to her new trunk with its unscuffed paint and shiny brass fittings and flung it open. She shook out, hung up, refolded, and put away her single day dress, her night clothes, and her change of drawers and two extra collars. She undid, brushed out, and repinned her tightly coiled hair, washed her face. The basin full, she washed her gloves, her removable black-dyed cuffs, her washcloth. She ran out of things to wash, ran out of things to do.

The floor's roll became more pronounced. Rigging creaked overhead. Crewmen shouted. Cassandra closed her porthole. A stevedore arrived with a simple meal of fresh mangoes and fried breadfruit and tea. She couldn't taste it, couldn't eat it. A different stevedore arrived and took it away. She sat a long time on her bunk and watched the shadows lengthen, her hands still, cold, in her lap. Go to bed, she told herself. Go to sleep. She got up, changed into her night shift, crawled under the covers. The ship rocked up and down, her thoughts drifted. The metal bracket holding the hanging lamp fixed to the wall somewhere to her right squeaked in time to the sea. She listened, tried not to listen. She couldn't sleep.

She thought of Rafe, wondered where he was, what he was doing. She wondered if he still blamed himself for what had happened between them. She wondered if he'd shared with Lenora what had happened, if she'd comforted him, if they had . . . She stopped wondering. It didn't matter.

She slept.

* * *

Rafe winced and fell heavily into his hammock. If he'd the breath to waste, he'd damn Nassau into the sea, it and its war speculators luring able seamen away from runs other than those for "the business," as blockade running had come to be called. He sighed. Available sailors were as unwilling to sign on for San Francisco as they'd proved unavailable for the *Good Fortune*'s run to Le Havre. He massaged his shoulder. Sailing short-handed had been frustrating as hell as the captain; it was damned exhausting as one of the overworked crew.

The scuttle banged and Rafe turned his head, watched Dom negotiate the gear jamming the unlighted fo'c'sle as the Acadian headed for his hammock. Rafe let his arm fall over his eyes. His uncle's stamina was as legendary as the man's short fuse and luck at cards. Damn him for making Rafe feel the older man. Rafe grimaced. Not older, old. *Jesu.*

"The boatswain, him." Dom grunted, banging his sea chest shut and springing nimbly into his hammock. "He—" With a roar he landed back on his feet. Rafe sat up so suddenly he banged his head. The other seamen, dragged from their sleep, glared, cursed.

"What the—" Rafe stopped. Dom was yanking his trousers up, swearing savagely. Behind him, his hammock swayed wildly from its moorings, weighted in its middle by the very animal Dom had spent the last five days at sea tripping over and vowing to toss to the sharks. Rafe grinned. Dom shot him a black glare, and Rafe looked down, covered his mouth with his hand. Grabbing the dog by the voluminous skin of its bull neck, the Acadian stomped out. Rafe lay back down. Could animals harbor death wishes?

The other crewmen, grumbling, mumbling, resettled, and the late hour's familiar night sounds returned. Rafe turned onto his good side and tried to ignore the cramped quarters, the stink of tar, the throbbing in his shoulder. He cursed silently. He was dead on his feet, but, off them, his mind took up and refused him the rest his body craved.

The week in Nassau had been no different. Then he'd sunk into the thick, goose-feather tick of Lenora's bed, and she had come to him, sensing his need, the upheaval at war within him. She knew him well, could tease him, please him, and bring from him more than any other woman he'd ever known. But for the first time, he'd held her afterward and listened to her breathing, felt her warm and soft and asleep against him, and felt sated but not soothed, released but not relaxed. Cassandra's face would come. As it came now.

Cassandra. Cassandra taking on Dom with fire in her eyes in the hold. Cassandra flying out of Doc's cabin like Satan's hounds were on her heels. Cassandra in her night shift making him so angry he couldn't see straight one moment, setting his loins on fire the next by merely looking up at him from her bunk. Cassandra laughing, running, swimming. Rafe rolled onto his back and scrubbed his face with his hands. Cassandra wild with shock, limp with grief. Cassandra, a shadow shrouded in black walking between Hadley and her friend's brother, standing with Hadley, disappearing below with Hadley—and never emerging.

Rafe's hands fisted. It was as if the Cassandra he carried in his mind had died, been wrapped in black and buried in a stateroom. He wanted her out, dammit. He wanted her ranting and raging and swinging and swearing—*alive*. But mostly, God strike him for the bastard seed of a bastard he was, he wanted her. He wanted Cassandra. Still.

"Haul taut the maintop bowlines! Maintop, there! Send a hand up and square the bunt gaskets of the topgallant sail!"

The booming orders, distant yet distinct, filtered with the sea sun through Cassandra's open porthole. She raised her head from where she knelt on the carpet; the rhythmic *snap snap* of her scissors cutting through the tartan plaid percale spread out about her slowed, stopped.

"Haul taut the starboard fore-topgallant sheet!"

Frowning, Cassandra bent back to work. Lenora had insisted Cassandra would be grateful for the length of percale she'd packed in the bottom of Cassandra's trunk with scissors and pins, tailors' chalk and threads and a supply of buttons, needles, and leftover trims from Lenora's well-stocked sewing basket. The woman had argued that Cassandra would welcome a gown of lighter weight when the temperatures soared beneath the autumn sun, when she tired of black in public and needed color to lift her spirits in the privacy of her rooms. Cassandra sat back on her heels, flexing her shoulders against the knot between her shoulder blades, wiping the perspiration from her face with her sleeve. Lenora had been right: Cassandra was grateful, grateful for a task that kept her in her stateroom, that kept her hands busy, her thoughts in cheek.

Her door, propped six inches ajar in an effort to coax a breeze through the porthole, swung wide and banged against the wall. Cassandra whirled as a blur of tan fur and yellow ribbon shot past her. She cried out as the invading dervish slid on the percale, yanking it from Cassandra's hands.

"Careful!" She found her voice and lunged all at once. A high-pitched bark split the air. Squirming, sharp-nailed paws and wadded material filled her arms.

"Oh! Oh, my. Siggy!" The door thudded shut.

Cassandra sat back, hard, on her bottom, tightened her hold on the jumping, jerking percale in her lap, and stared up at the woman from the deck. She was a sight, a fright in truth. Her matronly chignon had unraveled; the frizzed curls across her forehead were squashed. She stood panting, flushed, her plump hands clutched over her heaving bosom at her throat, her expression stricken. She looked at Cassandra, and her soft brown eyes filled.

"Forgive me, miss. Oh." Her gaze swept the floor and the tumbled, scattered sewing supplies.

A giant sneeze erupted from Cassandra's arms, and Sigmund, one ear turned inside out, his yellow bow asnarl, poked his head free of the plaid cloth and peered up at his master. He was undisciplined but not unintelligent, Cassandra decided. He didn't grin.

"Sigmund Samson Quiggly." The lady stiffened, her hands moving to her round hips. "You beast! Look what you've done. Look!" Her hand spread, palm up, indicating the chaos the dog had wrought. She looked back at Cassandra. Her chins wobbled, voice faltered. "I am so sorry. I . . . I will replace your material. I know that hardly amends for this . . . this . . ."

"Would you just take Sigmund so I can get up?" Cassandra asked.

Apologizing profusely, the woman hurried forward. It took both of them to separate dog from percale. Once freed, Sigmund was ordered to the corner and told to lie down. To Cassandra's amazement, he did exactly as bid, though his tail curling over his back jounced with wounded dignity. Cassandra pushed to her feet and shook out the wrinkled material. The elderly woman stooped for its other end. Together they smoothed it, laid it out on the carpet as before, and while the older woman retrieved the scattered supplies, Cassandra examined the percale for snags or other damage.

"You don't need to replace anything," Cassandra said, sitting back off her knees. "Truly." She cut off the woman's protest. "Look for yourself. He didn't hurt a thing."

"Certainly not his reputation," the older woman said. She glared pointedly at her dog. Sigmund, head on his paws, returned her look, his expression more patronizing than penitent. A plump finger wagged. "Don't you go looking down your nose at me, Sigmund." Cassandra rolled her eyes. Even if animals were capable of such behavior, the nose this dog boasted was practically flush with his bulging brown eyes. He was a most ugly specimen, really. She surveyed him critically. One with an equally odious reputation, it seemed. Well deserved! The lady's deep sigh as she sat down wearily on the room's chair interrupted Cassandra's uncharitable observations.

"I know he should be punished," the woman said.

Drowning might work, Cassandra was tempted to suggest out loud. She glanced over at the woman. The dejected droop of the elderly lady's shoulders and the sadness clouding her eyes as she studied her pet softened Cassandra's feelings, toward her if not toward Sigmund.

"The good captain has made it clear—most graciously, in all fairness—that one more incident such as this and Sigmund will be contained in the hold until we disembark."

"Nothing was damaged. I see no reason to bring this to the captain's attention." Embarrassed by the beaming gratitude trembling in the old woman's smile, Cassandra looked back at the dog. The ingrate was sound asleep, snoring!—oblivious to his master's distress or his own brush with banishment.

"You are a dear girl. I . . . I can't thank you enough." The woman chuckled, and Cassandra looked up. "Even if I could, I've just now realized I don't know your name."

Cassandra introduced herself.

"From Mobile?" The lady grinned and looked as perky beneath her disarranged hair as she'd looked beneath her disastrous bonnet a week ago. "I've been there. It's a beautiful city. Oh!" She flushed. "I'm Mrs. Winston Quiggly, dear, from Nassau these last many years but originally from Baltimore." She leaned forward. "I would so rather you call me Sophie, though. Would you mind?" Cassandra nodded her head, shook her head, a little overwhelmed by Sophie's barrage of words and innate friendliness. "Thank you." The lady beamed. "My, you have the most unusual eyes, Cassandra. May I call you Cassandra? They're not blue at all, are they? But a true pewter-grey." She leaned back into the chair. "It's quite noticeable, you know. Stunning." Cassandra looked down. "And you're as thin as my mother-in-law's chicken gravy. Have you been ill?"

Cassandra's head snapped up. There was a line thinner than bad gravy between friendliness and forwardness, and Sophie Quiggly was treading close to crossing it.

"No, I thought not," Sophie said. Cassandra frowned. "I'm so sorry, dear. You've only just gone into mourning, haven't you?"

"Mrs. Quiggly—Sophie," Cassandra corrected herself, "I do not wish to—"

"Of course you don't." Sophie smiled. "But you can't wish to stay locked away in your stateroom this entire journey either. You'll roast, for one thing, if you don't waste away first." She stood up. "Are you traveling alone, dear?" Cassandra took a breath, but Sophie read her look before Cassandra had time to voice it. "I'm a presumptuous old busybody. I know." She shrugged. Cassandra's eyes narrowed. Sophie and Sigmund had more in common than big brown eyes. "It's a freedom bestowed upon those of us tenacious enough to reach my age. Which"—her eyebrows rose—"is reason but no excuse. Would you like me to leave?"

Cassandra closed her eyes. How did one answer something like that? This woman was either harmlessly eccentric or intimidatingly sincere. Cassandra looked at her. Was it possible to be both? "I'm not sure," she answered slowly.

"Well said." Sophie's eyes softened, and her voice gentled. "I'd imagine you're not sure about much of anything right now." She sat back down in the chair. "That's to be expected, you know. And"—her eyes twinkled—"it's perfectly appropriate, acceptable, and nothing to be ashamed about."

Cassandra had reached her limit. "You don't know me. You don't know anything about me."

"True," Sophie said, ignoring Cassandra's outburst. "But I know a thing or two about bereavement. I know what it is to feel alone, to be left to my own devices. I know the desolation." She leaned forward. "And the anger." Her expression became serious. "What we know enables us to see what we see. And I know what I see in you, Cassandra, even without knowing your particular situation." She sat back. "Am I wrong?"

Cassandra turned on her heel and stalked to the porthole. "I'm not alone. I've a friend, one of the crew. And another friend sailing as a passenger." She turned, her chin out, voice steady once more. "There are four of us, actually, traveling to San Francisco together." She did want Sophie to leave. Now.

"I'm so glad." The lady looked genuinely relieved, until she frowned. "Where are they? Why are they allowing you to remain closeted away in here?" Cassandra opened her mouth, but Sophie hurried on. "I know that because I've been suffocating in my cabin for three days trying to keep Sigmund unincarcerated, and we're directly across from you."

"Maybe my friends are respecting my desire to be alone," Cassandra said evenly.

Sophie made a face. "Men friends, I take it." She stood up. "Well, Cassandra Mortier, I'm your friend now too. Don't forget that." She crossed to Sigmund, her wide yellow striped skirt mounding like melting butter about her as she stooped and gathered him into her arms. The dog blinked at Cassandra as Sophie walked to the door. She turned without opening it and smiled. "It may take a miracle, but I'm going to dress my hair. Then"—her tiny teeth flashed—"I'm taking Sigmund out for some fresh air. I would like you to join us."

Cassandra shook her head, motioning toward the plaid material spread on the floor between them. "I can only work in daylight."

Sophie's brow arched. "There's enough morning light between here and San Francisco to cut out a complete wardrobe. It is midday and one hundred degrees in this stifling stateroom."

Cassandra frowned. "Thank you, Sophie, but I don't think—"

"You don't think you need your health?"

"Of course I need my health!" If tenacity was what was required to reach an old age, Sophie Quiggly would outlive Methuselah. "I'm not up to chitchat about the wind, the war, or this morning's game of whist. I don't want to be with people right now, Sophie. Can't you respect that?"

"Of course," Sophie said. "But you'll only be with me, and I will refrain from all manner of chitchat." At Cassandra's look, she shifted her dog under her arm and raised a plump hand. "My word of honor." Sigmund barked, his back legs flailing, and Sophie rescued him from his undignified position. Cassandra was left to rescue herself.

She was beginning to enjoy Sophie's directness. It freed one to be likewise. "I doubt you can be quiet, and I know it would not be only us for very long." Stepping around her uncut material, she joined Sophie to reach behind her and open the door. Looking down at the much shorter older woman, Cassandra smiled, firmly. "No, thank you."

Sophie grinned. "It won't take me long to stuff this bush under a bonnet. You've nothing to worry about, dear. I've given my word, have I not? And I guarantee not one other passenger will approach us."

"You can't know that," Cassandra protested.

"Oh?" Sophie sighed, her shoulders drooping. "No one will even speak to us, my dear, as long as we are standing there with Sigmund."

Sophie proved as good as her word, and Sigmund proved good for something after all. It did feel good to be on deck, to feel the wind buffeting her, swirling her skirts about her ankles. Cassandra wished she could throw back her veil, remove her bonnet. It was a bittersweet thought. She would mourn her grandfather—and Jim—a full year in full mourning, no softer greys, no jet bead jewelry later on. She couldn't explain why, even to herself. She didn't need to explain it, knew only that that was how she needed to do it. In a year she would pack her black gowns away and mourn the gentleman and gentle man in her heart. Forever.

"Miss Mortier."

Cassandra turned, watched Lawrence Hadley striding toward them looking tall and fit in his dark brown frock coat that set off his lighter nankeen pants, his gait graceful, at one with the rolling deck.

"I didn't know you were venturing out today. I would have come for you." He stopped beside her, his smile welcoming, his light blue eyes searching her face. "Are you faring well? Is your stateroom satisfactory?"

"Yes. Thank you." It felt good to speak with someone she knew, to look up at a familiar face. "And thank you for the fruit basket and flowers," she added. Her cheeks heated. "Forgive me for not saying something sooner. It was—" She stopped, not used to feeling embarrassed about much of anything, and never as a result of a lack in the social graces. "I was lax, Mister Hadley. You've been very kind."

"You've had a difficult time of it, Miss Mortier." He frowned and looked over her head out to sea. "I only wish I could have delivered them to you on board a ship bound for France and your grandfather." He looked down at her. "I am sorry about . . . everything. It would mean a great deal to me if I thought you could believe that."

Cassandra studied him. It wasn't her. It was him. Lawrence's frown deepened the lines at the sides of his mouth. He looked down, brushed something off his sleeve, and she realized she was staring, and it was making him ill at ease. "You seem different," she said slowly.

His head snapped up, and his eyes held her gaze. "As God is my witness, Miss Mortier, I plan to be."

Sigmund barked, began squirming wildly in Sophie's arms. Cassandra and Lawrence turned toward the elderly woman struggling desperately to keep hold of her pet.

"Sigmund!" Sophie panted. Her bonnet tipped askew. The dog leaped free and nosedived onto the deck. Lawrence snatched him up before he had a chance to gather his four short legs beneath him and effect his escape.

"Thank you, sir," Sophie said, taking her pet back into her arms. "You are so quick. I thought surely—" She shuddered, not finishing her thought. "As for you." She glared at Sigmund. "Yes I see him and no you absolutely may not pester that poor, nice Acadian gentleman. He's busy!"

Cassandra stared at Sophie. "You can't be meaning—"

"Veasey," Lawrence said, slapping with disgusted swipes at the dog hairs deposited on his coat front and sleeves. He shot Sigmund a sour look. "That animal has taken a keen interest in our first mate, it seems."

"It's so odd," Sophie said, shaking her head. "Sigmund has always been a bit standoffish toward strangers. But"—she shrugged and shook her head at Cassandra—"from the first day he's been like . . . like this. It's as if they have a bond, or somesuch. See?" She nodded her head toward the foremast beyond them. Cassandra looked.

Dom was eighty feet above their heads, glaring at them. Cassandra grinned. She couldn't help it. Clinging to the ropes, the wind tearing at his black hair, he reminded her of her cat Lucifer, treed again by her father's hounds but more incensed that intimidated. From the corner of her eye she saw Sophie lift her arm, wave.

"Mister Veasey!" The woman's cheery voice carried on the wind. "Good day, sir. We're just out for some air. Beautiful day, is it not?" As surefooted as any cat, Dom swung down from the rigging and disappeared from sight. "Such a nice gentleman," Sophie sighed. She frowned at Sigmund. "Would you mind if I took Siggy below, Cassandra? I'll be right back."

"Of course not," Cassandra said. Sophie smiled and hurried off. Cassandra looked up at the tall supercargo beside her. "Such a nice gentleman?" she repeated.

"The woman's as daft as her dog," Lawrence said. His expression lightened. "But if she's behind getting you out of your stateroom, I owe her a debt of deepest gratitude. I've been . . ." He paused as if he was searching for words. "Concerned," he said finally.

"I'm grateful to her too." Cassandra smiled and looked out at the rolling Pacific. "It's good to be on deck."

"It's good to see you smile again." His smile at her look crinkled the lines at the sides of his eyes in a way that reminded Cassandra of Rafe's eyes when he smiled. She looked quickly back out to sea. Lawrence's voice became serious. "I thought never to see your smile again. I saw you go down with Navarre, tried to get to you, but was washed over the side tangled in debris myself." He stopped, and Cassandra remained as she was, waiting, willing him to continue.

"Most of the crew were lost with the ship." Cassandra winced. Many of those men had been Rafe's friends. He was holding himself responsible for their deaths, she was certain, and grieving, no less than she. Lawrence continued. "I drifted holding on to a splintered crossjackyard for what seemed an eternity. Long enough to know I was going to die of thirst, drown, or be eaten by sharks. It's a strange thing"—his voice lowered—"how differently one thinks about life, about one's own life particularly, when it seems to be over." Cassandra turned her head. He met her look, his eyes tortured, intense.

"I was ashamed of my life, Miss Mortier. And I was"—he frowned—"angry. It seemed so senseless to have finally realized how selfish, how . . . how inconsequential, my desires and all my manipulations had been my entire adult life when there was not a thing on this earth I could do about it, not one amend I could make. Nothing."

Cassandra closed her eyes and breathed slowly. Seeing the anguish in Lawrence's eyes was like looking into a mirror. Listening to his emotional words was like hearing her own thoughts, her own remorse spoken out loud.

"I was picked up by a British steamer and arrived in Nassau a week before you returned. I didn't run into Veasey or Jansen, avoided the waterfront, actually." He shrugged. "I was just so glad to be alive." He sighed. "And so guilty. It felt wrong to be the only one spared." He paused. "I thought about you, Miss Mortier. I would have given anything at that point to have been able to exchange my life for yours."

Cassandra reached out and placed her hand on Lawrence's sleeve, much as she had done with Clayton. "But I was spared, Mister Hadley. Rafe." She stopped. "Captain Buchanan got us off the *Fortune*. Dom and Mister Jansen got us back to Nassau. There's no need to feel guilty now, only grateful." Her words surprised her. They were for herself, she realized, as much as for Lawrence Hadley.

Lawrence's expression softened as he gazed down at her. He was a handsome man, Cassandra thought, when he allowed himself to be seen as mere man, not arrogant, aloof, self-righteous supercargo. "True," he said. "I don't know how Buchanan managed it, but I am grateful—more than grateful—that he did." He looked up, tossed the curly dark hair falling over his aristocratic forehead back, and faced into the wind. "I am going to be different, Miss Mortier. I vow it. I owe my uncle much and hope he will give me a chance, at least, to prove I can be trustworthy, honorable." He smiled, a twisted smile with no humor in it. "It might be better for you if Captain Buchanan introduced you to him, not me. Buchanan was thrown up to me so often as a model of sainthood that I fear I was primed to hate him before I'd ever laid eyes on him." He glanced at Cassandra. "I was wrong."

"We're all wrong at times," Cassandra said. "We all deserve a chance to start over and do differently." She smiled, and for the first time thinking of Randall Mortier brought a gentle warmth, not tearing pain. "My grandfather used to tell me that." Her smile reached her eyes. "Over and over and over, I'm afraid." Her eyes narrowed. "And I look forward to meeting your uncle, Mister Hadley. I want you to introduce me, no one else." Her chin rose. "Agreed?"

"Thank you," Lawrence said. He straightened. "Your friend is returning." He nodded toward Sophie, who waved as she worked her way between other passengers and negotiated around the ever-present clutter of cables and gear on deck.

"Mister Hadley," a gentleman called out, moving aside to let Sophie pass. "Are you joining us this afternoon?"

Lawrence raised his hand in reply and turned to Cassandra. "Our three o'clock poker game. It's a vice my uncle abhors, but I've no intention of giving it up until I see him." He smiled. "It's my means of income at present, I'm afraid." He bowed. "Would you excuse me, Miss Mortier?"

Cassandra nodded, watched him join the group forming about the other man, and disappear with them toward the saloon.

"One of your friends," Sophie said, reaching Cassandra's side.

"Yes." But, strangely, a friend she felt she'd only just met.

"He seems a nice man," Sophie said. "He doesn't care for dogs, though, do you think?" Cassandra pretended not to hear the question. "Is Mister Veasey the crewman you spoke of?"

Cassandra frowned. "No. I mean, yes." She avoided the older woman's look. "He's one of the four of us traveling together, yes." Thankfully, Sophie didn't seem to require any more information. They stood together silently, each of them content with their own thoughts. Cassandra's muscles eased, thoughts gentled.

"Sophie?"

"Yes, dear?"

"Do you think it possible for people to change? Really, truly change from how they've been their entire life?"

She sensed the older woman's smile beside her, heard her soft sigh that ended in something akin to a chuckle. "Life has a way of changing—and changing entirely at times."

"I agree," Cassandra said. How could she not? "But what about people? Us?" Lawrence Hadley. Herself. Rafe?

Sophie didn't answer right away. "Yes," she said at last. "But only by choice, not chance. We aren't in control of life, Cassandra, but we are responsible for our lives."

Chapter Twelve

RAFE LEANED BACK against the bulkhead behind him and stretched out his legs. He watched the ship's figurehead, a grinning dolphin, dip up and down ahead of him, welcomed the roaring, rhythmic hiss of salt spray, its cold dampness on his skin. His watch was over; his next one would begin before daylight if he wasn't needed before. He should be inside the fo'c'sle, not leaning against it, asleep in his hammock with the others. He wasn't sleepy.

They were making good time on a sound ship under an experienced master with an exhausted but seasoned crew. Only the passengers were restless. Rafe shrugged and closed his eyes. Passengers were always restless. "Sea life is an acquired taste, like that for tomatoes and olives," he'd read once. Carlyle? Dickens. No, Emerson. It didn't matter. He remembered it only because the account of life at sea as a passenger had made him laugh. Sailing for Bernard from New Orleans to San Francisco, he'd ever preferred cotton and cargo to cranky old women and, worse, coquettish young ones.

The picture Cassandra and her friend with the dog made came to him, strolling the main deck when there was room, standing apart from the others when there wasn't. Rafe chuckled. The old woman's determined friendliness was wearing even Dom down. Rafe had almost lost his footing overhead when he'd witnessed his arrant uncle doff his knit cap to the woman before scaling the ratline like a man half his age to join Rafe. When Rafe had shared his observation—he'd about lost his head. *Non.* Rafe lifted his arms, stretching the muscles across his shoulders and down his back. She was not a cranky old woman, that one. Looping his long arms about his pulled-up legs, Rafe rested his chin on one knee, his grin disappearing. And Cassandra was no coquette. He scowled.

She was out of her stateroom. She was walking, talking, had made a friend, apparently. But Cassandra was still missing.

Was she afraid she carried his seed? *Merde,* would she keep it from him if she found that she was? He swore under his breath. He understood grieving, the weight of it, the pall it cast over one's spirits. But Cassandra was carrying more than her grief. He frowned, glared blindly at the pitching figurehead. He sensed it in her walk, saw it in her once-animated, expressive hands now still at her sides or clenched about the railing. Or at rest on Lawrence Hadley's arm.

In a single, fluid motion, Rafe stood and stalked to the railing. A figure, more shadow than form, gasped and stepped back. Rafe turned full around. Cassandra.

"Rafe?"

Her voice was as he remembered it. Low, musical. But he'd forgotten how good his name sounded when she voiced it, how his breathing caught, pulse slowed. And raced.

"I didn't know—didn't think anyone was out here," she said.

"You shouldn't be out here alone. Especially at . . ."

Rafe's words faded as they both recalled the last time he'd said them. "At night," he finished. She looked so small, standing hidden in the dark, wrapped in her mourning blacks. Her head was bare, no bonnet, no veil. Her long hair hung loose about her shoulders, like a cape tossing about her in the wind. Rafe's fingers curled into his palms. Her hands moved, and she hugged herself. He could feel her unease.

"Are you cold?" he asked.

Their eyes locked, and Rafe held his breath. She was deciding how to answer, deciding if she would go. Or stay.

"A little," she said. He could barely hear her, but it was the answer he waited for. He swallowed, the relief—no, lightness rushing up inside him, startling him.

"Come here." He held out his hand. "Out of the wind." She hesitated. Rafe forced himself to wait, to keep his hand out, to hold it steady. And then her tiny hand was inside his, cold and squeezing his back . . . and feeling right as it had always felt right to have her hand in his. "Over here," he said, tugging her quickly with him as if he feared she'd change her mind and pull away.

He sat down between two water barrels, his back against the bulkhead as before, and guided Cassandra down between his knees. As before. "Better?" She nodded. It wasn't like before.

She remained stiff, poised for flight, unwilling to settle against him. He kept his hands on his knees. Together they watched the prow's crudely carved dolphin as they'd once watched the sea washing onto the beach in the moonlight. Rafe closed his eyes, aware of Cassandra's scent, her hair brushing his chin, her stillness. His jaw clenched. She was so close. So far away.

"I'm—" She stopped. "I found out—" She stopped

again. "I'm—" She cursed under her breath. Her shoulders slumped, her hair falling like a curtain around her face.

"You found out what, Cassandra?" Rafe asked. His hands fisted on his knees.

"You . . . you don't have to worry about . . . anything."

"You mean you're not—"

"No," she cut him off. "I mean yes, I'm not. *Oh.*" Her hands jerked up and covered her face, and Rafe damned himself an oafish idiot for embarrassing her.

He reached around her and pulled her back against him. She didn't protest. He felt her relax, slowly. She sighed, let her head fall back on his shoulder. And suddenly it was as it had been before: before the night on the beach, before the morning after with Doc. They were together, aware of each other. Comfortable with each other. Neither put it into words, but Rafe sensed Cassandra felt it as much as he.

"You couldn't sleep?" he asked.

"I needed some fresh air."

"Aye. Me too."

"It's beautiful up here at night. Look at the moon."

Rafe smiled and wondered if he'd ever look at the moon again and not hear Cassandra's awe, see Cassandra's moon-grey eyes. His smile left. He wondered if he'd ever hear her laugh, see those eyes spark with temper, dance with mischief.

"Are you worried about San Francisco?" he asked.

"Not so much now that I've gotten to know Lawrence."

"Lawrence?"

"You know. Mister Had—"

"I know who you mean." Cassandra turned and looked around at him. Rafe scowled and refused to meet her gaze. He heard her sigh, ignored it. She turned back and leaned against him.

"He's part of the reason I couldn't sleep, I think," she began. "We talked today, a long time, and—"

"If he's upsetting you I'll—"

"Stow it, Captain," Cassandra snapped, borrowing one of Rafe's phrases. He turned her by her shoulders in order to see her face.

"I'm serious, Cassandra." She tugged free of his hold and stood up. Rafe followed her to the railing. "If he's causing you concern, then I want to know about it."

"What we talked about was upsetting, not him," she said. She frowned in concentration as she gazed out at the waves and the night. Rafe studied her face and waited. "It seems his father was no better than yours or mine. After Lawrence's mother died they left wherever they were from and went from town to town. Cheap boarding houses and fistfights over cards. Those are Lawrence's earliest memories."

Her voice was so . . . sad. Rafe turned to stare out to sea and struggled to keep silent. *Merde,* what was Hadley thinking of, spewing this crap? If it hurt her to relate it now, Hadley must have seen how it hurt her to hear it.

"Their luck finally changed," she continued. "when his father married some rich man's daughter." Rafe scowled.

"Lady Luck dealt him a winning hand, then," he said. So what? he added silently.

"Only to lose it. The girl ran away." She paused. "I don't blame her. Not that running away is right," she added quickly. "It's not."

That sadness again. *Jesu*. Rafe wanted to take Cassandra into his arms, wanted to smash Hadley's face in. He wrapped his hands tightly about the railing.

"The girl's father was furious when his daughter, his only child, apparently, disappeared. He blamed Lawrence's father, threw him out." Cassandra's voice lowered. "One day they were in a mansion, the next day they were back in a filthy room over a . . . a brothel, I think. Lawrence wouldn't say, of course."

Of course, Rafe seethed. Such a gentleman, Lawrence Hadley. So concerned for Cassandra's tender sensibilities—without a thought to shredding her too tender, too vulnerable heart. "His father searched for her for years. Years, Rafe. Can you imagine? Nothing else mattered to him but his search for his missing heiress." Cassandra shuddered. "That's what Lawrence said he called her. Not his wife, his heiress. Poor girl."

"Did they find her?" Rafe wanted this topic of conversation done with and didn't disguise his impatience.

"Yes." She spoke softly, more to herself than to him. "She'd . . . died." Something in Cassandra's voice made Rafe turn toward her. She was hugging her arms again, shivering. Rafe frowned, pulled her into his arms. Something was wrong. His heart sped up. He held her closer, felt her chilled skin through the front of his shirt.

"What is it? What's the matter?" he asked.

"He saw his father murdered, Rafe. He saw it." Rafe closed his eyes and saw only Cassandra's tears gathering, felt only her distress. "He . . . he was only ten years old." She took in a ragged, steadying breath. "And . . . and that's why he . . . he ended up like . . . like he did, I think. Don't you think so?"

"I think that's what he wants you to think," Rafc said, but he no longer cared about Hadley. "Cassandra," he soothed. "It's all right." He rocked her in his arms. "It's all right. Dammit, Cassandra. Don't. Don't think about this anymore. He had a hellish childhood. He survived.

A lot of kids don't." The bastard, Rafe wanted to scream. He kept his voice low, steady. "It's all right."

Cassandra stopped shivering. Her breathing deepened, slowed. "I'm sorry." She spoke into his shirt. "I don't know why it upset me so much. But it did." Rafe hugged her tight, not trusting himself to speak. "Maybe because I . . . I am coming to like Lawrence. Or because he's . . . he's—"

"Don't tell me about men like Hadley." He couldn't control the loathing he knew Cassandra couldn't help but hear, didn't need to hear. She stilled, lifted her head to look up at him.

"No, Rafe." Her voice was calm. "He's changed."

Rafe closed his eyes and kept his mouth shut.

"He never knew his mother. You did. I barely remember mine, but I had my grandfather, and Lalie and Jim. Given the fathers we had, what kind of childhood would we have had but for those other people in our lives? What different people might we be today? Have you ever thought of that?"

"No," Rafe answered bluntly. He didn't want to think about it now. He didn't believe Hadley had changed. He didn't want Cassandra believing so either.

"The man who murdered Lawrence's father took Lawrence and got rid of him by putting him on board a ship, a China-bound tea ship. He went to sea at age ten, Rafe, just like you. His life was lived on ships, as a sailor, up until he joined his uncle's business. Did you know that?"

"No," Rafe said. He scowled. There was a bond among men who sailed, a tie deeper than shared skills or risks or attitudes. He wanted to keep seeing Lawrence Hadley as supercargo, as Bernard's arrogant nephew, one of them, not as a sailor, not like himself. He couldn't. *Dammit.* "He was worth three of any of the men he hired on in Havre the night the *Fortune* went down," he said, hating saying it, hating Cassandra's smug look. "Which means"—he straightened, went rigid as the thought crashed down on him—"which means that he hired incompetents knowingly, not out of ignorance. *Fils de putain.*" He stepped back from Cassandra, his anguish, his rage exploding. "Had the *Fortune* had a seasoned crew and a captain not laid out in a cabin, she might have weathered that storm. And your Mister-poor-dear-sailor-supercargo was directly responsible for both the crew and Navarre's knife!"

"True," Cassandra shot back. "And he holds himself as responsible for that as you do, Mister-spoiled-child-ranting-sailor-Captain!" Rafe swore, turned away. Cassandra's hand closed about his arm and yanked him back around. "And both of you hold yourselves responsible for the ship being lost, and you're both wrong!"

Her eyes were dark, stormy. Alive. Rafe stared down at her, physical warmth flooding his chest. If it took arguing about Lawrence Hadley, then by the Virgin and everything holy, thank God for the bastard. Cassandra had come out of hiding.

"Isn't that so?" Cassandra pounded his arm with her small fist. "Answer me, blast you."

"Isn't what so?" He bit back a grin at her enraged exasperation.

"I said"—she practically spit at him—"had the *Fortune* had a seasoned crew and the extremely competent Captain Rafael Buchanan at her helm, she still might have gone down in that storm. Right?"

He frowned. "Right." He hated it when she was right.

"Right," Cassandra echoed him. She sighed, the fight leaving her with her breath. He stood watching her watch him, sensing again that camaraderie winding about them, warming them both. Cassandra cocked her head, the smile that touched her lips wistful, beautiful. "I've missed you," she said quietly.

He grinned. "Missed pounding my arm and biting my head off?"

Her smile grew. "Yes. And arguing with you and talking to you and," she shrugged, "being with you. Like now. Like . . . before."

Before the night on the beach. They both knew it; neither would say it out loud.

"He's different, Rafe."

Rafe frowned. "Who?"

Cassandra rolled her eyes, shook her head. "Lawrence Hadley."

"Maybe." He became as serious as she. "But if Hadley was a joyless, self-serving pig's ear before, then he'll be a joyless, self-denying velvet purse now. We can change what we believe, maybe, and how we act." He paused. "But we can't stop being who we are, Cassandra, any more than any of us can go back and change how we got that way."

"Maybe," she conceded, frowning, thinking. Rafe watched her. Damn. He liked watching her think as much as he liked watching her hair curl in the mist and whip about her face. His thoughts jerked back to her words. "But he deserves a chance to be different, to be seen differently, taken"—her frown deepened—"for what he is, not for how he was." She raised her chin. "We all do."

"Aye." Rafe sighed, shrugged. Cassandra was different. Tonight with her was . . . different. "We go on," he said. "That's life."

Cassandra smiled suddenly, that smile he'd not seen before tonight. Wistful. "And we can go on too. I . . ."

She faltered. "I hope." She held out her hand as he had done from practically the same spot earlier. "Friends?"

Rafe looked at her hand, pale in the moonlight, small, soft. Steady. He stepped forward and took it, tugged her against him. Her hand slipped from his, both hands circling his waist. She gave him a short, hard hug and stepped back.

"I'm glad," she said. She raised herself on tiptoe, her lips brushing his cheek. She turned quickly, waved . . . and disappeared.

Rafe stood a long moment staring after her. He raised his hand, touched his cheek, let his hand drop to his side. He was different. He swore under his breath. Turning, leaning heavily on his hands at the railing, he swore again. He was in love with her. *Damn.*

"You're going to lead with that?" Lawrence asked, his brow furrowing as Sophie set a card on the crate between them. Beside him, Cassandra glanced up from the sewing in her lap.

"If it's not all right with you, it's perfectly fine with us," Mister Lyons chuckled.

"George," his wife and whist partner admonished.

Lawrence shrugged and nodded in her direction. "Your play, madam."

As the days had passed, one into the next, a lethargic routine had evolved, and this group came into being among like groups gathered on deck. They numbered five: Mister Lyons and his wife Isabelle, Sophie, Cassandra, and Lawrence. And Sigmund, of course, sitting at attention or sleeping and snorting at either Sophie's or Cassandra's feet. He was beside Cassandra this afternoon, his ribbon leash tied securely to the leg of Cassandra's chair. Which, she thought, glancing down at him, always made her uneasy. He grinned up at her, the bright green bow about his neck fluttering in the wind.

"Don't even think about it," Cassandra mouthed. From the corner of her eye she caught a familiar grin and the gleam of golden hair. She turned her head quickly, her cheeks warming. Rafe sat tailor fashion beyond them, head bent, working away at the sail spread about him, his larger needle pushing in and out of the canvas as nimble as hers. Her eyes narrowed. It was the five of them plus Sigmund and Rafe of late. She didn't trust either one of them to behave themselves, Sigmund with anyone, Rafe with Lawrence.

"Is something wrong?" Lawrence asked. He started to turn around.

"My veil." Cassandra reached up quickly. "The wind keeps catching it." She dropped a hatpin, and Lawrence bent to retrieve it. Sigmund growled at him.

"Siggy!" Sophie leaned sideways to eye her dog. "Mind your manners." Straightening, she transferred her arched brow to Cassandra, who took the pin from Lawrence and refused to acknowledge the older woman's look. The two of them argued every morning about Cassandra's refusal to leave her stateroom without her veil. "At least pin it back over your bonnet, dear," Sophie said. "How can you see to sew?"

Cassandra picked up her needle. "After years and years and uncounted hours in Sister Theodore's sewing room, one no longer needs to see in order to sew, Mrs. Quiggly."

Sophie snorted.

"You certainly learned well. You do beautiful work," Isabelle Lyons sighed.

"In San Francisco"—her husband reached across the crate to cover her forearm with his large hand—"you will have a sewing room, and help with the boys again, too, so you may stitch and sew to your heart's content." Cassandra swallowed, the warmth in the look passed between the couple in that moment making her throat ache. "I promise," he said.

Blushing to her hairline, Isabelle pulled back and made a show of rearranging her cards. "You're holding up the game, George."

Cassandra frowned and concentrated on the lace bertha she was altering and listened as Sophie shared her excitement about rejoining her nephew, as Lawrence expressed his concern that his uncle might not be so glad to see his nephew.

"Your good uncle will be elated to have you home, Mister Hadley," Isabelle said. "Ships can be replaced and losses recovered. One's family cannot."

Cassandra closed her eyes, took a slow breath, and resumed sewing. She didn't look up or slow her pace until Lawrence and Mister Lyons stood, excusing themselves for their daily poker game in the saloon as was their custom.

As always, Lawrence bowed over Cassandra's hand. "Would you join me at dinner this evening, Miss Mortier?"

As always, Cassandra withdrew her hand and declined. As Lawrence straightened, he stiffened. Cassandra held her breath and didn't have to look to know he and Rafe were staring each other down. At Mister Lyons's beckoning, Lawrence turned and the two wound their way down the cramped deck. Isabelle watched them, Sophie watched Cassandra, and Cassandra, oblivious to all of them, turned in her chair to glare at Rafe. He grinned innocently, raising his needle in salute. Cassandra turned her back to him, caught Sophie's eye, and, flustered, shook out the lace bertha with enough force to snap its seams.

"Mister Veasey's nephew," Sophie observed, gathering up the playing cards with a ruffling flourish. "He's a friend of yours but not of Mister Hadley's, I take it."

Cassandra leveled a warning look on the older woman. "Yes," she said. "A private misunderstanding, of sorts."

To her horror, Rafe chose that moment to stand and walk by them. He stopped. He was behind her. She couldn't see him; she felt him.

"Aye," he said.

Cassandra groaned silently, visualized too easily the exact grin on his face and the dangerous light dancing in those black eyes. She stared down at her lap, waiting.

"I thought I was captain of my ship. I misunderstood."

"Oh," Cassandra heard Isabelle gasp faintly.

"Miss Mortier. Ladies." With a nod he loped on his way, the sail draped over his wide shoulder.

"Give our regards to your uncle," Sophie called after him. Cassandra raised her head.

"What a . . . a strange man," Isabelle breathed, staring after him.

"He has a beautiful smile," Sophie said.

A beautiful smile indeed, Cassandra seethed.

She was still steaming hours later staring up at the low ceiling above her gently rocking bunk. "And I thought we could be friends," she said aloud. Blast. Who could be friends with someone who had so little compassion for his fellows, who went out of his way to cause her unease, and who possessed the social graces of . . . of a sailor!

She saw again Isabelle Lyons's shocked face. The

poor woman had looked as if she'd swallowed a double shot of whiskey—in a single gulp. Cassandra giggled. The young woman's five-year-old probably had as much knowledge of strong spirits as his gentle, naïve, doe-eyed mama.

"You're being nasty," Cassandra scolded herself. She liked the Lyonses. She loved their two boys, especially their five-year-old Georgie. Her grin returned, twice as big. She wouldn't be surprised if Georgie had gotten into the forbidden decanters in his father's study by now. She certainly had by the time she was his age. Sighing, Cassandra turned over on her side and stared at the grey circle of the porthole by moonlight. She wasn't angry anymore. She wasn't tired at all.

Her thoughts drifted. She thought of the Lyonses and their boys. She recalled the look the couple had shared that afternoon, the gruff voice George used when he corrected his older son that was negated by the exasperated love glowing in the man's eyes as he pulled the boy from the rigging or out of the hold every other half hour. She heard again Isabelle's quiet lullaby as she rocked their youngest asleep in her lap. And loneliness such as Cassandra had never experienced—not as a child after her father left, not in Denoir, not on board the *Fortune* or in the time since—welled up and ached inside her.

Family.

Sophie's eyes still shone when she spoke of her dear Mister Quiggly gone these many years. Sophie was going to join a nephew, a beloved boy she'd raised like a mother apparently. The Lyonses were going to whatever they were going to together. Cassandra envied them. Painfully.

"Stop it," she said and rolled out of the bunk. She walked to the porthole, breathed in the night air. San

Francisco loomed in her mind only days away somewhere beyond the night-hidden horizon.

"Can't sleep?"

Cassandra jumped at the deep voice inches from her face. She turned her head, searching, and stopped, catching her breath. Rafe leaned against the bulkhead beside her window.

"No," she said.

"You don't sleep well. Have you noticed?"

"Neither do you."

She could just barely see his grin, a white slash in the shadows cast by the bulkhead between them.

"No," he said. "Not since Havre." He turned his head and looked at her a long moment. "Can you come out here?"

Cassandra stared at him. The moon highlighted his light hair. The night magnified his dark eyes. She sighed.

"No," she said quietly.

"You've gained some sense, Cassandra Mortier."

It was Cassandra's turn to smile. "Aye, Captain Buchanan."

Rafe frowned out at sea, shifted against the wall, stilled. "What are you going to do in San Francisco? Have you thought about it? Do you know what you want?"

"I think about it." Cassandra rested her chin on her hands folded over the porthole's sill. "I might set up as a seamstress. Mrs. Tromby—one of the passengers—gave me the idea, said she'd be happy to recommend my work to her circle of friends."

"Bernard will help you, if that's what you want to do," Rafe said. "It's too bad his wife is gone. His spinster sister lives with them, though. I'd imagine a woman might be more helpful for that sort of thing."

"Lawrence insists I stay with them." Cassandra frowned. "I appreciate the offer, and I've not much choice." She smiled. "Sophie argued me into accepting that much."

"Mrs. Quiggly?"

"Yes."

"She's right." He turned his head to look at her. "And Hadley is right to insist on it." Cassandra smiled at his begrudging comment. "Don't push it," he growled and looked back out to sea.

She didn't. The night was gentle of a sudden, this moment in time too fragile. And needed, she realized. She followed his look and absorbed the night, the breeze and the sea-salted smells and the strumming cables and rigging. And Rafe Buchanan.

"I'll stay with Mister Cramer," she said after a while, resuming their conversation. "But I want my own life." She frowned. "More and more."

Rafe was looking at her, his eyes dark, steady. "I can't see you as a seamstress, or an idle woman of means, either. You want more than that."

"Yes." She looked away. "I want a home. I want to be a wife. I want to sing my babies to sleep at night and scold them every other half hour all day." Her throat tightened. "I want a family. Someday."

They were quiet a long time.

"What do you want, Rafe?"

He sighed, arched his head back against the bulkhead. "A ship, a crew, a cargo to deliver, a sea to sail. That's all I've ever wanted. Until the war." He frowned, and Cassandra waited. "I've no allegiance to a country so much as to people. I've cousins, Acadians that I care about, fighting for the Confederacy. Other cousins, Buchanans that I know about, doing the same.

But all I'm good for on land is spending my money out and marking my time until we sail again. Joining up didn't seem"—he shrugged—"like what I should be doing. Then or now." His frown deepened. "But running cargo between New Orleans and San Francisco like nothing was changed didn't seem right either. So Dom and I stopped sailing for Bernard and ran a centerboard through the blockade. But"—he glanced over at Cassandra and smiled—"you can't do it, not the way it needs to be done to make any difference. Not with a sailing ship.

"I think that's why the *Fortune* was so important. When Bernard got ahold of us and offered us that run, I jumped at it. It meant doing something I knew how to do, something that would make a difference."

"Maybe he'll offer it again. Is he a merchant like my grandfather, with a fleet of ships?" Cassandra ignored the pain that stabbed through her. Rafe didn't.

"He's got more ships. He's a good merchant, a good man. Cassandra. Look at me." She tried not to, failed. "Grieve him." His voice hoarsened. "But go on living. He would want you to have your babes and sing your chanties. You deserve it."

"And you deserve your ships and your cargoes and your seas to sail."

"Aye."

They stared at each other. The breeze was suddenly colder, the night sounds hollow, the sea infinite and lonely.

"Get some sleep," Rafe said. He raised his hand, touched Cassandra's cheek softly. "It's late." He stepped back.

"Good night," she called quietly as he walked away. She watched him until the night swallowed him, and his bare feet padded into silence. Turning, she returned to her bunk and lay quiet and still a long time. Then, for no reason she could name, she curled onto her side and slowly, silently cried herself to sleep.

Chapter Thirteen

CASSANDRA SAT ON the edge of the horsehair sofa in Mister Bernard Cramer's front parlor and told herself to relax. She glanced at the mantel clock. Its spidery hands hadn't moved. Lawrence had still been in his uncle's study across the hall only fifteen minutes. The bright cobalt sky and high, fast-moving clouds of an early December late afternoon in San Francisco beckoned beyond the room's tall windows. Cassandra stood, crossed to the window nearest the sofa and gazed out. And down.

She'd been in San Francisco all of three hours and already that was her most vivid impression of this bustling, foreign city. One looked down here, down on the waterfront and its wharves and warehouses, down at the bay itself, sparkling with whitecaps, sunlight, and sails. From Lawrence's uncle's parlor, Cassandra looked down on a forest of gabled rooftops and chimneys, the bay a bright slash in the distance. She closed her eyes, took a deep, slow breath, and let it go all at once. Sweet Mary, she was a wreck.

She wished she dared step out of the parlor back into the entry and the hall tree there with its beveled mirror. Nerves, she told herself. She knew how she looked: perfectly, primly appropriate and presentable, Sophie had sighed, frowning, upon seeing Cassandra off at the waterfront. Cassandra rolled her eyes and stared out the window, clasping and unclasping her gloved hands.

The study door opened. Cassandra took another breath, forced her hands to her sides, and turned around.

"Miss Mortier." A portly man dressed as severely as she in black broadcloth frock coat, vest, and rumpled pants crossed the threshold ahead of Lawrence and strode toward her, hand extended. Cassandra took his hand, returned his greeting. "Welcome to San Francisco, young lady." His smile was warm, his hair, what remained of it, as white as her grandfather's, though he didn't seem that old of a man otherwise. "And welcome especially to our home." The lines about his eyes creased with concern. "You've had quite a journey, Miss Mortier, from Le Havre to here. My nephew was right to bring you to us." His blue eyes gentled. Cassandra liked his eyes. "Accept my condolences on the loss of your grandfather and allow me and my sister Elizabeth to be at your service in every way."

"Thank you," Cassandra said. She felt herself beginning to breathe normally for the first time since the call had gone out that the Farallon Islands had been sighted. Rafe had dropped from the rigging, told her that meant the Golden Gate, the narrow entrance to San Francisco Bay, was not far off. "I appreciate your hospitality, Mister Cramer." She looked over at Lawrence, who had stopped just inside the doorway. He looked pale, she thought, and as relieved as she felt. "Lawrence has been a true friend to me since leaving Nassau." She turned back to the older man. "You should be proud of him."

Emotion showed plainly in the man's eyes. He nodded, then reached out and drew her hand through his arm. "Come. I will show you to your room."

"I'll bring in the trunks," Lawrence said, stepping aside to let his uncle and Cassandra leave the parlor ahead of him.

Cassandra walked with Bernard Cramer past the study door and down the hall. She glimpsed another, larger parlor, a dining room with a long table, an ornate china tea service gracing the table's polished surface. Mister Cramer released her hand and let her lead up a narrow flight of stairs. On the landing, Grecian statuary stood in two niches built into the corners. An octagon window gave a glimpse of the bay. The second flight of stairs led to a space more a room than a hallway. Cassandra gazed up at a gaslight fixture hanging from the ceiling's center; she'd not seen one before. Four bedroom doors were spaced about the walls.

"This is my room; that's Lawrence's." Mister Cramer pointed to the right. "My sister, Lawrence's aunt Elizabeth, uses that room there. She'll be delighted to have another woman about again." He smiled. "And this shall be your bedroom." He crossed to the door on the left nearest the stairs and opened it, stepping back and gesturing for her to enter first.

"It's lovely," Cassandra said. She knew a sudden urge to sigh and held it back. She'd forgotten such bedrooms as this existed since she'd been away from Leeland so long, away from bedrooms boasting more than a cot and study desk, with wardrobes instead of pegs for one's clothes, with pictures on papered walls and plants overflowing their rattan-worked baskets. A cherrywood fourposter with a crocheted cover dominated the room. It looked so big. Cassandra's gaze moved to the two tall windows where sunshine streamed through curtains crocheted in the same pattern as the bedcover.

"My wife's niece lived with us for a time. She did the room to suit her taste—which suited my wife's taste, apparently. A feat nigh miraculous." He smiled at Cassandra's look. "Dear Martha and her decorating disease, I called it." He laughed. "This was the only room in this house she didn't completely do over every spring."

Cassandra smiled for the first time.

"My." The older man sighed. "It's easy to see why Lawrence is smitten, Miss Mortier." Cassandra blinked, was stunned when Mister Cramer again took her hand, his eyes filling. "You can't know how I've prayed for something—someone—to come into my nephew's life and help him turn himself around." He squeezed her hand tightly. "You are a godsend, young lady. A godsend."

Lawrence cleared his throat in the doorway.

Cassandra and Mister Cramer stepped back from each other. Heat flooded Cassandra's cheeks. Nodding, beaming, Lawrence's uncle left the room promising to arrange a homecoming supper for seven o' clock sharp, which meant he must get to market else his sister serve up his head as the main course upon her return from her circle meeting.

Cassandra and Lawrence stood silently in the bedroom not meeting each other's eyes. The front door slammed below. Lawrence stepped around the trunk he'd brought in and crossed to a window. Cassandra looked down at her hands, at her trunk, her gaze settling on Lawrence's stiff, wide shoulders. She clasped and unclasped her hands once more in the silence stretching out between them.

"I owe you an apology, Miss Mortier." Lawrence remained at the window, his back to the room. "I'm afraid I was"—he paused—"more candid with my uncle than was perhaps wise." He turned, and Cassandra's gaze darted back to her hands. "Concerning my deep feelings for you." He moved toward her, and Cassandra wished she could flee the room, the house. She stood still, statue still, and Lawrence stopped in front of her. She forced herself to look at him. His light blue eyes searched her face. "Please believe me when I tell you I spoke for myself, about myself. I in no way meant to speak for you or to imply there was anything between us except"—he frowned—"our friendship."

"I believe you," Cassandra said quietly. Though she'd denied that Lawrence's feelings were moving beyond friendship—to Sophie, to Isabelle Lyons, to herself most of all—she couldn't feign surprise at hearing otherwise now. But she had no idea how to respond to this.

He reached out and took her hand in his two large ones. "Forgive me, Cassandra." He ducked his head in order to catch her eye. "Might I call you Cassandra?"

Cassandra raised her head. He looked so vulnerable, so hopeful. So distressed. "Of course," she said.

Lawrence straightened and let go a deep sigh. "This was most . . . ill-timed. I'd thought to give you a chance to get your bearings. To get to know my uncle and aunt." He smiled, a rare thing, she'd learned. "To come to know me better so as to better accept my hopes. For us."

Cassandra held his gaze. He was a strikingly handsome man with his dark wavy hair and bold blue eyes, his muscular shoulders and lean, long length bearing testimony to his sailor's life. He was a man women noticed, she was quite certain. And he had changed. She'd tolerated him on board the *Fortune* and been relieved to be out of his presence. She didn't feel that way now, and, if she was totally honest, she was not immune to either his appearance or his changed manner.

But he was so . . . intense. Joyless? Cassandra reined in her thoughts.

"I don't know what to say, Mister—" She stopped. "Lawrence. I've been so worried about how your uncle would receive me, about how I would feel about staying here, that I've not thought past today."

"And that's as it should be. I don't expect you to say anything. Not now. Not ever until you are ready." He squeezed her hand much as his uncle had done. "Maybe this is all for the best." Cassandra could see the strain easing in his face, hear it in his voice. She felt herself beginning to relax too. But only until he continued speaking.

"I vow to win your pledge, Cassandra. I know you are the woman I want to spend the rest of my life with, and I will do everything in my power to win you." His eyes burned with resolve. Black, midnight eyes rose up in her mind. Cassandra looked down. Her hands trembled within Lawrence's clasp. He steadied them, his voice low.

"I wish to win you, not overwhelm you." He placed his index finger under her chin and tilted her head up gently. "I want to live a new life. I want you beside me. I am a determined man. But"—his thumb skimmed her cheek—"I can be patient. For you."

Releasing her hands, he strode quickly from her room. Cassandra stared after him. Tears threatened, and she blinked them away, cursing herself for being a fool and a coward. It didn't help.

"Blast," she sighed, plopping down on the bed oblivious to its luxurious thickness, its exquisite cover. "I should have returned to Denoir."

True to his word, beginning at dinner that evening Lawrence treated her no differently than he'd treated her before, other than using her name. He must have spoken to his uncle, too, because Mister Cramer said no more to her, though he continued to beam at both of them. Elizabeth Cramer didn't look at any of them once the entire meal. Cassandra's nerves stretched that much tighter.

Exhausted, she retreated to her room only to sleep fitfully and awaken worrying about the quiet, reserved older woman with thin lips and downcast, disapproving eyes. Lawrence and his uncle left for the Cramer offices, and Cassandra endured the morning with Aunt Elizabeth. The woman was polite. But that was all. Cassandra was relieved when the lady retired to her room after their quiet luncheon. Mister Cramer's smile was like sunshine after a week-long deluge that evening, and it was all Cassandra could do to keep from hugging Lawrence Hadley as he came through the door she was so happy to see a familiar face.

"It's not you at all, Cassandra," Lawrence assured her later when his aunt declined joining them for dinner. "It's me. She is"—he looked out over the sloping yard where they walked behind the Cramer residence—"protective of my uncle. She never approved of me before." He shrugged. "She hasn't changed her opinion."

"Give her time," Cassandra said, her discomfort concerning Lawrence's aunt moving rapidly to dislike.

"It won't take her long to warm to you. I can guarantee that," Lawrence said. His gaze was as warm as his words, and Cassandra felt herself blushing though the night was turning cool, the breeze lifting Lawrence's dark hair and ruffling her skirts sea-scented and musky. They stood in the shadow cast by the house, squares of light from the windows spilling about them, giving Lawrence's sharply defined features a golden hue. He reached around her and settled her knit wrap more snugly about her shoulders. Unease skittered along Cassandra's nerve endings.

"We should go in," she said, hearing the catch in her voice, hating it. If Lawrence was disappointed at her abrupt end to their short time alone, he hid it well, and she was grateful. That he was not going to hide his desire for her hand he made clear beginning the next day.

Fresh-cut flowers graced her place at the breakfast table. Over the next four days small gifts arrived: a jet bead purse; a paper of pins and a tiny, gold thimble; a Dickens novel; tissue-wrapped scented soaps. Cassandra acknowledged each one each evening at dinner, touched, embarrassed.

And confused, she decided, taking the latest delivery from the still-distant, even thinner-lipped Aunt Elizabeth and retreating with undisguised haste to the privacy of her bedroom. Sighing, she walked to the window and fingered the ribbon bow tied about the small box in her hand. The day matched her mood: grey, overcast, the heaviness of rain in the air. The box was light. It felt like lead in her hands.

Frowning, she slipped off the ribbon and removed the lid. All she discovered was a folded piece of stationery. Setting the box aside, Cassandra snapped open the paper and glimpsed Lawrence's familiar handwriting. She groaned, looking up at the ceiling instead of at the paper in her hand. If this was an attempt at a love letter . . . She didn't finish the thought. Squaring her shoulders, she forced herself to read.

Cassandra,

I want you to come to think of San Francisco as your home, even as I dream—I trust not without hope—that you will come to regard me as a man worthy of providing you with a home.

Although my uncle and Aunt Elizabeth hold you in great esteem, as I knew they would, they must still seem as strangers to you. My duties at the office keep me away from you during the day.

Therefore, I have taken it upon myself to arrange a luncheon for you with Mrs. Quiggly this afternoon in hopes that an outing with your friend may brighten your day.

With only your happiness my greatest desire, I remain your true friend

L.H.

Cassandra broke into a broad smile. Lawrence was a true friend, a considerate, sensitive, wonderful friend. She twirled from the window, her spirits lifting for the first time all week. This wasn't a gift, it was a . . . a godsend—borrowing Mister Cramer's words. She looked over at the tiny clock on the gleaming cherry surface of the three-legged table beside the bed. Sweet Mary. She couldn't wait to tell dear Aunt Elizabeth that she wouldn't have to entertain—or pretend to entertain—Cassandra at lunch today. Cassandra smiled so wide her cheeks hurt. She couldn't wait to tell Sophie about Aunt Elizabeth.

"That poor, pitiful woman. She's of no consequence, dear. Be polite. Be gracious. And"—the waterfall of pink and green ribbons and bows spilling over Sophie's hat rippled—"be out of her presence as often as possible."

Cassandra smiled and sat back against the high oak chair, her shoulder muscles loosening, heart lightening. "Oh, how I've missed you," she sighed.

"You've missed yourself, Cassandra Mortier." Sophie's twinkling eyes became serious, and Cassandra prepared for a tongue-lashing. She wasn't disappointed. "You may not hide away again. This is San Francisco, city of a hundred hills, and you're going to traipse up and down every one of them if I have to tie one of Sigmund's ribbons about your pretty little neck and drag you." Their laughter floated between them as the waiter arrived with their meal.

Cassandra's first reservations about the restaurant when Mister Cramer's carriage had stopped in the middle of what had to be the city's business section disappeared. This tiny establishment tucked away amidst a labyrinth of offices and businesses was not the Poodle Dog to be sure, but its food was as delicious as its surroundings were nondescript.

"I knew my Daniel, poor bachelor that he is, took all his meals out, and it worried me," Sophie said. She took another bite, savored it, and sighed. "No more."

"Did he suggest this restaurant?" Cassandra asked.

"No. Mister Hadley arranged everything in advance. I'll bring Daniel back here soon, though, rest assured."

Cassandra ate; Sophie talked nonstop.

Cassandra learned more about Daniel, caught up on a week's worth of canine catastrophes, most of them involving Daniel's homicidal, possibly by now suicidal cat. Cassandra promised to get out of the house daily if for nothing more than a stroll about Mister Cramer's tiny, tilted backyard. She recalled unbidden how Lawrence had looked down at her there, how his strong fingers had lingered when he'd resettled her shawl, how she'd avoided being alone with him ever since.

"Cassandra?"

"Sorry." She looked up. "I was woolgathering."

Sophie leaned forward, her childlike teeth agrin. "I asked how Mister Hadley was faring with his uncle."

"Very well." Cassandra frowned down at her empty plate, knew without looking that the other woman's eyebrows were creeping upward. "His uncle thinks I'm a godsend, the answer to all his prayers"—she forced herself to look up—"for his Lawrence." Sophie's brows disappeared beneath the fringe of grey frizz poking out from her bonnet. Cassandra took a deep breath. "Mister Hadley wants to marry me."

Sophie's mouth pursed, her keen eyes alight, thoughtful. But it was her absolute and uncharacteristic silence that was disconcerting. Cassandra looked away, and, feeling unaccountably defensive, hurried on.

"He's a gentleman. He's established in his uncle's merchant business. He's sincere, I believe, in his desires for a . . . a home, a responsible life. He's . . ." She was babbling. Her cheeks were burning, but she couldn't seem to stop. "He's considerate, sensitive, generous. Today, for instance. He knew I would enjoy lunch with you." She stopped. She glanced at her friend. The woman's expression remained unchanged.

"Yes," Sophie agreed at length. "He's all of that." Cassandra stared down at her plate. "Not to mention quite manly to look upon."

Cassandra's head jerked up, and Sophie burst out laughing. Cassandra opened her mouth, closed it, and shook her head in surrender. "You are scandalous, Mrs. Quiggly."

"Nonsense," the older woman chortled. "I'm right." Her expression became thoughtful again. "Mister Lawrence Hadley. Every mother's desire for her daughter and every daughter's dream for a husband. Isn't that what Isabelle Lyons might say?" Her hat tilted to the side as she cocked her head. "But do you love him?"

Cassandra looked down. "I don't know that that's necessary," she said quietly. Frowning, she met Sophie's steady gaze. "Who one marries should be someone who wants the same things, values the same things. Even I know that."

"True. True." Sophie nodded, the sun from the window beyond them flashing dizzily in her pink and green mad milliner's nightmare of a hat. Her voice lowered. "But do you love him?"

Cassandra wrinkled her nose, her throat suddenly tight, her heart heavy in her chest. "Marriage is marriage, and love is . . ." Her words faded. She had no idea what love was. Rafe. His name echoed in her mind, in her heart. She knew desire. She knew need and fulfillment, caring and compassion. She knew loneliness and longing. And loss. Was that love? Sophie's pudgy hand closed over Cassandra's hand on the table between them.

"I would wish for my daughter differently than most mothers, I suppose."

"You've a daughter?" Cassandra asked.

Sophie sat back in her chair and smiled. "A beautiful, beautiful child. So bright. So full of mischief." Her lined face soft and tranquil, her usually sparkling eyes softer still, Sophie gazed at the table, but Cassandra sensed she saw the past. Cassandra reached for her coffee cup and waited.

"I married late myself." Sophie glanced up, the impish light back in her eyes. "Told my father I'd die a spinster before I'd marry just to be married like my five older sisters. He knew me well enough to let me be, and I wasn't unhappy keeping his house." The smile Cassandra had seen before came. "Until I met Mister Quiggly."

Shaking her head slightly, she continued. "We were well past the usual marrying age, and we were blessed with Emma later yet." A smile teased her lips. "I spoiled her. Admitted it then and admit it now. I couldn't help myself." She shrugged, sadness shading her smile. "I've never regretted it." She looked over at Cassandra. "I only had her for four years, but oh"—her eyes twinkled with merriment and tears—"they were such wonderful years."

Cassandra swallowed and set down her cup, fighting the growing ache in her throat. She could so easily see Sophie with her Emma, could even imagine Emma, spoiled and sprightly, awhirl in satin ribbons from head to toe. The ache became painful.

"There was a cholera outbreak that year." Sophie looked at the white linen tablecloth once more, still reposed, her voice poignantly matter-of-fact. "Strange enough, I don't recall if they ever came out and called it an epidemic." She frowned as if this forgotten fact bothered her, and Cassandra wanted to tell Sophie to stop. She felt in some way responsible for this painful turn in the conversation, searched frantically for words to turn it again before it went further.

"I lost Mister Quiggly and Emma within a week of each other."

Cassandra closed her eyes. The pain in her throat pushed down and filled her chest. Sophie went on. Cassandra closed her eyes tighter, forcing herself to listen.

"I remember the pain. There's never been any like it before or since." She paused. "Grief is a God-given thing, our right, our release. But"—she took a deep breath—"in my grief I raged against God, I think. Against life, I know."

Cassandra opened her eyes, and Sophie met her look.

"I spent the next three years of my life grieving for a life that was gone and rejecting any other one in its place. I was so angry. So wrong."

Cassandra shook her head. "You were . . . hurting."

"No." Sophie was as serious as Cassandra had ever seen or heard her. "I was raging furious. I was determined to never love like that again, never be hurt again. I was wrong." She sat back. "Could I bring back the past, Cassandra? Could I live it again, live it differently, live it better?" She shook her head and sighed. "Yesterdays are to be savored or severed. Todays are to be lived."

Cassandra traced the rim of the saucer beneath the chipped china cup holding coffee grown cold. "What . . . what happened?"

Sophie's familiar chortle made Cassandra look up. "Artemus, my prune-faced, Puritanical, penny-pinching, pathetically pompous missionary of a brother-in-law happened." She grinned at Cassandra's look. "My sister took ill, and I went to nurse her. Stayed on with her for a year, telling myself I was only being a faithful sister carrying out my Christian duty. But when Abigail passed on I found myself putting off leaving Nassau for one reason or another again and again until I finally admitted I wasn't leaving." Her grin widened. "You see, Abbey left behind the poorest excuse of a six-year-old you'd ever want to meet. Such a piteously put-upon child, all solemn and squeamish and scared of sins real and ridiculous and of his father most of all. About made me furious, and I wasn't about to leave and let Artemus finish the job." She shuddered melodramatically, and Cassandra grinned.

"Daniel?"

Sophie chuckled. "Daniel." Sighing, she smiled. "Whether you marry, when you marry, who you marry . . . Don't worry about all that, Cassandra. Just don't guard your heart. Let it heal, and then let it love again, and everything else will take care of itself."

Cassandra sat silently as their waiter cleared their table, watched a man and she assumed his wife be seated at a nearby table. The steady rumble of carriage traffic came and went as patrons entered or left through the door hidden from view by a small forest of potted ferns.

"Could you and Mister Hadley come for dinner tomorrow?" Sophie's question pulled Cassandra from her thoughtful silence.

"Tomorrow?"

The woman beamed. "Mister Veasey came by with a trunk that was misplaced, and I've invited him—and your friend the captain too." Cassandra's heart lifted, then sank in a single heartbeat.

"I think not," she said. "Mister Hadley and Captain Buchanan wouldn't enjoy themselves." She raised her hand when Sophie rolled her eyes in disgust. "Believe me," Cassandra said before Sophie could argue. "No one would enjoy them either."

"Then you two must come another time," Sophie insisted. She brightened. "I'll invite the Lyonses. Wouldn't that be fun?"

"Yes," Cassandra said. Seeing Rafe again would be . . . She frowned, suddenly unsure of how it would be—unsure if she even wanted to know. She shook free of her thoughts. "And we must do lunch again. Often."

"At my house." Sophie flushed. "I mean, Daniel's house, of course." She rushed on undaunted. "Today is Thursday. Every Thursday you must come for luncheon, and we will spend the remainder of the afternoon doing"—she spread her hands, palms up—"whatever. Agreed?"

"Agreed," Cassandra said. The hours and hours ahead with dear Aunt Elizabeth might be bearable knowing Thursday was coming. She glanced up as a group of four businessmen entered, their jovial moods and deep laughter ruffling the room's subdued atmosphere like a gust of wind on a still summer day. Her gaze snagged on the octagon oak clock hanging on the wall. "Sweet Mary." She looked over at Sophie. "We've talked the entire afternoon away today. It's almost three o'clock."

"Nonsense." Cassandra stared at Sophie's hat as her friend peered down at the small watch pinned to her bodice. Sophie looked up. "You're right. And"—she leaned forward, her voice dropping to a conspiratorial whisper—"that gentleman over there *has* been staring at us. Since we arrived!"

"What?" Cassandra turned and looked at the grey-haired, black-moustachioed man Sophie described. He was elderly, thin to the point of gauntness, and immaculately dressed in businessman's black. Cassandra's eyes narrowed. He was engrossed in his reading, in what looked to be several newspapers folded or spread out on his table, leaving little room for the coffeepot and derby hat also evident. "He's reading, Sophie."

"For three hours?"

"Maybe that's what he does Thursday afternoons, comes here and reads all those papers."

"I bet the only reading he's gotten done today is what he's looked down and done each time I've glanced his way," Sophie said, sitting back up straight. "I dismissed it at first and forgot all about him once our meal arrived and we got to talking, but"—she frowned—"he was here when we walked in, and he's still here and still looking over this way after all this time. Doesn't that seem odd to you?"

Cassandra shook her head, too used to the strange looks that so often followed in Sophie Quiggly's wake and not about to mention them. The only thing the least bit odd in this restaurant was Sophie's hat. And it was much worse than odd today; it was atrocious.

"Let's leave him to his newspapers," Cassandra said, tugging on her gloves. "Miss Cramer asked that the carriage be back by four o'clock." She looked pointedly at Sophie. "If we're to get together Thursday next, I'd best be prompt today, don't you think?"

The morning's dreary greyness had burned away with the afternoon sun. It settled now instead over Cassandra's spirit, growing heavier and heavier the farther away the carriage took her from the restaurant. Even Sophie's bubbling presence lost its power. Cassandra leaned and looked and admired and nodded at every house, garden, and Chinaman's pigtail the older woman pointed to on the way to Daniel's house. But the only site she truly scanned with any interest was the tall masts marking the waterfront and wharves in the distance.

She shook herself mentally. She didn't want to think about Rafe Buchanan. At Mister Cramer's this week, with Lawrence, with his horrid aunt, it had been easier. With Sophie babbling on and on about her dinner menu for tomorrow, it was next to impossible to keep thoughts of him at bay.

She wondered what he was going to do, if Mister Cramer was going to fit out another ship, if Rafe would be its master. She wondered where he was right now, wished she didn't know where he was going to be tomorrow. She wondered if there was a Lenora in San Francisco.

"Are you all right, dear?"

"Yes." Cassandra turned quickly from the window. The carriage clattered to a stop, and she spied Daniel's residence. A spreading hickory tree graced its front lawn, hiding much of the house from view. Sharp yaps punctuated the serene afternoon. Sigmund. He stood on his short hind legs, his front paws against the hickory's trunk, a pink ribbon snaking out behind him.

"Siggy!" Sophie was scolding before the driver could come around and open the door. "Leave that poor cat alone!" She clambered out and turned, breathless, two bright spots marking her round cheeks. "Good-bye, dear. I must go, or Sigmund will spy something else and be off like a flash and no catching him. See you Thursday. Here. Give Mister Hadley my regards. Siggy!"

Sophie scurried across the yard holding her hat on with one hand, shaking her gloved index finger furiously with her other. The carriage rocked as the driver took his seat, and Cassandra turned, watching Sophie until the street dipped down and the scene disappeared. An open carriage crested the hill. Cassandra started to face forward, stopped, and looked at the vehicle behind them more closely. Behind the driver she spied a derby hat. They turned a corner, and Cassandra felt gooseflesh rising on her arms. The passenger's hat. The black moustache. It was the man from the restaurant.

Cassandra whirled around forward and clasped her hands tightly in her lap. Coincidence? Perhaps, but her stomach denied it. She glanced out her window. The steep streets were unfamiliar, the residential homes parading past her no indication of her nearness to Mister Cramer's. She closed her eyes. It was three o'clock in the afternoon, she lectured herself. Broad daylight. She was with Mister Cramer's driver, not some hired stranger. She was being ridiculous. The carriage pulled to a stop.

Cassandra sat still, listened for a carriage to pass them from behind. She heard it approach, slow, and clatter to a halt behind them.

"Miss?"

Cassandra opened her eyes and stared at the man opening her door, offering his hand. It was him. Panic fluttered in her chest and must have shown in her eyes because the elderly man frowned and withdrew his hand.

"You know this gentleman, Miss Mortier?" Her driver appeared, his whip at his side but menacingly evident.

Cassandra shook her head. Her pulse slowed. Standing, the older man staring into the carriage looked even thinner. His hands at his sides were trembling.

"Here now, sir." The driver stepped forward and placed a meaty hand on the old man's arm. "We don't want no trouble. You've mistook this lady for someone else, I suspect. Go on, now. Let me help her down an' you go on about yer day."

The driver started to pull the old man away from the carriage door. The man didn't struggle, but his gaze remained fixed on Cassandra, his eyes enormous beneath the derby hat's rolled rim. They stared at her, beseeching, tormented.

"Wait," Cassandra said. The driver frowned but stopped his efforts.

"Mortier?" the old man said, his voice cracking. "Your name is Mortier?"

"Yes," she answered. She leaned forward, her fear gone. "Are you ill, sir? Can . . . can we help you in some way?" The driver scowled. Cassandra ignored him. The old man's hands were shaking more visibly, his color a slate-grey.

"You don't—" He stopped, wetting his lower lip beneath his thick moustache. "You don't know me, but I think . . ." His voice faded.

"No. I'm sorry." Whoever this poor man was and whatever had led him to follow her home, Cassandra's heart went out to him. "You've confused me with someone," she said gently. "I'm not from here, not from anywhere close to here, and I've only recently—"

"Your mother." The man reached forward, his hand curling over the side edge of the open carriage door. "What is your mother's name?"

"Miss." The driver stepped forward. Cassandra shushed him with a look.

"My mother is dead. Her name was Annalee. Annalee Maria—"

"Vannorman." The emotion that twisted the old man's face took Cassandra's breath. "Annalee Maria Vannorman. My daughter, Miss Mortier. *My daughter.*"

Chapter Fourteen

IT WAS THURSDAY next, and Cassandra had traipsed a hundred miles, not hills, across the thick Belgian carpets gracing Thomas Vannorman's stately home. The sun was gone, and the chill of San Francisco after dark joined the numbness fogging her thoughts. She no longer opened her eyes to crocheted window curtains, no longer worried about Elizabeth Cramer. She'd not lunched again with Sophie as planned.

She had a suite of rooms now, not a bedroom. She had no more worries—about acceptance, about a home, about the outcome of her grandfather's business affairs. And plans? Cassandra slowed, her feet drawn to the formal parlor's open double doors. She stopped, gazed from the threshold into the gaslit room. Sweet Mary, how did one plan a life that was daily whirling more out of her control and beyond her ability to cope, much less comprehend?

"Come in, Cassandra."

Thomas Vannorman's voice startled her. He sat, hidden but for his feet, in a wing chair facing the room's ornate but cold hearth directly across from where Cassandra stood. She crossed to him, her new high-button shoes sinking silently into the carpet, her black silk mourning gown tailor-made, rustling its worth and exquisite workmanship.

"Sit down. Please." The old man raised a frail, blue-veined hand and motioned to the matching chair beside him. "Forgive me for not standing."

"No," Cassandra said quickly. "It's quite all right." She sat down, smiled. Thomas Vannorman smiled in return, but even his smile looked sad, pained. Like his eyes. It was as if he'd been cast in cold marble melancholy and to be otherwise strained the skin stretched tightly across his skeletal frame. Cassandra hurt for him, if not with him. Wincing inwardly, she followed his look up to the full-length portrait hanging above the mantel.

It was like looking into a mirror.

Five days she'd been here, in the Vannorman high-windowed, four-storied mansion with its army of silent slippered Oriental servants, its monied extravagance, its manicured lawns at the base of Rincon Hill. She'd spent accumulated hours in that time staring up at this painting, at Annalee Maria Vannorman. And still Cassandra's heart jolted when she looked again now. She saw herself in a flowing Empire gown of another time, not her mother, not this sad, age-stiffened man's Annalee.

It was unnerving—and painfully familiar. The image Cassandra carried of her mother was truly an image, not a memory. When she thought of her mother, she saw another portrait, as large, as handsomely gilt-framed, its subject as achingly, hauntingly beautiful. If Leeland still stood, that painting still hung in the library there. As a child Cassandra had stared at it, studied it, wept silent, streaming tears before it, longing not for her mother but for her mother's . . . magic, her beauty, her gift. Cassandra's throat ached now at the memory. She'd longed for her mother's worth in her father's eyes. Six months ago in Denoir, Cassandra would have damned Leland Mortier and gone on about her business.

But the dam had broken. Feelings bubbled up and eddied and swirled. She looked up at the painting and saw herself, not herself as the exact image and age of Annalee when this portrait was painted, but herself as a child in the library back home. Her rage, her willfulness, her grandfather's love—whatever had held these feelings back then was swept away now in giant waves of hurt, confusion. Pain. Cassandra swallowed, blinked her vision clear, surprised by the rising tide of compassion running through it all. She clung to it, let it come. For her mother taken from life so soon. For her father so bitter and broken without her. But mostly it came for that lost little girl so left behind by both of them.

"She ran away."

Cassandra turned at Thomas Vannorman's gravelly, low-spoken words. He looked up at the portrait, and Cassandra was reminded of the way Sophie had stared at the table as she'd talked of her little Emma. But there all similarity ended. Where Sophie's words had come easily, her eyes sad but soft and glowing with love, the man beside Cassandra seemed caught up in an anguish so consuming it contorted his face and strangled his voice.

"A week after her wedding she just . . . disappeared."

"Her wedding?" Cassandra stared at him. Foreboding rippled through her, and she frowned. She'd realized only since coming into this man's house how little she knew about Annalee, how little she'd ever known. The stories Cassandra had begged from Lalie had always begun with how her father had arrived home from New York with a new wife on his arm and set New Orleans society a-wagging and sent Cassandra's *grandmère* to her bed an entire season. Jim's tales all bespoke Annalee's and her father's singular devotion to each other, stories Cassandra stopped asking to hear. Her unease deepened. Annalee had been the one topic about which Randall Mortier had remained reticent, unmoved by Cassandra's perfected, persuasive childhood pestering. She swallowed. Her parents married and then disappeared from this man's life forever? Why?

"My father brought her home. To New Orleans." Cassandra's voice echoed her incredulity. "You didn't know that?"

"All I knew was the thought of her leaving New York, living away from me, going away with some stranger—God forgive me, it made me insane. She was all I had. Everything." He stopped, his eyes closing above his sunken cheeks. "The child I'd refused nothing since the day she was born asked something of me for the first time in her life and"—his thick moustache quivered—"and I refused to even listen to her."

Bony fingers curled like claws over the ends of his chair's upholstered arms. "I wouldn't even allow her to tell me the boy's name." He turned his head to her, his eyes red-rimmed and ravaged with grief. "Mortier." Cassandra read his lips as much as heard him. His fingers uncoiled and hung limply from his wrists. "If I'd only known his name. . . . Then . . ." His voice faded into silence.

"My parents . . . eloped?" Cassandra asked. She knew her questions must be like fingernails raking across an open wound, but she couldn't stay her words. She needed to know. Thomas Vannorman stared again at the portrait, his voice as lifeless as his hands.

"Had I not forced her to marry, maybe then—later—she might have . . . forgiven me. Contacted me."

Cassandra frowned. "But—"

"That's been the heaviest to carry all these years. Knowing she would never know how badly I needed her forgiveness. How much I wanted to make . . . amends. I tried, Annalee. *I tried.*" He spoke to the girl in the painting.

Cassandra bit her lip. She felt as if she were eavesdropping and didn't wish to be, but there was no helping it, no escape.

"I hired people to find you," he whispered. "Would be sending them still if they would but go. But they couldn't find you. Not even Giles." His hands fisted, pounded the chair's arms. Cassandra gasped. "Giles," the old man groaned, his agitation seeping away like blood until his head sagged, his chin at rest upon his gold-threaded vest. "Too late I saw what you saw, knew what you begged to tell me. Too . . . late."

He sat so still. Cassandra leaned forward in her chair an inch at a time. Her heart began thudding.

"Mister Vannorman?" She reached out a tentative hand. "Grand—" She stopped. This man was not her *grandpère,* not Grandpapa. The man's greyed head rose until their gazes met, held. Long, cold fingers took hold of Cassandra's hand. His feeble grasp tightened. Without thinking, Cassandra squeezed back.

"I am glad you are here, Cassandra Mortier," he said. His voice was rough but strong, his sad eyes steady. "I left behind great wealth, came West to . . . forget. I accumulated only more wealth but no end to the pain of living with what I had done. With what I had lost." He swallowed. "Until . . . now." He closed his eyes, took a ragged, wheezy breath, and looked at Cassandra once more. "Let me make my amends to my Annalee. With you." His voice thickened. "Please."

Cassandra slipped from her chair to kneel beside him, his hand cradled in her lap. He was not her Grandpapa.

He was old and frail and broken. But he was her mother's father. She could not be his Annalee. She was young and wary and confused. But she was her mother's daughter—raised by wise, gentle Randall Mortier. Her heart stilled, mind calmed.

"I don't understand all that happened, can't know how Annalee came to think of it—of you—before she died." She stared down at Thomas Vannorman's hand, so white against her black skirt, so weak between her youth-strong palms. "But I do know she was happy, Mister Vannorman." Cassandra looked up. "All that I know tells me she was truly happy and truly, truly loved by my father. Cherished. Adored." She pushed past the pain that stabbed through her. "Grieved."

Pausing, Cassandra gathered her words and spoke as she knew Randall Mortier would have spoken. "Whatever happened, it must have hurt her very much. As it did you." Misery flashed bleak and stark in Thomas Vannorman's eyes. "But it didn't destroy her." Cassandra slowed, willed him to hear her, to believe her words. "She had an ability to give and receive great happiness, Mister Vannorman. And that, I think, says much about her . . . but even more about the one who raised her."

Tears tracked silently down the man's cavernous face, catching in his moustache. He closed his eyes, let his head fall against the chair's back. Cassandra stood and, hesitating, placed his hand gently in his lap.

"Thank . . . you," he whispered without opening his eyes. His fingers tightened about hers, released weakly. Cassandra turned. Hong Lew, the ancient cook, stood silently inside the doorway, the tray in his arthritic fingers holding long- and short-necked blue and green and amber-hued medicine bottles and vials. Heart twisting, Cassandra walked quickly from the parlor.

She couldn't sleep, couldn't even bring herself to remove her pinching shoes, change into her night shift. Staring into the darkness outside her window, the hazy glow of gaslights marking the street's winding downward slope to the bay, disconnected images drifted to mind. Four-year-old Emma. Had they called her Emmie? Thomas Vannorman's sad eyes came. Sophie's gay chortle. Her thoughts scattered, and Cassandra struggled to remember Annalee, not the girl in the portrait downstairs nor the young woman in the painting back home, but Annalee the mother.

Annie? Annalee!

Cassandra stilled. She closed her eyes to listen harder, remember better. Their parquet-floored entry hall in Mobile came, its white walls splashed by the sunshine spilling through the front door flung wide, her father's tall frame bending to heave his valise across the polished wood, straightening to stand and call up the balustered staircase where Cassandra huddled, watching, smiling. Waiting.

Annie!

Leland?

Cassandra heard her mother's light tread as if it approached this moment. She was coming, hurrying down the long upstairs hall, closer, faster. Cassandra saw again wide skirts billowing past her, a sighing cloud of pink brushing softly against her arm, smelled again the scent of jasmine, saw again her mother laughing, crying, being twirled round and round and round in her father's strong arms, skirts floating, swirling.

The entry, the sunlight, the stairs dissolved until there was only them, their laughter, their joy radiating out and up to her until Cassandra felt again how her grin had hurt her tiny face, how her giggles had bubbled up, how . . .

Cassandra's hand pressed hard against her mouth. How her mother had turned in her father's arms and seen her, beckoned to her.

Come down, baby love. Papa's home at last. Come!

"Mama?"

Cassandra's voice in her ears, not in her head, broke the spell. She sank to the carpet, bent double, but could not still her trembling, stop the tears that spilled freely, in wonder, in release. Grief is a God-given thing. . . . "Yes," Cassandra whispered. "Yes." She cried as she'd not known to cry at her mother's funeral, as she'd never cried over her father's rejection, as she'd only cried in Rafael Buchanan's protecting arms.

Rafe.

Her grieving became hurting. Groping to her feet, Cassandra fell across her bed, her sobs harder, choking. "Damn you!" She pounded her pillow viciously, wanted to smash something. "I . . . need . . . you." He'd sailed into her life, grinning, glowering. Holding. Healing. And sailors sailed away. They didn't settle, didn't come home every night and call up the stairs, sometimes didn't come home ever again. Have your babes and sing your chanties, Rafe had told her. She deserved it. "Yes," she choked. She did. "And I will have them. I will."

With Lawrence Hadley?

But do you love him? Sophie's question haunted her, hounded her, and let loose pelting, painful questions of her own. Did she like Lawrence? Yes. Could she visualize a life with him as husband and wife? Yes. Then why was she so avoiding him, holding her feelings so in check? Was she . . . guarding her heart? Afraid? Her tears came harder as the answer emerged, rending her heart, her soul.

No.

She wasn't hiding her heart. She wasn't afraid to risk being loved, risk loving. Her heart was breaking. Her heart loved—Rafe. Only Rafe. She wanted Rafe, wanted Rafe's strong arms catching her up, wanted their easy laughter, their damnable arguing, *their loving* swirling round and round her days, warming the smiles of towheaded babes with midnight eyes. How long she'd known it. How well she knew it. How hard the words finally came.

"I want . . . you. I need . . . you. I . . . love . . . you."

Her tears rocked her. The night deepened and wrapped about her, and exhaustion came, releasing her into the oblivion of sleep.

Rafe sat alone toward the back of the Gilded Rose, his chair tilted on its hind legs, his shoulders resting against the unpainted plank wall. He watched the Thursday night crowd jostling for drinks, for a stake in a card game, for girls. Thursday night, Friday night, Sunday night—it made little difference at the Gilded Rose or at any other like place here. This was San Francisco.

Frowning, Rafe raised his mug and drank deep. Frisco, Nassau, Le Havre, New Orleans, New York, Liverpool, Canton, Sydney. . . . He knew them all: their ways, their food, their pleasures, their dark sides. He knew what to expect, what to avoid. They were all different. His mug thumped onto the table, empty. They were all the same; they remained the same. It was he who was . . . different. He didn't like it.

He sat night after night, drink after drink, and felt restless, not relaxed. He bandied with the girls as easily, his gaze seeking out the prettiest ones as naturally, but it only made his heart ache, nothing else. There was no Lenora here, no friend, but he knew the houses where he'd be as welcomed and the women there as friendly. And somehow those houses had become like opium dens and pox-infested prostitute cribs: haunts to be avoided. *Non.* He wasn't himself. He didn't like it. He ordered another drink and leaned his head back against the wall, eyes closed.

His nose burned from the coal oil used in the lamps mixing with the cigars, offensive stogies to aromatic Havanas, smoking in every patron's hand save those with chew bulging their lower lips. The piano player across the room was drunk, playing loud and poorly and nonstop. Voices were rising, heating with tempers over the faro game beside him. Rafe blanked it all out, took himself in his mind to where there was only brisk wind and open sky. His jaw clenched. It wasn't the deck of a ship that offered escape anymore. It was a beach and a wave-pounded reef. And Cassandra.

"You asleep?"

Rafe's eyes snapped open, his chair clunking down on all fours. Dom sat down in the chair opposite him, the Acadian's dark eyes narrowed and too knowing. "You know me, Nonc," Rafe drawled, evading the concern creasing Dom's face. "Could sleep through a hurricane."

Dom didn't buy it. "You sick?"

Rafe's drink came; he ordered another for Dom. Turning from the serving girl, Rafe hunched forward, his elbows on the table, hands cradling his mug, and met Dom's gaze head-on. "I was not sleeping. I am not sick. I'm fine." A grin teased his mouth. "And how is Mrs. Quiggly this evening?"

Dom stiffened, blinked, his bushy moustache squirming beneath his oversized nose.

Rafe laughed outright and leaned back in his chair. "I've not been spying on you, Veasey." He raised his mug, pointed. "It's your hair."

Dom's gnarled hand flew to his head, and Rafe choked on his ale. "What is the matter with it, *aihn*?"

"Nothing." Rafe swallowed, eyes watering. "It's combed."

"So? You have not seen a man comb his hair?" Dom jerked his cards from inside his jacket—his new, unfashionably pressed, unbelievably loud hound's-tooth checked jacket—and snapped his cards as he shuffled them.

Rafe's grin widened. He knew better, but that had ever made little difference. "In all the years we've shipped together, nothing but the wind has arranged *your* hair." Dom's look blackened, but he refused to look up from his cards. Challenged, Rafe reached for certain suicide. "It's almost dogwatch, old man. You been over there all this time?"

Dom lunged across the table. Cards flew. Their drinks toppled. The air fogged blue with Acadian curses and Rafe's shouted laughter as the two rolled together off the table onto the uneven, filthy floor. The three tables nearest them emptied, the more experienced among those scrambling clear pushing past the gawkers in the bunch. The former misread the ruckus; the latter were disappointed. It was over as quickly as it started because Rafe offered no resistance save trying to protect his head with his arms, and Dom, always efficient, judged his point made after a jabbing score of blows well aimed and duly taken.

"Half-breed, shark's-meat whelp," the Acadian grunted, rolling off Rafe onto his back beneath the table with an oath, his arms falling limply out at his sides as he dragged in air. Wincing, still breathless from laughing, Rafe stumbled to his feet and reached under the table to help his uncle up. The space that had opened around them filled back up with men and smoke and noise, and, before Rafe had righted their chairs and Dom had retrieved all his cards, it was as if nothing had even happened.

Scowling, Dom used his sleeve to dry an ace that had landed in someone's drink, then dropped grumpily onto his chair and waited for Rafe to resettle opposite him. Fresh mugs thumped down between them. Rafe dug deep in his pocket, paid double for the new round, and, hefting a mug, brought it up to the side of his face, not his mouth. Dom smirked at the younger man's grimace.

"Been looking for you, man, half this night. Crazy crazy to worry after you, *aihn*?"

"You found me." Rafe groaned and closed his eyes. He'd be lucky to open his left one come morning. He sighed, at ease for the first time all night. Some things didn't change. "Ouch!" He jerked back as Dom's finger poked the swelling beneath his eye.

"Hurt?"

"Aye, it hurts!" Rafe tilted his chair back again, well out of Dom's reach, and cocked his head. "So. What's up?" Dom didn't waste punches or energy. If he'd come looking for Rafe, he had a reason. Dom's bushy brows came together over his nose. Rafe nursed his drink, waiting.

"Daniel, him." Dom glanced up from the blackjack hand he was dealing. "Sophie's boy." Rafe nodded. "His partner in the store, he is poorly and wanting to sell. Go back to his home port." When he didn't go on, Rafe set his cup aside and turned over his cards. He had nothing worth having.

"Sounds like a fair wind for Daniel to me, no older than he is."

"Aye." Dom took the hand and dealt again. "But he has not the money he needs, him, to weigh anchor."

"Mrs. Quiggly?" Rafe grimaced at his cards. "Hit me." Dom flipped him another card, equally as useless.

"Like you say, he is young, *aihn*? Too much pride, little little sense."

Rafe grinned. "He won't take her money." He shook his head. "He took mine, easy enough, when he sold me my—hey!" Rafe raised his hand at the fighting fire leaping into Dom's eyes. "It was good stuff, all right? And a fair deal." *Mon Dieu,* Dom had it bad. Another week of dinners at Sophie's and the Acadian would probably be championing that demon in dog's fur. Rafe sighed. The woman could cook, though. He glanced over at Dom. But her greatest charm, other than the way she smiled when she looked at his uncle, was the fact that she could almost beat the man at poker.

"Twenty-one." Dom grunted, taking the hand as easily as Daniel had taken Rafe's money. Rafe scowled as Dom restacked and shuffled. It was more than Rafe was going to come close to doing this evening. He looked up. Dom was still shuffling the cards?

"Daniel, him." Dom's lips pursed beneath his moustache. "He thinks maybe we might—" He scowled, stopped.

Rafe's mug froze halfway to his mouth. "We might what, Dom? Become *shopkeepers*?"

"It is a ships' store, not a damned dry goods," Dom shot back. He dropped a card, swore. "It is a livelihood off the sea but not away from it, yes?" Rafe cursed, and the older man leaned forward, his look killing. "It is an honor to be asked, and we will show him the same with an answer."

"Merde." Rafe let his chair hit the floor, set his drink aside. He raked his hair back from his forehead, but Cassandra's words, not Dom's, rang in his ears. *I want a home. I want to be a wife. I want a family*. Dammit! A shopkeeper could offer her that like a sailor never could. She'd known it. He knew it. He swore aloud, grabbed up his mug and drained it.

"I'm a sailor, Dom. That's what I do—hell, it's more that what I do. It's who I am. I can't be different than who I am."

"Aye." Dom's eyes narrowed. "You are . . . young."

His point was blunt, aim true. Rafe ignored it. "Deal, dammit." Only the cards snapped between them for five hands. Dom took them all. It took that many hands for Rafe to calm enough to think straight.

"We're busted, Dom. Have you forgotten? What we had we put in with Bernard to send to the families of the *Fortune*'s crew. Rightly so."

Dom shrugged. "Bernard would stake us."

It was the truth. Rafe pushed his cards across the table. He quit. Dom shuffled and laid out a solitaire game without him. Neither spoke. Rafe watched the cards flip over, watched them play out. Dom scooped them expertly into his palm and dealt a second game. Hours and hours they'd passed like this back when Rafe's legs still swung well above the floors of New Orleans sailors' haunts, or, later, when they curled beneath him on Anton's front stoop in the marshes. They'd sat thus at another table someplace else on Kearney Street here in Frisco years later, unexpectedly reunited, uncomfortably aware of each other's absence over the years, unsure of their desires concerning a future together.

Rafe looked away, took in the smoky room's noisome atmosphere with its strangers' faces and familiar crush, and knew he and Dom were each uncomfortable and unsure again. He didn't like it. But he accepted it.

"I meet with Bernard tomorrow," Rafe began. "He's giving up running the blockade, feels it's only a matter of time before the South collapses."

"Po yi." Dom sighed, folding and dealing again. He cursed the Yankees under his breath, the Northern armies nothing more than despised *Américains* in blue uniforms to his Acadian mind.

"He will offer me a ship, Dom. The *Orient Angel,* I'm thinking." Dom grunted. It was a square-rigged barque, Bernard's oldest but still seaworthy ship used in the lucrative tea trade.

"And Timmons?" Dom asked, referring to the *Angel*'s captain.

"There was trouble the last run," Rafe said. He grimaced. "Geoff's gotten too handy with his cattails once too often, and Bernard won't stomach it."

"Bernard, him, he owns his ships, knows what he knows. But he does not sail, *aihn*? Timmons is a good man. Bah!" Dom spit onto the floor. Rafe didn't agree, but he didn't argue. Dom stuffed his cards into his pocket. Rafe drew in a breath, held it.

"When do we sail?" the old man asked, his eyes steady.

Rafe stared at him. He'd been mentally readying to go to whatever lengths it took to convince Dom to remain at sea a while longer—had even been prepared to fail and act as if it didn't matter. He'd not expected this. But the distress that twisted his gut at his uncle's abrupt, unequivocating decision shocked him much more. Rafe studied his first mate, his only real family. His friend.

Dom's loyalty was unquestioned, unconditional. Dom's commitment to himself was one with his commitment to Rafe. He was irascible, irreverent, independent, and irritatingly at odds with Rafe half the time, and domineering and damned opinionated about it all the time. He was Dom.

And he was getting tired. Old.

Rafe looked and saw without wanting to the lines weathered into his uncle's face, recalled—grudgingly—how those lines softened under Sophie's smile, how he sat, that damned dog asleep on his old man's strong, bony knees, and grunted and groused and growled—and seemed as much at home sitting at Daniel's table as he was at ease sitting at this one with Rafe. Love for Dominic Alphonso Veasey swelled in Rafe's chest and twisted in his heart. It was time, time for Rafe to push the cards Dom was dealing him back across the table and let the man play solitaire.

"The *Angel* will sail in a month's time. If Bernard offers her to me, and"—he frowned down at his hands—"if I take her, my decision will be for me, not you, Dom." He looked up. "I can't see you a lousy landlubber, you Cajun cardsharp. But a ship's store stocked with a sailor's sense would be a good thing. A worthwhile thing." He met the Acadian's wary gaze. "I mean that.

"I think it shows great wisdom on my part, actually," Rafe continued, "given my youth and lack of sense." Dom swore, and Rafe laughed. "I'll let you test the waters. Then, if it goes well, I'll let you talk me into joining you later."

Dom shook his head, leaned back in his chair and stretched, arms raised over his head, legs stiffening and protruding out from under the table. "What I do," he said, realigning himself in his chair, "I decide for me, not you, yes? It is no different for me than for you." He shrugged. "We will wait. We will see."

"How is Mrs. Quiggly, by the way?" Rafe asked, turning their conversation to easier climes.

"She is . . . herself, *aihn*?" Dom said. "She is asking about you. Dinner tomorrow night, yes?"

"Fine," Rafe said.

"She is fussing over Daniel, him." Dom grinned. "The boy, he is as stubborn as her and does not yet know he has lost his shirt he is so worried about wearing his pants." Rafe laughed. He liked Sophie's nephew. But he was a rotten poker player. Dom had stood. Swiping haphazardly at his jacket front, he let his hands come to rest on the back of his chair as he pushed it under the table and prepared to leave. "And she is thinking that Cassandra, she will marry Hadley."

"What?"

Heads turned their direction. Rafe ignored them. Dom ignored Rafe and kept on walking right out of the saloon.

Chapter Fifteen

CASSANDRA OPENED HER eyes. Wincing, she rolled onto her back, could count the whalebone ribs of her corset squeezing the daylights out of her abused body. "God a'mighty," she groaned, sitting up. She couldn't believe she'd slept wearing this—this cage all night. But it was morning, just morning by the weak light struggling against the room's shadows.

Fumbling, cursing, Cassandra attacked the tiny buttons that closed her dress front from its high neck to dropped waist. She yanked her arms free and, not taking the time to stand and step out of the gown, pulled her chemise and corset cover over her head in order to get at the torturous undergarment's lacings. In more time than she liked, the corset dropped in a heap beside the bed with the other discards. Naked to her waist, Cassandra flopped backward on the rumpled bed cover and . . . breathed.

She swallowed. Her throat was sore. Her night's tears and torment returned but only to her mind. Cassandra closed her eyes. "What am I going to do?" she whispered into the quiet. She didn't know.

She remembered that she had agreed to meet Lawrence at his uncle Bernard's office on Mission Street for lunch today, a picnic lunch, weather permitting. Maybe it would rain. Cassandra wrinkled her nose. It wouldn't rain.

And she couldn't keep putting off his invitations. She hated her cowardliness. To carry it further bordered on cruelty, and she knew it. Her dress fittings were done—the saints be praised!—Thomas Vannorman had resumed going to his own offices during the day; she was . . . settled in. With a humorless laugh, Cassandra opened her eyes and gazed about her room. It was large and luxurious and—and she missed Martha Cramer's niece's bedroom, if not the strain she'd felt beyond its warm walls. At least someone had lived within that room once, someone young, Cassandra imagined, with a love of pretty things. Whoever the girl was, she'd left something of herself behind, and Cassandra understood why Bernard's wife had left the bedroom unchanged.

A breeze from a window left open in the night teased Cassandra's bare skin. It raised gooseflesh, felt good. She lifted her hand and traced with her fingers down her neck, between her breasts, her hand slowing to smooth the red marks left by the corset here, and here, and . . . She shivered, not from the morning's coldness but from the memory of Rafe's hands skimming over her, caressing her, kissing her. She didn't fight the memory. It came, warming her cheeks, filling her with a longing that glowed like embers from a fire. Her hand dropped to her side, and she willed the sensations to ebb away until the breeze brushing her skin felt cold, uncomfortable. Sitting up, she pushed off the bed and stepped out of her dress. It was morning, she told herself, her years at Denoir proving their worth in this at least.

"Move," she said aloud. "Get dressed. Get out of your room." She thought of Sophie. "Go outside." She crossed the bedroom with purposeful strides and banged open the wardrobe's heavy carved doors. Two more mourning gowns as expensively made as the one lying wrinkled on the carpet hung inside. She took one out, put it back. Her red tartan day dress hung away from the others. Her eyes narrowing, she fingered its lightweight percale. She wasn't going anywhere until later. Suddenly she wanted something more her own close about her, she couldn't say why. Raising her chin, she tugged the plaid dress free of its hanger and turned to lay it out almost reverently on the bed—and tripped over the corset. Cassandra snatched it up, eyed it, and tossed it, unconcerned when it missed the chair and slid dejectedly onto the floor. She felt better already.

Rafe took the three steps down from Thomas Vannorman's front door and headed toward the trellised opening in the high hedge the Chinese servant had pointed out. He strode quickly, his boots silent over the hand-clipped lawn, his hands deep in his pockets. He should turn around, leave while he still could. He should have left the Gilded Rose after Dom and slept, not walked the night through charting his course for everywhere but where he'd landed: Vannorman's brass-studded, leaded-paned, enormous front door. His feet slowed. *Mon Dieu.* One look at this place and he should be cured of whatever pox had infested his idiot brain. But his feet only slowed; they didn't stop.

He ducked beneath the trellis and through the hedge. The huge house and street disappeared once inside what Rafe discovered was a hidden garden with artfully sheared evergreens and spreading eucalyptus trees. And roses.

January was the season for roses in San Francisco. Their bright blooms graced the eye, even along the waterfront; their scent perfumed the air. But he'd not seen the likes of this.

Vannorman must covet roses like Cuffey'd collected shells. They exploded from iron trellis works, twined a two-foot fence of the same wrought-iron design bordering a man-made pond. Single bushes stood in pairs, in trios, in uncounted plantings, creating a kaleidoscope of scarlets and golds, creamy whites and softest pinks. Rafe stopped. And Cassandra. Her lap spilling over with blossoms, she sat in red glorious plaid on a garden bench in the middle of it all, eyes closed, head tilted to the sun.

Jesu.

He shouldn't be here. He swallowed, ordered his feet to back him away as silently as he'd come. He didn't move, wasn't going anywhere but to Hades. He swallowed the lump in his throat, winced at the knot where his stomach used to be. Seeing Cassandra like this, unaware, unguarded, after having vowed not to seek her out and having accepted never seeing her thus again was worth an eternity in hell, in a thousand hells. She turned her head. Rafe froze.

He watched her eyes widen, knew their exact shade of grey, how the color shifted from dark to light like the fog misting the bay at dawn. He could almost taste the sunshine soaking into her skin, feel the smallness of her hand inside his, the feather lightness of her touch, and he ached suddenly, not to hold her but to hear her voice and his name upon it.

"Rafe?"

He closed his eyes, couldn't find his own voice, didn't recognize it when he did. "Cassandra."

Cassandra smiled. For a moment she'd feared she'd conjured Rafe up, it seemed so right to look around and find him here. She didn't question his appearance further, was only glad he was here. She cocked her head. Here and looking as though he'd slept in a corset an entire week, one three sizes too small and laced just this side of suffocation.

Happiness fluttered in her stomach, sang in her heart. She didn't question that either. It just . . . was. Like discovering this tiny Eden this morning. She'd reveled in it, not paused to worry her wonder with recriminations about not having found it sooner. Rafe frowned, glanced from her to the pond, and Cassandra's smile gentled. He was feeling out of place, perhaps, out of sorts definitely. But he was here, and that was all that mattered.

"Hello," she said quietly.

His gaze jerked back to her. The sun warmed Cassandra's back, glinted in his finger-combed, disheveled hair. She breathed in, the air steeped with the tang of roses and dew. She knew why he was here, why he didn't want to be here. And it was all right.

"I love you, Rafe."

He cursed and turned, his shoulders rigid, head back as he scanned the sky, his hands fisted at his sides. Cassandra went to him, rose cuttings falling unheeded from her lap. Her steps slowed as she neared his back. She bit her lip, for the first time unsure. Closing the last foot between them, she slipped her hands tentatively around him, pressed her cheek to the space between his shoulders. He was silent, stiff. Here.

"I love you," he said hoarsely. *"Fils d'putain."* His large hands came up, curled about hers at his chest. Cassandra grinned, her eyes filling, heart soaring. That he cursed raggedly with his confession only made her grin wider, made his words more his own in her ears, in her heart. "This is"—his hands tightened about hers—"impossible."

Cassandra shrugged, knew he probably rolled his eyes at her movement. "An unavoidable disaster, Captain."

She released him and stepped back as he turned around. Reaching out, he cradled her face in his palms. She trembled, drank in his look, so grim; his eyes, so black; his nearness, so devastating to her senses.

He shook his head, the hint of a grin crooking one side of his mouth. "Unavoided, at least."

"At last," she parried.

His eyes narrowed. "Are you sure your name's not Lorelei?"

The teasing left her. "I'm not sure who I am anymore. So much has happened, so fast. It's"—she closed her eyes—"hard."

"Aye." Rafe's voice was deep. His fingers tightened where they tangled in her hair. Cassandra held her breath, her senses coming to attention—and ready when his kiss came.

She melded to him, her hands going round his waist, pulling him close, closer. Rafe's mouth slashed against hers, his need meeting hers, matching it, feeding the desire exploding between them. Cassandra's head reeled, heart tripped. Her hands fisted in the soft linen of his shirt.

He moved from her mouth to kiss her cheeks, moved on to plunder her ear, her other ear. Cassandra gasped, whimpered. Hands shaking, she tugged his shirt from his trousers, her fingers splaying against his skin. Rafe groaned and buried his face in the hair at her neck, crushing her against him, stilling her hands with his hug.

They clung to each other, both wanting, both fearing where the wanting would lead, but neither of them willing to let go.

"Cassandra." His voice brushed soft against her ear. "I need to hold you, just . . . hold you." He nuzzled her neck. "Kiss you." His hands cupped her breasts. "Taste you." She let her head fall back, let the flood of warmth his caresses let loose wash over her. "Touch you."

"Yes," she breathed.

They sank together onto the grass, undressed each other. Cassandra's eyes shy, her hands steady; Rafe's eyes bold, hands shaking.

It was not like the night on the beach. It couldn't be like that night, couldn't go where that night had taken them. It was not like anything Cassandra had known there was to know. It was not less. It was more.

The lawn their bed, their clothes their linens, they curled together, her softness pillowing Rafe's hard, muscled frame. Cassandra smiled into Rafe's serious eyes, and the garden's first gift of beauty and wonder became blessing, the warming sun's caress a benediction amidst a million bowed roses.

"Am I too heavy?" Rafe asked.

"No."

Cassandra's fingers traced his nose, his whisker-stubbled jaw. They slowed, circling his mouth. Her leg tucked over his hip so her foot might skim the backs of his legs, needing to see him, know him, not by sight but by touch, with her fingertips and toes. Rafe turned his head and captured her fingers, drawing them into the warm wetness of his mouth. She closed her eyes, trembled.

"You feel so good," Cassandra whispered. Her foot slowed down his leg. "You make me feel so . . . good."

Rafe pulled back from her hand. "Look at me." Cassandra opened her eyes. His eyes were shining, brilliant and black and beautiful. His arm reached up, his fingers tangling in her hair so that her neck arched and their gazes locked.

"That's because you are good, Cassandra Mortier. You," he bent and kissed her nose, "are," he kissed her chin, "good." His grin flashed.

He was quick, and Cassandra, her senses sated, was slow. She felt as if she only blinked and he was over her, his hands beneath her shoulders, his mouth nuzzling down her neck to capture her breast. She cried out, jolted by the dizzying pleasure his sensual ambush shot through her. He pulled harder, teasing and suckling until she thought she would go mad. He let go. Breathless, stunned, Cassandra stared up into his laughing eyes. "And you taste good, too."

He was grinning—gloating! Cassandra gloried in it, her laugh bubbling up between them. And when he thought he'd bested her long enough, she reached between them, her fingers curling about his shaft, and smiled up at him in triumph when he froze.

She teased. She stroked. She watched his eyes darken. Speaking only with their eyes, they shifted and fitted to each other, her fingers remaining about him, his fingers moving within her. And their playing became pleasuring.

Cassandra's eyelids fluttered closed. She was spinning, spinning. Thought slipped away. She heard Rafe's breathing, as shallow, as fast as hers, his words as garbled, as breathless. The giving and the receiving fused, Rafe's growling need heightening, hurrying hers until they clung to each other leading each other to their own release.

"Oh, God," she panted. She rolled over limply, lay on her back staring up at the sky, Rafe's shout still echoing in her mind, tremors still rippling through her body. She felt as if she'd been consumed yet left full, not emptied. Wonder full.

"This . . . is . . . crazy," Rafe managed beside her. Cassandra turned her head, smiled over at him where he sprawled, spread-eagled, the sun glistening down his gorgeous length. His brow lifted. "And probably . . . a sin . . . I think."

Cassandra shrugged and felt her bunched-up gown beneath her. "I wonder what's more stained: my soul or my dress?"

"*Merde.*" Rafe rolled off their clothes into the grass and sat up. The play of his muscles as he did so left Cassandra too weak to move. "Tumble up here, mate." He tugged at the plaid material, spilling her off it.

Smiling, silent, their fingers lingering but efficient, Rafe helped Cassandra back into her clothes. She sat down on the bench and, giving up on smoothing her skirt with her hands, pronounced the tartan no worse off than the gown she'd slept in last night.

"You slept in your clothes?" Rafe asked from inside his shirt. His head poked through. Looking down, he began stuffing the shirt's long tail into his buff-colored trousers. "Bad night?"

"Yes," Cassandra said quietly.

"You don't know who you are anymore." He fastened the last button closing his pants and looked up, his eyes steady, dark. "I don't know what's right anymore. For me." The crease deepened between his brows. "For you." Frowning, Rafe stooped, snatched up his boots and sat down beside Cassandra on the bench. "I spent last night trying to convince myself"—he shoved his foot into his left boot—"that loving you makes as much sense as rounding the Horn under full sail." He picked up the other boot.

Cassandra drank in the way the seam marking the width across his shoulders stretched as he bent forward, how his golden hair curled over his collarless shirt, how the muscles in his thighs stretched as he worked his foot into the new leather. She smiled wistfully.

"Aye, Captain Buchanan. That's just how it feels to be loved by you."

He straightened, twisting on the sun-warmed stone to glare at her—except that his exasperation miscarried in the face of those devil-dancing, merry grey eyes. His hand slid up her back to squeeze her neck, shaking her, then pulling her against his shoulder. "God, she's back," he sighed. "Thank God."

Cassandra lifted her head and stared up at him. "Who's back?"

"You, *minette*." Rafe grinned down at her, the lightness rushing through him unexpected, untamed. Like Cassandra. Irreverent, exasperating, sparkling, spontaneous. She was back.

Cassandra leaned her head on his shoulder. They talked, the sun warm, garden bright about them. Cassandra shared what she had learned about her mother. Rafe told her about the ship's store and the *Orient Angel*. They quieted. The sun warmed. The early morning was past, the day born and too quickly rushing up on them. They both knew it and remained still, neither of them wishing to hurry the inevitable.

But it was inevitable.

"I have to go," Rafe said, his hand around Cassandra's back stroking gently up and down her arm. "I'm meeting with Bernard at noon."

"If you wait, you can ride with me." Cassandra swallowed and studied the pond beyond them. "I'm meeting Lawrence. For lunch."

Rafe didn't answer. The tiny red primroses winding the wrought-iron fence around the pond jumbled in her vision. She was holding her breath.

"All right," he said.

As quickly as that, the tension dissolved between them, replaced by the quiet of before. They stood and walked back toward the trellis in the hedge, their pace slow, fingers twined, aware of each other, silent with their separate thoughts.

"Are you going to marry him?"

"Maybe. Not now."

"Why not now?"

"I don't love him."

"Are you going to marry me?"

Cassandra's feet slowed. "Are you going to ask me?"

Rafe's sigh was long and ended in an expletive. They reached the trellis, stopped inside its dark, humus-scented arch, and faced each other. Rafe took both her hands and watched his thumbs tracing slow circles over her soft skin. Cassandra studied his face as if his dark brows and straight nose and line-feathered eyes weren't already committed to memory.

"I don't know," he said. Cassandra nodded, once, a bowing to reality, its cost mirrored in Rafe's tensed jaw. He looked up. "Would you marry me if I did?"

Cassandra closed her eyes. His thumbs stilled on top of her hands. She took a breath, released it, and looked up at him, seeing him, needing him. Loving him. And telling him the truth.

"I don't know."

They stood, each at a loss, together. They stood silent, together. And finally they simply stood. Together. A grin teased Cassandra's mouth. She couldn't help it. Rafe saw it, caught it. They burst out laughing, not knowing why and caring less.

Rafe's arm looped over Cassandra's shoulders as they walked back toward the house. "We're going to shipwreck, Lorelei. I know it."

Cassandra slipped her hand about his waist. "No you don't." She peeked around to see his face. "That's why you're so blasted nervous." He glared at her. She laughed, and they entered Thomas Vannorman's front door together.

Cassandra sat in the Vannorman coach and waited while Rafe changed into clean clothes. She surveyed the boarding house where Rafe said he and Dom always stayed. The building was narrow, dwarfed by the livery on one side, drab compared to the fresh white paint and three-foot-high red lettering announcing the "Pirates Palace" on its other. What recommended the place was its menu, not its mien, apparently. Madame Mouledoux served the best jambalaya in town according to Rafe, and the only true cush-cush. Whatever that was, it was served for breakfast and Dominic Veasey relished it.

Sighing, Cassandra leaned back into the coach's rich upholstery and fussed with the black lace edging her glove. Rafe and Dom were eating Sophie's fried chicken tonight, not Madame's jambalaya. Rafe wanted her to come. She wanted to go. She probably shouldn't, she reasoned. She bit her bottom lip. She probably would.

The thought of seeing Sophie made her decision final. That they had originally planned to be together yesterday made her going seem almost legitimate. She called up her friend's sparkling eyes and quick laugh. Yes. It would be good to see Sophie again. Lawrence had truly gone to— Her smile disappeared and a heaviness settled in her chest as she thought of her other friend with his intense blue eyes and his rare smile. She had no doubt that Lawrence had gone to equally great lengths to surprise and treat her today.

"Blast." Cassandra gazed up at the sky. She didn't know how she was going to tell him. She didn't even know what she was going to tell him, exactly. She just knew she had to talk to him. Today. She closed her eyes. There wasn't a cloud in sight.

But there was a storm brewing, she sensed that the moment she walked into Bernard Cramer's Mission Street outer office with Rafe, and Lawrence looked up from his desk. His smile froze above his hard-starched collar and bow-tied cravat. His look as he spied Rafe's hand beneath Cassandra's elbow made Cassandra's mouth go dry. She started to pull free. Rafe's grip tightened. Lawrence stood up slowly behind his desk.

"Lawrence," she bubbled, smiling, babbling, wanting to knock both their heads in. "So this is where you hide all day."

One of the two doors opening off the room swung back, and Bernard Cramer hurried out, black suited, hand extended, looking so much as he'd looked the first time Cassandra had seen him she blinked. His smile, his genuine welcome was as it had been then as well, and she blessed the man and promised to light every candle in San Francisco if the saints would but let her and Lawrence Hadley get out of the office before Rafe and Lawrence glared each other to death. Or worse.

"Miss Mortier." Bernard had captured her hand. "So good to see you again. We miss you." He laughed and nodded toward his nephew. "Lawrence here has done nothing but pace and break pencil leads all morning. You've come to his rescue at last. And brought Captain Buchanan with you." He released Cassandra to shake Rafe's hand vigorously. "Come in to my office, Rafe. I've some matters to discuss with you that I'd as soon dispense with so we might relax and enjoy our meal."

Rafe nodded but looked down at Cassandra before he followed Bernard Cramer. "Will I see you tonight?"

"No," Lawrence said curtly, crossing to Cassandra's side.

"Listen, Hadley." Rafe moved to pull Cassandra from her place between them. Cassandra balked. Lawrence grabbed for Rafe's hand about her arm.

"Unhand her, you—"

"Gentlemen!" Bernard barked from his office doorway, and Cassandra had no doubt the man was as successful among his peers as he was genial within his home. He brooked no nonsense. Rafe and Lawrence eased back, leaving Cassandra between them unmolested but only too aware of how their contest continued in their eyes.

"Captain Buchanan," Bernard said more quietly but no less forcefully. "Come with me. Lawrence? Miss Mortier? Have a pleasant afternoon."

Rafe looked again to her, opened his mouth. Cassandra cut him off. "My plans for this evening—and every other morning, afternoon, and evening—are mine to make, and *neither* of you will be privy to them if *either* of you act like this in my presence again."

"Amen," Bernard said.

Cassandra glanced over at him and nodded. "Good day, Mister Cramer. My regards to your sister." She looked at Rafe, not nearly so warmly. "Captain." Turning, she took Lawrence's arm. "We were just leaving, I believe," she said evenly, stating as clearly with her look that if they didn't leave now they would not be leaving together at all.

They left.

Chapter Sixteen

JAW SET, SKIRTS rustling, the air crackling with tension, Cassandra set the pace when Lawrence motioned her to go left outside the office building, and they began walking up Mission Street. It was a fast pace.

She recognized the business district from the week before with Sophie but passed its shops and office buildings without interest, ignored the midday crush of hungry shoppers and businessmen, barely heard the coach and dray and wagon traffic rumbling beside them. Lawrence reached for her arm and turned them onto Fifth Street.

"Were you with Buchanan this morning?" he asked, his words clipped.

"Yes," she said as shortly. She was too angry to care what he thought. Who she spent her mornings with was none of his business. Who she lunched with was none of Rafe's business either. They turned up Market, turned again onto Powell. She walked faster, oblivious to the looks they received from their fellow pedestrians.

"Are you planning on seeing him again?"

Cassandra tugged her elbow free of Lawrence's hand. "Yes." So much for worrying about what to say or how to say it, she seethed. The bay blurred ahead of them, alive with lateen-rigged fishing boats and the taller sails and black smoke of ocean vessels coming in from the sea. Smaller craft ferried passengers. Private sailboats boasted families out in the sunshine after the weeks and weeks of rain.

A long wharf jutting in the familiar right angle over the water was their destination. Blindly, she let Lawrence lead her to a light sailing skiff and help her climb over its side. He seated her in the bow. His hands were shaking. But only when Cassandra realized he was casting off, did her anger let loose of her thoughts.

"We're taking this out alone?" Her veil, pinned back over her bonnet, whipped wildly in the wind as the single sail filled, and they pulled away from the wharf. She had to hold on to her bonnet with one hand. "What are you doing?"

"Taking you for a sail on the bay." He'd doffed his frock coat and looked and moved like the skilled sailor he was. But without his usual grace. "I thought you would enjoy it."

Cassandra's conscience pricked. He spoke woodenly, without looking at her. The wind was blowing his dark hair back from his face, and she saw for the first time how pale he was, how grim the lines at his mouth. He'd been so kind to her, gone to so much trouble for her, wanted to marry her.

He was so angry with her.

"Lawrence," she began. She wished she could touch him, make him look at her. "Please listen. Try to understand."

"We were going to sail over to Saucelito, buy some wine and cheese—whatever else you wanted from a fisherman and his wife I know there."

"Lawrence. We can still do that. We are still—"

"Then I was going to take you up in the hills. There." He pointed. "See it? Mount Tamalpais." Cassandra didn't turn to look across the choppy water. He didn't notice. "It's beautiful up there. The view. The trees—huge, some of them. You've never seen anything like it. Ever."

Cassandra shut her eyes, his stiff words dripping like acid into her heart.

"No people. No noise. Beautiful. I knew you'd like it. It's like being on top of the world, the only people in the world." His voice warmed, became his own again. "And we'd spread the blanket I brought and have our picnic there." Cassandra, eyes still closed, could almost envision sitting in the sun under giant trees, the bay's blues and sea-greens sparkling below them, the sky big and bright above them. "And then we'd eat and talk and I'd listen to you laugh. I like it when you laugh." Cassandra smiled. "I was going to ply you with food until you were full and wine until you were sleepy. And then I was going to seduce you."

Cassandra's eyes jerked open. "Lawrence!" Her amused laugh died. He was finally looking at her, his gaze steady, cold. And dead serious. She stared at him, stunned.

"We belong together, you and I. You would have realized that after today, wanted me as I want you. And we would neither of us have wanted to wait any longer to begin our life together as man and wife." His look cooled, and his voice roughened. "I thought you were different, thought you cared. But you're like her after all. Just like her."

Cassandra glanced behind him. The wharves were distant. Vessels big and small were everywhere, but they were near none of them and skimming farther and farther away from all of them. Her heart thudded in her chest.

"Lawrence." She spoke slowly, refusing to be afraid. "If someone else hurt you before, I'm sorry. But I'm not her—I'm me. And we are friends. I want us to remain friends."

"Everything was perfect. And she ruined it. Just like you."

"Take me back," Cassandra blurted out. She didn't like this, didn't like Lawrence acting like this, talking like this. If he was so upset about this morning, so angry with her that he wished to frighten her, he'd succeeded.

"She got away with it." Lawrence stood, trimmed out. "He only thought he could—thought he had." His large hand curled about the rudder. "He was wrong." Lawrence stopped scanning the way ahead and fixed his look on Cassandra. "Like you were wrong to get mixed up with that Cajun Buchanan." Cassandra's breathing became forced, shallow. This wasn't anger. It was deeper, uglier.

"You are mine, Cassandra Mortier. Justice, not coincidence, took me to Havre. Justice, not blackmail, drained Leland Mortier of his money and his manhood."

"What?" Cassandra sank against the planking at her back. "What did you say?"

"And *justice,* not chance, delivered you to me on board the *Fortune*. To me!" His eyes were wide, unfocused. The sail luffed; the boat lurched. Cassandra's bonnet sailed over the water. Lawrence swore and leaped up. The craft steadied.

Cassandra clung to the sides of her seat, her thoughts churning. She wet her lips, tasted the salt of the perspiration breaking out on her lip, felt it trickling secretly down her back. She stared at Lawrence Hadley. "Are you saying you know why someone was blackmailing Leland Mortier?"

Lawrence whirled. "Blackmail?" His voice was tormented, his face twisted. "What could I take from him that could begin to equal what he took from me? What?" he screamed. "Was it my fault my bastard father was obsessed with finding his runaway wife? Reclaiming his place, her fortune? Was it my fault the bitch didn't tell your father she was already married? Was it? You tell me!"

"Holy Mary." Cassandra choked, struggling for breath. Was Lawrence saying her mother had run away from his father, that her mother was his father's wife, his heiress? How could that be?

Without wanting to, she recalled the night in Thomas Vannorman's parlor, and the old man's anguish and guilt. *If only I'd not forced her to marry.* It hadn't made sense at the time, but it was making sense now. Annalee had asked to marry Leland Mortier—a boy who would take her away? No! she wanted to scream. It was all coming too fast, colliding, crashing inside her head. Lawrence's father's murder. Lawrence's forced life at sea. She pressed her hands to each side of her head, to keep it from exploding, to keep Lawrence's words out.

"Tell me!" he raged. "Did I deserve any of it? The terror? The beatings? The years and years and years of being passed from master to master, from hell ship to hell ship, sailing for opium, for slaves, for everyone else's ill gain and my own destruction dare I do less than they wanted or say more than 'Aye, sir,' 'Aye, sir,' '*Aye aye, sir.*' "

"Stop!" Cassandra held up her hand. "Don't." She couldn't bear any more, hear any more. Her father was a murderer? Worse than a murderer for what he'd done to Lawrence, to an innocent boy. Damn him. Hot tears burned her eyes. He'd deserved worse than blackmail. She hoped he was burning in . . . Cassandra's mouth went dry. Was her mother condemned for eternity as a . . . a bigamist?

"Alfredo!" Lawrence called.

Cassandra jerked her head up. They'd left the bay and were gliding across a tiny cove toward a houseboat and a dinghy alongside it tied up to a half-submerged dock. Smoke drifted up from the rusty stove pipe protruding from the boat's patchwork-quilted shingling, but no answering shout sounded. Cursing, Lawrence maneuvered them closer. The bow banged against the dock.

In the time it had taken them to cross the bay to wherever they were now, Lawrence Hadley had aged a score of years. Cassandra stared at him, at the lines carved deep on each side of his mouth. His face was drawn, the skin tight, as taut as the skin stretching over Thomas Vannorman's tortured features. But unlike the old man, Lawrence's eyes snapped and gleamed.

"We're getting out here," he said. "Alfredo!"

Cassandra winced at his shout. She stood, stumbled as the boat tipped with their shifting weight. She knew when Lawrence swooped her up, stepped precariously onto the swaying dock. She heard his cursing, the rotting planks groaning. But the thoughts breaking loose inside her head were more real. Leland and Annalee. No wonder he'd not been able to stand the sight of his dead wife's daughter and fled to France. His precious Annalee had never truly been his wife. For all he knew, her daughter might not even be—

Stiffening, heart pounding, Cassandra pushed at Lawrence's chest. "I can walk. Put me down." He set her on the dock.

"Wait here," he ordered. He leaped onto the houseboat deck, and she watched him disappear inside the deckhouse without seeing him. She favored her mother, not the dark-eyed Creole Mortiers. So what? her mind raced, raged. It mattered not whose blood ran in her veins. She'd just as soon think that Leland Mortier's didn't! Tears stung her eyes. But what of Randall Mortier? Was he still hers? Was he still her Grandpapa? A worse thought reared up. It sickened her.

"No," she sobbed aloud. The dock creaked and tilted, and Lawrence again stood beside her. Cassandra grabbed his arm. "Tell me," she said. "My grandfather. Randall Mortier." She closed her eyes. "Did he know what happened to your father? To you?"

"Cassandra. Sweet Cassandra." Lawrence sighed. There was a deep sadness in his words, even gentleness. Cassandra trembled, jerked back when his thumb wiped a tear from her cheek.

"Tell me!"

"Justice," he continued as before, but gently, his tone heavy, resigned. "She is a hard mistress. I would not have had it so hard, Cassandra. Believe me." His hands moved up and down her arms. She wanted to scream, shove him away. But she would know the truth, all of it. She stood still. The dock bobbed beneath them.

"Tell me," she whispered. Her hands fisted at her sides.

"I was done. I was satisfied. I was on my way to the life I'd planned and worked to make possible. With what I had and with what I would have after Nassau I had enough. But justice wanted more."

"My grandfather." Cassandra spoke through clenched teeth.

"He'd never have been able to find me. But he stumbled out of the dark a day too soon, Cassandra." His voice hardened. "All he found was your father's altered ledgers. They told him what money had gone where, but not why. Stupid, self-righteous old man! He knew nothing about anything. But did he ask? Did he care? No! He wanted me to pay for his precious son's honor. Ranted on about—"

Cassandra screamed, lurching back from him. "You? You murdered him? You! And Jim? Did you murder Jim too?" She flew at him. "All he knew was that you'd robbed from his son, hurt his son. And he loved his son." Her fists landed with her words, pounding Hadley's vest. "His weak, life-destroying coward of a son."

Hadley caught her wrists. "Justice, Cassandra! It was justice killed them."

"Justice for what?" she shouted, blinded by her tears, her horror. "Grandpapa never hurt you. Jim didn't hurt you. You could have gotten away, stopped them without killing them!"

"Shut up!" he screamed. He shoved her away from him. Cassandra reeled back, slammed into one of the thick posts anchoring the dock over the cove. The fog she'd sunken into crossing the bay cleared. Dragging in air, pressing her hand to her forehead, she noticed the woods all around them for the first time, saw how they were hidden from the ships dotting the bay. Lawrence hurried toward her, and her mind snapped into the present along with her senses.

"Forgive me. Cassandra." He grabbed her, pulled her against his chest. "I . . . I didn't mean to hurt you. Truly. I would never hurt you." He stepped back, his hands biting into her arms. "Your grandfather." His face twisted. "It had to be, can't you see? I wish there could have been another way, an easier way. For you!"

"Who's there?" a voice shouted from the woods.

Lawrence frowned down at Cassandra. "Wait here, Cassandra. We will talk." She forced herself to nod, smile, and held her breath until Lawrence's long stride took him into the wood's edge and out of sight. Her legs weak, heart crashing against her ribs, Cassandra glanced at the water, the boat they'd crossed in, the woods. Run! Run! her mind screamed. Grabbing up her skirts, she bolted down the dock and veered into the brush opposite the way Lawrence had taken. Her mother, her father, even Jim and her grandfather no longer mattered. She stumbled over a fallen limb, regained her footing and ran faster. Lawrence Hadley no longer needed to seduce her; he needed to silence her.

Cassandra crouched and pressed her side against the steep bank. Her heart hammered, pulse roared in her ears, but she denied her lungs air with short, shallow breaths. Her greater need was silence else the two men tromping through the brush along the bank's edge above her head discover her hiding place. Twice before she'd fled the approach of Lawrence Hadley and the man Alfredo. A third time would not be charmed. Cassandra couldn't run anymore. Even if—no, when!—they moved past her out of earshot, Cassandra would remain where she was until dark, until . . . She shook her head. Thinking only made the fear worse.

"Cassandra!" She tensed at Lawrence's call. "This is futile. Trust me. I won't hurt you. I could never hurt you. Cassandra!"

His steps crunched in the tangled undergrowth as he worked his way toward her, calling, cajoling. She closed her eyes and clutched the gnarled root of a willow sapling, prayed its spray of branches and dusk's lengthening shadows hid her skirts from above.

If she made a sound, she never heard it, but the silence shattered into shouts and chaos. Whipping leaves slashed her face, twigs crashed. The sapling tore from her hand. Without thinking Cassandra lunged blindly down the bank. Her feet skidded, sank into mud as she sloshed blindly into the cove. Everywhere was water, shouts, screaming. And hands, fisting in her hair, yanking her arm, circling her waist.

"No!" She kicked, clawed, and was half-dragged, half-carried up the bank. "Murderer! Murderer!"

Cassandra's back slammed against the ground, the impact knocking the wind from her. Fighting for breath, Cassandra stared up at Lawrence Hadley straddling her hips, his weight trapping her. He was shouting, but it was his face that stilled her bucking beneath him. Wide-eyed, Cassandra stared up at the nightmare face that had chased her out of sleep and haunted her childhood.

She threw her arms over her head, but it came on, rushing up, careening toward her. "No!" She heard her scream, heard Lawrence's voice. But it wouldn't stop. It came, and came not as nightmare but as memory. Cassandra began shaking, shuddering.

The library. She was in the library, huddled behind the huge desk. And afraid. So afraid! Trapped, she stared though she didn't want to see, couldn't move though she wanted to run, flee. The man was screaming at her father. He wouldn't stop. She saw her father lunging at him, both men crashing onto the floor, rolling, fighting. The poker from the hearth raised. "No! No!" It fell. And fell and fell and fell. Cassandra cried out as she'd not been able to cry out then. Tears streamed down her cheeks.

"Oh, God. Oh, God." She'd seen it, *been there*. It had been Lawrence's father's face she'd fled, his death shrieks that had lodged in her mind to echo and echo ever afterward, her own terror that had buried it all deep in unnamed nightmare. "Murderer!"

"Cassandra!" Hands pried her arms away from her face.

Lawrence, pale, trembling, pinned her wrists to the ground. "No, Cassandra," he panted, his tormented blue eyes inches from hers. "Not . . . murder. Justice." His desperate eyes filled. "Not . . . murderer. *Husband*." The chaos crashing inside Cassandra's head swallowed her deeper. "Don't . . . don't you see?" His grip hurt her, pressed her hands so hard against the ground the debris jabbed through her gloves and gouged the skin of her hands. "You . . . are . . . mine. It's meant. Ordained! It is . . . *justice*." He closed his eyes, gathered his breath, and stared down at her, his words steadier, his eyes too bright.

"I . . . I didn't believe it at first either. But I didn't fight it. I let it happen, let it come as it would." He smiled, such a rare smile, a wondrous, eye-lighting, little-boy smile. "And it came, Cassandra. Can't you see? It all fell into place, better than anything I could have planned—than anyone could have dreamed!" Cassandra closed her eyes. Little boy lost. Tossed away and battered. Broken. "Don't fight this, Cassandra. You said it. Said it yourself." Cassandra shook her head mutely, her thoughts slowing, numbing. "You are you, not her. You are mine. You will know that if—"

"This is crazy. I'm out of it." The man Cassandra hadn't even noticed pushed to his feet. Lawrence jumped up, dragging Cassandra up with him. He yanked the man back around with his free hand.

"You owe me, Alfredo!"

The man swore and twisted free of Hadley's hold. "I owe you nothing! *You* hightailed it out of Frisco when we cheated the wrong man's dandified son out of a measly night's winnings, and *I* kept my trap shut. I say that makes us even, old friend. More than even!" His paunch heaved over his filthy trousers. "I laid low, an' you lived like a prince free as a canary bird in France. I call that pretty damn even!"

"I could have fingered you and stayed here, you bastard. Did you ever think of that?" Hadley swore. "All that doesn't matter anymore. All I want from you right now is use of your pitiful houseboat, all right? I can pay you. Name your price, Alfredo. How much for your houseboat and your silence?"

The man hesitated, and Cassandra pulled free of the spinning emotions numbing her brain.

"Don't," she said. "Don't listen to him. If you want to help yourself, help me."

Lawrence yanked Cassandra in front of him, his hand covering her mouth. "Heroism is hard to spend, Alfredo. I can find someplace else easy enough if you've a woman's stomach and no need of my money. Make up your mind. Now!"

The stranger's hooded gaze ricocheted from Cassandra to Lawrence. Cassandra stood still, only her mind moving, telling her to save her strength, gather her wits.

"Fine," the man grunted. Cassandra closed her eyes. "But I want nothin' to do with kidnapping. Nothin'!"

Cassandra felt Lawrence relax though his hand remained as tightly clamped against her mouth. "Just let me keep her here. That's all. I'll be back as soon as I— Hold, damn you!" He cut off the man's protest. "I've business to finish. You want your money or not?"

"How long? I gotta know how long this is going to take!"

Cassandra stilled. She could almost smell the stranger's fear: fear of losing out on the money, fear of becoming involved, fear of making the wrong decision.

If Lawrence left her in this terrified man's charge, then maybe she'd have a chance. A chance, she prayed. Give me a chance.

"If I leave the girl here with you, I've got to sail across the bay and back again. That would be safer," Lawrence said. "But it would be faster if we all went across in your houseboat. Then you only have to keep her quiet for as long as it takes me to go into town, get what I need, and return to the wharf."

"We'll take the houseboat." The man turned and crashed away from them along the bank's ledge, his curses filtering back and mingling with Cassandra's rising hopes.

"Sweet, sweet Cassandra." Lawrence spoke sadly. He sighed and nudged her forward still guarding her silence with his hand. "This is not what I'd planned. It could have been so different." His voice, his concern, set her teeth on edge. "But I forgive you, Cassandra." She tripped. His hand released her mouth as he reached to keep her from falling.

She whirled. "You forgive—"

"Hush." His finger pressed her lips. His eyes stilled her tongue. "You must forgive me. It is only right." His smile came. Cassandra shuddered. "Don't be sad," he crooned. "Don't be sad, sweet Cassandra. Not on our wedding day."

Chapter Seventeen

SILVERWARE CHINKED AGAINST heavy china, loud in the pressing silence. Rafe gave up pushing his food around on his plate and tossed down his fork. Only Dom was eating with some semblance of an appetite. Even Sophie was quiet, her round face sad, eyes downcast.

Rafe watched his finger tracing the rim of his cup, silently cursing himself for the thousandth time for making an ass of himself at Bernard's with Hadley.

"Is your eye bothering you, Captain?" Sophie asked.

Dom snorted and stabbed another piece of chicken from the platter in front of his plate. "It is not his eye that hurts him but his mouth that hurts his eye, yes?"

Rafe exchanged a quick look with Sophie. For a woman, she handled Dom's blunt sagacity pretty well: she ignored it.

"My eye is fine," Rafe said. He looked back at his cup. It was his life that was a mess, his heart that felt like raw meat. Damn her. He could still curse her to Davy Jones's locker and back, but he could no longer tell himself he didn't love her or wouldn't try to see her again. He did, and he would. If she chose to continue seeing Hadley, he'd have to accept that. His finger curled back, his hand fisting. Like hell. He grimaced and looked up.

"I'm sorry, Mrs. Quiggly. I'm not much company tonight. I think I should go."

"Nonsense." Sophie reached for Rafe's cup and stood up. Crossing to the kitchen door, she pushed the screen open and tossed the cold coffee outside. "Daniel will be back as soon as he's finished up that late order." The screen banged as she returned to the table and her seat. "Here." She poured fresh coffee for all three of them. "He'll be disappointed if you leave before he gets home. Drink your coffee."

Rafe picked up his cup but didn't consider it coffee. Somehow, he associated coffee with his memories of his maman, wanted it to taste the way hers had tasted. To this day unless Dom brewed it, he hardly drank it at sea. Unless he was in New Orleans or staying here at Madame Mouledoux's, he didn't drink it at all. Strange, he thought, the things one took with one into life.

He sat back in the ladder-backed, cane-bottomed chair and watched quietly as Sophie cleared the table, her chirrupy voice and Dom's gruff one a backdrop to his thoughts. The older man's pipe tobacco floated in the lamplight, its pungent aroma soothing. Sigmund sneezed and growled at his place at Dom's feet under the table.

As rotten as Rafe felt about how he'd behaved in Bernard's office, as upset as it made him to think of Cassandra with Hadley, as disappointed as he was at not being with her now, he was glad he'd stayed in Sophie's kitchen. Or in Daniel's kitchen, he supposed.

He glanced down at the oak tabletop, clear now of supper and tablecloth. Daniel. He liked him. He was short and round and even chirrupy like his aunt. He was a hard worker; more telling than that, he was an eager worker. Eager to learn, eager to please, eager to succeed. He would do well. He was a born shopkeeper.

Rafe glanced over at Dom. The Acadian sat sideways at the table, talking to Sophie, who was sloshing dishes through water at the counter opposite them. Rafe's uncle raised a muscled, scrawny arm, his pipe jabbing a point home in midair, and Sophie dimpled and told the man he was full of duck feathers. Rafe looked down, her light chortle and Dom's deep chuckle pleasant in his ears.

Dom was happy here, at home here. He fit in here, at this table, in this tiny kitchen, squatting on the steps out front, gazing up at the sky from the yard out back, always with Sigmund underfoot and Sophie busy nearby. Rafe frowned. And Dom was a born sailor.

But an old one, Rafe's mind argued. A tired sailor ready for an easier berth. Rafe wasn't. He knew it, hated it at times like now when he was missing Cassandra so badly his stomach was in a knot. He had hated it worse in Bernard's office when his friend and employer had not mentioned the *Orient Angel*. They'd gone over old business, gone over things they'd finished up before or Bernard could have done on his own concerning the *Fortune*. And lunch, which they both had looked forward to sharing and both should have enjoyed, had been about as quiet as Sophie's table tonight.

Hadley.

Rafe breathed in through his nose to keep from cursing out loud. If he wanted to be with Cassandra, if he wanted to sail again for Bernard, he was going to have to come to terms with Lawrence Hadley. He couldn't.

Cassandra argued the man deserved a chance to be seen differently. Why couldn't he accept that, believe that? Bernard Cramer did. Bernard was a decent man prone to seeing people kindly—but not falsely. He'd sent his nephew away to France in the wake of some scandal and in admitted defeat. And he'd changed his mind in the time since. Why? And why couldn't Rafe do likewise? Rafe's eyes narrowed. Was it something in Hadley or something in himself that blinded him to what others saw?

He stared at his coffee that wasn't coffee. Did Hadley remind him too much of the bastard *Américain*? His father's towering height and light hair flashed in Rafe's mind's eye, but it was the man's proud, privileged arrogance that Rafe remembered best. Terrence Buchanan had sauntered through life like some sort of god, his word sacred, his needs paramount, his will unquestionable.

Women adored him. Rafe's jaw clenched. His maman had run from him, been terrified of him, but she'd loved him, had cried out for him with her last breath. His peers had pandered for his approval, his servants quaked at his displeasure. Only his son, his only son, his illegitimate son, had denied him allegiance. In name only did Rafe acknowledge Terrence Buchanan, and in that only because his mother had given him his name and was proud of it.

Rafe's hand circled the cup. He wished it was a tankard. He'd long ago forgiven Anton. The trapper had ever been self-serving and quick-money-loving and had never claimed to be less or more than he was. Rafe had forgiven Dom for not coming and taking him away, wished today he had the power to remove the guilt his uncle carried all on his own. But he'd never forgiven his father for using his mother, for treating his son like reclaimed property. Like his taste for thick, black coffee, Rafe carried his hatred to this day. Was it time to put it away?

A muffled bark rumbled, exploded into high-pitched frenzy and a flash of tan fur as Sigmund shot from under the table and streaked from the kitchen down the hall, paws sliding, nails clicking. Dom swore, pushed up from his chair. Rapid knocks sounded at the front door. Sophie, wiping her hands on her apron, smiled brightly at Rafe as she hurried after Dom and dog.

Rafe forced himself to stand, hope and dread scattering his thoughts, slowing his feet. He followed Sophie, heard the door, Dom's and Sophie's familiar tones—and an unfamiliar voice. A man's voice. The barking ceased, the sudden silence as jarring as the disappointment ripping through him.

"Rafe!" Dom said. He and Sophie struggled to hold up a man who must have collapsed into their arms.

"Here, Sophie. Let me have him." Rafe hurried forward.

"The sofa. Lay him on the sofa."

Dom and Rafe followed Sophie into the small sitting room off the entry, the next moments a rush of hurried movement: Rafe taking care of the stranger, Dom lighting the lamp, Sophie scurrying for an afghan, Sigmund snorting and prancing in circles.

Frowning, Rafe straightened and moved out of the way so Sophie could finish tucking the blanket about the man's limp form. Dom returned from closing the front door and came and stood beside Rafe.

"There is a carriage outside," the Acadian said. "Fancy fancy."

"A driver?"

"Non."

"Goodness!" Both men looked at Sophie kneeling beside the sofa. She sat back on her heels. "It's the man who was staring at us."

Dom bristled; Rafe frowned, and the two spoke at once.

"When? Where?"

"Who?"

Sophie turned her head to look at them, eyes wide. "This is Cassandra's grandfather."

"You must help me! Please!"

Rafe's hand shot out as he bent over to keep the man from sitting up. Only his hand on the old man's heaving chest was steady.

"Vannorman? What is it? Why are you here?" The old man stared wildly, blindly about the room. "Vannorman!"

"Easy, Rafe." Dom placed his hand on Sophie's shoulder.

Sophie smoothed the disoriented man's hair back from his eyes. "Mister Vannorman." She spoke gently, firmly. "We will help you."

"Help . . . me." Vannorman's gaze fixed on Sophie's face. With a giant shudder, he closed his eyes. "I . . . must see her. Talk . . . to her. Please."

Rafe swore. "What's happened?" he ground out.

"I can't . . . let it happen . . . again. Oh, God." Tears trickled back into his thin grey hair. "It's not necessary. Tell her. Must . . . tell her. *Please*."

Sophie glanced up at Rafe. Frowning, she gripped Vannorman's frail hand. "Has something happened to Cassandra?" Her voice steadied. "You must tell us, Mister Vannorman. You must talk sense."

The old man dragged in a shaky breath, nodding, calming. Rafe waited, was aware of nothing save Thomas Vannorman's face, Thomas Vannorman's heart pounding beneath his hand on the man's chest—and his own fear racing with it.

"The letter," the man began. "It was there. When I got home."

"From Cassandra?" Sophie asked.

"Yes—no."

With an oath, Rafe straightened and faced away from the sofa. Vannorman's next words caught Rafe unprepared and stabbed through him like a knife in the back.

"Cassandra is . . . eloping. Tonight."

Sophie's gasp, Dom's curse; Rafe heard them and ignored them. As if he listened from a great distance, he heard the little more left to tell that Vannorman shared. She and Lawrence were leaving for Europe, would marry en route, didn't know when they would return. The room was spinning around him, his mind numb, hands shaking. Rafe moved woodenly to a chair beyond the three at the sofa and sank into it.

Vannorman's weeping came to him, the old man's garbled thoughts spilling into broken words.

"It doesn't make any *sense,*" Vannorman rambled. No, Rafe thought. But what about him and Cassandra had ever made sense? "She . . . she hates Hadley." No, Rafe closed his eyes. He was the one who hated Hadley. Had his hate pushed her into his arms? In anger? In spite? His own fury sparked. Cassandra could be so goddamned reckless. When she got her dander up. When she got pushed. When she—

"Hadley doesn't . . . love her."

"Mister Vannorman," Sophie soothed. "You can't know that. Mister Hadley has been good to Cassandra. He truly has. And maybe she has discovered that she loves him."

Non. Rafe shook his head. He didn't know why Cassandra was doing this, not after this morning in the garden. But he knew who she loved. Loss and rage tightened in his throat as a ragged laugh tore from Thomas Vannorman.

"Giles Hadley? He doesn't love anyone. Only himself."

"Lawrence," Sophie said. "Lawrence Hadley."

The bastard, Rafe wanted to scream.

Thomas Vannorman stared at Sophie, blinking rapidly as if waking from a deep sleep. "Wait." Struggling, he sat up and fumbled in his frock coat pockets. The afghan slipped in a heap onto the floor. Sophie pushed up from her knees, and Dom wrapped his arm about her shoulders. The old man snapped open a crumpled sheet of paper, stared down at it.

"My God," he breathed. "This can't be." He looked up at Sophie and Dom. "Lawrence. This was written by Lawrence. But I thought he was dead." Vannorman's face creased. "They are both dead. Drowned."

Dom spoke for the first time. *"Non."* He cursed. Rafe looked up for the first time. "This Lawrence Hadley, he is very much alive, him. She wants to run away with him? More fool her. Bah! They deserve each other, yes."

"Dominic!" Sophie whirled, eyes snapping.

"Hold." Rafe stood and crossed quickly to the sofa, his thoughts racing, mind clearing, filling like a sail catching wind. He knelt down in front of Thomas Vannorman. "Who drowned, Mister Vannorman? Explain."

"Giles and the boy. They both drowned, together."

"Who was Giles Hadley?"

The older man winced, but he was again in the room, back in the present. "The man I forced my daughter to marry." His voice shook. "I wouldn't listen. And"—he took a shallow breath—"and she ran away."

Rafe nodded. It was all making sense, falling into line. A dark, dangerous line. "And Hadley? What happened to Hadley and his son when your daughter left?"

"When I wouldn't let him stay longer in my house, he . . . he became threatening, vowed he would return with Annalee. And when he did, he would keep her from me, but I would never be able to keep him from her money." Thomas Vannorman looked away, disgust and revulsion giving life to his blood-drained features. "*His* money, he called it, earned by working for me and marrying her." He met Rafe's eyes. "He took his son and left. I never saw them again."

Sigmund whined. Dom spoke in crude French, and the dog quieted.

"Cassandra's father." Rafe frowned. "He either didn't know all this and married your daughter, or knew it and married her anyway. Mister Vannorman." The old man waited, eyes wary. "I think Giles Hadley may have found your daughter." Thomas Vannorman shook his head.

"No. He would have come back. He wanted my money, not her. I got one letter." His mouth twisted. "From a creditor. That's how I learned Hadley and his son had been drowned."

"Or murdered." And worse, Rafe added silently, his loathing for Cassandra's father deepening.

Sophie gasped.

Dom cursed. "Rafe. You are talking crazy."

"No." Rafe silenced Dom with a look. "Mister Vannorman. This is important. How old was Hadley's boy when they left? Can you remember?"

"Young. A mere child. I don't know." The other man sat up straighter. "Who are you? Why are you asking—"

"Not now." Rafe leaned forward. "*Think.* How many years after they left did you learn that they'd died? Could the boy have been about ten? Ten years old?"

"Oh my," Sophie breathed beyond them. Rafe heard Dom start to speak, saw Sophie wave him silent out of the corner of his eye. Rafe concentrated on Thomas Vannorman, willing him to remember, praying he could remember.

"I was here. The letter reached me here, in San Francisco." Vannorman was thinking out loud. His eyes squinted, brow furrowed. "It took a while to get here because it went to New York first. It was from"—Rafe held his breath—"Mobile. Mobile, Alabama." Rafe sat back, his hand clutching the arm of the sofa. He listened but didn't need to hear any more. "Yes." The old man's head lifted. "Yes. He might have been ten." It was his turn to lean toward Rafe. "Why? What does this have to do with Cassandra?"

"A boy of ten visited Cassandra's home when she was a little girl," Rafe said. His thoughts were racing well ahead of his words. Had Cassandra learned any of this? "He came with his father and was mean to her cat." Was she still with Hadley? Was she all right? "Soon after they left, Cassandra's father left for France and never came back."

"And"—Sophie took up when Rafe stopped, her words as low, as horrified as his—"when Lawrence, the Lawrence Hadley we know, was ten, he saw his father murdered and was sent to sea by the man who did it."

"You are thinking that they are the same ones?" Dom demanded. "Hadley. It is not such a strange name, no? Mobile. It is a big city, a port. Lots of people drown. You stretch this, Rafe. Too far."

"No." Rafe stood. He began pacing. "Do lots of people commit bigamy, knowingly or unknowingly, Dom? Do lots of people leave their home and never come back and never say why?"

"*Non.*" Dom's eyes narrowed. "And not so many, them, they become victims of blackmail."

"What are you talking about?" Thomas Vannorman said, standing, his voice rising, shaking. "Where is Cassandra? What's happening now matters to me, not yesterday's mistakes and misdeeds. I must talk to—"

"Wait, Mister Vannorman." Sophie held up her hand. "Are you saying Mister Hadley kept his identity from Cassandra because he's a . . . a thief?"

Rafe's blood chilled. He stopped pacing. "Worse, Sophie." He looked at the three at the sofa. "Try murderer."

"The mate, him, and her grandfather." Dom's voice was low, dangerous. *"Merde."*

"We have to find her." Sophie grabbed Dom's arm. "She can't marry that man, not until we know. We can't let her!"

"Cassandra hasn't run off to marry anyone," Rafe said.

"What are you saying?" Vannorman exploded.

Sophie stared at Rafe, stricken.

"She's not eloped, Mister Vannorman," Rafe began. He couldn't finish. All of it crashed down on him. He felt the blood leaving his face, heard Dom through the roaring in his ears.

"Aye. More likely, she's been shanghaied, her."

"That's preposterous!" Bernard rose behind his desk, unable to contain his fury. "Miss Mortier told me herself how and why she boarded the *Fortune*. And Lawrence didn't know anyone here but the people I introduced him to, other than lowlifes and gamblers of his own choosing. Certainly not Thomas Vannorman! And you are saying he knew something about them that neither of them knew themselves?"

Rafe spun on his heel and stalked across Bernard's study to the door. He was wasting his time, and they were out of time, had run it out combing the waterfront, wracking their brains. Hadley and Cassandra hadn't been seen. If Hadley had purchased passage out of Frisco, he'd used another name. Rafe twisted the doorknob, stopped. There was nowhere else left to go. Dom and Daniel were still at it, but Rafe couldn't take any more questions. He wanted answers.

With an exploding oath, he smashed his fist against the door, whirled and strode back to the desk and the grim-lipped man behind it.

"Facts? You want facts? You've not heard a thing I've said!" Rafe stopped, forced his voice to lower, calm. "I *know* Hadley was blackmailing Cassandra's father, Bernard. Her grandfather was murdered the night before we sailed because *he* knew it. Fact! Hadley was interested in Cassandra, not in her welfare, from the start—he was courting her, dammit! Long before the wreck and his goddamned change of heart! And whether he had one or not, whether he loves her now or not is *irrelevant*."

"And the fact you've every good reason to hate Lawrence isn't relevant?" Bernard charged, waving his hand. "Is all this fact? Or is it because Miss Mortier has chosen Lawrence over you and you can't accept it?"

"Listen to me!" Rafe exploded, lunging over the desk and grabbing Bernard by his frock coat. "Leave me out of it. What of Cassandra?" His hands fisted in Bernard's lapels, shook with his desire to make Bernard hear, help. The blood drained from Bernard's face. "What if I'm right? Think, damn you! She's either choosing to marry a man she doesn't know a thing about, or"—fear stabbed through Rafe's gut—"she's being held against her will by the man responsible for her father's destruction, her grandfather's murder." Rafe's words tightened with his fists. "Are you willing to live with what might happen to her if I'm right, Bernard?" He released the coat lapels, and Bernard fell back and sank into the desk chair.

"Are you?" Rafe shouted when the older man didn't speak.

Bernard winced, looked down at the desk and his scattered papers. "No," he said. With trembling fingers he fumbled with the papers, smoothing them, restacking them. "This running away together. It upset me. Didn't make sense to me." He shook his white head. "But Lawrence seemed so . . . I've never seen him so excited. Happy." His hands spread on his desk and stilled. He looked up. "I pray you are wrong, Captain, but"—he frowned—"for my own peace of mind—for Miss Mortier—I need to know that you are wrong before they leave San Francisco."

Rafe's heart slowed, thudded hard in his chest. He took a breath. "Do you know where they are?"

"No." Rafe cursed, closed his eyes. "But Lawrence asked I send a man with his bags and personal papers. To Meiggs Wharf. I was getting them together when—" Bernard stopped. Rafe's pounding steps were already at the front door.

"Powell Street," Rafe bellowed as he clambered up beside the hired driver waiting outside. The Virgin bless the bastard for waiting. "Meiggs Wharf. Hurry!"

Chapter Eighteen

WAKE UP. WAKE up. Cassandra moaned. She couldn't move, couldn't wake up. She stopped fighting. Her phantom. She prayed for her phantom, not the nightmare face, to come. He would find her, help her. "Help," she called aloud, called to her dream.

The dark mists swirling about her shifted. Clouds. Silvery clouds in a midnight, windswept sky. She was floating with them, higher and higher, lifting. To the moon. Bright light in the widening blackness. Life light in the spreading fear. Light. Light. The clouds dissolved. There was only the moon. Bright moon. Light moon. Cassandra stilled. Phantom moon.

His features emerged slowly. His nose. A chin. He was smiling, smiling down at her. And she could see it—see him! Warmth rushed through her, wrapped round her. *Don't be afraid,* minette. *You don't have to be afraid.* She smiled. She was not afraid, not now. She had never been afraid of him, with him. His face rippled like a reflection on water being tossed by a rising wind. No, Cassandra wanted to shout. Don't! Don't go! The rippling eased, face smoothed, and Cassandra saw her phantom. She stared at his face, at a face clear and close. And known. At eyes dark and desiring. At a smile warm and quick. Pain jolted through her like lightning splintering a night sky. "Oh God," she whimpered, fighting the knowing, fighting the pain. Rafe. It was Rafe.

"Lady? Lady!" Cassandra jerked awake to Alfredo's greasy black curls and drooping moustache bobbing in her face, his frightened voice scraping her ears. "You all right, lady?"

The man, the filthy deckhouse, the hard bunk, and the ropes cutting into her wrists crashed back into focus. Cassandra pressed into the lumpy pallet away from the man bending over her. The stink of stale garlic and whiskey stung her nose. His face blurred. She turned her head.

"Leave me alone," she said, her throat tight. "Or help me." She looked back, desperation drying her tears. "You don't need to be party to this. All the money in the world won't help you when—"

"I am party to nothing." The man jerked upright and crossed the littered floor to a knapsack half-filled on the rough-sawed table in the room's center. He resumed stuffing things into it, his back to Cassandra on the bunk.

"To nothing?" Cassandra's voice cracked. "Isn't this your houseboat? Your bed? Your ropes tying me to it?"

"No!" Alfredo whirled to face her, his eyes wild, his greyed shirt stretching at its buttonholes with his rapid breathing. "My houseboat is missing! I found a skiff in its place when I returned from Saucelito to the cove. If they find me and if they ask me, that is all I will know to tell them!" He turned back to his work, cursing under his breath.

Cassandra watched him, listened to him, and gathered her wits. "Alfredo," she said quietly. He stopped cursing but didn't slow his packing or turn around. "If you untie me before you go, I will not say anything about your part in any of this. I will support your story, tell the authorities that Lawrence took me to the cove, and we got in the houseboat that was anchored there, and we left again." Cassandra waited, watched the man's hands slow, shoulders round. "Think well, Alfredo," she pressed. "If I tell them what happened and you tell them your version, who will they believe? But if we both tell them the same thing . . ." She let her words fade, let the import of her words sink in of its own weight.

"And if Hadley comes back to no one," the man said, "and finds me before he finds you, or before the authorities find him? No." He shook his head. "I will take my chances, lady. If you are here, he will leave with you, and you will not be talking to anyone about me or anything else."

"Because I will be dead, Alfredo." Cassandra's words became ice. "Murder is not the same as cheating the wrong man's son. Lawrence will not evade a charge of murder, and those who will not rest until he's hung will have no mercy on those who might have saved me and did not." She sat up as far as the ropes at her wrists tied to the bunk's sides allowed.

"It is they you are taking your chances with, Alfredo, not with me or with Lawrence Hadley. Their wealth. Their power. Their rage. This is your houseboat. Lawrence is your friend." The man whirled from the table and faced her. She met his look. "Are they going to believe you? Have mercy on you? Or are they going to avenge my murder?"

Footsteps pounded down the wharf outside. Both Cassandra and Alfredo went rigid, stared at the door.

"Alfredo!" Lawrence shouted from beyond it. "Come here!"

"Wait!" Cassandra called out. The door slammed behind the cursing trapper as he bolted out on deck. Cassandra stared after him. It was over. Lawrence was back. His pitiful friend was gone. She closed her eyes and tried to think of nothing, tried to blank out the low voices floating to her, tried to press back the cold, the chilling fear spreading through her and beading on her skin. The door banged open, shut. Alfredo moved to his knapsack, yanked it open, and stuffed a leather pouch deep inside it.

"Your money?" she said. "It will not help you."

"Shut up, lady!" Alfredo heaved the pack over his shoulder. "He's waiting for someone on the wharf. It's too late now. I can't help you—only me!" He swung toward the door, stopped. With an oath, he turned and crossed to the bunk. He stood over her, his paunch heaving, eyes red-rimmed. "I'm sorry." His words were hoarse, strangled. "I don't have no hero in me."

He stooped suddenly, his pack thudding loudly onto the floor. Metal gleamed in the weak lamplight. A knife. He was wielding a knife. Cassandra sucked in her breath—and swallowed her scream. He was cutting her free, hurriedly, savagely. She grimaced to keep from crying out. She was free.

The man stood, tossed the knife into her lap, and grabbed up his knapsack. "You're on your own, lady. An' I ain't ever seen you before in my life." He turned and slammed out into the night.

Cassandra leaped from the bunk. She stopped at the door, staying an uncontrollable urge to fling it wide and run. Cursing her trembling legs, she pressed her ear to the unpainted wood. Lawrence and Alfredo were arguing. She could make out only Lawrence's anger, Alfredo's fear. She heard them scuffling; then hurried footsteps pounded down the long wharf, faded. Cassandra closed her eyes.

"You're on your own, lady," she breathed. She turned and leaned against the door, her every sense tuned to the slightest noise from outside, her eyes scanning the cluttered room. The place was a floating pigsty. Her gaze darted over discarded clothes, scattered fishing nets and gear, and food-encrusted tinware. A lone salami rolled gently to and fro under the table in time with the creak of the soot-blackened smoking lantern dangling from the ceiling. The knife. Its eight-inch blade glinted in the unsteady light, the single polished thing in the room. Cassandra pushed away from the door and, hesitating only a heartbeat, scooped the knife up from the floor beside the bunk.

It was heavy, its weight balanced and solid in her palm. Cassandra bit her lip. She didn't know how to use it and didn't want to use it. She glanced back at the door. She had to get away. Now. But the door faced the wharf, and Lawrence was out there waiting for someone on the wharf.

"Damn." Cassandra willed herself to think, move. With the light spilling from the boat's lantern a floating beacon in the night, sneaking out the door unnoticed was impossible. For like reasons, blowing the light out would be about as good as hanging her head from a window and announcing—

"The window!" There were only two windows not boarded up from the inside; a large one on the bulkhead facing the stern, shuttered but usable, and a much smaller one over the bunk—on the bulkhead opposite the door.

Cassandra scrambled onto the bunk as fast as she'd scrambled out of it. Hands steady, heart racing, she dropped the knife at her feet and yanked her heavy, layered skirts up to her waist. Head first didn't work. She started over, legs first. Splinters gouged. The rough wood shredded her stockings, scraped her shins, her thighs. Squirming, twisting, she hung at last half in and half out of the window, balanced on her stomach, her tangled curls sweeping the rumpled pallet like a broom made of hair. Taking a deep breath, Cassandra pressed her elbows tight against her sides, grasped the window's bottom edge, and pushed off.

"Who's there?" Lawrence straightened from where he leaned against a piling. "Cassandra?" His eyes scanned the deckhouse's squat profile rocking gently under the night's rising full moon, searched the darker vessels on either side of it. A loose cable banged in the wind. From the street end of the wharf the pounding of an approaching horse and rig rang clearly over the water. Lawrence whirled. With an oath, he headed toward the street, keeping well in the shadows cast by the fishing fleet lining the way.

Meigg's Wharf loomed ahead, and Rafe grabbed the driver's arm. "Slow down." The other man's muscular arms began sawing at the reins. Rafe slipped his knife from his boot, his eyes fixed on the lone figure moving secretly along the wharf. "You carry a blade, mate?"

"No, sir," the man grunted beside him. He stole a quick glance from his horse to Rafe. "Don't court trouble"—he looked back to his reins—"don't like running at night." They swung around at the end of the street. "Never was no good with no knife."

"Aye." Rafe grimaced. "I've never been any good with a horse." They clattered to a stop, and Rafe leaped to the street, putting the hack between him and the water. "Remember the two men and the coach where I hailed you?" The driver, panting from exertion, stared down from his perch and nodded. "Find them. Send them here with any help they can get and get back before I get my throat slit if you want your fare for this night's trouble."

The driver scowled. "You ain't got no money on ya?"

"Go!" Rafe ordered with a captain's bark and blacker look. "You handle that horse, and I'll handle this"—he slashed the air—"and we'll both be well enough when it's over. *Go*!"

"Who's there?"

The driver swung his head toward the wharf. Rafe stepped back, his knife shifting, becoming a part of his hand. Hadley emerged from the shadows. Rafe heard him but couldn't see him.

"Answer!" Hadley called. "Are you come from Bernard Cramer?"

"Aye, Mister Supercargo."

Hadley swore.

"Aw, shit." The driver reached for his whip. The horse and hack bolted forward, throwing rocks, spewing dust. The two men left behind didn't move. The limestone cloud settled. The horse's thundering hooves faded. Moonlight and shadow and the slosh of water and the creak of empty vessels remained. And still, the two men didn't move.

"Buchanan."

"Aye." Rafe echoed Hadley's snarl, mirrored the other man's loose, battle-ready stance. "Where is she?"

"Fool." Hadley's smile made Rafe's eyes narrow. "Mortier. The old man. You. All of you. Fools."

"Where is she?" Rafe repeated. Hadley's smile tightened. "Forget it, Buchanan. It's almost over now. Justice." His voice lowered. "She amazes me, champions me. And Cassandra. She is mine."

They circled each other, the opposites of each other in hair, in eyes, in fine woven linen and faded chambray shirtsleeves. They measured each other, the equal of each other, twin blades glinting death in the pale moonlight, sailor's blades wielded in the like-skilled hands of men hardened and honed by the sea.

"Navarre isn't here, Mister Supercargo. When was the last time you dealt an honest hand? Can you even remember how to play, Hadley? Without a stacked deck and five aces up your sleeve?"

"Come on," Hadley taunted. "Come at me, you Cajun bastard. I'll play."

"Fold, Hadley, while you still can. All I want is Cassandra. I don't want to hurt you."

"Liar!" He lunged, his knife hissing in a lightning arc. Rafe leaped and recovered, a thin red line widening down the length of his arm. Hadley grinned. "You want to hurt me." His face hardened. "Because I'm going to kill you."

Cassandra clutched the corner edge of the deckhouse, paralyzed by the scene unfolding at the wharf's end. The figures were far off and indistinct, disappearing and reappearing in and out of shadows. They slashed, slammed together, leaped apart. Cassandra's nails bit into the wood, her fear and horror choking her. They were going to kill each other.

She sagged against the bulkhead, her helplessness overwhelming her in strangled, tearing sobs. She was five again, huddled in terror under the desk. Full grown she couldn't stop it from happening again. Reason wouldn't stop them. Her screams wouldn't stop them. Her puny weight against theirs wouldn't stop them. They were going to kill each other. And she was going to be left with it, left with the memory and the horror and helplessness. She raised her head from her arm. And the loss. Again.

"No." The word was more mouthed than spoken but it rocked through her, vibrating with a power that took hold and sparked and flamed, part reason, part resolve, and all rage.

"No!" she screamed, pushing blindly away from the bulkhead. She stumbled around to the front of the deckhouse and yanked open the door. The knife. What had she done with Alfredo's knife? She ran to the bunk, her hands skimming its filthy covers, her fingers closing about the knife's smooth wooden handle.

Cassandra straightened, stared down at the blade. She wouldn't be able to stop them. "I don't care!" she shouted. Neither could she stand by sobbing helpless, stupid, fruitless tears when she could . . . It came then, unbidden, came fully formed and in full-blown simplicity. She spun, the knife clunking onto the floor. "Not when I can stop them."

She climbed up on the table, reached for the lamp's base and tugged. She burned her fingers in her haste. Swearing, she yanked harder, and the twine knotted to the nail hook in the ceiling tore free. Cassandra toppled backward, nearly falling off the tabletop. Leaping down, she stepped back from the table, turned her face away, and flung the lamp with every bit of rage in her. Glass shattered. She cried out and stumbled back. She stopped, looked. The base rolled off the table, spilling flame with its fuel. Angel-led, it banged onto the floor, bounced, and wobbled the remaining feet to the tossed cover hanging over the bunk's side. The stench of wool and billowing smoke filled Cassandra's nose, burned her eyes. She whirled and fled out the door, banging it shut behind her. She didn't slow until she had made the wharf and stood clinging to the nearest piling, dragging in air and searching for the two she prayed would react as one.

"Yes," she panted. She heard Lawrence scream her name. A shout. Running feet. "Yes." She saw them. Saw him. Rafe. Knife gone, he was yanking his shredded shirt over his head as he ran, the muscles in his legs bulging. His shirt clutched in his hand, he ran faster, drew closer. "Yes," she breathed, his hair golden as it caught the fire's glow. She pushed free of the piling, moved to step forward to stop him—and froze as Lawrence, knife raised, shot out of the darkness behind him.

"Rafe!" Her scream echoed above the roar of the boat's deckhouse outer walls going up in flame. Lawrence and Rafe crashed together onto the wharf's planking. Kicking. Punching. Lawrence's blade gleamed now above them, now between them. The fire's hot breath scorched Cassandra's back, but she couldn't move. Her mouth wouldn't open.

Rafe rolled on top. Gaining purchase, he reared back, found his footing, and lunged to his feet dragging Lawrence up with him by the man's vest front. His arm drew back, the muscles cording along his blood-spattered shoulders as he buried his fist in Lawrence's stomach. Lawrence doubled over, stumbled backward.

With a roar Lawrence reversed direction and plowed into Rafe full force. The planks beneath them bucked under their exploding impact. With brute force, with an animal's frenzy, Lawrence jerked back on his feet and began kicking Rafe's inert form. The sickening thud of leather pounding skin unleashed Cassandra's scream. Lawrence whirled, his face a mask of twisting emotion, his eyes riveting on the pyre of roaring flame the houseboat had become.

"Cassandra!" he shrieked. Rafe swore, weaved onto his knees. Lawrence turned. "She's mine!" he screamed. He bent, flung Rafe over one shoulder, and with inhuman, vicious strength, hurled him the width of the wharf. Cassandra flew out from the piling as Rafe crashed and lay still.

"No!" she sobbed. She collided with Lawrence, then grabbed onto his arm when he tried to shove past her and keep running. "Stop!" she choked. "Lawrence! It's me! I'm—"

She felt her feet lifting from the wharf's deck, her hands tearing loose from Lawrence's sleeve. Leaping orange hues spun past her vision, but it was her name she heard. Someone calling her name. Rafe? Icy water filled her mouth, her nose. She choked, breathed in, and knew too late there was no air, only water. Cassandra fought, kicked, but she had no air, couldn't get back up to the air. The water was sucking her down, pulling her, swallowing her. Water. Everywhere was water.

She stopped fighting. The fire in her lungs stopped burning. She was floating, spinning, freed of the water's weight, free in the water's soothing caress. She was waltzing. Water waltzing. Caught up in some silent, swirling, water-wondrous dance. With Rafe.

With Rafe and the moon.

Rafe in the moon's light.

"Cassandra? Answer me. *Look at me.*"

She smiled. It was so easy to look at Rafe in the moonlight. She saw him beside her porthole outside San Francisco. His eyes serious, voice low. Sad. She saw him on the cay, at the lagoon, above her, his shoulders caped in moonlight, his eyes black with desire for her, brimming with his gift of awe for her. She trembled. She saw him silhouetted by the moon and the night in her cabin on board the *Fortune,* felt again how his profile stole her breath, how his hands had shaken and his eyes burned when he'd stuffed her between the covers. Myriad visions of Rafe came to her until Cassandra stood again in her room, the garden bell clanging.

She was flying again down the stairs, skidding along the crushed-shell path, yanking back the heavy gate, and sailing into his arms. She felt again her arms wrapped round his neck. His thick hair, taut muscles. She struggled to see, to speak, and stared at last up at his face, bronzed in the red-orange glow. And his were still the blackest, most beautiful eyes she'd ever seen.

"Cassandra?" Rafe's fingers, cold, shaking, moved up her shoulders, her neck, and came to rest on each side of her face. "Cassandra?"

She smiled. "What took you . . . so long?"

Chapter Nineteen

HE WAS HERE.

Cassandra gave her mirror a last searching scrutiny. Her color was high, eyes serene, but her fingers gave her away. They trembled as she smoothed her prim collar, fumbled when she fussed with her full sleeves.

"Relax," she breathed. "You look fine." But she wanted to look perfect.

For eleven long months she'd waited for this day—this night as it turned out. That nightmare night when Rafe had dragged her up from the bay's bottom and Dom and Daniel had dragged them both onto the wharf, Cassandra had been oblivious to the crowd that had filled the empty night with shouts and questions and crowded the lonely wharf with pounding feet and pressing onlookers. She'd seen only Rafe, wanted only Rafe. He'd not left her side.

Cassandra smiled. He'd not left her bedside afterward, not for Dom, not for Sophie, not for Thomas Vannorman's physician in all his mutton-chopped, teeth-clenched, fuming ferocity. Rafe had been by turns passive, impassioned, and unapproachable, but he'd remained present. For her.

Her smile faded. The morning after she'd been pronounced well and fit to be up and about her life again, she'd opened her eyes and discovered no Rafe to be up and about it with. Her eyes narrowed, were no longer serene. It rankled still.

He'd left her alone to sort through all the events that had transpired, both wondrous and wicked, from their morning in the rose garden to Lawrence's death in the fire. He'd left her alone to miss him and hate missing him and then hate him for making her miss him when she hated missing him so much. Damn him! Her features softened in the mirror, eyes calmed. He'd left her to wait for him and to decide once and for all if she wanted that, wanted him.

Cassandra turned, her bright green silk skirts rustling softly over her stiff crinolines, and headed for the parlor downstairs. She'd done it. She'd cried and raged and wondered. And walked. Her feet slowed on the stairs. She'd taken Sophie's advice and gotten out of the house and walked and walked and walked this city. She'd grown familiar with its hills and fascinated with its people: their dizzying diversity of colors and cultures; their shared dreams and exuberant vitality. She reached the last step and stopped, her hand tensing on the banister's polished, smooth wood.

The rope burns about her wrists were hardly noticeable now. What scars remained on her heart were healing. And she had decided. Her gaze darted to the light spilling from the parlor's open door into the hall. Rafe was here, and he had decided too.

Rafe stood, feet apart, hands clasped behind his back, facing the fireplace and hearth. He heard Cassandra coming down the hall, heard the carpet steal her footsteps, felt her gaze on his back when she stopped inside the room. He stared up at her mother's portrait and saw only the girl's daughter in his mind.

"Rafe?"

He turned around. It cost him; he'd known it would. *Jesu.* After months at sea, months of living on his memories of her until he'd tried to damn them all to Hades or go mad, seeing her an arm's length in front of him all well, all soft, all grey, grey eyes was so hard. So good.

"Hello," he said. Cassandra's brow arched. Rafe forgot his unease, bit back a grin. Aye, it was good. Cassandra out of mourning and in high color with mutiny sparking in those gorgeous eyes.

"That's progress," she said.

" 'Hello' is progress?"

"It is for someone who left without even saying goodbye!"

"Oh." Rafe frowned and studied her face, wished he could read her as easily as one read the sky. "I didn't know how," he said simply. He still didn't, he knew now but didn't say it out loud. "You want me to go?"

Her expression turned murderous. "*Damn* you!"

Rafe closed his eyes, his deepest dread and dire misgivings rushing up. Maybe she'd come to her senses if she had any, was going to serve him his due and go on to hers. He looked at her. But, the saints protect him, he needed to hold her once more before he was tossed out on his ear never to know her touch again save in memory and madness.

He reached out, his finger twining a curl next to her ear. She went still, the ache spreading in his gut mirrored in her eyes. His palm slid up and cupped the side of her face. "I am guilty as charged," he said.

"Yes," Cassandra said, her voice small, unsteady. "You are worse than guilty. You are . . ." She caught her breath as Rafe's thumb traced her cheek. His other hand circled her waist and pulled her to him. She was so soft, felt so right against him. He didn't have to touch her. Just watching her eyes darken made his knees weak. "You are stubborn," she resumed, her whisper forced, "and arrogant and . . ."

"And?" He bent close to her face, to hear her fading words, drink in her scent, feel her hair tease his nose.

"I missed you."

Her hands curled around his neck, and Rafe crushed her to him. It was her heart she gave in her kiss. Shock and joy and wonder shot through him. Clinging to each other, they tumbled into desire. Out of breath, Rafe raised his head. She kissed his neck, his ear, and traced his jaw back to his mouth.

"I missed you," he groaned. He kissed her nose, her eyes. "I missed you. I missed you." His hands skimmed over her. "God, Cassandra." He yanked her hard against him, her softness melding to him. They were shaking. Rafe frowned and pulled back to look down at her. She was crying.

"Come here, *minette*." He pillowed her head against his shoulder. Her arms wrapped around his waist. He rocked her. She hugged him harder, sniffed into his shirt. His grin, her giggle, and the laughter came. Bubbling, building, it exploded into merriment onto mayhem and a whirling sea jig that undid Cassandra's hair and destroyed Rafe's paper collar.

They collapsed, laughing and winded, onto the parlor's settee. Turning their heads resting against the horsehair upholstery, they watched each other as their breathing slowed. Rafe swallowed.

"I want"—he spoke between breaths—"to tear your clothes off . . . and lay you down right here . . . in Vannorman's parlor." He watched Cassandra redden—and not bat an eyelash. "Progress?"

She smiled. "Perdition."

Cassandra watched the lines crinkle at the sides of Rafe's eyes, cherished the warmth that was his laugh. Sweet Mary, she loved this sailor, this simple-complicated, steady-surprising, crazy–crazy-making man. Every towering inch of him.

"Come on." Rafe stood and dragged her up by her arm. Before she could speak, they were across the parlor and swinging into the hall.

"Rafe!"

"Where's your grandfather? I need to borrow you and his coach. Does he have a driver?"

Thomas Vannorman was found, accosted, and left grinning ear to ear behind his library desk. When his driver wasn't to be found inside the carriage house nor hailed outside it, Rafe attacked the tracings and hooked the horse up himself. They rattled down the drive beside each other on the driver's seat. Neither had any business being there.

An unplanned U-turn and three near accidents later Cassandra wasn't wondering where they were going so much as praying they got there alive. She held on tighter, got quieter and quieter, was treated to the deepest depths of Rafe's multilingual vocabulary, and came to a jolting stop in some narrow, unpaved alley somewhere along the waterfront with a renewed faith in the existence of guardian angels. Rafe looped the reins around the brake and sat back, draping his arm about her shoulders.

"We're here," he said.

"In one piece." Cassandra shot him a look. "I think."

He grinned. "Progress."

Cassandra shook her head. "Providence, Captain Buchanan." She leaned her head back on his arm, heard his sigh echo hers. They stared up at the night sky and quieted.

San Francisco didn't sleep. She could hear the muted refrain of a piano, hurried footsteps, and the rumble of carriages and hacks up and down the street they'd turned off into the alley, the hardy hails raised between mates and fellows. But here beside Rafe it was dark and still, and the sky was big and silent overhead. She frowned.

"No moon?"

"There's a moon," Rafe said. "It's too early."

Cassandra smiled and disagreed. It wasn't too early. Her moon was here and none too soon. "Why did we come here?" she asked. When he didn't answer, she turned her head and looked at him.

Rafe stared up at the stars and remained silent. Cassandra curled her fingers into her palm in her lap, resisting the urge to trace the profile he presented. His straight nose, square chin, strong neck. Arrogant, stubborn, uncompromising, Rafael Buchanan could be all of those things. But he was beautiful. Beautiful to look upon, yes, but more beautiful inside.

"When I left"—his low words claimed her thoughts—"I didn't know how things would be when I got back. Bernard came to me and offered me the *Angel,* and I took it."

Cassandra closed her eyes. Poor Mister Cramer. "He's a good man," she said quietly.

"Aye." Rafe turned his head. "He said he'd talked with you."

Cassandra nodded and looked back at the stars. She'd ended up at his office one day on one of her walks, and he'd left to walk with her back to her grandfather's. "I think," she said, calling up that day's conversation, "that Lawrence Hadley committed monstrous acts"—

she frowned—"but he was not a monster." Rafe didn't speak, and when she sensed he was listening, waiting for her to go on, she did so. "He thought I was still in the houseboat and lost his life trying to spare mine." She trembled. Rafe's hold tightened. "That doesn't take away what he did. He caused so much hurt and did so much wrong"—the stars blurred overhead—"but he hurt himself most of all, Rafe." She turned her head, and Rafe's dark eyes reflected her pain. "I don't hate him; I hurt for him. Today."

Rafe pulled her closer against his side. She settled her head against his strong shoulder. "I know," was all he said. Cassandra sensed that he did know, and her tensed muscles loosened, the ache in her throat eased. He'd done for himself on the deck of his ship what she'd done walking the streets of San Francisco. She wasn't surprised. She wasn't relieved. She was simply grateful that he was who he was and how he was.

"I knew I wasn't ready to become a shopkeeper with Dom," he resumed as before. "I talked with Bernard before I left, convinced him I was ready to be a shipowner as well as master." He sighed. Cassandra frowned, listening. "So, beginning with this run, I'm in the process of getting enough together to buy and fit out a ship of my own." He stopped. Cassandra took a steadying breath. He was a sailor. She hated missing him. She loved him.

"That's wonderful, Rafe. It won't take you long." She shrugged, her smile small but true. "You could end up with a merchant fleet—who's to say? You'll be good at whatever you do, and this is . . ."—she shrugged again—"perfect."

Rafe scowled up at the sky. "Is it?"

"What?"

"The idea of owning a ship still feels as right as it felt then. More right." His frown deepened. "But how good it will be . . ." He gazed down at her, his eyes dark, his thoughts hidden. "I'm not so sure about that anymore." Squeezing her shoulder with his hand, Rafe removed his arm from behind her back. "Stay here." He leaped to the ground. "I'll be right back."

"Rafe? Rafe!"

He disappeared between the two buildings beside them without answering, without a backward glance. Mumbling, cursing under her breath, Cassandra gathered up her skirts and clambered with ill grace in mood and movement down from the driver's seat. A light flickered, brightened, and the alley window of the shop they'd stopped behind glowed. She stomped over to peer through the filth and insect remains of the cobwebs curtaining the window's cracked glass. Rafe's tall, shadowy form moved about on the other side. A door she'd not seen in the darkness creaked open and the shop's light spilled into the alley.

"Cassandra?" Rafe called.

"Do I look like Sigmund?" Cassandra huffed. Rafe's gaze swung to her at the window. Her hand shot out, pointing to the coach. "You weren't even going to come out and help me down?"

His eyes narrowed. "Aye, that is a pretty high horse you're riding, Miss Mortier." His laugh drowned out her curse. He reached her in two strides, grabbed her elbow. "Come inside." He shuffled her out of the alley and through the door, closing it behind them. "You must be slowing down. I was rushing to get the lantern lit before you crashed in after me in the dark and broke your stiff little neck."

"*I've* a stiff neck?" Cassandra whirled to face him.

"On occasion." He tugged her the rest of the way to him and took her next words in his kiss. Cassandra stilled, surrendered. Their kiss deepened. It took her breath, made her dizzy. Rafe moved from her mouth to her ear. She let her head fall back, and he groaned and nuzzled her neck, with his tongue, his nose, his lips. His hands fisted in her hair.

"Jesu."

Cassandra smiled, suspended in the layers and layers of sensations and emotions setting her nerve endings atingle, making her limbs wobbly. Rafe slumped back against the door. Cassandra burrowed deeper into his arms. They leaned together, shaking, trying to remember how to breathe normally.

"Where are we?" she asked into his shoulder.

"Not where I want to be." He sighed. *"Merde."*

She turned her head and looked at the room. Wood shavings covered the floor in broom-made piles and foot-made disarray. Wood. The scent of it, the sight of it in all its forms: fresh-felled logs; logs standing denuded of bark; blocks of wood sprouting faces and wings; finished pieces, statues of wood. An eagle with a twelve-foot wingspan took up the tiny room's cleared work space. A school of fish, some realistic, some imagined, lined one wall. Cassandra frowned and pushed away from Rafe to turn and see them better. Not statues, figureheads. They stood made and in the making in the lantern's warm glow, all of them destined to grace the prows of unknown ships and ride, in majesty or whimsy, into the wind over the seas.

Rafe's arms circled her waist from behind. He pulled her back, and she leaned against him as before but facing the room. "This is Old Man Martin's shop. He's a master craftsman."

"He's an artist," Cassandra said. She turned her head to look up at Rafe. "He leaves his shop open like this?"

Rafe smiled. "He's also an old friend." Rafe's eyes became suddenly serious, his expression guarded. He looked out at the room. "This was the last place I stopped before I left on the *Angel*." Cassandra's eyes widened.

"You ordered a figurehead? For your ship!" She turned, her gaze darting about the room. There were so many. "Which one? Which one is yours? Is it finished?"

"I don't know. It's either finished or just begun."

Something in his tone made Cassandra turn. The way he was watching her made her heart quicken. "The figurehead?"

"She's finished."

She. His ship would chase a lady. Of course. Wrinkling her nose, Cassandra again searched the wooden figures, concentrating on the images of maidenhood present in abundance, most of them with bosoms in equally great abundance, she discovered. Of course. If Rafe Buchanan had dragged her into the night, robbed her of a year's growth with his driving skills, and brought her here to show her the lady he'd decided to spend eleven months of every year with instead of her then— Her gaze stopped, fixed on the figurehead sitting back from the others.

"Sweet Mary," she breathed. She walked to it, wood shavings catching her hem. She was a lady. Like all this lady's sisters Cassandra had ever seen, she had long, flowing hair forever flying in the wind. That was all she had that was expected. It wasn't all that was familiar.

Cassandra stared: at the figure's man's vest complete with tatters and tears; at the fragile shell she cradled like a Madonna with child in her slender hands; at her own likeness looking back at her carved in wood. "Lorelei." Cassandra read the name on the fluttering scroll at the figure's base resting amidst a carved cloud of tropical palms and ferns. Rafe came and stood behind her.

"She's finished," he repeated. "It's the reason *for* her that I'm waiting to know."

"What do you mean?" Cassandra asked, unable to look away from the figurehead.

"Before I left I figured I'd either have her to remind me of my wife or to remind me that my life was sailing, and—"

"Stop." Cassandra turned, her attention focused only on Rafe Buchanan. "Your life is sailing, Captain Rafe Buchanan, and your wife had best know that." She raised her chin. "I love you, Rafe. How you are, what you are, all you are—it's all . . . you."

Rafe stared down at her. "You cannot be a sailor's wife, Cassandra."

Cassandra shook her head. "I would be your wife." She shrugged. "And you are a sailor."

His thumb reached for her cheek. "You cannot be this sailor's wife." Cassandra tried to look down, away. Rafe's hand cupped her face and would not allow it. "Hold," he ordered. She met his eyes. It was the hardest thing she had ever done. "I no longer want this figurehead to remind me of a wife I never see. Not enough. Not if that wife is you." His other hand came up. He framed her face. "If you cannot sail with me, I won't sail. I'll go in with Bernard and learn to be a shipowner and not need to be a master too. Not like I need to be a husband. If it's with you." He closed his eyes.

"No."

Rafe's eyes snapped open. Cassandra watched their color darken, his skin tighten across his high cheekbones. She raised her chin between his hands.

"You are going to sail your *Lorelei,* Captain Buchanan. And she is not going to remind you of me. I am." The color deepened now in Rafe's cheeks. Cassandra discovered her captain's voice. "And when you tire of chasing me and I tire of chasing our babes up and down the ratlines, we will settle and—"

Rafe caught her up and twirled her high in the air, round and round. He stopped. She slid slowly down his front, the room still spinning about her head. Her hands curled round his neck as he pulled her down with him amidst the wood shavings and sawdust and kissed her like she needed to be kissed.

"And we'll try our damnedest to act like civilized landlubbers, and I'll go be a merchant shipowner with Bernard and buy a derby hat and a carriage—" He raised his head. "What do you think? Are we making progress yet, Miss Mortier?"

"I think"—mischief glinted in her eyes—"I think I'm glad I like to walk."

FREE
Romance
(a $4.50 value)
Send in the Coupon Below
To get your FREE historical romance and start saving, fill out the coupon below and mail it today. As soon as we receive it we'll send you your FREE Book along with your first month's selections.